DYNASTY

33

The Dancing Years

Cynthia Harrod-Eagles

sphere

SPHERE

First published in Great Britain in 2010 by Sphere
This paperback edition published in 2011 by Sphere
Reprinted 2011 (twice), 2012

A CIP catalogue record for this book
is available from the British Library.

ISBN 978-0-7515-3772-7

Typeset in Plantin by Palimpsest Book Production Limited,
Falkirk, Stirlingshire
Printed and bound in Great Britain by
Clays Ltd, St Ives plc

Papers used by Sphere are from well-managed forests
and other responsible sources.

MIX
Paper from
responsible sources

FSC
www.fsc.org FSC® C104740

Sphere
An imprint of
Little, Brown Book Group
100 Victoria Embankment
London EC4Y 0DY

An Hachette UK Company
www.hachette.co.uk

www.littlebrown.co.uk

...ia **Harrod-Eagles** is the author of the contem-
...y Bill Slider Mystery series as well as the Morland
...sty novels. Her passions are music, wine, horses,
...ecture and the English countryside.

Visit the author's website at:
www.cynthiaharrodeagles.com

Also in the *Dynasty* series

To Tony, with love

THE MORLANDS OF MORLAND PLACE

James

Lucy — THE LONDON MORLANDS (qv)

Benedict
1812–1870
m(1) Rosalind Fleetham
m(2) Sibella Mayhew

Regina
1857–1907
m. Sir Peregrine Parke, Bt

TEDDY
b.1850
m(1) Charlotte Byng
m(2) Alice Meynell

George
1849–1885

HENRIETTA
b.1853
m(1) Edgar Fortescue
m(2) Jerome Compton

BERTIE
b.1876
m.1909
(1) Maud (2) Jessie Puddephat Morland

POLLY
b.1900

JAMES
1910

LIZZIE
b1872
m. 1897
Ashley Morland

JACK
b.1886
m.1915
Helen Ormerod

ROBERT
1887–1918
m.1909
Ethel Cornleigh

FRANK
1889–1916
m.1916
Maria Stanhope

JESSIE
b.1890
m.1911
Ned Morland

Richard
1912–1917

Thomas
b.1918

NED
1885–1915
m.1911
Jessie Compton

Martial
b.1898

Rupert
b.1899

Rose
b.1909

Basil
b.1916

Barbara
b.1917

Roberta
b.1911

Jeremy
b.1912

Harriet
b.1915

John
b.1916

Martin
b.1916

THE LONDON MORLANDS

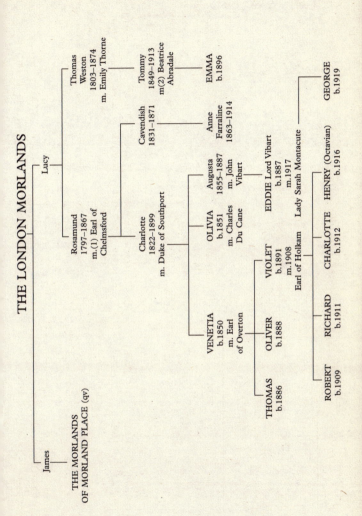

BOOK ONE

The Aftermath

Men remember alien ardours
As the dusk unearths old mournful odours.
In the garden unborn child souls wail
And the dead scribble on walls.
Though their own child cry for them in tears,
Women weep but hear no sound upstairs.
They believe in loves they had not lived
And in passion past the reach of the stairs
To the world's towers or stars.

Wilfred Owen: 'The Roads Also'

CHAPTER ONE

May 1919

In the housekeeper's room at Morland Place there was a large, ancient desk with a big leather chair, where generations of housekeepers had prepared their accounts, written letters, scrutinised tradesmen's bills, and rebuked erring servants. The high walls were lined from floor to ceiling with panelled cupboards, where they kept good things locked away. When she was little, Henrietta had sometimes been sent here with a message for Mrs Holicar, and sometimes Holicar had given her a handful of raisins or a little bit of stem ginger in reward. The dim, cool room smelled, as it had then, of tea, coffee, spices and cake.

Henrietta had always been a small person, and age was shrinking her further: her hands looked tiny on the arms of the chair and her feet barely touched the floor. She was mistress of the house, running it for her widowed brother Teddy; and this morning she was interviewing housemaids. The war was really over: even six months ago it would have been a luxury beyond dream to take on more staff. Now the demobilised men were reclaiming the jobs girls had done for four years, and the girls were having to come back to domestic service.

The war had changed them, as it had everyone. The

specimen before her now, a buxom, florid-faced young woman, was looking about her with a bold, assessing eye and no shadow of reserve.

'Where were you before, Betty?' Henrietta asked.

The answer came in a self-assured torrent. 'Well, ma'am, Ah were working in t' shell factory, but Ah never liked it there. Nasty, dirty work it were, and they were right strict if you were late on, or stopped a minute just to catch your breath. Treat you like dirt, them supervisors – 'rate you for just nothing at all! So the minute the Armistice went off, me and me friend Aggie put us coats on and walked out. That self an' same minute! Ah'm not jestin' nor jokin'! Ah wanted to go on t' trams – I'd like that, me – but me mam said it weren't right to be takin' jobs t' boys'd want, comin' back from t' war, so Ah went to work for Mrs Lloyd in Clifton, ma'am, as house-parlourmaid.'

'I don't know Mrs Lloyd. Have you a reference from her?'

'Oh, yes, ma'am, a right good 'un,' Betty said, handing it over.

Henrietta read it. It didn't say anything specific, but seemed eager that Betty should be taken on by someone else. 'Why did you leave Mrs Lloyd?' she asked.

'The work were too hard,' Betty said with disastrous frankness. 'And it were only me an' Cook, there, and it were right dull, just the two of us. Ah like a bit more company, me.' She looked round approvingly. 'Ah thought a big house'd be better.'

Better for you, perhaps, Henrietta thought, not for us. Too flighty, too lazy, too sure of herself. And at – what, nineteen, twenty? – already too old to train. She imagined, with a shudder, how Sawry, the butler, would take to being looked in the eye and answered back. 'I'm sorry,

4

Betty. I don't think you'll suit. Thank you for coming. Send the next girl in, if you please.'

It took Betty a moment to realise she had been rejected, and then she shrugged, gave an exaggerated sigh and flounced off. 'It's too far from t' shops an' t' cinema, anyroad,' she declared, saving face as she headed for the door.

Henrietta sorrowed over the ruination of maids – another thing to be laid to the war's account. But the next girl looked much more likely: younger, shy and hopeful, almost tiptoeing up and peeping about her in awe. She gave her name as Sally Gowthorpe.

'Gowthorpe?' Henrietta said. 'From Walton?' The girl nodded. 'I had a sewing-maid who married a Gowthorpe from Walton. Would that be your mother?'

'Me gran, ma'am,' the girl corrected, making Henrietta realise in those few words how much water had passed under her particular bridge since she had been running Morland Place.

'Of course,' she said. 'How is she?'

'She lives at our 'ouse since Granddad passed on. It was her what said I should come up the Place, ma'am.'

'How old are you, Sally?'

'Fifteen, ma'am.'

'And have you any experience of housework?'

'No, ma'am,' she admitted in a whisper, her eyes down. 'Just helping me mother in the house and with the little ones, ever since I left school. But now me dad's home from t' war, he says I've to get a job. He says—' She stopped herself, blushing, for talking too much.

'Well, Sally, if you come here to Morland Place we'll train you in our ways, so your lack of experience won't matter a bit.' In fact, breaking girls of habits learned in other houses was much harder. 'I think you'll suit us very well. You can start on the first of the month.'

By the time she reached the end of the candidates she had found another suitable novice, and an older girl she thought worth trying out as a sewing-maid: she would not do for a housemaid because she had a child and wanted to live out, but she was well-spoken, and seemed grateful for the work. Henrietta would have liked to find out her story, suspecting some deep misfortune, but it was not the time to ask. There were so many personal tragedies behind women's faces these days.

At the end Sawry, the butler, came in. He had been interviewing footmen, an even more unimaginable luxury. The male staff had been shrinking with every army call-up, and Sawry had to do more and more, despite his advancing years.

'Have you had any luck?' Henrietta enquired.

He looked glum. '*Not* a promising morning, madam. I suppose it's the war, but there wasn't one of them had what I'd call the right *demeanour* for a servant.'

'I suppose we should expect that,' Henrietta said. A man who had been to France and fought in the trenches was not going to be like the men from before the war, who had never been further from their own village than Leeds market. Experience and wider horizons, not to mention facing death on a daily basis, would naturally rub away the deference Sawry had looked for in vain. 'Was there no-one, then?'

'Well, madam, there is one who might just do. He says he was a footman before the war, and he's been batman to an officer since 1916. He's well set-up, clean and smart.'

Henrietta cocked her head. 'What are your doubts about him?'

Sawry shook his head, finding it hard to put into words. Daniel was all he had said, and intelligent besides, but there was something about the directness of his gaze, the self-assurance of his military bearing, which was not servantlike. 'I doubt he'd stick, madam,' was all he could say in the end.

'Well, perhaps we could try him, at any rate,' Henrietta said. 'Unless you prefer to wait?'

Sawry's legs ached all the time, and his back twinged from bending over the lamp-room table, having to fill all the lamps because there was no-one else to do it. He longed to be a butler and nothing else again. 'I think we might try him, madam, if you approve. Would you care to see him? He's waiting outside.'

Henrietta smiled inwardly. Sawry wouldn't have had the man wait if he hadn't wanted him taken on. 'Yes, send him in,' she said.

As she was crossing the great hall later, she discovered Teddy just come in, standing in a swirl of dogs by the side table, taking off his gloves.

'Did you find someone?' he asked her.

'Two housemaids, young enough to train,' she responded. 'And a footman.'

'Thank God! Poor old Sawry's ready to drop.' And his man, Brown, who helped out, was not getting any younger, he thought.

'But Sawry doesn't think he'll stay,' Henrietta added.

'Why not?'

'Too independent. I'm not sure, though. There's something about him that I like – a sort of quietness. I think he may do.'

'Was he in the war?'

'He was someone's batman. I wrote the name down – I thought it might be someone you know,' she said. 'And before the war he was a footman at Garrowby Hall.'

'Well, that's something we can check, at any rate,' said Teddy. 'But how old is he? If he was working before the war . . .'

'Twenty-six,' Henrietta said. Teddy shook his head doubtfully. 'I think he has a story to tell,' she mused, 'but I doubt he'll ever tell it.'

Teddy smiled. 'You always think everyone has a story to tell. Is there going to be any tea?'

'Come into the drawing-room and I'll ring,' Henrietta said, linking arms with him comfortably. They had been growing closer over the years. Ever since he had given her and her family a home with him, she had been running the house: his wife, Alice, a gentle, inactive person, had never wanted the job. But since Alice had died last autumn of the Spanish flu, Teddy had turned even more to his sister for comfort and companionship. They drew together as they had in childhood, in the shadow of their older brother.

'There weren't as many candidates for footman as I expected,' Henrietta said, as they crossed the staircase hall. The dogs, knowing the time as well as anyone, followed hopefully. 'I thought the boys coming home from the war would be looking for work.'

'Demobilisation has a long way to go yet,' Teddy said. He opened the drawing-room door for Henrietta. The sunshine coming in at the southerly windows struck a gleam from the mellow old furniture, and the clock on the overmantel ticked a calm, quiet welcome. 'And with the women leaving the wartime jobs, there are plenty of vacancies to soak up the men,' he went on, following his sister in.

'There was one girl here today who said she'd left the munitions factory the minute Armistice was declared.'

'There's a lot of pressure on the women to give up their jobs, even if they don't want to,' Teddy said, taking up his usual stance in front of the fire, though the grate held nothing more than its summer fan of paper.

'You mean their husbands won't want them to work?' she asked.

'That's one thing. And of course, the unmarried ones will be eager to *get* married. There'll be a lot of weddings this year.'

'Which means a lot of babies next year,' Henrietta said. For years the news had all been of deaths.

'And besides that,' Teddy concluded, 'it's their patriotic duty to give up their job for an ex-soldier. It's in all the papers.'

'It was their patriotic duty to take the job in the first place,' said Henrietta. 'Dear me, they do put so much on women these days.'

'You wanted the vote,' Teddy said.

'Not me,' she disclaimed.

'The point is, what with one thing and another, I don't think there'll be too much unemployment. The government's giving three months' unemployment insurance to all ex-servicemen, so they'll have a chance to look around. There's bound to be a post-war boom, so they'll get soaked up quickly enough.'

'Why will there be a boom?' Henrietta asked, sitting down and absently caressing the spaniel's head that was immediately thrust under her hands.

'All the world will be hungry for our goods, and with the men coming back, the factories will be able to go into full production again,' Teddy said confidently. As well as textiles factories, he owned three department stores called Makepeace's, one in York, one in Leeds and one in Manchester. 'There's the servicemen's war gratuity to be spent – anything up to forty pounds a head. They'll want civilian clothes. And the women will want new dresses after four years of making do. What with all the weddings, and setting up new households – sheets, table-cloths, curtains – and baby clothes to come, we can't fail!'

'But won't you lose the army contracts?'

'There are still more than a million men in uniform. The army won't get back to peacetime levels this year.'

'But eventually?'

'Oh, eventually I'll need something else for my factories to do. But I've already thought about that.' It was wonderful to Henrietta how her brother had become such a complete merchant. He had never been more than ordi-narily bright as a young man, but he seemed to have a sort of instinct for business. 'Ships, my dear – passenger liners! People have been confined so long, they're going to be mad for travel. The liners will come out of military service and they'll all want refitting. Sheets instead of army shirts.' He rubbed his hands. 'I'm looking forward to seeing the ocean racers back in business. White Star will come to me, after our long association, but I don't see why I can't make a bid for Cunard as well.'

Henrietta laughed. 'Is there no end to your ambition? You'll be monarch of the seas before you're done.'

'I've a son and a daughter to provide for,' Teddy said. His nine-year-old heir, James, had had the flu as well, striking panic into Teddy's heart, but he had recovered, and the illness had even caused a spurt of growth in the boy, who had shot up two inches since Christmas.

10

Polly, his beloved, beautiful daughter, had escaped the flu, though she had had a bad cold at Christmas. Physically she was well, but she was not herself, too quiet, mopish. She had always been so bright and energetic, up to everything: if anyone could be said to have enjoyed the war, she had. But now . . .

'Hen, what's *wrong* with Polly?' he asked plaintively.

'Oh dear, I don't know,' Henrietta said. She had noticed the change in Polly too. 'Perhaps it's just her age. Nineteen is a difficult time for a girl. Lennie's still in France, and I don't believe she's heard from Captain Holford in a while—'

'Lennie's just a cousin and I don't believe she ever cared for Holford,' Teddy said sharply.

'Maybe that's what's wrong,' Henrietta suggested.

'No, no,' Teddy objected. 'Girls get lovelorn when they're *in* love. They don't get glumpish because they're *not*.'

'Well, perhaps she's just feeling a bit flat, now there's not so much excitement. Perhaps she needs a change.'

'There's been too much change altogether in the last four years,' Teddy objected.

'The war's affected us all, one way or another,' Henrietta said. 'Things can't be the same again. We have to make the best of it.'

They were quiet a moment, and then Teddy's face brightened as the door opened and Sawry and a maid came in with the tea things. 'Ah, muffins!' he said. 'Now there's one thing that never changes – and thank God for it! I tell you what, Hen – we ought to have a party. A grand victory ball. Invite everybody. That would cheer us all up.'

Henrietta caught Sawry's eye, and understanding

11

passed between man and mistress. The work involved in a grand ball . . . 'We'd need at least one more footman. And a pastry cook. And kitchen-maids.'

'Get 'em,' Teddy said largely, oblivious to all difficulties.

In her house in Manchester Square, Venetia looked up from the eyepiece of her microscope as her son appeared in the doorway of her laboratory. 'Dearest boy! I didn't know you were here.'

'I wasn't,' Oliver said. 'I was in Sidcup. I've been up all night.'

He looked it. He had dark shadows round his eyes, his hair was ruffled, his clothing awry. 'You are a little *mal soigné*,' she agreed mildly.

'*Mal* everything.' He leaned against the door frame and kicked moodily at the carpet. 'We lost Flighty.'

'Oh, my dear! I'm so sorry. What was it?'

'Immediate cause, heart failure. But it was the infection that sapped his strength.' Oliver sighed deeply. 'It's probably a mercy that he went quickly, because sepsis was sloughing away everything. But after so long, and so many operations . . . He was one of our pets.'

'I know, dear.'

Venetia understood the depths of the frustration Oliver felt. After serving with the RAMC in France, he had joined the specialist plastics unit at the Queen's Hospital in Sidcup, where servicemen with terrible face and hand injuries were given a chance of new life through the pioneer techniques of Harold Gillies. Oliver had always had an interest in plastic surgery, and his experiences at the Front had given it direction. The Sidcup unit was small and tightly knit. Venetia had visited several times and, like Oliver, had been impressed by the stoical courage of the men in bearing not only great pain and a future of multiple operations but their own disfigurement. They rarely left the unit, because their appearance made ordinary people turn away in horror; but inside 'the zoo', as they called it, they had acceptance, companionship and hope.

Harold 'Flighty' Bird had been an observer in the Royal Flying Corps until being shot down near Plug Street. The wreck had caught fire, which had robbed him of most of his fingers and half his face. He was one of the longest-serving members of the zoo, and had endured numerous operations to restore him to a semblance of humanity, and to give him hands with which he could at least dress and feed himself. He was always cheerful. He said of himself that he looked like the worst cheese-nightmare of your life, but self-pity got you nowhere.

Flighty was usually the first person a patient saw when coming round from the anaesthetic – mumbling, as they all seemed to, a string of filthy language.

'Now then, none o' that,' Flighty would say, leaning over the bed. 'Ladies present.' And when they moaned, he would say, 'Here, look at me! Now then, cock, if you can stand that, you can stand anything. You're an oil painting compared with me, mate. Have a fag.'

Oliver had lately been engaged in giving Flighty a new nose, first raising a pedicle of flesh from his abdomen to his forearm, then raising it from the forearm to the forehead. Flighty had gone several weeks with his arm supported in that position while the blood supply established itself; he joked that it was the longest salute in the history of the army. When the pedicle was detached from his arm, it was to be moved down into position over the hole in his face where his original nose had been.

'It won't look too bad, though I says it as shouldn't,' Oliver had told him only a week ago. 'Though I'm afraid your belly was not as hairless as a girl's, Flighty old man. You're going to have a nose you'll have to shave every morning.'

'I'll take that, Doc,' Flighty had said. 'Just so long as I've got something to blow when I got a cold. Doesn't arf make a mess when all you've got is a bleeding great hole in your phiz.'

But somehow, despite all precautions, sepsis had struck, and now Flighty was dead.

'We take such care,' Oliver said bitterly. 'We do everything, *everything*, to keep things sterile.'

'I know,' Venetia said again. She had been one of the pioneers of antisepsis, fighting an almost lone battle at a time when surgeons operated in blood-encrusted coats down which they wiped their hands, and stropped their scalpels on their boot soles. 'But these things happen, despite all our efforts.'

'What we *need*,' Oliver said, 'is a reliable bactericide that will operate inside the bloodstream to kill the staphylococci.'

'Obviously,' Venetia said drily. 'We've been wanting that ever since Lister told us infection wasn't God's judgement on bad behaviour.'

'Well, you'd think someone would have discovered it by now,' Oliver cried in frustration. 'It must exist out there somewhere. Nature creates the problem, nature must contain the antidote. Why doesn't someone find it?'

'Why don't *you*? You're more than capable of doing the research.'

'When would I have time?' he said indignantly.

'The same could be said for all of us,' Venetia pointed out. She saw his black mood was passing. 'And do stop kicking the paintwork, darling.'

'Sorry.' He gave her a weary smile. 'Sinking into self-pity.' He nodded towards the microscope. 'What's that? Koch's jolly old bacilli?'

'Happily, no. The absence thereof. One of my subjects seems to be curing himself. I can't believe it's anything I did. I've been looking for a cure for tuber-culosis most of my professional life, and I've never even come near it.'

'Maybe it's the same thing,' Oliver said. 'Maybe some-thing that could kill staph would also kill Koch's.'

'Perhaps. Just find it for me, would you, darling?'

'All right, Mother dear. I'll have a look later.' He yawned. 'Meanwhile, me for a bath and bed for a couple of hours. I'm off for a couple of days.'

'I suppose that means you'll be dancing until four in the morning?'

'If I can find someone to dance with.'

'Can't you dance with Verena?' Venetia had been pleased these past months to see Oliver, her chronically bachelor son, pay attention to Lady Verena Felbrigg, daughter of the Earl of Roughton, who was a nurse in the VAD. Venetia liked the girl immensely, and was keen to see her son settle down and be happy.

'She's on night duty. You have to admire her,' he went on. 'Other girls would have given up nursing by now, but her contract doesn't end until July and she won't break it.'

'She's a very good sort of girl,' Venetia said. 'Pretty, too.'

Oliver looked at her sidelong. 'If you're cooking up a

romance for me, Mother dear, you should remember that I am very nearly out of a job, and in no position to ask anyone to be my wife.'

Venetia was secretly pleased: the fact that he had mentioned the word 'wife' was a good sign. 'You won't have any difficulty in getting something,' she said.

'With all the other demobbed army doctors to compete with? A guinea here and there for assisting is not going to add up to a life a chap could ask a girl to share – especially not an earl's daughter.'

'Take your fellowship,' Venetia said calmly, 'and then we'll see.'

'We'll see, all right,' he said gloomily, kicking the door frame again.

'Oliver!'

'Sorry.' He stretched his shoulders. 'Anyway, I don't want to talk about it now. I'm off to bed. You keep dashed early hours, old thing, otherwise I'd suggest we meet for breakfast when I get up around half past eleven. But I suppose you've had yours?'

'You suppose right. Besides, I shall be going out at half past eleven.'

'Oh, Lord, yes, it's the funeral, isn't it? Look, I'll have Ash call me at eleven, and I'll escort you as far as the door of the Abbey, and go on and have breakfast at the club.'

'Will you, darling? That'll be nice.'

When he had gone, she didn't immediately go back to her slides. His interruption had set so many trains of thought in motion. Poor Flighty – infection – Koch's bacillus – a bactericide. At Morland Place, she remembered, the grooms put mouldy bread on horses' cuts to

16

make them heal cleanly; and her great hero, the surgeon Joseph Lister, had done experiments back in 1871, showing that bacteria would not grow in urine samples contaminated with mould. He had even cured a patient's infected wound with a mould he identified as *Penicillium glaucum*. And a few years later in Paris, Pasteur had inhibited the growth of anthrax with a mould – though he identified it, she recollected, as *Penicillium notatum*. There was certainly something worth looking into there. *Nature creates the problem, nature must contain the antidote*.

The trouble was that *Penicillium glaucum* was a catch-all term for a certain class of moulds, and no-one knew what the active principle was, or in which moulds it could be found, still less how to extract it. Would the *Penicillium* principle kill Koch's? She toyed with the idea of injecting mould into her subjects. But nothing anyone had injected into consumptives – tar, gold, God knew what else as well – had so far proved efficacious. The sanatorium treatment was all there was – absolute rest, fresh air, good food. All very well for the comfortably off, but the working classes could not afford a rest cure, especially one that might take months or even years.

No, prevention was definitely better than cure when it came to tuberculosis. Education about avoiding infection, and training in basic hygiene could only do so much: the disease was fostered by the conditions the lower classes lived in: cheek by jowl, foul air, poor nourishment. But vaccination: it had virtually eliminated smallpox, that terrible scourge of the last century. Oh, for a vaccine against tuberculosis, to clear the slums of the wasting death that snatched away children and young mothers and burly working men indiscriminately . . .

17

There had been some interesting work going on before the war in the Pasteur Institute in Lille – Calmette and Guérin had developed a culture of non-virulent bacilli from bovine tuberculosis. If a vaccine from cowpox could prevent smallpox, perhaps the same principle could work for human tuberculosis. Definitely worth looking into . . .

How tired Oliver looked! He worked tremendously long hours, and when he was off duty he would not rest, but went out 'helling' – as the American troops lingering in London called it: drinking and dancing and visiting nightclubs. Dancing seemed to have become the obsession of the young people back from the war – and those who had never gone. The mood of almost violent merrymaking that had burst out at the Armistice seemed not to have died down. Everyone had something to forget.

Verena . . . She wished he would settle down with Verena, but of course it was true, he would be discharged from the army very soon and it would take time for him to establish himself in some specialty. She could afford to keep him, but she knew his pride would not let him, and he would never allow his wife to be kept. She must find some subtle way of helping him. And they would just have to hope that Verena would wait, and wasn't put off by all this wild dancing.

Of course, Oliver was taking the loss of his brother very badly – worse than Venetia would have expected. He and Thomas had been close as boys, but their lives had grown apart, particularly since Thomas had gone to Russia as military attaché to the Romanov court. When the Romanovs had disappeared, Thomas had disappeared too. The army had posted him as 'missing believed killed', and if he did not reappear – which for various reasons Venetia thought impossible – Oliver would inherit the earldom in a little under seven years' time. He had never wanted to be earl, and helpless anger about that situation added to his natural sorrow for his brother.

As to Venetia, the war had taken not only her first-born, but her beloved husband, too. But she was sixty-nine years old, and if age taught you nothing else, it taught you to make the best of things. She had Oliver who, whatever he thought, would make a creditable earl one day, and might do sterling service in the House on behalf of his profession; and her lovely daughter Violet, who had given her four grandchildren.

And she had her work. The war was over, bar the talking, and at last she was free of those irksome committees and meetings and fund-raising activities. She had given the X-ray ambulances, which she had worked so hard to buy and equip, to the Red Cross; she had closed her office and refused all requests to take on other charities or public offices. The sense of liberty and uncluttered time at her disposal was almost dizzying. For almost the first time in her life, she was free to follow her interests and work at her own pace.

On that pleasing thought, she returned to the microscope, removed the slide and inserted another. She had two hours before she would have to go and get dressed.

The newspapers the next morning were full of the State Funeral. Teddy read out bits at breakfast, and passed around the pages with photographs. The body of nurse Edith Cavell, executed in 1915 by the Germans for helping Allied soldiers to escape from Belgium, had been exhumed on the 14th of May and conveyed with a military escort to Ostende, where it had been put aboard the destroyer

19

HMS *Rowena* for Dover. Then on the 15th it had been taken by train to Victoria, put on a gun carriage, draped with the Union flag, and conveyed through the streets, with a company of soldiers and two bands, to Westminster Abbey for a state funeral at noon.

'Venetia was there,' Henrietta said. 'She told me she'd been invited. I think she said she'd met Nurse Cavell while she was training.'

'The King was represented by the Earl of Athlone,' Teddy read. 'That's the Queen's brother,' he explained to his daughter, who was listlessly pushing buttered eggs around her plate.

'Hmm?' said Polly indifferently.

'It wasn't a very long service,' Teddy said, still reading. 'Just half an hour. But the crowds in the street were immense. The whole route was lined, both going to the Abbey and afterwards all the way to Liverpool Street. It says, "A profound silence fell as the gun carriage passed, and every head was bowed." Strange that of all the people who died over there, only her body should be brought back.'

'Our soldiers are always buried where they fall,' Jessie said.

She had been quiet lately, too, Henrietta thought, trying to examine her daughter without appearing to – ever since she had come back from spending Easter with Violet in London, she had seemed to have something on her mind.

'All the same . . .' Teddy said, but didn't finish the thought. Morland Place had given its share: his son Ned – Jessie's first husband – missing at Loos; Henrietta's son Frank, fallen at the Somme, and his brother Robert, dead of typhoid caught in Palestine. And there were footmen and estate workers and tenants and villagers who had paid the ultimate price. Everyone you knew had lost someone.

'I don't see why we can't bring them back, now the war's over,' said Ethel, Robert's widow, raising a frequent complaint of hers. Uncle Teddy was rich, he had friends in high places: surely it would be a little thing to him to bring Robert back from the hospital cemetery in Malta.

'Think of the chaos,' Jessie said, 'if everyone did it.'

'And the resentment of those who couldn't afford it,' said Maria, Frank's widow. 'As it is, everyone had the same burial and the same headstone, men and officers alike. No-one's sacrifice was greater than another's.'

Ethel sniffed. 'That's a matter of opinion. Some people had wives and children. Yet they bring Nurse Cavell back . . .' Her tone was resentful. *Who cares about her?*

'We'll have our War Memorial,' Henrietta said soothingly. 'It will be beautiful, and all our dear ones will be remembered on it.'

Teddy said, 'You know, we might have a trip over to France some time, to visit the graves. I'm sure a lot of people will be going. It will take time for the army to clear things up, and for all the boys to come home. But next year, perhaps . . . I'd like to visit some of the battlefields, see how they match up to my imagination. You can't really tell enough from a map.'

'But Ned doesn't have a grave,' Ethel objected. 'And Robbie's buried in Malta. I'd like to go to Malta, with the children, so they can see his gravestone.'

'I don't think it's healthy to dwell on such things,' Maria said. 'Now the war's over, I just want to forget it.'

Ethel, who didn't like Maria – she was suspicious of clever people, and Maria suffered fools badly – looked triumphant, her nostrils quivering. 'So, you want to forget poor Frank, do you? I can't say I'm surprised. And I don't suppose he'd be expecting you to visit his grave, given that it hasn't taken you long to get over him, which he must know, if he's looking down.'

'*Ethel!*' Henrietta said, scandalised. It was fortunate that Father Palgrave, the chaplain, to whom Maria was now engaged to be married, was not at the table, having been summoned early to a sickbed in the village. Maria merely looked indifferent, but Henrietta couldn't believe she wasn't hurt all the same, as *she* would have been.

Ethel was unabashed. 'Well,' she said, 'all I can say is I'd think it was an insult to poor Robbie if I was to fall in love with another man when he was hardly cold in his grave. It isn't decent.'

'That's enough,' Henrietta said firmly.

'It's quite all right,' Maria said quietly. 'Nothing Ethel says can offend me. If you'll excuse me, I have some letters to attend to.' She rose and left the table.

Finding everyone looking at her, Ethel tossed her head and muttered, 'I speak as I find.' And then, with an attempt at pathos, 'I can't help it if I miss Robbie. I can't sleep for crying most nights. I don't know what to do with myself without him.'

'We all miss him,' Henrietta said.

Polly stood up abruptly. 'I'm going out for a ride,' she said. She looked pale. 'Excuse me please, Aunt Hen – Papa.'

Ethel made a muttered excuse and took her departure too, leaving Teddy, Henrietta and Jessie in a slightly awkward silence.

Then Henrietta said, 'Oh dear.'

'I wish Helen was here,' Teddy said. 'She always seems to keep things comfortable. The house is too quiet without her and Jack and the children.'

Jessie looked up from the toast she was buttering. 'Quiet?'

'Oh – you know what I mean.' He frowned over his coffee cup. 'Dash it,' he exploded – though mildly, all things considered, 'we've all suffered losses in this war. Why does Ethel have to make more noise about it than anyone else? And Maria only makes things worse. She doesn't seem to know the meaning of tact. Why can't everyone just get along, the way they used to?'

'It's the war,' Henrietta said soothingly. 'Everything's changed. You have to expect it.'

Jessie gave her a faint smile. 'I wonder how long we're going to rely on that excuse? I hear it just about every day.'

Teddy drained his cup and stood up. 'Well, war or no war, I have to go and see a man about some pigs. And then I have a meeting of the railway board, so I shan't be home to luncheon, Hen dear.'

'Everything's unsettled,' Jessie said when she and her mother were alone. 'It's this waiting period, not knowing how things are going to come out.' She frowned at her hands. 'It's funny, all through the war we thought that as soon as it was over, everything would go instantly back to normal. Bells would ring, uniforms would be thrown away, and we'd all take up where we left off. But it isn't that easy.' She looked up and saw her mother's troubled face. This seemed a good time to share something pleasant with her. 'I'm having another baby.'

Henrietta's face lit. 'I *thought* you might be! Darling, I'm so glad! Does Bertie know?'

'I wrote to him last week.'

Jessie had had two miscarriages before the birth of Thomas last year. 'You'll have to be careful from now on,' Henrietta said. 'No more riding, to begin with.'

Jessie smiled. 'I knew you'd say that. Poor Hotspur – how he'll miss me! And I'll miss him. I *wish* Bertie would come home,' she went on. 'I hate this waiting. I keep feeling that something's going to go wrong.'

'He's safe now,' Henrietta said. 'There's no fighting in Cologne.'

'I know that, but . . .' Under the table, her dog Bran sensed her unease and pushed his head up onto her knees. 'He was supposed to be coming home in June,' she sighed, 'but here it is, the middle of May, and he hasn't said anything about it. And now they've promoted him to brigadier.'

'But that's good,' Henrietta said. 'He deserves it – your uncle says it ought to have happened months ago.'

'Yes, Mother, but they won't want to let someone go when they've just promoted him.'

'Oh, I don't know about that,' Henrietta said, searching for a way to comfort her. 'They give people medals when they leave, don't they? Like prize-giving on the last day of school.'

Jessie laughed. 'Mother!'

'Well, you know what I mean. Jessie, have you got that dog under the table? You know how I feel about that.'

'Sorry, he just crept in,' Jessie said. 'I'll take him out. I have to go, anyway. I'm wanted at Twelvetrees.' The stud stables belonged to her, and orders for horses were at last picking up.

'You're not going to ride over, are you?'

'Just this one last time,' Jessie said. 'Don't fuss, Mother.

I won't go out of a walk, I promise. What are you doing today?'

'Mrs Tomlinson wants me to go over the table linens this morning. And this afternoon it's the Hospital Relief Committee meeting, about aid to limbless soldiers. They can't decide whether it should come out of the Chronic Illness Fund or the Industrial Injuries Fund.'

'I don't suppose the limbless soldiers will mind.'

'Probably not, but you have to get the money in before you can give it out,' Henrietta said, 'and people always want to know where their donations are going.'

'Well, don't work too hard.' Jessie came round the table to rest her hands a moment on her mother's shoulders. 'There's not enough of you to go round.'

Henrietta watched her go, glad that at least she had distracted her for the moment from her worries.

CHAPTER TWO

Fairoaks was a substantial house built in the early 1880s, standing square in four acres of garden in Weybridge. It had all the solid benefits of upper-middle-class comfort – a carriage sweep, shrubberies, tennis lawn, coke boiler in its own brick outhouse to fire the central heating – but none of those hostages to taste so common to the period: no balconies, wrought ironwork, mock-Tudor chimneys or mock-mediaeval curlicues. Mr Ormerod, Helen's father, had had electricity and the telephone put in before the war and had toyed with the idea of a motor-car; but it was only a short walk to the station, and there was a taxi-rank for emergencies or wet evenings.

Before the war the tradesmen had delivered, and Mrs Ormerod had had no need to discover that the shops were also a short walk away. The changes the war had wrought had been a shock to her system. Deliveries had stopped, the tradesmen disappeared. Male servants were called up, and female ones left to work in factories, or to serve in the shops to which a bewildered Mrs Ormerod now had to walk to buy her own meat and groceries – only to find them in short supply or downright non-existent.

The taxi-rank developed alarming female drivers; the postman turned into a woman; you couldn't find a window-cleaner for love nor money. Conversations with previously comfortable acquaintances became full of pitfalls, as sons, brothers, nephews and cousins fell in battle. There was no-one to play bridge with any more, and the vicar's sermons became *most* peculiar. And the newspapers were full of things that caused Mr Ormerod to look grim at breakfast, just when the table was naked of those things that might have softened him, such as real butter, and marmalade, and decent coffee.

It was a comfort that their son, Freddie, was too important in engineering to be made to go to the war. On the other hand, Helen had disgraced the family by taking a job – delivering aeroplanes from the factory to the military units – and then their younger daughter Molly had insisted on learning to type and gone to work for the Ministry of Munitions. Two daughters in paid employment! However much it was explained to her that war work was a patriotic duty, Mrs Ormerod could not get past the horror of having wage-earning daughters.

Her pet dachshunds could not cope with the descent from a diet of choice meat to one of kitchen scraps and had faded away. And then in February 1918, Mr Ormerod had died from a heart attack, and Mrs Ormerod's rout was complete.

'I'm afraid she's losing her grasp of things,' Helen said to Jack, as they sat in the garden in the June sunshine, watching Rug run about, nose to the ground, searching for his old friends the dachies. Mrs Ormerod was upstairs having her afternoon rest. Helen had helped her mother take off her shoes and dress, placed the eiderdown over her and drawn the curtains, and Mrs Ormerod had murmured, 'Thank you, Connors,' as Helen had left her. 'Connors was at least two maids ago.'

Jack grunted acknowledgement. He had troubles of his own. He had been shot down in March 1918, had spent the last eight months of the war as a prisoner, and had come home in such impaired health that he had still not returned to normal.

Flying was not only his profession but his passion, and one of the things he had long dreamed of was being the first man to fly the Atlantic. Back in 1914 the *Daily Mail* had offered a ten-thousand-pound prize for the first non-stop crossing, which had never been claimed, and as soon as the war was over, it had renewed the challenge. Last month, his old friend Tom Sopwith had set up an attempt, with a remodelled Sopwith B1 bomber and a two-man team, to fly from St John's in Newfoundland to Ireland.

Had Jack been fit, he was convinced he would have been asked to be part of it: he and the Australian Harry Hawker had been Sopwith's test pilots before the war, and both of them were also engineers and designers. It would have been natural for Sopwith to choose him. But when Hawker and the crated aircraft had set off for America in March, Jack was still far from well, and the second man in the team was some fellow Jack had barely heard of.

As it happened, the attempt had failed: the engine had overheated and they had been forced to ditch in mid-ocean, as soon as they had found a ship that could pick them up. Even with the peevishness of long convalescence, Jack did not quite suggest that if he had gone along it would not have happened; but he could not help feeling, deep and unspoken in his heart, that things might have been different.

Helen knew, of course: she always knew what he was

thinking. Aloud she told him that it was damned bad luck, but there would be other chances. Inwardly she was glad not to have been in the position of Muriel Hawker: the ship that picked the men up had had no radio, and for a desperate week it was believed they were dead. The King had even sent a telegram of condolence. Helen had lived through all that once, when Jack had been shot down and posted 'missing', and once was enough.

One reason they had left Morland Place to come and stay at Fairoaks was so that Jack could go and see Tom Sopwith about a job. The RAF had released him in January, and he had a wife and two children to support: he must look towards the commercial sector to make his living. The other reason was Mrs Ormerod's failing health, and a desperate plea from Molly for help in looking after her. Molly's job had also disappeared when the Ministry of Munitions was disbanded, but with her skills and experience she could easily get another. She didn't want to dwindle into the 'daughter at home' looking after her mother.

She came out from the house, now – a tall, firm-featured girl with straight dark hair pulled back into a bun, dressed in a plain skirt a modest four inches above the ankle and a mannish white shirt. She carried Barbara on her arm and held Basil by the hand, the latter looking ominously mulish, the former alarmingly angelic.

'Oh dear, what have they been up to?' Helen asked, hoping her offspring hadn't been wrecking the house. They were extremely handsome children and remarkably alike, with Jack's good looks and Helen's colouring, but they had a propensity for devilment and egged each other on.

29

'Nothing serious, but Nanny's rather frazzled, so I've brought them out for some fresh air while she soothes herself with the mending,' Molly said cheerfully, dumping two-year-old Barbara in her mother's lap. Basil, a year older, gave his parents no more than a glance before dashing off to play with Rug. Animals were far more interesting than people.

'Poor thing, she's finding her elevation rather a strain,' Helen said. They had 'borrowed' Mina from Morland Place, where she had been merely a nursery-maid. She had volunteered for the trip, and had been excited by her promotion to 'Nanny Mina', but Basil was a handful and Barbara had recently discovered the delights of screaming when she didn't get her own way. 'They're at a difficult age. They're very good with you, though,' she added, smiling at her sister.

Molly made a face. 'I know what that means. Next you're going to say what a waste it is that I haven't got married and had some of my own.'

'I wouldn't say anything so tactless,' Helen protested. 'You forget Mother had been despairing of me for seven years before I got married. It takes time to find the right man.'

'Yes, and yours is perfect. Can't expect both of us to have such luck,' Molly said, with a teasing glance at Jack.

'Don't spare my blushes,' he said. 'Here, I'll take Barbara to look at the shrubbery and leave you two to gossip in private.' He lifted his daughter from Helen's lap. She wriggled to get down, but consented to take his hand and walk off with him.

'We don't "gossip", I'll have you know,' Molly called after him. 'It's called "intellectual conversation".' They watched him join Basil and Rug and disappear into the shrubbery. 'How is he, really?' Molly asked. 'I haven't had a chance yet to speak to you alone.'

'Much better,' Helen said.

'He doesn't look it.'

Helen winced. 'Your famed frankness.'

'No sense in covering things up – not between us, anyway. I was shocked at how poorly he looked. It was the prison camp, was it?'

'Confinement, poor food and no medical attention,' Helen said. 'It sapped his strength, and then he got that terrible cold during the winter. Of course we thought it was the Spanish flu. I was afraid we were going to lose him.'

'Poor you,' Molly said, with a look of real sympathy. The sisters were separated by ten years, so they had not been close growing up, but they had become fond of each other since Helen's marriage.

'And he was covered with terrible sores that just *wouldn't* heal,' Helen went on. 'I can't tell you how lowering that was. But it's the damage to his spirit that really worries me. He won't talk about it, though we always talked about everything before. There was something about being locked up that was very hard for him.'

'I shouldn't think anyone would like it.'

'No, but some stand it better than others. And he must be remembering that long period after he was shot down the time before, when his ankle wouldn't heal and he thought he'd never fly again. He *needs* to fly. He's like a caged skylark.'

Molly's mouth quirked at the poetic image. '*Very* like a skylark.'

'I can't help it,' Helen said. 'He might not look like one, but he's suffering inside, and missing out on the Atlantic

31

crossing only added to it. I hope and pray Tom Sopwith can give him a job, or I don't know what we'll do.'

'When's he seeing him?'

'He's going down to the works tomorrow. I'm sure Tom will give him a good hearing,' she concluded doubtfully.

Molly knew what she was thinking. 'As long as he doesn't look at him too closely. But you can always go back to Morland Place. Uncle Teddy would never cast you out to starve.'

'I know. And the children love it there – frankly, I'm sure they'd rather live at Morland Place than anywhere else in the world. But Jack needs to support his own family.'

Molly was thinking. 'If Mr Sopwith gives Jack a job, you'll have to live down here, won't you?'

'Yes, of course. I know what you're thinking.'

'Mother can't cope on her own any more. When Freddie was here last Sunday he murmured something about having her come to live with him.'

Helen's eyes widened. 'Oh dear, that would never work. He'd bother her to death. I can't imagine why he even suggested it.'

'Because it would be no trouble to him,' Molly said. 'He'd be at the office. It would be Joan who'd have her all day long.'

'And Mother doesn't like Joan.'

'Nobody likes Joan, except Freddie. Actually, I'm not sure even he likes her much.'

'Molly!'

'But then the same rule applies – he's at work all day and doesn't see much of her.'

'Poor Joan.'

'Well, to be fair, she doesn't like Mother, either. She

resents it when Mother criticises the way the children are brought up.'

'It's hard for women to live under the same roof as their husband's mother,' Helen said. 'Of course, it's different for me at Morland Place.'

'Very different sort of roof,' Molly observed. 'A castle with hundreds of servants, rather than "The Laurels" with a cook and two housemaids.'

Helen laughed. 'You will have your fantasy. But it is a different sort of household. And my mother-in-law is a dear: we get on very well. And,' she added, 'I don't bring up my children – the nursery does that.'

'Do I detect a gripe in that sentence?'

'Only a very little one,' Helen said. 'It's wonderful not being bothered by them – or it was, when I had a proper job to do. But if I'm not to have a job outside the home, I think I might as well make my husband and children my job.'

'Very old-fashioned and proper of you.'

'You needn't sound disapproving.'

'I wasn't, really, but it wouldn't do for me,' Molly said. 'I've had a taste of a life on my own terms, and I don't want to give it up. Which brings us back to Mother.'

'You've had a good long "go" of looking after her,' Helen said. 'All through the war, really, because Daddy wasn't up to much most of the time. You deserve to have your own time now, if it can be managed.'

'If Jack gets a job in Kingston, it would make sense for you to live here,' Molly said. 'And then I could get a job in London with a clear conscience.'

'Do you have anything in mind?'

'Oh, one of the other ministries. I know plenty of people who will put in a good word for me if I ask.'

'But you'd still live here?'

'Golly, of course I would! Mother would have a fit if I set up alone as a "bachelor girl". Besides, I couldn't afford a proper flat and I'd hate living in lodgings, with a hatchet-faced landlady steaming open your letters, and having to eat brown Windsor and boiled haddock at the communal board, with travelling salesmen and depressed spinsters who smell of mothballs.'

Helen laughed. 'Your imagination! You should write stories for one of the magazines.'

'Perhaps I will,' Molly said. 'But it's all true. I've heard Jack's tales about his landladies, before he married you. And I've heard what other girls at the ministry say. No diggings for me, Hel. I'll stay here and keep you sane. You'll need me after a day alone with children, servants and Mother.'

'It hasn't happened yet,' Helen reminded her. 'He has to see Tom Sopwith first.'

So much rested on it, she thought, watching her husband on his knees with the children and Rug, examining something on the ground – a beetle, probably. Basil was at the age when insects were a fascination, and Rug would sniff anything that moved. If Jack got a job in Kingston, they could live here, which would solve the problem of housing and Mother in one neat package. Mother had her own income, which would pay for the upkeep of the house, and it would provide more spacious and comfortable accommodation than they could hope for on Jack's salary. Mother would have someone to run it for her, and tell her what to do; the children would have a nice big garden to run about in, and a nursery suite designed for the purpose (Helen and Freddie had grown up together there – it gave a little twist to her

34

heart to think of Basil and Barbara following them); and Molly would have the freedom to live her life as she wished. Naturally Helen hoped that that life would sooner or later involve a very nice man and a brace of children: she couldn't help having a good opinion of matrimony. Molly called her the tailless fox; but Molly liked to make a joke out of everything.

Tom Sopwith hadn't changed. His handsome, genial face had a few more lines in it, but he was the same eager, enthusiastic, warm-hearted man Jack had grown to know and like from the early days at Rankin Marine down in Southampton. Sopwith's first shocked look suggested he found Jack changed, but he concealed the expression swiftly and smoothly, grasped his hand and beamed a smile of welcome as he pumped it. 'It's been a long war, old fellow. I read about your DSO – congratulations. Jolly good show!'

'Oh, it was nothing.'

'I bet it wasn't nothing! And your being taken prisoner. That must have been rotten.'

'Could have been worse.'

'You weren't involved in the daring escape that was in all the papers?'

'I helped with it, but I wasn't one of the escapers. They'd already picked them before I arrived. I read about your Atlantic attempt, by the way. Jolly bad luck!'

'Yes, and it all looked set fair, too. We tested everything for weeks on end down at Brooklands.'

'What happened, exactly?'

'Well, they took off around half past three, local time, and everything was going well, until just about nightfall the water temperature started climbing.'

'Blockage in the water pipe?'

'That's what Harry assumed . . .'

A satisfyingly technical conversation followed, during which Jack discovered all the things he had wanted to know about the Atlantic attempt, except why the engine had overheated – a secret the aeroplane had taken to its watery grave. Speculation, however, was both free and absorbing.

When they had finally exhausted the subject, Jack asked, 'How's business?'

The genial face lengthened somewhat. 'Not good,' Sopwith said. 'The loss of the government contracts was immediate. They've been winding down much faster than anyone anticipated. The peacetime RAF is going to be tiny, and of course they've got plenty of machines to be going on with. By the end of the war we had three and a half thousand people working here at the four plants, a third of them women. Most of the older men and almost all the women left of their own accord after the Armistice, but still it's a struggle to keep the rest of them busy. I've been retooling since January so that we can diversify. We're making motorcycles now, doing coachwork, even making furniture, but it's hand-to-mouth stuff.'

'What about civilian aviation?'

'We brought out our first civil aircraft last month – the Dove. We thought that was an appropriate name for peacetime.'

'Yes, I read about it,' Jack said. 'From what I gather it's basically a two-seater Pup, isn't it?' Another technical conversation later, he asked, 'How is it going?'

'Nothing doing so far,' Sopwith admitted. 'The market just isn't there. I still believe flying is the future – the

Prince of Wales is very keen: took him up for a test flight at Hounslow when we launched the Dove – but for the moment anyone who wants to buy an aeroplane, and has the money to do so, can get all the ex-RAF buses they like for a fraction of the price. We're being undercut by our own second-hand Snipes and Pups,' he concluded ruefully. 'It's heartbreaking.'

'But things will pick up?'

'Bound to, in the long run,' Sopwith said with his bedrock optimism, 'but it's hard going at the moment. Even Harry's talking about going over to motor-racing.'

Jack gave him a frank look. 'I came hoping you'd have something for me – a position.'

'I guessed you did. Of course I'll find room for you somewhere, but I don't think it will be anything you'll like.' He mused. 'Perhaps you might fit in somewhere at the showroom.'

'You have a showroom?'

'In Molton Street,' Sopwith said, and then, seeing the misunderstanding, 'For the motorcycles.'

'I don't know anything about motorcycles,' Jack said blankly.

'You'd soon pick it up,' Sopwith said. He regarded his friend with sympathy. 'Times are bad all over. Martinsyde is struggling. Airco is in trouble. Glendower, Portholme, Kingsbury Aviation. Proctor's are talking about going over to agricultural machinery. The bottom's fallen out of aviation for the moment. What about Rankin Marine? Have you thought about going back to them?'

'They closed down during the war. The government used the plant for ship repairs until the Armistice.'

There was a silence. 'Well,' said Sopwith, 'at any rate,

let's go over to the Canbury plant and I'll show you over the old place. And then, what say we have a bite to eat together, for old times?'

'It was no good,' Jack told Helen, when he got back to Weybridge later that day. He told her what had been said, and of the offer of working in the showroom.

'It's better than nothing,' Helen said cautiously. She could see he was unhappy and didn't want to provoke him, but she *did* want them to live at Fairoaks. It would solve so many problems. 'An engine's an engine, surely.'

'I don't even like motorcycles.'

Helen laughed. 'Oh, come! They're hideously noisy, dirty, smelly, dangerous to the driver and a menace to pedestrians. What is there not to like about them?' She managed to elicit only the quirk of a corner of his mouth in response. She grew serious. 'Jack, it's a job,' she urged.

'It's charity,' he retorted.

'So you've turned it down?'

He got up and moved away from her restlessly. 'Tom's left it open. But there must be something else. There are still other places to try. I'm going to Brooklands tomorrow, see who's there. Something will come up.'

If he had said it cheerfully she would have been glad of his optimism, but it sounded more like desperation. 'Of course something will,' she said firmly. 'Tom was the first person you asked.' She stood up, seeking to distract him. 'Do you want to come and see the children have their bath?'

'No, thanks. I'm going outside for a smoke.'

He's tired, she thought, watching him go. She just wished he wasn't always tired.

★ ★ ★

38

The train slid and sighed into the sumptuous curve of York station, under the high vaulted glass roof that gave it a cathedral-like quality. Bertie reflected a moment on the many homecomings to this same station in the course of his life: as a boy from school, longing to see his mother and siblings, painfully aware of the bad school report burning a hole in his overcoat pocket; as a youth from university, equally aware of the debts he had run up, which would be winging their way behind him like faithful homing pigeons to his father's desk.

There had been the returns of his idle young-manhood, from house parties and hunting weekends in the shires – unhappy returns, as his relationship with his father had deteriorated into sullenness on one side and hostility on the other. Returns from South Africa, to an England that seemed impossibly small and green after the vast bleached plains of the veldt. The shocking return from India after his father's death, when the guilt of his unreconciled quarrel, and the loneliness of sudden responsibility, had driven him into the unsuitable marriage with Maud.

Wartime returns to her and the boy: cool indifference from her, burning excitement from Richard, his precious son, who always had a jar of tadpoles or a beetle in a matchbox to show him, whose trusting, grubby hand would be placed instantly in his with the urgent injunction to 'Come and see, Daddy!' The war had taken them both: Richard blown into unidentifiable shreds by a German bomb; Maud dying of a head injury in a car crash.

All these things flitted through his mind in an instant, as the echoing loudspeaker made its announcement. The train gave a few preliminary jerks as it slowed, and Bertie stood up to pull his bag from the overhead rack – he had not brought Cooper, his servant, with him.

She was there. He had seen her from a long way back: small, neat, fair, unremarkable – except that every new sight of her astonished him with the intensity of his love for her. She had come alone – he was glad. Uncle Teddy's liking for meeting trains was legendary, but he wanted her undivided attention. She was accompanied only by her young hound, Bran, who was sitting quietly at her side as a good dog should. She would be right opposite his carriage when the train came to a halt – of course she knew where first class stopped – but because of the angle of light on the windows she couldn't have seen him yet. It was a small treat for him to have those few extra seconds of gazing at her.

Now she saw him, and her face lit as though there was a candle behind it. It made him shiver to be loved so much. She was a Morland and certain standards had to be maintained, so she was wearing a wide-brimmed hat he hadn't seen before, trimmed with artificial daisies. She had on a smart summer suit of fawn linen but, being Jessie, it was roomy and comfortably cut. Besides, she had written to him that she was pregnant.

He stepped down. Their emotion was too great for words just at first. Instead he said, 'New hat?'

Foolishly she touched it. 'Do you like it?'

'Very fetching.'

'Is that all your luggage?' She turned to the elderly porter hovering behind her. 'That's all right, Dowding, we won't need you.'

The last time he had come home there had been a female ticket-collector. Now it was a man – sign of the times, he thought: a young man with a prematurely old

40

face. His knowing eyes scanned Bertie's uniform and he drew himself automatically to attention, accepted and clipped Bertie's outward half, and nodded to Jessie. 'Thank you, Lady Parke.' No Morland had ever had to buy a platform ticket, not for York station, which wouldn't have existed if it hadn't been for them.

Outside in the strong June sunshine she said, 'Someone's had a word with him. He called me "Miss Jessie" when I arrived.'

'Was he one of yours?'

'He didn't work at the house but his mother did. And his father was a railwayman so of course he's steeped in family tradition.' Bertie was automatically looking for the motor, but she smiled and gestured and said, 'See what I've got, to take the conquering hero home in style?'

A little way along a boy was holding the head of a smartly turned-out pony between the shafts of a dog-cart. Bertie laughed. 'Good job Cooper isn't here! He's very keen on my dignity these days.'

'Bother dignity. I thought you'd enjoy it – a nice change.'

He felt in his pocket for a coin for the boy, but she had one ready, paid him, and climbed in, taking up the reins. He might have known she wouldn't let him drive. Bran jumped up and Bertie threw in his bag and took his place beside her. The boy stepped away, touching his cap. Jessie clicked to the pony, it threw itself into the collar eagerly, and they were off.

The pony moved well, and Jessie was a good driver. The sound of its hoofs on the road, the rumble of the wheels and the fresh air and sunshine were like a tonic after the trains, boat and taxis. 'You're absolutely right,' he said. 'You were wonderful to think of it.' The rough-coated dog was between them, radiating heat, his tongue unfurled and dripping, gazing eagerly ahead. Bertie had a mental image of what he must look like. If Cooper had seen his brigadier in such a ridiculous situation he'd have had a fit. Bertie smiled inwardly. He didn't care! He was home for a few precious hours, and his dignity was on holiday. If it weren't against regulations he would have taken off his cap and tossed it into the air.

'Besides,' Jessie added, as they came out onto Blossom Street, 'Uncle Teddy's away with the Benz, and Helen and Jack took their car to London.' She smiled sidelong at him. 'In a nice reversal of the usual order, they sent the children by train and went in the car themselves. Took a couple of days about it and stayed overnight at an inn. Helen was quite excited about it – said it would be like another honeymoon. Of course, Jack had his leg in plaster the first time around, so what with wheelchairs and crutches it probably wasn't a young girl's dream.'

'So they've gone to Helen's mother's house?' Bertie said. 'How long will they be away?'

'I don't know. A few weeks at least, which is why they took the children. Uncle Teddy wasn't keen, of course. He says the house is too quiet now.' She laughed. 'Only Uncle Teddy could think a house in which there are still seven children and seven adults is too quiet. Although I must say it *is* quieter in the nursery without Basil. That child manages to seem like a crowd all on his own. He must get the devilment from Helen, because Jack was always as sweet as a plum, Mother says.'

'Perhaps she doesn't remember,' Bertie suggested.

'Oh, I think she would. She and Papa were living in a small house in London when he was little, so he would

42

have been everywhere, not far away in the nursery like at Morland Place. Thomas is longing to see you.'

Bertie shook his head. 'Darling, you're buttering me up. He's only one year old. He doesn't even know me.'

'I'll bet he remembers you when he sees you.' She hesitated, and then said, a little consciously, 'I hope the next one is a girl.'

'I do, too. A little girl who looks just like you.' He reached out past the dog to lay a hand on her knee a moment. Bran naturally thought the gesture meant for him, laid a paw graciously over the arm and licked Bertie's face until he was forced to withdraw in self-defence.

Jessie laughed. 'Wait until we're off the road. Meanwhile, tell me about the peace conference. Are they ever going to get to the end of it?'

'It can't be much longer,' Bertie said, more in hope than conviction. The conference had been going on in Paris since January, and seemed to suck in more people and more considerations by the week. Diplomats rubbed shoulders with kings, prime ministers, foreign ministers, crowds of hangers-on and advisers, journalists, industrialists, academics and lobbyists for a hundred disparate causes from women's rights to national independence, all clamouring for their particular interest to be taken into account.

'I rather wonder whether, if they had held it in Preston or Peterborough instead of Paris, so many people would have been eager to flock there and stay on for months. They might have got the business over in half the time.'

'But what *is* the business?' Jessie asked. 'Uncle Teddy tries to explain it to me but he doesn't manage to make it clear.'

'And you expect a clear and succinct précis from me?'

43

'Yes, and before we reach the track, if you please, because I shall have other things to think about then.'

'Oh dear. Well, then, to boil it down as far as possible, the three main nations, England, France and America, all have different aims. France wants Germany to be weakened so it can never attack her again. England wants the German fleet dismantled, various German territories confiscated, and the Ottoman Empire carved up between us and France. And America has a lot of high-minded ideals about a new world order of universal peace and brotherhood. That's why they want a League of Nations: all disputes to be argued out round a conference table, and no more treaties made between one set of countries against another set.'

'Well, that sounds nice,' Jessie said.

'Yes, except that France wants a private treaty with America and us, guaranteeing intervention if Germany should attack again. America doesn't want that. It wants independence for the Ottoman states, which England and France won't agree to. It isn't keen on harsh reparations from Germany, which France insists on. And it demands an independent Polish state, which nobody else wants. Meanwhile there are representations from Italy, Austria, Hungary, Japan, the Balkan states – oh, and what does one do about Russia?'

'Enough!' Jessie protested. 'I see now why Uncle Teddy can't make it make sense for me. They'll be there until Doomsday.'

'I think they will have to agree on a core treaty and work the rest out afterwards. No-one can afford to keep maintaining the situation as it is. The biggest mistake,' he added gravely, 'was in letting the German Army march home under arms. They should have been disarmed and sent back as prisoners.'

44

'What difference does it make?'

'All the difference. Already we're hearing mutterings from the Germans that they weren't really defeated. Agitators say they were betrayed by certain politicians and generals, otherwise they would have won in a few weeks more. We should have made it absolutely clear that they were beaten, *kaput*. As it is, a new generation will grow up wanting to set the record straight some time in the future.'

'You don't mean another war?'

'I'm afraid we may have it all to do again,' Bertie said. 'It's not only my opinion – most of the senior staff think that way. At the end, we were all desperate for peace, but only peace through victory. However bad things were, *we* never wanted to call it a draw.'

Jessie turned the pony off the road onto the track for Morland Place, and drove in silence for a minute or two, thinking about what he had said. Surely he couldn't be right. It had been the war to end all wars; it was unthinkable that it could ever happen again. 'Perhaps the Americans are right about their League of Nations,' she said, hesitant about offering an opinion on something she didn't really understand.

He pulled himself together. He didn't want to alarm her. 'Yes, perhaps it will be a resounding success. And Germany won't be in any state to cause trouble for many years to come. Even without the reparations – if they're ever agreed on – she's falling into chaos: riots on the street, strikes, rampant socialism, Communist militias seizing territories. We don't need to worry about them for a long time.'

'Poor things,' Jessie said. She drove round a bend of the track so that they were out of sight from the road, and halted the pony in the shade of some trees. Bran looked at her for permission and she gave him a shove to encourage him to get down. 'Go and sniff at something. There's altogether too much of you.' Another shove, and he clambered past them and jumped down to dash nose first into some interesting bushes. The cart seemed suddenly roomy without him.

'Goodbye to the chaperone,' Bertie said. 'Did you really think you needed him? I wouldn't shame you in public, Lady Parke.'

'It still sounds strange – Lady Parke.'

'Strange nice or strange nasty?'

'Strange wonderful,' she said. She pulled off her hat. He drew her to him and they kissed long and luxuriously.

'Privacy at last,' he murmured into her ear, when they drew breath.

'Wait until tonight,' she promised.

'Will it be all right?' Maud hadn't let him near her for eight of the nine months of carrying Richard.

'It will be all right,' she said, and they kissed some more.

The pony sneezed, and shook his long mane against the flies. Bran had disappeared – run off home, probably. The stillness of afternoon settled over the landscape as the sun slid down from the zenith and the tree shadow deepened. Somewhere nearby a dove croodled softly and monotonously. Bertie lit a cigarette, and Jessie leaned her head on his shoulder, safe in the circle of his arm. It was perfect peace.

'I suppose we should go,' she said at last, reluctantly. The crown and three pips of his rank on his shoulder strap were becoming uncomfortable, though she'd have borne more than that to be with him. 'They'll be wondering where we are.'

'Not just yet,' Bertie said, stubbing his cigarette carefully. 'There's something I want to talk to you about.'

She sat up and straightened her hair. 'That sounds ominous.'

'No, it's nothing to worry about, but it's something we have to discuss.' He turned sideways on the seat so he could face her. 'Did you not wonder why I'm here?'

'I was a bit surprised that you had leave so close to being stood down,' she said, 'but I thought you'd wangled it.' She looked alarmed as the implication came to her. 'Bertie, don't tell me you're not being stood down?'

'We're being kept a few weeks longer,' he admitted, 'but I'm promised the battalion will be coming home next month and will be paid off before the end of July.'

'Oh. Well, that's not so bad, then,' she said. 'I suppose I can bear a few more weeks if I have to.'

'But that's not what I wanted to tell you.' He plunged in: 'Darling, they want me to stay on. They desperately need senior officers, especially with combat experience.'

'Bertie, no!'

'Not in Germany,' he said hastily. 'It would be at Horseguards. Absolutely no going overseas. It would be pretty much like an office job – daytime only, bar the occasional function, coming home to you every night. We could have a nice house in some pleasant part of London, and be just like a suburban bank clerk and his wife.'

'Oh,' she said, thinking about it. 'Do you really want to do it?'

'It's my duty,' he said. 'And it would only be for two years. After that, we'd be free to go where we want and do what we please. Would you mind living in London for two years? Violet's there, Cousin Venetia and Oliver, and Emma will be coming back soon, I imagine. And if we picked somewhere near a park you could ride. Could you bear it?'

'As long as I'm with you, I can bear anything,' she said. 'But, oh, Bertie, what about Mother and Uncle Teddy?'

'Yes, I had thought about that.'

'Mother wouldn't say anything, of course, but she'll miss me so much. And Uncle Teddy will hate it. Maria and Father Palgrave are going to be moving out once they marry, and if Jack and Helen go too – which I suppose they're bound to, when Jack's fit again and gets a job – he'll be bereft. There'll only be Ethel, who's no help to anyone, and Polly. And Mother will have to run the house all alone.'

'She has Tomlinson,' he reminded her gently. Mary Tomlinson had been Jessie's personal maid, but when Jessie moved back to Morland Place she had become housekeeper.

That was one more realisation. 'I suppose I'd have to leave Tomlinson behind.' She had become as much a friend as a servant. Jessie would miss her.

Bertie watched her face. 'There's an alternative,' he said. She looked hopeful. 'I could take a flat in London and you could stay here with the children. I could come down most weekends, and you could come up and visit sometimes. It might not be too bad, just for two years.'

'Oh, Bertie, I don't want to be apart from you. We've waited so long.'

'Then perhaps I had better say no,' he said neutrally. Not neutrally enough – she could read his mind. He had never shirked a duty. 'No,' she said at last. 'You must do what you have to. But we'll live together, in London. I can't be away from you. It will be hard on Mother and Uncle Teddy, but it can't be helped.'

He picked up her hand and kissed it. 'I hoped you'd say that. And we can visit them. It's only a few hours on the train.'

She gathered the reins, waking the pony from its doze. 'I'd better get us back. Bertie, don't say anything about this at home. Let me tell them in my own way, when the time's right. Just say you'll be out there a few weeks longer. How long do you have, by the way?'

'I have to be back on Monday, but I can take the milk train on Monday morning.'

'The rest of today and two whole days more,' she said. 'Bliss!'

He laughed. 'What will you say when we're together every day? I suppose you'll get used to it and won't care.'

'It will still be bliss,' she said, clicking to the pony. 'Tea will be waiting. I'm pining for a cup. And Mrs Stark was making curd tarts and parkin this morning in your honour.'

They came out from under the trees and Bertie looked around with content. The sweet June afternoon lay like butter over the familiar fields. The pony trotted through the ford of the beck with a jingle of harness, and the cold smell of the water came to him, and a hint of damp, bruised grass and peppery nettle. It was good to be home.

CHAPTER THREE

Jack stared glumly at the advertisement in the newspaper.

> Ex-officer, distinguished service in war, will act as driver/guide to private motor parties wishing to tour Western Front, Battlefields, Cemeteries etc. Expert knowledge. Fluent French. Fair German. All arrangements discreetly made. Box No. 283.

It had caught his eye as he turned a page, and now he found himself drawn almost ghoulishly to it again and again. Was it someone he knew? Someone he had served beside? Did he have a wife and family? How did he feel about having to sell himself like that? Was it better than being dead? He supposed the wife and family, if any, must think so.

Here was another, even more pathetic.

> Ex-officer, excellent war record, dependent mother to support, urgently seeks employment. Anything respectable considered. Box 220.

And, of course, here was the other side of the coin:

Lady, fiancé killed in war, wishes to marry blind or otherwise disabled officer, for mutual comfort and support. Box 531.

This was the pathetic flotsam left by the passage of the worst conflict mankind had ever known; these and the men one saw on the street, men in wheelchairs, on crutches, men with folded sleeves or trouser ends, men – perhaps worst of all – shuffling along with their heads sunk into their collars, trying to keep out of sight a face that flying metal had butchered into a nightmare. And the women with dead eyes, and mouths that had forgotten how to smile, and the girls who would never have a chance of marriage. *Lady, husband killed in war, seeks employment as live-in companion.*

He wished he didn't feel so down. He wished he didn't feel so damned tired all the time. He had always been a cheerful, positive person. It wasn't like him. He didn't like being like this. It didn't help that Helen kept quietly cheerful, facing up to the new realities of life as if nothing mattered as long as they were together. She was patient with him – too patient. The only time she had snapped at him was when the cook had left, worn down with having to make meals without ingredients, and Helen had had to take on the cooking, with the help of the kitchen-maid. She had made no fuss about it, apologised lightly for her failures and laughed off burns and cuts and dropped dishes and disasters that a lesser woman would have wept over. She managed the whole thing so gracefully that it had made him feel even more guilty, until he made the mistake of telling her so.

'Why should you feel guilty?' she had asked, and he ought to have heard the warning in her voice.

'Because my wife shouldn't have to cook. I ought to support you properly.'

'Bosh. You didn't make the cook leave. Besides, it's only temporary. I'm teaching the kitchen-maid everything I learn, and as soon as she can do the job, she can have it.'

'It's not right. It's humiliating,' he began, and *then* she snapped.

'Humiliating for *you*, that's what you mean. You're not thinking about me. As it happens, I really don't mind cooking – and if I did, what then? Someone has to do it – just as someone had to deliver aeroplanes during the war. You didn't complain about that, did you?' He tried to speak and she overrode him. 'Everything isn't about you, Jack.'

'If only you weren't so damned cheerful about it,' he said feebly.

'Being cheerful helps me get through,' she said sharply, 'and if it bothers you, I'm sorry. No,' she corrected herself, nostrils flaring, 'I'm not sorry. It's just too bad for you! Stew in your own juice, if you like, but don't expect me to join you.' And she walked out.

They had hardly ever quarrelled, and he was devastated. Later he apologised, and she kissed him and held him and said it was her fault too, and asked his forgiveness.

'I shouldn't snap at you. I know you feel tired and ill and discouraged. But we'll get through, Jack. Just be patient.'

'You're a hero,' he said with a rueful laugh.

And she looked at him with frank astonishment. 'You went to war. You risked your life for me and the children and your country. You were shot down, and injured, and imprisoned. *You*'re the hero, and don't you forget it.'

He tried, he really tried, but it was hard even to feign cheerfulness when he felt so awful most of the time, and when he found himself becoming one of the personal columns' fraternity of *ex-officer, good war record, seeks honest employment.*

There was a further blow to his hopes in mid-June when the newspapers were suddenly full of the heroic exploits of two airmen, John Alcock and Arthur Brown. With the lure of the still-unclaimed *Daily Mail* prize, the Vickers company had modified a twin-engined bomber, the Vickers Vimy IV, and shipped it and their pilot and navigator to St John's in Newfoundland.

The two men took off at about half past one on the afternoon of the 14th of June. As the newspapers reported with enormous relish, the flight was attended by many difficulties, including engine trouble and fog, which were only overcome by feats of the same sort of heroism as had recently won the war. Brown had to climb out onto the wings again and again to free the air-intakes of ice, while Alcock frequently had to fly blind, and at times with the cockpit filling up with snow. They reached the coast of Ireland early in the morning of the 15th. Alcock tried to put down on what seemed to be a nice, smooth green field, but which turned out to be a bog, so the adventure ended in a crash-landing. Fortunately it was also a soft landing, so pilot and navigator escaped injury.

Thus they became the first men in the world to fly across the Atlantic non-stop, and the excitement and acclaim were enormous. The newspapers were full of charts and maps, 'expert' analyses, photographs of the take-off and landing, and imaginary representations of everything in between, drawn by fevered duty-artists with a love of the dramatic and little understanding of aerodynamics. Children's comics brought out their own versions of the story. The faces of the heroes became instantly as familiar to every schoolboy as that of Monsieur Blériot, and cigarette cards changed hands at inflated juvenile prices.

Alcock and Brown won not only the *Daily Mail*'s ten thousand pounds, but a thousand pounds from a private well-wisher and two thousand guineas from an Irish tobacco company. Within days the King had put the nation's seal on the achievement by knighting both men.

Jack managed not to say at any point *That should have been me*. He answered Basil's excited questions with patience, helped him cut out the pictures for his scrap book, and smiled as he agreed with Mrs Ormerod's opinion that Alcock and Brown deserved every honour the nation could bestow. But he couldn't quite meet Helen's eye when Molly said brightly at the breakfast table, 'Oh dear, what does that leave for you, Jack?'

Now it was nearing the end of June, and he seemed a long way even from getting a proper job. He had written to all the aircraft companies he knew of, offering his design and engineering skills, but nothing was doing. He haunted the airfields, and found a depressing number of other airmen idling about, hands in pockets, also looking for a job. So far he had only had casual employment, taking people up for pleasure flights at Brooklands, a demonstration flight at Hendon, giving a lesson here and there. There was no money in flying at the moment, and no-one would offer airmen anything more than piece work. It was not enough to support a family.

Yes, he had a family to support. He gave himself a shake, put the newspaper aside, put on his hat and caught the train up to Town. It was time to bite the bullet. He made his way from the station to Molton Street, where Tom Sopwith's motorcycle showroom was. As Helen had said, what man didn't like motorcycles? He could learn to love them. But reaching the showroom, and passing by for an anonymous look before going in, he saw at once that the offer of a job had indeed been charity. It was plain they didn't need him there, that in fact there was not enough trade to support the manager and assistant already in attendance. He stood on the other side of the road and watched for half an hour, and there wasn't a sign of a customer, nor did the telephone ring once.

He decided on the instant not to take Tom Sopwith up on his offer, even if it meant becoming a battlefield courier instead. He wouldn't rob his old friend.

'If it comes to taking charity,' he told Helen that night in bed, 'I'd sooner take Uncle Teddy's. At least he's family.'

'You're right,' she said. 'One doesn't leech off one's friends.'

He sighed. 'But what do I *do*? I wish I knew.'

'Just keep plugging on,' Helen said.

She didn't want to go back to Morland Place, and not only because she didn't want her husband to be branded in his own mind with failure. She was comfortable here in her childhood home, and the children were settling down and behaving better – Nanny Mina was learning the knack of handling them. Her mother had improved greatly now the worry of running the house had been taken off her shoulders: she was more alert and less confused, and was even talking about playing bridge again.

And Molly had been interviewed for a job in the new

55

Department of Health, which had just been formed out of the Local Government Board – a post that would be a promotion from her previous position. Helen didn't want to scupper that for her. But most of all, she wanted Jack to get back on his feet, and she didn't believe that would happen if they went back to live on tolerance at Morland Place.

She thought he had fallen asleep, but after a bit he murmured, 'If only I didn't feel so rotten.'

'You've been very ill.'

'I ought to have recovered by now. Damnit, I can't excuse myself that way.'

'You must be kinder to yourself. You'll feel better when you get a job,' she said. 'Try not to worry about it. Luck will change. It always does.'

It did change, and within two days. Jack went to Hendon, where an air show had been taking place for much of the month, in the hope of at least getting another display flight. The first person he bumped into – literally – was a lean, rangy man with a long, mobile, attractive face, who stared at him for an instant, lifting his hat in apology, and then broke into a smile of recognition.

'Jack Compton, by all that's wonderful!' They shook hands heartily. 'I had no idea you were back in circulation. I heard you were damnably ill after that prisoner-of-war camp. I'm glad to see you're back on your feet.'

'Thank you,' Jack said, equally delighted with the encounter. 'You're looking very well, Geoffrey. Prosperous, in fact. How's business?'

'Oh, pottering along, you know. Up and down. But look here, let's go and have a spot of something, and you can tell me what's been going on in your life.'

Geoffrey de Havilland, a parson's son a couple of years

older than Jack, was a flyer, but though he had joined the RFC when the war broke out, a crash in 1913 had left him unfit for combat. He had turned his talents instead to aircraft design. He and Jack had met from time to time at the Royal Aircraft Factory: de Havilland designed aeroplanes for the War Office, and in fact his BE2 had become a standard RFC machine.

He and Jack had often discussed their different reactions to the same problem: while Jack had fretted because his injury at the beginning of the war had kept him grounded, de Havilland was grateful to be let off flying so that he could concentrate on design, where he believed his real talent lay. The government evidently agreed with him, for they bought several of his prototypes – all given the prefix DH, after his initials – and put them into production. Towards the end of the war, even the American Airforce had five thousand DH4s, and it was their most successful bomber.

There was no doubt that designing had left him more prosperous at the end of the war than flying had Jack; but it was doubtful either regretted the way their lives had diverged.

'How's Helen?' de Havilland asked, as they walked across the ground towards the refreshment tent. 'And the children?'

'All very bonny. How's Louie?' De Havilland had married the woman who had been governess to his younger siblings, a warm and level-headed person whom everyone liked. 'And the boys?'

'We had another last year – I don't know if you heard? A third boy. I'm sure Louie was hoping for a girl this time, but she won't admit it.'

'Girls bring their own special problems,' Jack said,

'but I must confess I wouldn't change Barbara, even though she can be a little fiend at times.'

He laughed. 'Can't they all? I say,' he paused, 'I'm not dragging you off to the beer tent against your will, when you'd rather be watching the show?'

'Not at all. I didn't come here to watch,' Jack said. They continued walking. 'How are things at Airco?'

De Havilland was the chief designer at the Aircraft Manufacturing Company, always known as Airco. He shrugged. 'It's the same pretty well everywhere these days. Too many spare buses left over from the war, and not enough customers.'

'I saw Tom Sopwith recently, and he said the same.'

'Ah, but we're not sitting down under it,' de Havilland said. 'I'll tell you about our plans. What will you have?'

They got two glasses of beer and found a quiet corner to sit.

'We were rather spoiled in the war as far as aircraft manufacture was concerned,' de Havilland resumed when they were settled. 'I don't think any of us anticipated how quickly they'd run down the RAF after the Armistice.'

'Indecent haste,' Jack agreed.

'Quite. But there's nothing to be gained from indulging in nostalgia. We've got to adjust to the new world and make something of it. Commercial passenger flights are the future. It'll be hard going to begin with, but I believe the appetite for travel is there, and the money will follow eventually. So we've made a start, redesigning the nine-ack for passengers.' The nine-ack was the DH9A bomber. 'We're calling it the DH16. We've given it a wider fuselage, onto which we've fitted an enclosed passenger cabin. Takes four passengers – comfortable seats, nice little portholes along the sides to enjoy the view. We flew the prototype here at Hendon in March – needed a few adjustments, but on the whole I'm pretty happy with it. Now we've got the bigger Rolls-Royce engines it's a reasonably comfortable flyer.'

They discussed some technical points, and then Jack said, 'But have you found any customers for them?'

'The first ones are going to AT&T.' He gave Jack a pleased look. 'Interesting things are afoot, Jack old man. Did you know the government's agreed to a passenger airport at Hounslow Heath, with its own permanent Customs hall, to be opened next month?'

'I hadn't heard that. But what's it for?'

'For all the passengers who'll be flying back and forth to the newly liberated continent! Look, Paris and London are two hundred miles apart, but by train and boat and then train again, with all the nuisance of changing, it feels like much further. And given that the railways in northern France have been bombed to ruin, it can take all day to get there. Not to mention that the Channel might well be rough. No pleasure in that. But what if you could step into a nice little bus at Hounslow, and step out two hours later in Le Bourget? You could even come back the same day if you wanted to. Welcome to the wonderful new world of air travel!'

Jack laughed. 'You don't need to convince me, old man. It's them out there as 'as to stump up the fare.' He jerked his thumb towards the general public outside.

'Well, if someone doesn't try it, we'll never know, will we?'

Aircraft Transport and Travel – AT&T – was a subsidiary of Airco, whose factory was conveniently at Hendon, a short hop from the airstrip at Hounslow Heath. Jack had memories, though not fond ones, of Hounslow: he had been posted to Home Defence there for a time in 1916 when he had been longing to get back to active duty in France. 'Won't the costs be rather high, though, compared with the train and boat?' he asked. 'Will people be able to afford the fare?'

'Initially it will be expensive,' de Havilland agreed. 'We'll have to rely on the novelty of it to bring in passengers. But once we've got a regular service going, we'll apply for a mail-carrying contract and that should bring the fares down considerably. Then there are the possible government contracts – flying diplomats and Cabinet ministers back and forth. *They* won't cavil at the cost. And freight should help, too – newspapers, for instance, and luxury goods. Not heavy freight, of course, but things that need quick transport. Perishables.'

'Strawberries and clotted cream,' Jack suggested.

'Now you're getting the idea! Look here,' he finished his beer in a swallow, 'how would you like to toddle over to the hangars and have a look at the Sixteen? We've got one here – going to do a trial flight to Paris next month, get an idea of speed and fuel consumption.'

'I'd love to. Like to take her up, too,' Jack added wistfully, not thinking it would be possible.

'Are you flying again?' de Havilland asked.

'Hoping to. I'm fit, all right. I've been doing demonstration flights and lessons, and "sixpenny sicks" at Brooklands.'

'Once round the lighthouse in the Saucy Sue?'

'It keeps the wolf from the door, but if I can't get a proper flying job soon, I'll have to find something on the ground. That's why I came here today, in the hope of hearing of a billet.'

De Havilland looked thoughtful. 'Sorry, old chap, I

didn't realise what you meant when you said you didn't come to see the show. But look here, don't think about that now. Come over to the hangars and see our new girl. And I don't see why we can't take her up for a tool around. No point in being head boy if you can't nab some privileges now and then.'

Jack brightened. 'I'd love that! Thanks tremendously, old man. I'll be interested to see how she handles. Of course, I was a fighter pilot . . .'

'The principle's the same. You'll find the handling a bit different, but after all, if you can fly a Camel, you can fly anything.'

Some hours later they were back on the ground. 'Thanks awfully,' Jack said. 'I don't know when I've enjoyed anything more. Having an expert along to chat to – and not only an expert, but *the* expert, the man who designed the bally thing – made it very special.'

'I enjoyed it too,' said de Havilland. 'You're a talented flyer, Jack. I hope you won't be offended when I tell you part of the reason we went up was so that I could be sure of that.'

Jack felt a heat behind his face. 'What do you mean? I don't understand.'

'You said you're looking for a flying job. How would you like to join AT&T and fly the London to Paris passenger route?'

'Are you serious? You're offering me the job?'

'It will be tremendously good for us,' de Havilland said. 'Think how that will look on the advertisements: "Your pilot for the trip will be Major Jack Compton, DSO, hero of the Western Front."' He waved away Jack's laughing protest, and went on, 'Not only that, but there's the element of trust. People will be nervous at first, but they're more inclined to trust an ex-service pilot, and the higher his rank the better they'll like it. Now look here, you don't have to decide right away. Take time to think about it – discuss it with Helen, sleep on it. But don't take too long, will you, old chap? We're doing a couple of proving-flights next month and we want to start the service in August.'

'I don't need to think about it,' Jack said. 'And I know what Helen will say. I'll do it. I can't thank you enough.'

'I've got my motor here – why don't we go over to the office and work out the details together?' He smiled. 'It could turn out to be the briefest job in history, you know, if we don't get any passengers, so don't be too grateful too soon.'

On the journey Jack reflected on how far things had come in such a short time, historically speaking: from his childhood at the turn of the century when he had drawn flying machines and everyone told him heavier-than-air flight was impossible; to the first time he had left solid earth, when Henry Farman had taken him up at the Paris Air Show in 1909; through his service in the war, in flying machines that were also killing machines; to this moment, when flight seemed at last about to be harnessed to the peaceful purposes it was meant for. He had not been the first man to cross the Channel, or to cross the Atlantic non-stop, but perhaps he could be the first man to fly a commercial passenger service. That would be something, wouldn't it? And if flying had come so far in twenty years, where might it not go in the future? He was still young – he had his part to play.

He felt energy running through his veins for the first

time in a year; and reflected that Helen had, as always, been right: he did feel better now he had a job.

The news that Jack had got himself a flying job – and such an interesting one – was received at Morland Place in varying ways. Jessie was simply pleased for him. 'Good old Jack! Now he'll be happy. He's never really comfortable with both feet on the ground.'

Teddy was intrigued. 'A passenger flight to Paris, eh? Now that's something I'd like to try.'

Henrietta had a mother's anxieties. 'I hope he really is feeling better. And that it won't be too much of a strain on him. Flying with passengers must mean more responsibility than flying on your own. I wish he'd chosen a less dangerous profession.'

Polly said only, 'I wonder if they'll let him take Rug with him.'

And Ethel said, rather sniffily, 'When it comes down to it, it's no better than being a tram driver, is it? Nothing to get excited about.'

Palgrave, the chaplain-tutor, said, 'The children will be excited about it, anyway. I shall be able to get a number of lessons out of it – geography and physics and trade and sheer adventure. It's a story that has everything! It's always so much easier to teach with a good example to draw on.'

'Wouldn't it be fine, Hen,' said Teddy to his sister, 'if you could fly all the way across the Atlantic? Go and see the family without having to spend a week on a ship?'

'It will come one day,' Jessie said. 'If those two men can do it – Alcock and Brown – it won't be long before they'll be taking passengers.'

Henrietta shuddered. 'It's bad enough thinking of

crossing the Atlantic in a ship,' she said – she had almost lost her daughter and grandchildren, as well as Teddy, when *Titanic* foundered, and she would never entirely trust the sea again, 'but the idea of *flying* over it, hanging in the empty air with nothing to hold you up – no, thank you! You'll never persuade me to ride in one of those things. If it fell down you'd be killed. You wouldn't have any chance.'

'Jack's aeroplanes have "fallen down", as you put it, lots of times,' Jessie said, 'and he wasn't killed. Aeroplanes are made to glide, Mother. Even if the engine stops they can still get down safely.'

'The venture may not flourish,' Palgrave said, to comfort Henrietta. 'I dare say the tickets will be very expensive. It may be that no-one will be able to afford them. I'm afraid Jack's job may not last very long.'

'Oh, there will always be rich people,' Teddy said, 'looking for a new way to spend their money.'

Only Maria seemed to have nothing to say on the subject. She was often quiet during these family discussions, for she felt something of an outsider, not a Morland by blood, and without Ethel's sense of grievance to drive her. No-one particularly noticed her silence, except her betrothed lover, who gave her a thoughtful glance, and bided his time until he could be alone with her.

The moment arrived at tea-time when, having settled the children with some drawing, he went down to the drawing-room and found Maria there alone, sitting at the round table, sewing lace onto a fine cotton garment. She looked up as he came in, and said, 'By tradition you aren't supposed to see my wedding clothes until the day, but as this is only a petticoat I suppose it doesn't count.'

'I would think tradition must dictate that I shouldn't

see your underclothes until *after* the event,' he replied solemnly.

'Only if I'm wearing them,' she smiled.

'I shall turn my eyes away just in case.'

'Don't trouble. I'll put it away. I wanted to talk to you.'

'Am I early or is tea late?'

'You're early, but only by five minutes. I shan't ring until Mother-in-law gets here.' She put the sewing back into the basket and he turned another chair out from the table and sat facing her. She had almost died from the Spanish flu last autumn, and if anything could have made her more dear to him, it was the possibility of losing her. Seven months on she was fully recovered from the debilitating illness, but there was a difference in her. She was quieter, less ready to laugh. Her face was thinner and paler, though no less beautiful to him. Even before the illness she had found her life at Morland Place limiting, but now she seemed sometimes actually oppressed by it.

He had been willing to take her right away after their marriage, but Uncle Teddy had begged so hard for them not to go too far that a compromise had been reached: Palgrave was to remain as chaplain-tutor but he and Maria were to 'live out', in a small cottage on the estate where they could have their privacy and Maria could take care of Martin, her three-year-old son by Frank. Palgrave had been glad not to have to find another post in the present climate. The shell-shock that had caused his release from the army did not trouble him too much now, but he still had relapses from time to time – terrible nightmares and episodes of helpless, shivering debility. They were caused by any unusual strain on the nerves, and a new post away from Morland Place was bound to be more of a strain than being here where he was comfortable. And, of course, he would have to reveal the disability to any potential employer, which would make finding another post much harder.

Maria had agreed to the compromise when it was proposed in March. She had taken her choice between the three houses suggested by Uncle Teddy (she had picked the cottage furthest away from Morland Place), and had seemed to enjoy in her quiet way talking over, sometimes with Palgrave and sometimes with Jessie, schemes of decoration and convenience, what to do with the garden, whether to get a cat and other pleasant domestic trivia.

She had only had five days with Frank, something of which Palgrave was painfully aware, because it was hard sometimes not to be grateful that there could be no comparisons. He was looking forward to the intimacy of married life in a small house, with Maria presiding over the teapot and the child underfoot, though he did worry that she might be taking on too much. She *said* she was perfectly strong again, but sometimes she looked tired, and if she so much as cleared her throat he found himself wondering anxiously what would happen if she fell ill while alone with the child in the cottage – which was quite isolated – while he was at his work.

He could see, now, that something was on her mind, but he didn't have to wait to find out what it was. Maria never beat around the bush.

'You know what this means, don't you?' she said. 'Jack getting this flying job. It means he and Helen and the children will have to live down there.'

'I imagine they'll live in her mother's house,' he said,

66

not seeing the difficulty. 'I know Helen was worried about her mother anyway. She'll be glad to be able to be on the spot.'

'No doubt,' said Maria. 'And when Bertie comes home, Jessie and the baby will be going to live with him in London. Don't you see? If we go to the cottage it will leave Uncle Teddy and Mother-in-law all alone here with only Ethel for company.'

'And Polly.'

'Polly's no company for anyone these days, and she's no match for Ethel. Can't you imagine it at mealtimes, with Mother-in-law listening to Ethel's constant stream and Polly drooping, silent, at the other end? It's too cruel.'

'But—'

'Uncle Teddy hasn't worked it out yet, but he will. By dinner tonight he'll have realised how many people he's losing and he'll start trying to persuade you to stay here.'

'Us, you mean,' Palgrave corrected.

'He'll work on you,' Maria said, meeting his eyes with a penetratingly frank gaze, 'because he knows *you* don't really want to go.'

'That's not true,' he protested. 'I'm looking forward to living with you in the cottage.'

'No, my love, you're looking forward to living with me,' she said. 'The cottage is a means to an end.'

'Well . . .' He hesitated, knowing there was truth in this.

'And it will be inconvenient for you not to be in residence here, and having the villagers and estate people not knowing where you are.'

'It will involve a lot of messages being passed back and forth,' he admitted, 'but we'll manage.'

'And there will be times when you'll want to stay on – when a child is ill, or a servant has a crisis – but you'll feel you have to come home to supper or disappoint me, and you'll be torn.'

'Priests are always being torn,' he said, trying to lighten the mood.

'Besides, you actively *like* living here. I don't think you're a cottage sort of person at heart.'

'Are you?' he countered.

'No,' she said, always truthful, 'but I want to be alone with you, so I'm willing to accept the inconveniences. If you had been destitute,' she added, 'I'd have lived under a hedge with you. It doesn't make me a hedge person.'

'But, Maria, my dearest, what are you saying?' he asked anxiously. Was she thinking better of marrying him?

'I'm saying we'll have to live here after we're married. The cottage is not a possibility.'

'Don't say that! I know what it means to you.'

'No, you don't,' she said quietly, 'but it doesn't matter. I can't be so unkind to Uncle Teddy and Mother-in-law, and I can't be so selfish towards you. And I couldn't stand up to the pleading and coaxing that would go on. I'd sooner give in now than go through it.'

'You don't mean it?' he said, trying not to feel relieved.

'Of course I do. I never say things I don't mean.'

'If we did stay,' he said carefully, 'it need only be for a while, until Jessie and Bertie come back.'

'No,' she said. 'If we don't go now, we never will. It doesn't matter. I suppose I always knew how it would be. The cottage was never more than a fantasy.'

'Is that why . . .?' he began hesitantly, not knowing quite how to put it. Though she had inspected the cottage and talked about how it would be, she had never seemed in any hurry to put the plans into action. Necessary repairs to windows and roof had been undertaken by Uncle Teddy, but Maria had not given the orders for the alterations or refurbishments. She had said that when they came back from their honeymoon it would be soon enough to arrange everything, and it had been in no-one's interest to urge her.

But this seemed too delicate an area to explore, and he changed what he was going to say. 'In any case, in a few years, once the children have grown up and gone to school, my job here will be ended, and we can go and start a new life together anywhere in the world.'

'It won't let us go,' she said. 'This house. It devours you. When Frank died, it demanded me and Martin in reparation, and now we're part of it. It will never let me go. Even the ghosts can't escape.'

'Dearest,' he protested, 'the house isn't a living thing. It can't demand or devour anything. And there are no such things as ghosts.'

'You haven't seen them,' she said. 'I have.'

'When?'

'When I was ill.'

'But you were feverish then. You imagined things. This is all nonsense, Maria – a morbid fantasy. It isn't like you. This is just an old house, nothing more. You talk as if it were some kind of idol, demanding sacrifice.'

She looked at him. 'Ah, but you're a willing victim. You and Uncle Teddy.' She might have said more, but at that moment the door opened. 'Here's tea,' she said. 'And Mother-in-law.' Henrietta appeared, leading the way for Daniel with the tray. 'At least we can be sure of making one person happy.'

Polly and Jessie came in behind them. Ethel was at her parents' house – her father had been unwell.

'Making someone happy?' Jessie said, catching the last words. 'That sounds like a good idea.'

The dogs surged past and rushed up to Maria, milling about her with upthrust smiles and waving sterns. She patted them and pushed them away. She had had to get used to being assaulted by the love of large dogs whenever she entered a room – one of the many strange things about life at Morland Place that had taken some adjustment for a person brought up in genteel poverty in a suburban villa. Life, she reflected, could hardly have taken her further from everything she had assumed was the norm. If only I had been a boy, she thought wistfully, I could have 'listed as a soldier.

'Is the master coming in for tea?' Henrietta asked Daniel, counting cups.

'Yes, madam. He rode in a minute since. He's just talking to the boy about a loose shoe, and then he'll be in.'

And so my fate is sealed, thought Maria.

CHAPTER FOUR

Helen and Jack left the children with Nanny Mina and a rather nervous grandma ('But what shall I *do* with them? Do they play cards?') when they travelled down to York for the wedding, but they took Rug with them. It was deliciously peaceful in the railway carriage, even though they travelled third class, and Helen realised for the first time how much noise and activity children generated when you had them around you all day. There was something to be said for the nursery system of big houses like Morland Place. She was enjoying her spell of domesticity, but she didn't think she'd like it for a permanency. Fortunately in the natural course of things Basil and Barbara would grow up and become rational in a few years' time, and she would be able to find something else to do. She rather fancied going back to delivering aeroplanes, if ever – no, she must say *when* – the industry picked up again.

For the few days they would be away, Molly would keep a distant eye on things. She was taking up her new position on Monday and was excited about it. She had also had a letter from France from her friend Emma Weston, who was still out there with the FANY, saying that she would be coming home at last in the middle of July. Molly had asked Helen if she could invite Emma to stay until she had decided what to do with herself.

'I'm sure Mother won't mind,' Helen said. 'Emma's just the sort of house-guest she approved of before the war. If she accepts.'

'Why wouldn't she?' Molly said.

'Because, darling, we're down here and she might want to be in London. And she might have already made arrangements with Violet. And don't forget you'll be at the office from Monday to Friday, so you won't be around to amuse her.'

'Oh glory, I'd forgotten about that,' Molly said. 'Bother this job. Why didn't it start in August instead?'

'Now you're discovering the joys of regular employment,' Helen said, laughing. 'Spoilt little rich girl!'

'Bosh! Who worked all through the war – every day, mind you, not just tooling off to fly an aeroplane for an hour or two when the fancy took her?'

Jessie met them from the train, standing with Bran beside her just as she had for Bertie, but this time in the wrong place. 'I didn't realise you'd be travelling in third,' she said. 'Hello, Rug, old chap.' She fended him off, and he bounced around Bran instead, plainly glad to be back. He had found it hard suddenly to be an 'only dog'.

'We have to save pennies now,' Helen answered. 'You're looking well, Jessie dear.' She was beginning to show a little, Helen thought.

'So are you!' Jessie exclaimed to Jack, as he stooped to kiss her. 'So much better! Mother will be mortified. What have you been feeding him on, Helen?'

'Success,' Jack answered for her. 'Helen said I'd feel better once I got a job, and she's right. Suddenly all that

72

greyness and tiredness just went away, like fog being sucked up by the sun.'

'We're all thrilled about your new job,' Jessie said, leading the way out of the station. 'Uncle Teddy's planning to find some excuse for a trip to Paris just so he can try you out. Here, now, look what splendour we have for you.'

It was not the chauffeur-driven Benz, nor yet the dog cart, but something quite new, a four-seat touring motor in smart grey and black with red leather seats. The sunshine gleamed on the chrome of its bull-nosed radiator; Rug followed Bran, who ran ahead, and both ceremonially marked a tyre.

'It's a Morris Oxford,' Jessie said. 'Practically brand new – Uncle Teddy bought it from a major in the Howards who'd bought it for his son, who didn't come back. The poor man couldn't bear the sight of it, so he was selling it to buy something else. It has a 1548 cc four-cylinder engine, and four-wheel brakes.'

'Ah, so that's—' Jack began.

'Stop right there,' Helen commanded. 'I don't want to sit through a technical discussion from you two before we get to the important part. Why did Uncle Teddy buy it? To oblige the major?'

'Yes, but not only that. Since he sold the Renault during the war, and I sold my little Austin when I went to nurse, there isn't a small car at Morland Place for when he's away with the Benz. And even when he isn't, the Benz isn't suitable for Polly to drive.'

'Polly doesn't drive,' Helen objected.

'She started to, years ago, and she wants to learn properly now. So Uncle Teddy bought her this car in anticipation.'

Jack laughed. 'Isn't that just like him? Shall I drive?'

'Not on your life,' Jessie said. 'I want to have as much fun as I can before I sink into motherhood again.' They climbed in, with Helen kindly taking the back seat so that Jack could be in front and examine everything. The dogs jumped in with her, and Jessie drove out of the station yard.

'So this is Polly's car?' Helen said, holding on to her hat.

'Yes, but I'm to drive it when I want to, or when it's needed. And Uncle Teddy thought it would be a good thing for Father Palgrave to be able to drive, for when he gets a call from a sick villager or someone in one of the outlying cottages. It makes sense now he and Maria aren't going to the cottage.'

'I didn't know Father Palgrave could drive,' Jack said.

'He can't. I'm to teach them both. It keeps me busy until Bertie comes home.'

'Is Maria very disappointed about the cottage?' Helen asked. Jack had not made the connection between their leaving and Maria's decision, but she had guessed it, though she refused to feel guilty.

'She doesn't seem to be, but it's hard to tell with Maria. She doesn't say much, and what she says is always to the point.'

'Why should she be disappointed?' Jack said. 'They'll be much more comfortable staying put. It will save Father Palgrave a journey every day. Anyway,' he added, 'no-one makes Maria do anything. It was her own decision.'

Helen and Jessie both let that pass. Women's lives had to be subordinate to men's, or how would the world get on?

★   ★   ★

74

The wedding was charming, everyone said afterwards. The weather kept its promise of the past weeks – it really had been a glorious summer. The chapel was decked with roses and lilies, and the vicar from the village officiated, since Palgrave could hardly marry himself. Maria's mother had declined, through ill-health, to attend, even though Uncle Teddy had offered to send the motor for her – Jessie mentioned to Helen that she thought Mrs Stanhope was growing a little strange. Since Palgrave had no near relatives, Uncle Teddy had invited various friends and prominent neighbours to fill out the numbers. He argued that Palgrave, as chaplain, had a public face, so it was quite appropriate to invite people outside the family.

Maria's dress, which she had made herself, with help from the women of the house, was of cream lace over lavender silk, soft shades that suited her colouring; it was ankle-length, with the newly fashionable low waistline, and had chiffon under-sleeves, much easier to fit than silk. With the lace removed – so ran Maria's thrifty thinking – it would make a suitable evening-gown; while Henrietta pointed out that the lace could be saved for the wedding of the daughter she would have one day.

Maria's thick brown hair was drawn back into a chignon and decorated with white rosebuds. She didn't think it appropriate, as a widow, to wear a veil. She didn't want to carry flowers, either, but at the last minute Harriet, Ethel's four-year-old daughter, who was watching her being dressed by Sweetlove and Tomlinson, discovered this and assured her earnestly that brides always had flowers. She had seen pictures, and they always, always had 'a big bucket of flowers'. Convinced it would jeopardise the whole legitimacy of the wedding process, she slipped out of the room and returned a short time later with three roses she had filched from a vase downstairs which she begged Maria almost tearfully to carry.

Sweetlove told her not to be so silly, but catching Maria's eye, Tomlinson took the flowers, found a bit of material to bind round the stems, and put in a couple of stitches to hold it together. Harriet beamed with relief and Maria felt suddenly almost unbearably touched. She had never had a sister, and imagined that perhaps this was what it would have felt like.

Maria had wanted Polly as the only bridesmaid, and had resisted all Ethel's hints and, finally, urgings to have Roberta and Harriet as well. In the end, purely for the sake of peace, she had accepted another of Ethel's ideas, to have her own three-year-old son Martin as a pageboy in a white satin Gainsborough suit. She did not care for children being used in such roles, just as some people have an aversion to animals being dressed up in human clothes. But Polly managed Martin very well. He clutched her hand, bewildered by all the eyes on him and wondering whether to howl or suck his thumb, but with a few reassuring squeezes and some murmured encouragement from Polly he did neither, and took his mother's flowers from her at the right moment, with a solemn look that almost undid her.

He turned out to be the sensation of the wedding (which would have been gratifying if Maria had had that sort of vanity). Everyone said afterwards that it was the *sweetest* sight and the *completest* thing, that he had been a *little gentleman* and made a perfectly *charming* addition to the wedding procession. Several people secretly planned to have a Gainsborough-suited pageboy (or why not *two*?) at their own daughter's forthcoming wedding and smiled complacently in the certainty that no-one else would have thought of it and they would lead the fashion.

Uncle Teddy and Henrietta had not scrimped on the wedding feast, though neither bride nor groom was a blood relative. It was the first proper celebration since the end of the war, and the months since November had been hard ones in many ways. It was time to be happy again. There was champagne for the toasts, Mrs Stark had made an enormous cake, and there was a handsome cold collation, which had all eyes brightening, for it was a long time since anyone had seen such a spread of roasts and pies and salads, jellies and creams and tarts.

After the eating and drinking and the speeches, a small band was brought in from the servants' hall where they had been waiting, and there was dancing. Denis Palgrave danced with his wife for the first time, and though neither of them was a good dancer, having had very little practice, they circled in each other's arms in such a state of bliss that no-one would have noticed any lack of skill. The dancing had been Teddy's idea, and mainly for the sake of Polly, whom he loved to see dance. In her bridesmaid's dress of white muslin, with yellow roses in her golden hair, she looked exactly like an angel, he thought. She danced every dance, but almost as if she were in a dream, hardly speaking to her partners. Teddy thought with a sigh of mixed pleasure and pain that she had never looked more beautiful; and that all too soon it would be her wedding he would be arranging. The thought of seeing her off on her honeymoon was painful; he only hoped she would be coming back, as Maria would be.

Maria and her husband went up to change, and a taxi came at length to take them to the station. Everyone crowded into the Great Hall to see them off with kisses and congratulations, good wishes and a few tears from those who always cried at weddings. They were pursued to the taxi by quantities of rice, thrown for luck by the servants, and a large number of dogs and children in an extreme condition of excitement and too much cake. They were going by railway to Scarborough for two weeks, and then to London, to call on Maria's mother, and to spend another two weeks seeing the shows and enjoying whatever other amusements the capital might offer. Each had secretly worried that a whole month in Scarborough would be too dull for the other, and each was quite mistaken.

When they were gone, the guests shortly took their leave, and the family was left feeling rather flat. The nursery-maids fell on the over-excited children and bore them away to the upper regions, and the adults gathered in the drawing-room wondering what to do with themselves.

'Polly, dear, why don't you play something for us?' Henrietta suggested, to break an awkward silence. Polly obediently drifted over to the piano and began to play the piece that was lying there.

Teddy stood before the fireplace, his hands behind his back. 'Well,' he said. 'Well.' He looked about them enquiringly.

'It was a very pretty wedding,' Helen supplied.

'I'm sure they'll be happy,' Henrietta added. 'It's a pleasure to see two people so suited.'

'Frank would have liked him,' Jack said. 'I think he would have approved.'

In a moment of silence they remembered Frank; and Robbie; and Ned. It was strange, Jack thought, to be the only one of them left; it seemed especially strange here, at Morland Place, where they had grown up together.

He would not have been surprised if the drawing-room door had opened and one or all of them had come in: pleased, yes, but oddly, not surprised.

The door did open, but it was Sawry, to enquire on Mrs Stark's behalf about supper. Henrietta dealt with the matter, the servant departed, and Helen, of her good nature, was about to propose a hand of whist to keep Uncle Teddy amused. Polly stopped playing, having had difficulty in turning the page because the piece was so well worn, and Jessie got up to go and turn for her, but stopped halfway to the piano with an indrawn breath and a widening of her eyes. Remembering with alarm her history, before Thomas's birth, of miscarriages, Helen took half a step towards her and said, 'What's the matter?'

But Jessie turned a shining face towards her and said, 'Nothing's wrong. I felt the baby move for the first time.'

The Treaty of Versailles was signed in the Hall of Mirrors on the 28th of June 1919 – the anniversary of the assassination of Archduke Franz Ferdinand, which was widely held to be the immediate cause of the war. The Treaty marked the official ending of the war between Germany and the Allied Powers, and required Germany to accept sole responsibility for the war, to disarm, and to make reparation in the form of monetary compensation and yield of territory.

Bertie wrote to Jessie:

Nobody got everything they wanted, which I suppose is inevitable when you consider that twenty-seven nations were involved. France wanted Germany to be much more harshly treated so as to crush them, and we and the Americans wanted more lenient terms so as to reconcile them. Proverbially a compromise satisfies no-one, and it seems from what I read that Germany will be neither pacified, conciliated, nor permanently weakened, only made to feel resentful, which will just store up trouble for the future. Italy didn't get Fiume, so they're cross, and Japan didn't get their clause proscribing discrimination on the grounds of race or nationality, so they're angry with Australia, who vetoed it. The League of Nations has been created to appease the Americans, but nobody believes it will ever amount to much. And the Austro-Hungarian Empire has been broken up, which simply creates a multitude of weak states incapable of forming a barrier to German expansion. But it's a peace treaty, when all's said and done, and probably the only one we could have got in the circumstances.

The French aim of crippling Germany so that it could never attack anyone again was superficially attractive, but America and Britain both had reservations. France wanted the rich industrial lands of Alsace-Lorraine back, but also wanted to confiscate the German power-house of the Rhinelands. This, in Britain's opinion, would have made France too powerful, and Britain never would entirely trust the Old Enemy, even having fought a long and costly war to save her.

As to the punitive reparation, a figure the equivalent of £11.3 billion in gold had been set, but it seemed doubtful, given the state of Germany – starving and falling into chaos and socialist revolution – that it would be paid. Furthermore, before the war Germany had been a principal customer of both Britain and the USA, and a prosperous Germany was needed to establish a stable European trading environment. A penniless Germany and an over-mighty France would not contribute to the balance that both the English-speaking nations required for their commerce and their peace of mind.

Still, there was a universal sense of relief among the people, as opposed to the politicians, that they could now really count the war as over. The Paris conference went on, grinding out the details, but at home all eyes were now focused on the plans for the peace celebrations. The government had set up a Peace Committee in May, under the foreign secretary, Lord Curzon, and originally a four-day festival in August had been mooted. But with the signing of the treaty everyone wanted the date moved up, and this and the national state of finance required it to be scaled down to one day, Saturday the 19th of July, which was to be called Peace Day.

The official event was to be held in London, but every town, almost every village, meant to have its own celebration. There were dissenting voices: some thought the money would be better spent on giving support to demobbed soldiers or pensions to war widows. Others wrote to the newspapers to say that making merry when so many were bereaved and so many more crippled and disfigured from their wounds was in the worst of taste. Most celebrations would involve a march of some sort, and there were complaints that the war had been fought to kill off militarism, not promote it at home. But this minority had no chance against the salient English characteristic of liking to have a good time, and the majority threw themselves into the preparations with a will.

*   *   *

Lord Holkam came home for a few days at the beginning of July. He had been in Paris since November, having begun as one of Field Marshal Haig's aides, and having been transferred to military liaison with the British delegation. There was no doubt he was an Important Person, and that his future career looked likely to be gilded. None of this impinged very much on his wife, Violet. She might have gone to Paris and become a leading hostess, but she had no particular desire for the glamour, and he was no longer quite sure enough of her to press the matter. Besides, life as a bachelor in what had become the *de facto* capital of world government had its compensations.

Arriving home, he bathed and changed, went to Downing Street, the House, Horseguards, and his club, returned to St James's Square to pay a brief visit to his children in the nursery – a distinction they could happily have done without, since they hardly knew him, and his stern formal manner made them frightened of him – then asked the butler, Deeping, where her ladyship was.

Deeping, a new man since the war began – Varden had been called up – was elderly and slow, but at least he had been properly trained, and in a noble house. Violet had got him when his master died and his mistress had been forced to close up the house and go and live in the lodge for economy's sake. He was glad to get the job, and Holkam was a good, old title, but the changes war had brought and the lack of traditional formality distressed him. Her ladyship was a very beautiful lady and well connected, but the household was naturally much depleted and there was no entertaining. He was hoping with the peace that his lordship would return and things would get back to what he considered normal: a large household, regular entertaining, and the bustle of important visitors to whom to display his knowledge of etiquette and genealogy. He looked forward to saying things like, 'Yes, indeed, your grace, I had the pleasure of serving her dowager grace at Marlsham before the war,' and to explaining to new housemaids the delicate distinctions of rank and precedence he had learned over a lifetime.

To his lordship's current question, however, he could only answer, 'I believe her ladyship is in the green parlour, my lord,' a short phrase that left him no scope to express by nuance any of his feelings about the situation.

The green parlour was a small room at the back of the house into which Violet had retreated as the household shrank, and which she now used almost to the exclusion of the rest of the house. Holkam found her there reading letters at the table by the window; her two Pekingeses were curled on the sofa. The room was papered in a dark sea-green, which, with the green damask of the upholstery, gave the room its name. The sunlight outside made it seem darker; in the winter, with the fire lit, it was more cosy than gloomy.

Violet looked up as he entered. At twenty-eight she seemed to him, incredibly, more beautiful than ever. Her delicate features, violet-blue eyes, porcelain skin and dark hair had withstood the passage of time, the birth of four children, and the grief of losing her father, her eldest brother and her lover to the war. Holkam did not like to think about the latter, or the fact that his youngest son had not been fathered by him. She had been a prize when he married her, not only the most beautiful debutante of her Season, but rich as well – and his fortune had been dispersed by a profligate father. He had loved her for those things, and for the fact that she seemed well brought up, meek and obedient, and likely to enhance his stature in the world. She had produced the three children he had wanted, and was a popular hostess, but she had disappointed him by taking a lover in horribly public circumstances, and by proving to have a mind of her own in several inconvenient ways.

However, the lover was dead, he had accepted the child, and the scandal seemed to have been forgotten. She was undoubtedly still beautiful, and could still be an asset. On the whole, he thought life after the war could be satisfactory. He was even prepared to allow her to take another lover, as long as it was done discreetly. He had sufficient children and did not require her sexual services: he preferred to take his pleasures elsewhere. He had always been attracted to women of the lower sort. Paris had provided them in plenty – with the peace conference installed there, it had sucked in girls from all over the country, and had been to him like a tuck-box to a greedy schoolboy. But he had always been able to find what he wanted in London, too.

'Holkam,' Violet said. 'I heard you were here. How long are you staying?'

'Only until Monday – I must catch the evening train. Are you engaged tonight?'

'I'm dining at Eddie's, but I'm sure they will be happy to have you, too.'

He nodded approvingly. Eddie was her cousin, Lord Vibart, who was equerry to the Prince of Wales, had married a marquess's daughter, and had a new son to whom the prince had stood sponsor at his christening. Nothing could have been more suitable.

'I'll go with you gladly,' he said.

Violet rose. 'I'll write a note to send round to Piccadilly,' she said. The Vibarts lived in a tall house close to Hyde Park Corner, a short walk for a servant with a message.

'Just a moment,' Holkam said. She looked at him enquiringly. 'Sit down, won't you, my dear?'

Violet sat obediently, and looked up at him. He was tall and still handsome, though rather heavier than when she had first met him, both in the face and the body. The war had suited him, bringing him status and confidence. He was a powerful man. She remembered with distant surprise how much she had loved him when, as a seventeen-year-old and fresh from the schoolroom, she had been courted by him. He had been the 'catch of the season', a young man of such looks, charm and address that every mother had wanted him for her daughter. Hardly anyone had been surprised when he picked Violet, whose beauty seemed to deserve him. But her parents had been doubtful about him, and it was only because she had begged to be allowed to have him that they had consented to the match. Her father had been worried by his lack of fortune; Venetia had found something cold and hollow about him. But Violet had adored him, had endured the many restrictions he placed on her, and a distressing breach with her parents, and the love had survived until the moment she discovered that he was unfaithful to her. Then it had stopped as though turned off with a switch, and she had resigned herself to a life without love, until she had met Laidislaw.

Well, that was over, too. Now the war was ended, she would have to find some other way to fill her life.

'What is it?' she asked her husband calmly. 'What do you want?'

He seemed uneasy, which was not like him. He cleared his throat awkwardly. 'I would like to speak to you,' he said.

'You are doing so,' she pointed out unhelpfully.

He stuck his hands behind his back, cleared his throat again, and took refuge in formality. 'You will no doubt have read about the Treaty of Versailles?'

She raised her eyebrows. 'I know that such a thing exists,' she said. It was too much to expect her to have read the details. She had never claimed to be an intellectual.

'Quite,' said Holkam, who had no illusions about her brain. 'The treaty formally ends the war.'

'And I suppose that means you will be coming home,' she said to help him along.

'Not immediately. There is a great deal of work left to do. In fact, I would be surprised if the conference closed before next year.'

'And you will be staying on in Paris?' she said.

Was there something of satisfaction in the way she said that? He eyed her cautiously. 'Yes,' he said. 'For some months more at least. But I will eventually come home, and that's what I want to talk to you about.'

She nodded, waiting for him to continue.

'Violet,' he said, 'you are my wife.'

'Yes,' she assented cautiously.

'We agreed, did we not, to a certain arrangement, for the sake of the children? And for reputation.'

'Yes,' she said again. 'I adhere to the agreement. What is it that you want?'

'I want,' he said, with an air of plunging in, 'a comfortable marriage. I think I am entitled to that. I want to get back to normality. I want to entertain here with you

86

as my hostess, and to accept invitations with you on my arm, to be seen with you in society. I want,' he concluded, 'a happy marriage.'

Violet considered. 'I will, of course, be your hostess and appear in public with you, but as to your happiness – I have not been essential to that for many years. I don't see how I can secure it for you.'

'Just by being friends with me again,' he said. 'Can't we go back to that?'

'I don't think we were ever friends,' she said, but not in a hostile manner.

'Then can't we begin? Add a modicum of warmth to our politeness. Be in private what we seem in public, a contented couple. I will not interfere with your private life. Make what friends you wish, do as you please, as long as the decencies are maintained.'

'You, of course, will carry on as before with your private life,' she said, a little coldly.

'Don't let us bring up old quarrels. I have no wish to quarrel with you. I want us to be – reconciled. We are young and healthy, and have many years of marriage ahead of us. Wouldn't it be foolish not to arrange them as comfortably as possible?'

That was certainly a point. 'Friends,' she said musingly.

'We have the children to think of, too,' he urged, thinking he was making headway.

'I am prepared to be friendly,' Violet said. It would be a relief, in a way. 'But there must be rules.'

His face darkened. He did not expect to be dictated to. 'You want to place conditions on friendship?'

'In a friendship there must be equality,' Violet said. 'Either side must be free to make or reject conditions.'

'Well,' he said impatiently, 'what are they?'

'Old quarrels are to be set aside. You will never bring up the subject of Laidislaw.'

'If you do not, I will not,' he said, tight-lipped.

'And Octavian is to be treated no differently from the others.'

'His name is Henry!'

She turned her face away. 'You see, it is impossible for us to agree.'

He tried to suppress his impatience. 'My dear, you cannot expect me to present the child to the world as my son, bearing the name which everyone knows was that of your lover. That is unreasonable.' She did not answer. 'I will promise to treat him no differently from the others if you will call him Henry, which is after all his given name.'

'Very well,' she said, after a moment. Her child would always be Octavian to her, no matter what name she said aloud. 'Next—'

'*More* conditions?'

'Just one more. You will never let me find out about any of your women. Do as you please, but they must not exist for me. No breath must ever reach me.'

'I agree,' he said. 'And equally, I must never know about anyone of yours.'

She looked surprised. 'I do not have a lover.'

'You may, one day.'

'No,' she said. 'That's all over for me. You needn't worry. When you are from home, Freddie shall escort me.' Sir Frederick Copthall had been her faithful companion since she was first married, one of those well-conducted bachelors welcomed everywhere by hostesses keen to keep their numbers even.

'You depend too much on him. What if he should get married?'

She stared an instant and then laughed. 'Married? Freddie?' She stood up. 'Well, if that is all, I must send off that note, and then we ought to think about going up to change.'

'There's time before the dressing bell,' he said. He pulled the rope. 'Let me send for sherry. I haven't chatted to you for a long time.'

'Is this the beginning of the new dispensation?' she said, but pleasantly. She took up one of the dogs and placed it in her lap to make room on the sofa. Holkam drew up a chair. 'What shall we talk about? The Peace Day celebrations? I suppose you will be back for those?'

'I expect I shall be taking part, but there will be private parties after the close of festivities, too. I think we ought to give a dinner in the evening. We must get the invitations out quickly, if we are to secure the best guests – we won't be the only people to think of it. Is your present cook capable of a dinner for, say, twenty?'

'It depends rather – ah, Deeping. Bring sherry, will you? And I must send a note to Lady Vibart. Wait there while I write it, and then have it taken straight away.'

'Yes, my lady.'

Deeping managed a covert look from his mistress to his master, and saw the latter sitting in a relaxed pose by the unlit fire and actually *smiling*. It seemed to the old man a good omen for the house.

The FANY unit at Poperinghe was disbanded in the middle of June, with the final tribute of being asked to tea with Princess Mary. The desperate need to clean up for it had caused something of panic, and they arrived reeking of petrol, where they had been trying to get the oil stains out of their uniforms. The princess gallantly refused to notice.

After that there was a brief period of packing up and the majority of the women went home. But Emma could not yet face the prospect of abandoning the comfortable khaki and going back to the trials of mufti, and attached herself to an American woman who had bought a small lorry and was still running a service between the various military installations, the hospitals and the docks. But at the end of the first week of July even she gave up, and Emma had no choice but to pack her meagre luggage and, with her mongrel dog Benson beside her, take ship at Calais for England.

She felt very tired, grubby and rather depressed. She could not say she had thoroughly enjoyed the work for the last few months, but going home presented her with large problems. She was an orphan, extremely wealthy, and the world should have been at her feet. But her fiancé had fallen at Ypres two years ago; and then in 1918 a man she had felt she could one day care about had been killed. Most girls went home from France with the intention or at least the hope of getting married; she didn't even have a mother and father to welcome her, and had no idea what she was to do with the rest of her life.

She arrived on Friday night and in accordance with Molly's urgent plea went first to Fairoaks, where she was to stay Saturday and Sunday and travel up to London on Monday morning with Molly. Mrs Ormerod welcomed her with old-fashioned formality, though unable to prevent a horrified glance at Emma's hair, which she had cut short in the hardest days of the surge in 1918 and found it convenient to keep short ever since. Benson and Rug had a happy reunion, starting with ecstatic sniffing and tail wagging, which exploded into a grand tussle and wild chase that took them all round the garden. Emma found Helen and Jack very soothing people to come home to, calm and blessedly free from questions. They had dinner in the pleasantly lamplit dining room – after all that time in France, dining tables and electric lamps were wonderful luxuries, not to say four courses and fine linen napkins – and afterwards Helen played the piano so that no-one had to talk much, until Emma went early to bed.

The next morning she met the children and spent a happy hour with them. Basil had questions about the war: which had the larger moustache, the Kaiser or General Haig; what was General Haig's horse called; why didn't France have a king; did Germans eat anything apart from sausages; could tanks drive backwards as well as forwards; and when you lived in a trench did you still have to wash your hands before meals? Emma answered them seriously. Then he drew her an aeroplane 'like Daddy's'. Barbara showed her her best china baby and asked, perhaps ominously, if dollies ever had their hair cut.

On Saturday afternoon Helen took Molly and Emma out for a run in her motor-car and they had tea in a little village, which was already busy smartening itself up for Peace Day. On Sunday everyone went to church, so Emma went too, so as not to cause discord, though she had felt very far from God ever since Wentworth had been killed, not really on speaking terms with Him. During the hymns she looked around at the faces, the mouths opening and shutting, singing the words as if they meant something, and wondered if it were a pleasant club from which she alone was excluded, or a mass exercise in self-delusion. The war, in all its multi-layered atrocity, seemed as good a proof of the non-existence of God as you could hope to have; or, if there were a God, it must be one with an unpleasant sense of humour.

In the afternoon she had a long chat alone with Molly, walking round the garden, following the sun from bench to bench.

'Everything's so green,' she said. 'And there are so many birds. After a while you get used to the way France looks and you start to believe it's normal – the mud, the ruins, the tree stumps, the bits of bodies.'

'You have to forget about it. I know it will be hard, but you have to. It *wasn't* normal, and it will never happen again.'

'There are lots of us,' Emma said. 'You see it in people's eyes. Coming over on the boat, I walked round the deck, and everyone I passed, I could look at their eyes and know what they'd seen. Some hadn't been over long, you could tell, and they'd go back and adjust all right. But others – they weren't seeing what they were looking at. It's a queer sort of emptiness you get to recognise.'

'You're tired,' Molly said. 'When you've been back a few weeks you'll start to feel better and then you'll be yourself again.'

'I'm not sure who myself is any more,' Emma said.

'I won't have that,' Molly said vigorously. 'You have to pull yourself together and snap out of it, because the alternative is to give up, and you're not that sort of person. What would Major Fenniman say? He didn't die just to have you give up. That would be an insult to him.'

'Oh, Molly, you're so full of energy you wear me out,' Emma protested weakly.

'But you know I'm right.'

'Yes.' Emma sighed. 'I know you're right.'

'All right, then – here's what's going to happen. You'll go and stay with Violet for a bit and see the people you have to see. And perhaps we'll spend Peace Day together, if you haven't any other plans by then. All departments are closing for it. And after that, we'll think about what job you're going to do. Because you can't spend your life in idleness. And you know we talked about living together? Now Helen and Jack are here, I won't feel bad about leaving Mother, and I'd love to live in London. I don't really fancy diggings, but you're so rich you could rent a whole flat to yourself, and then,' she concluded with satisfaction, 'you'd need someone to live with you, because it wouldn't be nice to live alone, and here I am, ready and willing.'

And now Emma laughed. 'You do one so much good! Well, I promise if I rent a flat, I won't live in it with anyone but you.'

'Good. And I've got lots of ideas about things you might do, not all of them jobs, but all good, useful things that might be fun, too. I assume you want to have fun.'

Emma thought of the long months of struggle and privation she had spent in France, and the death and suffering she had witnessed. 'Oh, yes,' she said. Benson came running up from his latest race with Rug, his tongue hanging out of the side of his mouth, to make sure she was still there. She stroked his head. 'I certainly mean to have fun.'

93

CHAPTER FIVE

Venetia heard about the plans for Peace Day through her friend Christopher Addison who, as head of the new Department of Health, was a member of the Cabinet. She had known him for many years as a doctor – he had taken his degree at University College, and was a fellow of the Royal College of Surgeons – and through his work on the link between housing and health, something she had always been interested in. He liked to call on her from time to time to discuss his achievements and disappointments, enjoying her intelligent sympathy and, if he called at tea-time, her cook's Vienna slices.

His first object as minister for health was to get through his Housing Bill, which would provide government funding for local councils to build housing for the lower classes. The housing shortage had been getting worse ever since the 1890s, but all private house building had ceased in 1914, so the situation had deteriorated sharply during the war years. Furthermore, there were thousands of inadequate houses and downright slums that ought to be replaced; and now the men were coming home from the war and getting married.

'We estimate that nationally we need something in the order of six hundred thousand houses,' Addison told Venetia, in her private parlour, one warm afternoon. His long, narrow face grew animated, and his deep-set dark eyes bright with enthusiasm for his subject. 'We can't put an obligation onto the councils to clear their slums without giving them some sort of subsidy. The rents they will be able to charge, if the houses are to go to those who need them most, won't cover the full cost of building. And we can't force local people to pay for them through their rates.'

'I had no idea the shortfall was so drastic.'

'Without some serious effort now, we are storing up a health problem for the future. We know the connection between poor housing and public health. You remember the cholera epidemics of the last century?'

She nodded, pouring tea.

'Besides, we campaigned at the election last year on the promise of building a land fit for heroes,' he concluded. 'Surely the first thing a hero needs is a decent home.'

'Forgive me, but this does smack of socialism to me.'

He ate a piece of bread-and-butter. 'I am beginning to find that word not quite so hateful as I once did. The ordinary working man cannot build his own house, and it's quite evident that private enterprise can't or won't do it at a rent he can afford.'

'For sound economic reasons.'

'No doubt. But then what do we do? We've agreed we can't leave them crowded into tenements and slums.'

'But at bottom, is housing a man really the government's business?'

'It's the government's business to send a man to war; isn't it the government's business to see he has a decent place to live when he comes back?'

'If it is, what else becomes the government's business? You build a man a house, then you find yourself wanting to give him a job. So the government starts employing people. You control their wages, which means private enterprise can't compete, and eventually the government becomes the only employer. You want your employees to eat properly so you have government food shops, which means you control the prices. Then you have to take over farming, too, so that you can fix the production costs. Eventually the government controls everything. But who controls them?'

He smiled. 'I had no idea you had such a fertile imagination. That could never happen.'

'My dear, I will tell you *how* it could happen: if you do things for a man, rather than letting him do them for himself, you sap his moral fibre. Soon he doesn't *want* to act for himself – it's easier to be looked after. And once he's in that state, he won't question or even notice what else his political masters do. He will vote for the man who promises him the most, like a dog wagging his tail for the biscuit tin. The government will be free to indulge in any kind of corruption and chicanery it pleases while it enslaves the nation. And there's an end to freedom.'

'Perhaps freedom is overrated. Isn't it better for a man to be taken care of than to be free, if freedom means hunger and homelessness and disease?'

'That, my dear Christopher, is exactly the question,' Venetia said, with a smile. 'It's what the southern states of America proposed regarding the Negroes.'

'But you paint an extreme case. And I repeat, it could never happen.'

'It's happening already in Russia.'

'But Russia has always been corrupt, and its people have always been slaves. We are a free, proud people. Besides,' he concluded, with an attempt at pathos, 'all I want to do is build a few houses for the returning soldiers.'

Venetia laughed. 'You're a good man, and there's no arguing with you, especially when you call six hundred thousand "a few".'

'We all have our rhetorical devices,' he said.

'Have a Vienna slice. Mrs Cannon made them specially for you.'

'Thank you. And look, just to reassure you, let me point out that these council houses won't be given to the men for nothing. They'll pay rent. It's just that we want to cap the rent at the 1914 level, without overburdening the local taxpayer.'

'And who is to build these houses?' Venetia asked, filling up his teacup.

'Oh, private contractors – you see, I don't mean to have gangs of government builders roaming from place to place like navvies, or an official government design they all have to copy. There'll be local diversity, and freedom for councils to do what's best in their own circumstances. I may be beginning to see some advantages in socialism, Venetia, but I'm a long way from being a Comrade Lenin.'

Venetia raised her hands. 'I surrender. For my part, you shall have your houses. I'd be as glad as anyone to see the slums razed. And now tell me about the plans for Peace Day. How is it all coming along?'

He told her of the initial struggle between Lord Curzon, who had wanted something splendid, and Lloyd George, who had pressed for economy. 'But of course now we've brought the date forward we've had to strike a compromise. Splendour *with* economy.' His eyes twinkled. 'We achieved the impossible – both sides won!'

'This Victory March I've been hearing about . . .?'

'Lloyd George was rather taken by the French plan to have a march on Bastille Day, with troops passing a great catafalque representing the war dead and saluting it. Our monument, of course, must be bigger and better than theirs.'

'You'll need an architect.'

'Yes – Mond at the Board of Works suggested Lutyens.'

'Excellent idea,' said Venetia. Sir Edwin Lutyens had been appointed as one of the three principal architects to the Imperial War Graves Commission, to design cemeteries and memorials in France, and she had seen some of his ideas and approved of them.

'We called him in to Downing Street and gave him two weeks to come up with a design, but he presented us with detailed plans within hours,' said Addison. 'It turned out that Mond had sounded him out about the project at the beginning of June.'

'What is his monument like?'

'Absolutely modern, but based on classical geometry – quite plain, but somehow very grand. We didn't want anything overtly religious because of the differing faiths among the Allies, especially the Empire troops. It's a tall, stepped monolith, thirty-five feet high, with a tomb on the top. There won't be a body in it, of course,' he added, as she raised an eyebrow. 'In fact, Lutyens suggested the name Cenotaph for it, from the Greek *kenos* and *taphos*, meaning empty tomb.'

'Yes, I see.'

'The Ancient Greeks set great store by the proper observance of burial rituals, and when the body wasn't available – because it had been overtaken by battle or was lost at sea, for instance – they built a catafalque with an empty tomb to represent it.'

'So many of our fallen have never been found,' Venetia said, 'and the rest are buried where they fell, and will never come home. It is appropriate.'

'We all felt so. The only division among us is on how to pronounce the word,' he added with a smile. 'Most seem to favour "sennotaph", but others insist that since the word begins with *kappa* and *eta* in Greek, it should be pronounced with a hard *c* and a long *e* – "keenotaph".'

'And which will prevail?'

'Lloyd George is not a Greek scholar,' he said succinctly. 'Anyway, it's to be erected halfway up Whitehall for the troops to salute as they pass.'

'Time is rather short for construction, surely?' Venetia said.

'It'll be made in wood and plaster, rendered to look like stone. As it's only temporary, it doesn't need to be too substantial. Lutyens says it will stand up for a week or ten days, but we'll be taking it down immediately, so that will be quite long enough.'

Violet was shocked when she first saw Emma, who had come in a taxi from Waterloo and was shown in to her in the morning room. She was so thin, and brown from the weather, and the liveliness and sparkle had gone from her face. Her mouth looked almost grim, Violet thought; but the words that escaped her were 'Oh, Emma, your poor hair!' Her own gleaming, blue-black tresses reached almost to her waist when let loose. For an instant she remembered how Laidislaw had loved to play with them.

A woman's hair was one of her greatest assets. *But no-one will ever again see my hair loose,* she thought.

Emma smiled uncertainly and touched her shorn head. 'I know it can be rather a shock,' she said, 'but it's so much more practical for work, especially in this hot weather.'

Violet was ashamed of her outburst. 'I only meant it looks rather ragged. Have you been cutting it yourself?'

'Yes, and without a mirror. Sometimes one has no choice.'

'Sanders is a great hand with hair – you must let me ask her to trim it for you.'

'With pleasure,' Emma said. 'You look wonderful, Violet. Not a day older.'

Violet seemed embarrassed. 'You did so much for the war effort, while all I did was sit on a few committees. But at least now I can make sure that you have some pleasure. You will be staying with me, I assume?'

'It's very kind of you.'

'Not at all. I've been longing for you to come home. What are your plans?'

'I shall have to go down to see Uncle Bruce and Aunt Betty, but apart from that I haven't any.' She looked bleak. 'I feel completely cut loose, like a rowing-boat on the ocean. Without any oars. There isn't anything I have to do, or want to do. To tell you the truth, I'm rather afraid of the future.'

Violet laid a hand on her arm. 'Then don't think about it. It's natural you should feel at a loss at first. Just stay here with me, and let me entertain you, and I'm sure in a few weeks you'll think of something you want to do. London's going to be very lively, with Peace Day coming up; and then we can all go down to the country.'

'All? Is Lord Holkam coming home?' Emma asked.

'He's going to be in Paris at least until next year,' Violet said. 'I meant us and the children. Speaking of which—'

'Yes, I would love to go up and see them.'

'And do bring Benson. They adore animals.'

'Her ladyship has arrived, sir. She is waiting for you in the suite.'

'Thank you, Witcher.'

Witcher had been the head porter at Brown's Hotel for thirty-five years, and had seen many touching reunions, particularly during the war years, but, as he told Mrs Witcher that evening, he had never seen anything quite as nice and satisfactory as the way Sir Perceval Parke's face lit up – 'just like a Christmas tree' – at the thought of seeing his wife, or the way he almost ran up the stairs, too eager even to wait for the lift. It was a very pretty thing to witness. Brigadier Sir 'Bertie' Parke, as he was known, was a double DSO and VC and a genuine hero, he informed Mrs Witcher – who knew that anyway because she'd seen the news reel at the cinema of the King presenting the VC medal – so it was right that he should have a bit of happiness now the war was over.

The genuine hero bounded into the sitting-room of the suite to be greeted by the ecstatic tail of a very large brindled hound, and very shortly afterwards by his lady wife, who emerged from the bedroom at the sound of the door opening and flung herself at him with a glad cry of 'Bertie!'

A silence followed, at the end of which, still in his arms but allowed to breathe at last, Jessie looked up into his dear, dear face and said, 'Is this it, then? Finally, finally? You're really home for good?'

'Really,' he said, pushing a wayward curl of hair from her brow so that he could kiss it.

'No more going overseas?'

'Not without you, my love. You smell delicious,' he added.

'You feel wonderful,' she returned. Her arms were as far round him as she could reach. 'So solid.'

'I'll take that as a compliment,' he laughed. 'You, on the other hand, are a veritable sylph. I could do with a little more of you, darling one.'

'There'll be plenty more in a month or two.'

'How is the baby? Behaving himself?'

'He's started moving. I'd forgotten how exciting that feels.'

'And you're well?'

'Tired, sometimes, but very well.'

Bran, eager for attention, thrust himself between them, and they broke apart at last. 'How did the hotel management take to him?' Bertie asked.

'They weren't very welcoming. Other ladies have Pekes and Poms and poodles.'

'I see the problem,' Bertie said, stroking the great rough head. 'They probably thought he was a pony.'

'But then I said that you adore him, and they couldn't really refuse anything to a war hero, so here we are. Exercising him will give me something to do when you're busy, and I couldn't really leave the poor fellow – he pines when I'm away.'

'She brings the dog but leaves our child behind.'

'Thomas has lots of attention, and as soon as we have somewhere to live, I'll go and fetch him. You can't imagine how much planning it would have needed – and he would cause far more chaos in a hotel room than Bran.'

'How do you like the suite?'

'It's sumptuous,' Jessie said.

'*Sumptuous?*'

'There's no other word for it,' she assured him solemnly. 'Can you really afford it?'

'Oh yes. Remember, I haven't been spending very much for the last year or so – no estate to keep up, no household expenses. I'm quite in funds.'

'If you'd been a bachelor, you could have stayed at your club.'

'Given the endless rounds of drinks I'd have had to buy, it probably wouldn't have been any cheaper.' He cocked his head. 'Any more objections? You sound as though you don't like it after all.'

'Oh, I do. It's just that during the war we all got used to doing without. It almost feels sinful now, to have such luxury. It's silly, really.'

'Very silly. This isn't luxury, it's a hotel. Luxury will be when we have a home. And to keep you occupied, when you're not walking the dog, you can start looking for a house for us. If you're sure you really want to stay in London through the summer?'

'If you have to be here, I want to be here too.'

'I do have to. But you could take a nice little place at the seaside and I could come down and visit,' he urged. He didn't want to part with her, but he was concerned for her health.

She shook her head firmly. 'No bon,' she said, making him smile with the soldiers' slang. 'You can't get rid of me that easily.'

He took her into his arms again. 'This is how much I want to be rid of you. What would you like to do this evening?'

'You haven't any engagements?'

'Nary a one. I'm yours until tomorrow morning.'

'Then I would like to go for a walk in the Park – I'm sure Bran would like to get out.'

'We'll look like a French Impressionist painting: *Lady and military gentleman with large dog by a lake, with ducks.* And where would you like to dine?'

'All alone with you at a little restaurant, if you know of one.'

'Of course I do. Soho is full of them. Somewhere *très intime*?'

'With a checked tablecloth,' she said gravely. 'I insist on a checked tablecloth.'

'And a Gypsy fiddler who will try to come and play for us, until I give him a shilling to go and bother someone else.'

She laughed. 'Foolish!'

'I feel foolish with you. I want to be foolish – light-hearted and happy and never sad or worried or weighted with regrets again.' He was serious suddenly. 'There are so many ghosts in our pasts. It doesn't dishonour them if we decide not to think about them. We've been given this chance of life together. We mustn't waste it.'

'We won't,' she said. She laid her head against his chest. She knew what he meant. A great many people had had to die for them to be here, as they were, together, but they had not sought it or engineered it. There were so many dead to grieve for, at the end of the most costly war in history: it would be all too easy to become paralysed by it. If her experience in France had taught her one thing, it was that life was to be cherished and used to the full.

Bran interrupted them again, whining and scraping at the door. She broke away hurriedly to stop him.

'We'd better take him out before he lands us with a bill for damages,' Bertie said. He extended his arm to her. 'Will you walk with me, my lady?'

When they reached the Park, and had seen to the relief of the dog, they took up a leisurely pace arm in arm, and Bertie said, 'I haven't told you my news yet. We've been chosen to take part in the Peace Day parade.'

'We? The West Herts, you mean?'

'Not the whole regiment. A representative group of sixty. I shall have to select them from around my four companies. It's a great honour.'

'Of course it is – and no more than you deserve,' Jessie said. His old battalion had come back at the beginning of the month, and they had gone first to barracks at Sandridge for the demobilisation process, which would take two weeks. For those he chose for the march, it would be their last military engagement. To his surprise his servant, Cooper, who had been with him right through the war, had declined to continue in his service for the next two years.

'No, sir, thanking you all the same,' he had said. 'I done my bit. I ain't signin' on again. When we got into this 'ere lot, back in 'fourteen, they was sayin' it'd be all over by Christmas. You and me, sir, we knew it wasn't goin' to be that easy. But we never knew 'ow 'ard it'd be, and that's the trufe. So I'm gettin' out while I still got some gettin' in me.'

'I shall miss you, Cooper,' Bertie had said, and meant it. They had been through a lot, and while Cooper was an incorrigible grumbler, he was also a first-class wangler, who had kept his master supplied with the essentials and even, sometimes, luxuries. He had shown great courage on occasion, and great devotion. There had been no need

105

for Cooper to follow him back across the battlefield under the German guns at the Somme, for instance, but he had done it. It was a miracle they had both survived. 'What will you do? You haven't any family, I believe?' he asked.

'None that'll own me. But don't you worry, sir. I got plans.'

'I'd be interested to hear them,' Bertie said, not thinking he would tell him. Cooper liked to be mysterious.

But, to his surprise, Cooper told him quite freely. There was a pub, it seemed, back in his native Hertfordshire, called The Case Is Altered. He had drunk in it as a young man, and had conceived all those years ago a desire one day to own it. Having never married, he'd had nothing to spend his money on, and had salted it away year on year over his long military career, together with the fruits of various 'wangles' and 'deals', which he described collectively as 'business'. Now with his demob bounty he had enough.

'I always meant to run a pub when I retired from the army.'

'Yes, a lot of soldiers say that,' Bertie said.

'A lot of blokes *says* it, sir, but that's as far as they gets.'

'Well, I wish you good luck with it, Cooper, and if ever I'm that way, I shall call in on you and buy a pint of your best.'

'That you shan't, sir,' Cooper said indignantly. 'Beer you shall have, or whisky, or whatever you fancy, but I shan't take your money for it.'

His last service to Cooper would be to pick him for the Peace Day March. 'He and I have been in since

August 1914, and there are only five others left in the battalion who were at Mons. They'll march in the front rank. For the others I'll pick the longest serving and any with especially meritorious records.'

'And you'll be at their head?' Jessie asked. 'On horseback?'

He nodded. 'Just for the occasion. The present colonel sportingly insisted.'

'So he should. I shall be proud fit to burst,' she said.

'I'd hoped I might watch the parade with you,' he said.

'No, no, this is so much better. I'm so pleased for you. How will it be arranged? You won't march all the way from Sandridge?'

'No, darling, of course not. I'll parade the chosen men at barracks and have a rehearsal. But there's to be a military camp set up in Kensington Gardens, and we'll march out from there.'

'Well, don't worry about me,' Jessie said. 'I shall place myself unequivocally in Cousin Venetia's hands. She's bound to have secured some first-class place to watch from.'

'As soon as I'm released I shall come and join you.'

'It's going to be quite a day,' Jessie said. 'I do hope the weather's kind. I really feel everyone needs a celebration now. It's been so hard for them at home, with the rationing and air raids and waiting for telegrams.'

'Harder for them in some ways than for us,' Bertie said.

People started to pour into London on Friday the 18th of July. All hotels and guesthouses were full, and those without relatives or friends to board with spent the night sleeping in the parks or on the streets. One enterprising group of women climbed onto the wall around the Victoria Memorial Gardens and stayed there for the next sixteen hours. Kensington Gardens had been turned into a military camp and the fifteen thousand soldiers and fifteen hundred officers who were to take part in the parade were bivouacked there under strict guard, not so much to keep them from the temptations of drink and women but to keep the drink and women from getting in.

Extra trains were put on and arrived all through the night, delivering thousands more spectators, and by six the next morning the scramble for the best places along the processional route was well under way. By eight o'clock it was impossible to cross Trafalgar Square. Whitehall was packed from end to end, and the temporary Cenotaph was unveiled that morning to a murmur of admiration. The Mall was solid, with an overspill into the Park, and outside Buckingham Palace there was a temporary pavilion where the King would review the parade.

The streets had been decorated with flowers and flags, strings of bunting and coloured ribbon, and looked very gay. Oxford Street, with its big stores, had made a special effort, and attracted thousands of the visitors from out of town and from the suburbs, coming up with their children to see the decorations. The façade of Marshall & Snelgrove was glorious with garlands of flowers and wreaths of foliage interspersed with flags, and above it all in huge gilt letters the word 'VICTORY' between the dates 1914 and 1918. Selfridges, not to be outdone, had similar decorations, but at either end were pedestals on which were mounted huge plaster groups of heroic figures representing the three services, with the Angel of Victory holding out a laurel wreath over their heads.

The official programme for the day, price one penny, was sold in hundreds of thousands; there were the usual souvenir sellers; and others hawking buns, pies, fruit and lemonade to the waiting crowds. The day was a hot one, and the pubs anywhere near the route were soon sold out, so that anyone selling anything to drink was very welcome. A story got about that a man with a bottle of ginger beer had shouted out that he was prepared to auction it, and was severely hurt in the resulting rush. But the crowds were universally good-humoured. Children were passed down to the front for a better view, and old men with medals and wounded soldiers were accorded the best spots.

Venetia had been lucky enough to be assigned a window in the Home Office, which was right opposite the Cenotaph. She had meant to hold a breakfast party, but after discussion with Oliver and Violet it was decided everyone should assemble at Violet's house, since it would be near impossible to get from Manchester Square to Whitehall afterwards. From St James's Square they could walk across the Park and through Downing Street.

So Violet held the breakfast party. Lord Holkam was not there – he had already left for an official breakfast at Horseguards – but Freddie Copthall stood by her side as he had so often before. Venetia came early with Oliver, who was accompanied by his friend Kit, Lord Westhoven, lately returned from France on the expiry of his contract with the RAMC. Emma was there, and Jessie – Bertie was also at Horseguards – but though the Vibarts had been invited, they were otherwise engaged. It made a pleasantly intimate party of seven.

'Just as well,' Venetia said, to comfort Violet, who had imagined a much larger gathering. 'The window wouldn't have afforded a view to any more.'

The breakfast was splendid – a vast ham, sausages, eggs, bacon, kedgeree, kidneys, piles of fruit, coffee, champagne – and Emma found herself staring at it in a sort of shocked wonder, almost unable to take it in. They had been adequately fed in the FANY, but the food in France had always been plain. Often simply a cup of coffee was beyond their scope – *ersatz* had been the best they could hope for. She hardly knew where to begin – the superabundance defeated her.

'Rather a change from one fried rasher on a tin plate,' said Kit Westhoven at her elbow.

She looked up at him. He was tall, very handsome, with a lean, Grecian face, blue eyes and rather unruly fair hair, which today, however, was sleeked into polite submission for the occasion. 'How did you guess what I was thinking?' she asked.

'It wasn't difficult. I was thinking it myself. You and I are the most recently returned from France.'

'Freddie only came back yesterday,' Emma said, in fairness.

'Paris isn't quite the same thing,' he said. 'I don't think they've been stinting themselves at the peace conference. You've been at Pop, haven't you?'

'Yes, until two weeks ago.'

'Ypres is not a pretty place. I've been at St Omer, but I've had to go to Ypres from time to time since the Armistice.'

'I was at St Omer before,' she said.

'Yes, so Oliver told me. Did you know a restaurant, Chez Gustave?'

110

She smiled. 'Oh, yes! We went there as often as we could. His meatballs!'

'The man was a genius. I swear he could have made bully taste like duck *à l'orange*!'

'How strange. Here we are talking about food again,' Emma said. 'It was all we ever seemed to do over there. And yet with all this feast before us, we both have empty plates.'

'Well, let's plunge in together. I'll serve you and you can serve me.'

'All right. But not too much.'

He eased an egg onto her plate. 'I think you should have a little of everything.' He looked down just as she looked up, and their eyes met in a swift rush of sympathy. 'I say,' he said, to cover the moment, 'I do like your haircut. I hope it's not impertinent to say so. It's tremendously modern.'

'Thank you,' she said. 'You're the first person who hasn't rolled their eyes in horror at the thought of a girl with short hair.'

'It suits you. I'd like to see more girls bob. Perhaps you can start a fashion.'

She laughed. 'I suppose that would be something to do with my life. I must find some purpose.'

'Do you feel at a loose end, too?'

'As if I've been cut adrift. But you're a doctor – you won't have any difficulty in making a future for yourself.'

'I don't know,' he said. 'The things I've seen and had to do in France have rather put me off the whole thing. At the moment I don't care if I never see the inside of a hospital again.'

'I hope I never do,' said Emma.

Across the room, Venetia said to Oliver, 'Emma and Kit seem to be getting on well together.'

Oliver looked. 'Yes,' he said, 'and why shouldn't they?'

'What do you mean?'

'Only that they make a pretty couple. Both handsome, Emma rich, and Kit with a title.'

Venetia smiled. 'Ah, you're making a romance between them.'

'It wouldn't be such a bad thing, would it? Better than either of them marrying a stranger and being lost to us.'

'Selfish reasons are always the best.'

'And Emma's doings with the FANY have given her a rather different view on the world from the majority of females, which might make it hard for her to settle with your average man. Kit will know exactly what's made her as she is. It might be the best thing for both of them.'

'You wouldn't mind?' Venetia asked.

'Why should I?'

'Because you had plans for you and Kit to set up in practice together.'

'Well, that can still happen.'

She shook her head. 'If he marries, he'll be a different Kit. He'll be Lord Westhoven of Lutterworth, with the estate and the seat in the Lords and the necessity of breeding an heir. He won't have time for doctoring.'

Oliver shrugged. 'Oh, well, I've had to face that possibility anyway. At least this way I know I'll like his wife.'

The Cenotaph, they all agreed, looked most impressive, standing in the centre of Whitehall, its summit crowned with a great laurel wreath holding in place a Union Flag draped loosely over the tomb. The sides bore the flags of the White Ensign, the Red Ensign and the Union Flag, representing the different arms of the services.

'You'd never guess it was just wood and plaster,' Jessie said. 'It looks so solid.'

Venetia explained to the best of her ability the principle on which it was built: the apparently straight lines, vertical and horizontal, were actually curves, but on such a huge radius they seemed straight. The planes of the monument were, in fact, all parts of a vast invisible sphere. 'If you extended them, they would meet up nine hundred feet below ground and nine hundred feet above it.'

'I like that,' Jessie said. 'It has its roots in the ground and its head in the stars. Perhaps that's why it looks so permanent.'

'People have been putting flowers there,' Violet observed. There were a few homemade wreaths on the steps, and one or two small bunches of ordinary garden flowers, which somehow looked both pathetic and touching in the context of the massive, uncompromising monument. 'I wish we'd thought of doing that for Papa and Thomas.'

The parade was impressive, solid bodies of men marching in perfect step, and in a silence made somehow more profound for the massed sound of their boots on the pavement, a martial beat that roused a ghostly echo from the surrounding buildings. It made Venetia shiver. Men from the three services were there, with representative bodies from the Allies and the Empire. It was a proud moment for her that women from the three women's services were included. When she had voted for the first time the previous year, it had been an extraordinary experience, but the sight of those uniformed WAACs and WAAFs and WRNS marching in silence in the hot sunshine among the men seemed better proof of what they had achieved.

She was standing beside Jessie when the West Herts came along, with Bertie at their head, and heard her draw a little breath of pleasure and pride. Bertie knew where they would be, and lifted his eyes a moment as he passed, but she did not think he could have seen them.

The generals, Pershing, Foch and Haig, came past, and saluted the monument. Lord Holkam was behind Haig, among his aides. Violet looked down at him dispassionately and thought of how Jessie had looked down at Bertie. Life had dealt them such different hands. Holkam knew where they were, too, and looked up, and she thought he smiled slightly under his moustache, but couldn't be sure. Then they were past and gone.

When the whole parade had passed, the solemnity of the moment was broken and they could talk again.

'Didn't Bertie look splendid?' Jessie said, still at the window.

Behind her, Oliver said, 'Yes, dear. And so many medals. He quite dazzled.' But he patted her shoulder, to show it was only teasing.

'Of the three leaders,' Kit said, 'I thought Foch looked the most impressive.'

'It's all the gold lace. The French uniform's too gaudy for my taste,' Oliver countered.

'It's a pity Haig is such a little grey old man,' Kit said.

'Handsome is as handsome does,' said Freddie. 'I know which one I'd sooner follow into battle.'

Almost as soon as the parade had passed, the crowd had pressed forward into the road to go up to the Cenotaph and examine it, some of them bowing their heads in prayer. More people were now leaving tributes of flowers, their summer colours small and bright against the grey-white of the steps.

In the afternoon there were entertainments in the parks, tableaux organised by the League of Arts in St James's, Shakespeare performed by the National Organisation of Girls' Clubs in Regent's Park, and a grand concert in Hyde Park, with combined choirs providing ten thousand voices, and the massed bands of the Brigade of Guards. Venetia's party attended the concert, and during the afternoon the King and Queen made an appearance, to rapturous cheers.

And in the evening there was Violet's dinner party. Holkam was released from official receptions in time to host it, and Bertie arrived from Kensington Gardens. Eddie Vibart was off duty that evening, and he and Sarah were among the guests. Violet sparkled with jewels and the satisfaction of organising a successful occasion, and Holkam was most attentive to her – almost affectionate, those who were close to the couple noted.

The official celebrations were to be rounded off that night by a grand fireworks display in Hyde Park. Eddie proposed that they should decamp after dinner to the house of Lord Tonbridge in Mount Street to see the spectacle. 'He's holding open house, so I know we'll be welcome.'

'You go, if you like,' Violet said good-naturedly.

But Lord Holkam clearly thought this very rude, and Sarah gave Eddie a meaning look, upon which he withdrew the suggestion meekly. After dinner the ladies went upstairs, where they were soon joined by the younger men, who had quickly tired of the political conversation of Lord Holkam and their elders. The hour for the fireworks display arrived, and Violet said suddenly, 'You know, I believe we could see them from the leads. The house is so tall. Shall we go up and see?'

Everyone thought this a good idea, and trooped upstairs. It was a warm evening, a little overcast but windless, and there were plenty of flat spaces on the roof for them to stand and move easily.

'What a good idea of yours, Violet,' Jessie said, as the first rockets shattered the dark sky. 'It's a very fine view, bar the odd chimney stack.'

'I doubt we'd have been able to get a taxi,' Freddie said. 'We'd have probably still been walking, and missed it all.'

Oliver told his mother the next day that it was as well they hadn't gone, as the evening at Mount Street had been spoilt by an unfortunate accident. One of the guests, Lady Diana Cooper – the society beauty, daughter of the Duke of Rutland, who had recently married the dashing officer Alfred Duff Cooper – had fallen through a skylight into an attic bedroom, hitting the floor twenty feet below and breaking her thigh. 'Which rather took the shine out of the pyrotechnics,' he concluded.

CHAPTER SIX

Outside the capital, celebrations had taken a similar course. Every town or village that could muster some soldiers had had a march and a thanksgiving service, and temporary monuments, many of them small copies of the Cenotaph, had been erected for the day. There had been civic banquets, open-air theatricals, water pageants, tableaux, fairs, shows of all kinds; and as soon as it fell dark, bonfires were lit up and down the country to imitate the beacons that had announced the defeat of the Armada.

York had its own festivities, with a concert in the Minster in the afternoon and a ball at the Assembly House in the evening. Henrietta had persuaded Teddy that it would be more suitable for the Morlands to join in with them than to hold their own separate entertainments. 'In any case, now the war's over we can have the August fair again,' she pointed out. Morland Place had hosted a grand fair and ball every year before the war, and Teddy's face brightened at the thought.

'Yes, you're right. It won't do to be having two balls so close together – looks like showing off. I just wanted to see Polly dance.'

'You can see her dance at the Assembly House.'

★   ★   ★

Polly was beautiful, an heiress, and had always been popular: she had never lacked for partners, even when, because of the war, they were thin on the ground. So she danced every dance at the Assembly House ball; she listened and nodded and sometimes even smiled as she revolved elegantly; but she said little herself, and even those bold enough to think they might have a chance with her retired baffled. There was something remote about her, they thought, trying to remember how it had been before the war. Surely she had been much livelier, much more fun? But she had been a schoolgirl then. It seemed Miss Morland had grown up into a Snow Queen. They paid their homage, and went on to dance with more chatty girls.

Teddy didn't at all mind her keeping her distance from the boys, graciously as she did it. He was in no hurry for her to get married.

Henrietta might worry: 'She doesn't seem to show any interest in any of them. It isn't natural in a girl her age.'

But Teddy said, 'She has the sense to know none of them is good enough for her.'

'You'll never think anyone is, but if she gets a reputation as untouchable, what then? You must want her to get married one day. You can't want her to be an old maid.'

And Teddy stirred restively. 'Oh, there's plenty of time – no need to worry about that yet.'

Polly knew all this. She saw her aunt's anxious looks and her father's complacent ones. She heard enough of whispered conversations to know that the boys found her hard to fathom and the girls not very friendly. She heard her smile called 'enigmatic' and quite liked that. She had no desire to have girl friends to chatter to, and while she liked the boys admiring her, she wanted it to be from a distance. She *felt* remote. It was as if everything she saw and heard was on the other side of a wall of glass. She lived inside her mind, where Erich Küppel could still be found, where she could see his face and hear his voice, remember the times they had been together, and imagine being with him again in some dim and ill-defined future.

She had stopped moping about the house. Her object was to avoid enquiry, so she went to Makepeace's, the shop in Coney Street that would one day be hers, and involved herself in the business. She went to dances and tennis parties. She went out riding a lot, because then she could be alone, which was what she liked most. On horseback she could revisit the places he had been: his handiwork remained in hedges he had laid and walls he had repaired. And when the longing for him became too great she could gallop over the moors until the speed wore it out of her and the wind dried her tears on her face. That she seemed to everyone, except perhaps Henrietta, to be normal was a tribute to the control she had learned to exercise over herself. It was what she wanted – simply to be left alone.

Maria, back from honeymoon, was surprised to notice that Polly was reading the newspaper every day when Teddy had finished with it. Polly had never interested herself in the wider world before. Maria was intrigued, and when a little detective work revealed that it was the overseas news she was reading, she could make nothing of it. She could only see that reading it gave Polly no pleasure.

It made Polly feel sick to read about the things that were happening in Germany. Attempted Communist revolution, violent strikes in the Ruhr, Bavaria taken over

119

by armed socialists, Munich occupied, food riots in German towns. *Where was he? Was he safe?* They said people were starving to death in Germany, because paying for the war had ruined them, and now reparations would keep them from recovering. But he was a country man: his father owned an estate. You couldn't starve in the country, not really – there was always something to eat. And he was resourceful, strong and clever. He *would* survive.

She lived on her memories of him, and fantasies of how she would see him again one day. She would go to Germany. When she was twenty-one she would be free to go where she liked, and her father would surely give her a larger allowance. She would save until she had enough for the fare, and go and find him. Or he would come to her. He had told her that Germans would be hated for years, perhaps for ever, and would not be allowed to come back to England. But his love for her would surely find a way.

She would see him again. In the mean time, she had simply to go on, smiling from behind the glass wall so that people never found out she had fallen in love with a hated Hun soldier, for that was something they would not understand, and would never, never forgive.

Jessie, spurred by the desire to have her son with her, searched with great energy and within days had found a small house in Dover Street that she told Bertie would do. It was an easy stroll for him to Horseguards from there; Jessie would be able to walk the dog in the Park, and it was five minutes from Violet's house if she wanted company.

It was a tall and narrow building with a dining-room

on the ground floor, a double drawing-room on the first, three bedrooms and a bathroom on the second, three more on the third, which would do for a nursery floor, and servants' bedrooms in the attic. The kitchens were in the basement, as usual in that sort of house, and there was a servant's bedroom down there, which presumably had originally been the butler's room. Jessie did not mean to bother with a male servant, and thought it would be good for the cook, since most cooks she had ever met were fat and would not relish climbing all those stairs to go to bed.

Her next port of call was the employment exchange in Oxford Street that Cousin Venetia had recommended. She had Bertie's authority to employ a cook, two housemaids and a kitchen-maid. He agreed that with a nursery-maid, and perhaps a charwoman once a week, that was all they would need. They would send their laundry out. Living so handily in London they would not need a motor or carriage and the tiny garden at the back could be tended by an occasional gardener. 'And if we entertain you can always hire extra staff by the evening,' he pointed out.

'Yes, I remember Mother saying she used to do that when we lived in London.'

Finding a nursery-maid was harder. She still hadn't found one she liked when she went down to Yorkshire to collect Thomas.

'The problem was the same in my day,' Henrietta said. 'As I recall, we always took country girls for nursery staff. That's how we got Nanny Emma from Norfolk, and look how well that worked out. She's still with us all these years later.'

'You should take a local girl back with you,' Teddy said. 'Nothing could be better than a Yorkshire girl.'

'But would they want to come?' Jessie said. 'And it would be so far for them to visit their families, poor things.'

'I suppose we could lend you one of the girls for a week or two,' Henrietta said, 'until you get settled.'

'Can you spare one?'

'With Thomas gone, and the older children doing lessons, there'll only be Martin, John and Harriet to look after. Nanny Emma ought to cope with two girls. As to *wanting* to go,' she concluded, 'I should think any girl would jump at the chance of a few weeks in London.'

Nanny Emma was harder to persuade. 'Nasty, dirty, smooky ole place to be taking my babby,' she said, holding Thomas possessively to her. As the nursery's youngest he was naturally her own private property and she didn't see why she should part with him. 'You can't bring up children right in London. That ent healthy.'

'But, Nanny, you brought us up there,' Jessie pointed out, aching to hold her baby but unable, short of snatching him, to get hold of him.

'Twarn't my choice,' she said firmly.

'And we were all quite healthy.'

Nanny Emma shifted ground. 'We went to the seaside in August. I can't see the reason of taking my babby away now. Noobody stays in London in August and September. You could leave him hare with me until you get settled in,' she went on beguilingly, 'and fetch him in October, when it gets cooler.'

'I miss him and want him with me,' Jessie said. 'I'm his mother.'

'That doon't mean you have to be hanging round his neck every minute,' Nanny Emma sniffed. 'Babbies are best left to them as knows what to do. Parents can visit when they wants. Within reason.'

But Jessie had smiled at Thomas, and now he beamed back at her, and was holding out his arms. Firmly she took hold of him, and Nanny Emma had no choice but to release him.

'I'm sorry, Nanny, but I must have him,' Jessie said, and added kindly, 'Don't worry, Maria will be increasing soon, and then you'll have a whole new family to take care of.'

Nanny Emma took the point, and was almost placated. It had been hard, with nothing but widows in the house, to contemplate the prospect of no more babies – she had never expected Helen and Jack to stay after the war. Jessie marrying Bertie had reopened the door, only to slam it closed with this going-to-London nonsense. But, of course, there was Maria. She had forgotten Maria. She didn't look the type to have a large family, in Nanny Emma's professional opinion, but surely there would be two at least, and that would tide them over until Jessie came back, or Miss Polly got married. Like Teddy, she had never imagined Polly living anywhere but Morland Place, even after marriage.

Emma was having tea at the Ritz with Vera Polk. Vera had invited her several times to her house at Paulton's Square, which she shared with several other women, but Emma had been too busy to accept. Finally the invitations had become embarrassing to refuse, and Emma had suggested tea instead. She chose the Ritz without thought, as being the nearest place, and having the nicest tea, but Vera was obviously not comfortable with her surroundings. She looked out of place, with her severe and rather shabby clothes, although at least now her bobbed hair didn't look so odd. It wasn't quite a fashion yet, but even here in the Ritz there was another female besides Emma and Vera with short hair. But it was Vera's attitude that was most awkward. She stared around her with evident disapproval and, when she spoke, did not lower her voice, so that several neighbouring tables had to pretend not to hear her disparagements.

'I suppose I should have expected you to pick somewhere like this,' she said.

'I thought you'd like it. The tea is very good,' Emma said.

'Like it? I suppose it's all right for the rich and idle,' Vera said. 'I'm just surprised at you, trying to impress me with your wealth. I thought better of you, Emma, after you went to France with the FANY. I thought you were a proper person.'

Emma blushed with vexation. 'What do you mean?'

'I suppose I should have taken the hint when you kept refusing to see me. Your old friends aren't good enough for you now, are they? Now the war's over and you can go back to a life of meaningless pleasure with your titled friends. But that's what rich people do. Use people and drop them.'

'I didn't. I haven't. I don't know what you're talking about,' Emma said, head up, upset.

'Why did you refuse to come and see me?' Vera demanded.

'I didn't refuse. I had other engagements, that's all. The first free moment I had, I asked you to tea. And here you are.'

'The first free moment. So busy all of a sudden! But you haven't seen any of your old FANY friends, have you? You haven't been seen at Headquarters. You didn't even go to the reunion dinner.'

124

A first reunion dinner had taken place at the Florence restaurant in London in July, with a hundred and eighteen members and guests.

'Everyone was there,' Vera pursued. 'Even MacDougall, who was ill, sent a telegram. But not a word from Weston.'

Emma shook her head unhappily. 'I just felt – it seems to me that the FANY has served its purpose. The war's over. We had a job to do and we did it. Now that's in the past.'

'Once a FANY, always a FANY,' Vera said. 'We haven't disbanded. We haven't given up. We're all working hard to find a role for the corps in peacetime, because we believe in it. Besides the good it does to others, it transforms the lives of its members. How can you forget the friendship, and all we achieved, so easily?'

'I haven't forgotten,' Emma said in a low voice. 'But I can't remember the FANY without remembering the rest of it, the horror, and death. I want to forget. I want to forget the whole war. It was hideous and hateful and it took away everything I valued.'

'I see. You don't value us, then.'

'You wilfully misunderstand me,' Emma said angrily. 'You know what I mean.'

Vera nodded grimly. 'Yes, your fiancé, and then that fellow Wentworth. Men, always men! You define yourself by them. To you, the men in your life were the only things that mattered. It seems we taught you nothing.'

Emma saw that Vera was hurt, and despite everything felt sorry for her. She said, trying for kindness, 'I don't feel that. The friendship of the others in France was wonderful. And you've been very good to me too. Your letters kept me going through some of the worst times.'

Vera softened at once. 'I wish I could have been with

you. You know I'd have gone myself if it hadn't been for my wretched leg.' She had been injured by a shell while driving blankets up to the Front earlier in the war.

'I know. You're very brave.'

Vera leaned across the table and clasped Emma's hand. 'I don't want to see you leave the corps. I don't think you're strong enough to manage on your own. You'll go wrong without us. You need your sisters around you, our support and friendship. There's still plenty for us to do, even in peacetime. We owe our duty to the women of this country to lead by example.'

'Yes,' said Emma. A woman at the next table was looking at them, and she was embarrassed. She tried to slide her hand free, but Vera held it more tightly.

'And with your money, there's untold good you could do. The women's cause is as important as ever. There are so many injustices to put right. You're rich and well connected – you can take office and use your influence. You could be commandant of the FANY in a year or two. I don't want to see you fritter yourself away in marriage, like so many of these silly women.'

'I'm not going to get married,' Emma said bleakly.

'Good,' said Vera, removing her hand. She sat up straight and drank some tea. 'I must say I'm relieved to hear it. I was hoping you would come back from France unattached. It's a good thing, really, that Fenniman and Wentworth died, because attachments like that only demean you. Men always want to make slaves of you, but real love can only exist between equals. That's why the only true love is the love of women for women.'

Suddenly Emma felt sick of her, wanted only to get away and be left alone. Vera went on talking about how men always wanted to tell you what to do and wouldn't let you be yourself. But she was doing exactly the same thing, wasn't she? Telling Emma what she should do with her life. Emma was all for self-determination, but she liked politeness and tact and tolerance and kindness too, and she didn't want to live in Vera's world, where everything was combative and harsh. And the love of women – she had truly loved her fellow FANYs – could not replace for her the love of men. Whatever Vera said, she still *wanted* to get married, though she didn't believe it would ever happen now: she would never be able to love anyone else enough to marry them.

On the 25th of August, at ten past nine in the morning, Jack took off from Hounslow Heath in the DH16 for Paris, with a cargo of newspapers, Devonshire cream, sacks of mail, some fine leather goods and, among the passengers, a reporter from the *Evening Standard*, who was going to write a very useful piece on how he flew on the world's first regular daily scheduled international passenger flight. There were an awful lot of qualifiers there, Jack thought, but at least he had managed to be first at something.

The weather was fine and he had no difficulty in finding the way, having flown so often over northern France. They made Paris in two hours. There were reporters waiting at Le Bourget, and photographers too. Jack thought of Helen, and posed obediently on the wing for his photograph, realising with a sort of surprise that he would be able to buy a copy of the paper for her when he came back tomorrow. The advantages of regular air services came home to him in a very personal way.

The other newspapers picked up the story from the *Standard*, and the *Daily Mail*, true to form, wanted something more personal. Their reporter made enquiries about Jack and found not only that he had been decorated in the war, which was good, but that he had flown with his little dog in the cockpit, which was better. In vain Jack said he had never taken Rug up on operations: they wrote the story the way they wanted it. And they wanted the right photograph, too; so, since it would be such good publicity for the AT&T service, he took Rug with him to Hounslow and posed in the cockpit with him on his lap, wearing his flying hat and goggles. Thus for one day, at least, Rug accompanied him on the flight to Paris. Rug adored flying, but it was rather different on the converted bomber. He couldn't sit with his head out of the window as he could in a small single- or two-seater, and Jack thought he found the flight rather boring, and very noisy. When he got home that evening, he told Helen that he wouldn't take him again. 'He can come with me on pleasure flights, from Brooklands.'

'You don't think you'll have had enough flying, doing the Paris service?' Helen said in surprise.

Jack smiled sheepishly. 'Frankly, I feel a bit like Rug. It isn't the same. I was a fighter pilot – I like to hear the wind in the wires.'

Helen planted a kiss on his forehead. 'Fly all you like, my darling. In fact, we can go to Brooklands next time you're free and go up together in a two-seater.'

He kissed her back. 'I could never have married anyone but you. You *understand*!'

The servants' hall at Morland Place took the *Daily Mail*, and Sawry brought it in at family breakfast time to show the photograph, which was rather ingeniously captioned 'The Dogs of War'.

'Well, this is very amusing,' Teddy said, passing it round the table. 'And a good advertisement for the company.'

Henrietta marvelled, and passed the paper to Ethel. 'Isn't it odd how the war has changed our attitude to newspapers? "Getting into the papers" was always rather shameful, even if it was for doing something good.'

'It's mostly about the dog,' Ethel said.

'I dare say those cinema news reels have blunted our finer feelings,' said Denis Palgrave.

'It was a very fine thing to see Bertie being decorated by the King,' said Teddy, who had gone to the cinema on purpose to see it. 'Nothing to be ashamed of there.' He sighed. 'I'm pleased for Jack that he's got himself a job, and doing something he likes, too, but I suppose it means they won't come back.'

'I don't think so, Teddy dear,' Henrietta said. 'But they'll visit.'

Teddy brightened. 'On the subject of visits, I saw charwomen going in to Shawes when I was out that way this morning. It won't be long.' Venetia, Violet and the children were coming down to Shawes for a few weeks. 'We should have some jollity while they're here.'

'My Jeremy will enjoy playing with Violet's boys,' Ethel said. 'They're just the sort of boys Robbie and I always wanted as friends for them.'

'It will be so good to see Venetia again,' said Henrietta. 'But what a shame Emma won't be with them.'

'It's right and natural that she should visit her uncle and aunt,' Palgrave said. 'And perhaps she'll call in on her way home.'

'I wonder how the war will have changed her,' Henrietta continued. 'She must have seen some terrible things out there.'

'No more terrible than the things Jessie saw,' said Teddy, loyally.

'But Jessie was older. And she has Bertie now. Poor Emma lost her fiancé.'

'She's young,' said Palgrave, 'and very pretty and very rich. I'm sure she won't stay single for long.'

'She may not want another attachment,' Ethel said. 'Some people stay faithful in their hearts to their first love. And I must say it's hard to hear you talk about "poor Emma" when I don't hear anyone saying "poor Ethel".'

Henrietta was stricken. 'Oh, Ethel, dear, we don't forget – how could we? We do pity you with all our hearts. It's just that we happened to be talking about Emma.'

'Well, my loss was much greater than hers,' Ethel objected. 'She only knew Major Fenniman for a few months. There's no comparison.'

'You can't measure the depth of a love in days and weeks,' Polly said, surprising everyone, since she rarely joined in conversations these days.

'Who's talking about weeks?' Ethel said. 'I was married to Robbie for *years*. And what do you know about love anyway? Flirting with boys is not the same thing at all.'

For a breathless moment it looked as though Polly was about to retort, but Father Palgrave smoothly intervened, addressing Teddy on another topic, one dear to his heart. 'I hear that York Corporation is looking at some land in Heworth, sir, with a view to building new houses for the working classes. Do you know anything about that?'

Emma went to Scotland driven by a strong sense of duty, and with no expectation of enjoying it. She was

130

fond of her uncle and aunt, who had been her guardians since her father died when she was seventeen. They had always tried to do the right thing by her, even though it was not always what *she* thought was the right thing. But she had never liked Scotland and had fled to London when she reached twenty-one, like a prisoner fleeing durance vile. In the last months of her incarceration her guardians had done everything they could to get her respectably married to a man they could approve of, and it had taken all her strength of character to resist them.

The war had changed her. She was more patient now, more accustomed to doing her duty rather than seeking pleasure. She was aware of the value of family ties, conscious that life was short and uncertain, and that showing respect and gratitude to her elders had better not be put off. And, of course, she had tasted independence and developed the character of a woman of self-determination. She did not come into her fortune until January 1921, when she was twenty-five, but her allowance was so ample that she could please herself as to where and how she lived. She had nothing to fear from Uncle Bruce and Aunt Betty.

That they found her changed was evident from the first moment. Their tender solicitude told her they were upset by how much older, sadder and wiser she was; Aunt Betty said she looked as though she had seen things no female should see; Uncle Bruce said her complexion was sadly brown, which meant much the same thing. They both made a determined effort to be cheerful, and deliberately did not ask about her experiences, plainly thinking it was something best forgotten. They did not mention Major Fenniman, either. Emma had brought him to be introduced to them when she had become engaged, and they had thought him quite unsuitable; but they could not be glad about his death or her grief, so it seemed best to avoid the subject.

The three of them were awkward together at first. She thought they had aged a great deal, and become more set in their ways. But now it was she who made things easy for them, falling in with their daily routine, chatting to them about the topics that mattered to them, mentioning only those things in their past together that raised no unhappy memories.

Aberlarich was a remote, rain-swept stronghold, a fortified manor house of impenetrable granite, rising like a grim grey dolmen from its rolling acres of curlew-haunted moor and crow-dark forest. In that storm-lashed part of western Scotland, fires had to be lit all year round: when the sun shone, which it did occasionally, it was colder inside than outside, because of the thickness of the walls. In France Emma had longed for peace and quiet, but here there was too much emptiness, too much silence. It left her at the mercy of her thoughts.

And she had nothing to do. During the day, when the weather was anything other than impossible, she went out of doors, but the Abradales kept no horses, and the terrain was so wild and primitive that walking never seemed to get you anywhere: one patch of heather and stunted thorn seemed much like another. Even Benson found it daunting, for he was not a tall dog, and Emma often found herself carrying him as she waded through knee-high heather and bracken. He got his exercise running around the small square of lawn and topiary surrounding the house that constituted Aberlarich's garden.

In the evenings the Abradales liked to talk, or to have her play for them. Sometimes Uncle Bruce got out the chess board, and Emma would challenge him while Aunt Betty knitted. One evening, to vary the monotony, they had a dinner party for the nearest neighbours: middle-aged and elderly folk, the men in kilts and the women in faded satin, much *décolleté*, with tartan sash and vast diamond and amethyst brooches. The former displayed bare knees as impervious as pumice stone, the latter brave acres of puckered chicken-flesh. *Décolletage* being the order of the day, if Emma hadn't been hardened by the winters under canvas in northern France, she doubted she could have survived.

It was on the morning after the dinner party that Aunt Betty said at breakfast – a full-blooded meal intended to fortify you for the rigours of the day, 'I'm conscious, Emma dear, that it's a little dull here for a young person like yourself.'

Emma was too honest to speak a downright lie, but she managed a deprecatory sort of murmur.

'No, dear, I know it's quiet, and you must want company of your own age. So your uncle and I have accepted an invitation from the Cardows. Lord Cardow is an old friend of your uncle – they were at school together. He has a shooting party every year on his estate at Glen Kingie. It's always quite a large affair, so there'll be young people there as well.'

'There was no need, really,' Emma protested. 'I'm quite content. And I know Uncle doesn't like going away.'

'Och, you'll enjoy it. And your uncle will like blethering with Jock Cardow. I dare say he'll even take a gun out. It's a shame you didn't bring a maid with you, but Lady Cardow will provide you with a housemaid.'

Emma made no more objections, only reflected that a lady's maid would have very little to do. Her service in France had taught her to dress herself, and her head needed nothing but a vigorous wielding of the brush. The only point on which she stood out was when Aunt Betty suggested that there was no need to take her 'wee dog' with her. Benson, Emma said firmly, would pine without her.

The journey was long, slow and tedious. They arrived at the castle just before tea-time, and were shown to their rooms, Lord and Lady Abradale by the housekeeper, and Emma by a plain, dark-haired housemaid who said, 'I'm Jeannie, miss. I'm to take care of you.'

Emma's room, though not big in floor space, seemed cavernous because of the height of the ceiling and the tall, narrow window. There was a fire in the grate, and the air was a degree less than Arctic, but there was a strong smell of damp, which told her this was a room not often used. She tried the bed and found the mattress had apparently been stuffed with small rocks, but that was always the case in country houses. There was no bathroom, but the garderobe in the corner had been converted into a water-closet and provided with a door, and there was a wash-stand. 'Will I bring you up some hot water now, miss?'

When she had gone, Emma got out Benson's blanket and spread it on the armchair beside the fire, and he jumped up and said this would do very well. 'I'll take you for a walk between tea and dinner,' she promised him.

The water took a long time to arrive, and Emma had done her own unpacking by the time Jeannie appeared with a tall jug. She apologised breathlessly about the distance to the kitchen, which Emma could guess from the fact that the water was only just warm.

'What's the form here?' she asked. 'Do we change for tea?'

'No, miss, you'll be fine as you are,' Jeannie said, cocking her head critically. 'P'raps just a wee brooch or something.'

So Emma washed her hands and face and went down to tea in her tweed skirt and pink silk blouse, leaving Benson by the fire. A footman directed her to the drawing-room, a vast, long chamber with panelled walls, a tartan carpet, heavy dark furniture and an enormous fireplace in which a fire had already been lit. The walls were decorated with stags' antlers and crossed claymores, in between family portraits of the School of Lely, of men in uniform and women with plump chins and long coils of hair. It was all much as she had expected.

There was quite a crowd there already, and the dispensing of tea was well under way, with a round table almost groaning with good things: they took the meal seriously in this part of the world. The level of conversation was cheeringly high after a week of the silences of Aberlarich, and Emma was suddenly glad her uncle and aunt had had this attack of conscience.

Then her attention was claimed by someone at her elbow saying, 'What? No Benson? Surely you can't have left the little tyke behind.'

'Knoydart!' she exclaimed, with all the pleasure of seeing a familiar face in an unfamiliar place. She had last seen Angus Knoydart in uniform, in Ypres, just before his unit had been stood down. His handsome fair face was wreathed with smiles. 'What are you doing here?'

'The same as you, I imagine. I was invited. I've been

135

on my estate ever since I was demobilised – there's a great deal to do – so it was nice to be forced into a bit of pleasure for a change. But you didn't answer about Benson.'

'Oh, he's upstairs in my room.'

'Good. In a changing world it's important for some things to stay as they are. Trooper Weston without Benson would cast me adrift on a sea of uncertainty. When did you get back to England?'

They fell into a comfortable conversation about Ypres and what they had been doing since and the fates of various acquaintances. It was good, Emma thought, to be with someone who had seen the same things and didn't ask foolish questions – someone who *understood*. He did not comment or even look at her hair, having seen her in France with a brutal cut and knowing the reason for it. Others came and joined them, some local people that Lord Knoydart had known all his life, some who had met Emma before she fled south. She was alarmed to discover one of her former suitors among them: Sir Walter Colliston, a big, stout young man, red-faced and gingery-haired, who had been Uncle Bruce's second favourite in the Emma Stakes, after Knoydart. That he practically owned Arbroath had not compensated, in her view, for his loud voice and complete lack of anything interesting to say with it, and his insensitivity to any rebuff from her. He had been convinced she would marry him.

But Colliston had been to the war since then, had turned his stoutness into muscle. Though his face was still red, his voice was less loud, and the old unthinking arrogance had died with his men at Poelcapelle. He had many things of interest to talk about now. He had heard that Emma had joined the FANY, and was full of admiration for the corps. 'First Anywhere, that's what our chaps always said it stood for.'

Soon she was the centre of the most voluble group in the room. Every soldier was glad to talk to a pretty girl who understood. Somehow she acquired a cup of tea and some things to eat without having to move from the spot or interrupt the flow of conversation. She was aware that several of the men around her were vying for her attention, but it was in a discreet and sensible way: she was their equal; she was not patronised. She was sorry to have to extricate herself from the party, but the clock told her the dressing bell was approaching, and she had to take Benson out.

When she came down with him, she found Knoydart lingering in the hall. 'I had to see my old friend Benson again,' he said, and when she cocked an eye at him he smiled deprecatingly and said, 'All right, I don't know him that well, but a breath of fresh air before dinner seems like a good idea. Should you object to my company?'

'Come with us and welcome,' she said.

Outside it was growing dusk, and the peat-smelling air had a chill in it that said summer was over.

'How quickly August slips into autumn,' Knoydart said. Benson bounded ahead, glad to be out, snapping at the little white moths that came out at twilight. The sun was a wobbling red line along the cloud bank to the west. The distances were smoky and blue, and an unseen curlew made melancholy calls of loss, memory, and innocence never to be regained. 'My country,' he went on. 'I dreamed of it so often when I was in France – especially when I thought I'd never see it again. It's a beautiful country, but somehow always sad.'

'All of us who were out there are sad,' Emma said. 'We invest places with our own feelings.'

'I thought Scotland was sad even before the war,' he said. 'I suppose,' he added, trying for lightness, 'it's something to do with the weather. When the sky weeps all the time, it's hard to feel it's a happy place.'

'But you still love it,' Emma said.

'I love it, but I don't think I can live here. I'll always come back, but I think I have to make my life somewhere that doesn't fill me with such painful longing.'

'For what?'

'I don't know,' he said. 'That's the devil of it,' he added, in a low voice. They completed the walk in silence, but a comfortable silence of old friends. The dressing bell recalled them to the house as Emma began to shiver. The thread of crimson was gone from the sky and the blue dusk was growing colder.

A great effort had been made by the Cardows, with enormous fires in all the public rooms, tapestries and hangings over walls and doors and heavy curtains keeping out the draughts from windows. The result was that Kingie Castle was no colder than other country houses, which meant that away from the immediate vicinity of the fire, it was chilly. Emma changed into her evening gown beside the fire, half envying Benson, who was settled into his comfortable armchair for the night. But Jeannie explained that, in accordance with Lady Cardow's sensible standing instruction, a warm shawl was provided for each of the ladies, and their maids would accompany them downstairs and receive the shawl from them at the drawing-room door so that they might enter bareshouldered but not blue.

'And the same when you go to bed, miss. Lady Cardow rings and we come and fetch you.'

The evening did not begin auspiciously for Emma, for when she entered the drawing-room she saw that all the gentlemen were in dress kilt. It was no more than to be expected, but she was a Londoner to her bones and had an unreasoning prejudice against the kilt. She couldn't help feeling it was a ridiculous garb for a man. Even Knoydart was diminished in her eyes, though his figure displayed to advantage in his native dress.

But at least when they were all seated at the dining table she could see only the gentlemen's top halves; and since she was seated between Knoydart and Lord Kilmelford, who had been at Third Ypres, the conversation was interesting and sensible. The food was not particularly good, but she had not had great expectations of it: in a house still lit with candles she supposed the kitchens were fairly primitive, and the distance from them to the dining-room meant that the dishes would always be cold.

After half an hour in the drawing-room, with the tinkling talk of the ladies, while the gentlemen were discussing their port and cigars, she was quite glad to learn that Lady Cardow favoured early nights. There was to be no dancing, and no parlour games or charades: she did not approve of them. There was a billiard room, and card tables were set up in an ante-room for those who insisted on bridge, but she made it clear she expected only gentlemen to require these diversions.

The men rejoined them, cold coffee was served, and at ten thirty Lady Cardow rose and said, 'I shall ring for the candles.'

*　*　*

So the visit passed with a mixture of pleasantness and boredom. Emma did not care to go out with the guns, so she spent Saturday morning flicking through a magazine, listening to the other women's talk, and walking with Benson, who gave her the perfect excuse to get away and out of doors. They all went out in the brake to have luncheon on the moor with the gentlemen, who returned to tea before going off to dress for dinner. The evening went much as the previous one had, except that the dinner was grander, with evening guests coming in from outside, and after dinner there was dancing in the garden room to a wind-up gramophone brought in by one of them at the request of Lord Cardow, who thought the young people might need diverting.

The older gentlemen played cards or discussed politics, and a group of the middling ones played billiards. Emma danced with just about every young male in the party, and was aware that every so often her uncle appeared in the doorway to watch her for a few moments and nod in satisfaction. When he did so she would make a point of smiling happily at him, to let him know he had succeeded in giving her a good time, though in truth she was longing to go back to London where she would not have to dance with a man wearing a shorter skirt than her own.

On Sunday there was church to vary the routine, followed by a walk round outside with Lord Cardow for the men and a tour of the house with Lady Cardow for the women. Emma managed to absent herself with Benson as the excuse, and had a pleasant wander around the gardens, which were more extensive than at Aberlarich, but equally devoid of flowers: lawns, hedges and topiary seemed to take up all the gardeners' energy, and all was shades of green, interspersed with dark conifers and rather weather-beaten statues of heroes and graces.

She was not entirely surprised to be joined as she walked down an avenue of yew by Lord Knoydart, decently clad in a tweed suit with no knees on display. She thought he had not looked enraptured when the gentlemen's walk was announced.

'Another escapee,' he said, as he came towards her. 'I guessed I'd find you here.'

'I'm realising what a good thing it was to bring Benson,' she said. 'Not that I mind looking round houses as a general rule, but I was longing for fresh air.'

'You haven't missed anything. Lady C is very thorough, but her subject matter doesn't match her diligence. No decent furniture or china, and the portraits are all "studio of".'

'And an awful lot of old weapons and dead animals,' Emma sighed. 'You'd almost think that having anything beautiful or desirable in your house was somehow sinful. I'm wondering whether that melancholy you spoke about before is something to do with a national dislike of being comfortable.'

He laughed. 'Oh, poor Emma!'

'I'm all right,' she said. 'I didn't come down here expecting to enjoy myself, but to do the right thing by Uncle and Aunt. The trouble is, they seem to have me on their conscience. I half suspect they engineered this invitation deliberately for me.'

'They did,' said Knoydart. 'But that's not to say Lord Cardow wouldn't have invited them anyway. This August shoot is a fixture in the calendar, apparently.'

'Apparently? Don't you always come?'

'I've been away at the war, remember.'

'But before that?'

'Oh, well, the Cardows aren't exactly my generation.'

'But I assumed you knew their son, or your parents knew them, or something.'

He looked slightly uncomfortable. 'Well, to tell the truth, I think Lord Abradale asked Lord Cardow to invite me.'

Emma began to feel cold down her spine. 'You think that, do you?'

'Well, I know so, really.' He laughed unconvincingly. 'Your uncle wanted you to enjoy yourself, and meet some old friends. There's nothing wrong with that, is there?'

She considered the presence of Sir Walter Colliston, Lord Kilmelford, James Stuart-Kerr – all former suitors of hers. She stopped walking and turned to face her companion; her expression was hard.

'Tell me the truth, Knoydart – and I shall know if you're lying. What are you really doing here?'

He scanned her face a moment, and then said, 'Your uncle thought this would be a good opportunity for me to meet you again. He said you often spoke about me and he thought – if we had some time together, perhaps it might – you might—'

'In fact,' Emma interrupted, 'he's trying to get me married off. Hence the presence of those others.'

'What others?'

'Colliston and Kilmelford and the rest.'

'I don't know anything about them. I just wanted to see you. Is that so wrong?'

'And when were you planning to propose? What were Uncle's *instructions* about that?'

He blushed with annoyance. 'I'm not here on your uncle's instructions. I like you, Emma. There's no secret about that. I thought I made it plain when we met in Ypres. I like you very much.'

'You weren't going to propose?'

'If I did, it would be because I want to marry you, not because I was told to.'

'Then I'll save you the trouble, just in case you're still considering it,' she said angrily. 'I won't marry you. Nothing would make me marry a man who lives in Scotland and wears the kilt. And you can tell my uncle that if he meddles in my affairs I'll never see him again.'

Knoydart was angry too, but he controlled his face and voice. 'You had better tell him that yourself. I'm not your messenger. I'm sorry if I upset you, Emma. It was not meant.' And he turned on his heel and left her.

Somehow she got through Sunday evening and Monday breakfast. It all seemed a blur, as she kept the flame of her anger alive for when she and her aunt and uncle should be safely back at Aberlarich. Then she confronted them.

'I only want the best for you,' Lord Abradale said, shaken but unabashed. 'A young female like you needs to be married.'

'What do you mean, "like me"?' Emma demanded.

'All girls should be married,' her aunt said. 'It's the natural way.'

'I shall never marry.'

'You are an heiress, Emma,' Abradale said. 'You will inherit a very large sum in a few years' time. Moreover, you know that I will be leaving my fortune to you. You will be one of the most important heiresses in the country. It is not fitting that you should remain single – in fact, it is impossible. You must have a husband to take care of things for you.'

'I shall have a solicitor to do that,' Emma said.

'It's not the same at all, and you know it. You need a husband.'

'If I wanted a husband, I would choose one for myself,' Emma retorted.

'That is not fitting. You see where it got you before, this independent way of doing things. That young man, Fenniman.'

'Yes,' Emma said bitterly, 'Fenniman, the man I loved. He took me to see his father and I brought him to see you. We didn't need to ask you. If we hadn't wasted time seeking your approval we could have been married, at least for a few months. We would have had that.' She choked back a sob. 'I might even have had his child. As it is, I have nothing of him. I blame you for that. And now you're trying to interfere again. Well, I won't have it!'

'Emma!' Aunt Betty cried. 'You will not speak to your uncle like that!'

'I'm sorry.' She controlled herself. 'I think I had better leave.'

Abradale, who was looking profoundly shocked, said automatically, 'You can't leave now. There's no train before tomorrow.'

'Then I'll go into town and stay in an hotel.'

'You'll do no such thing!' Aunt Betty said, aghast.

Abradale silenced her with a look and said quietly, 'I will have McTear drive you to the train tomorrow morning, if that is what you wish. But do not let us part with ill blood. I have never wanted anything but your happiness.'

Emma stared at him. It was not her happiness he had always wanted but her respectability. But perhaps to him it was the same thing. He could not hurt her now. Her allowance was enough until she came into her fortune, and he could not take that from her, or make her marry against her will.

'I will leave tomorrow,' she said, 'but not in anger. I'm sorry if I spoke too freely. Our ideas are very different. We will never see eye to eye. But you needn't worry about me. I am not a frivolous girl any more. I can take care of myself.'

'You should not have to,' said Lord Abradale, but more in sorrow than anger.

So Emma fled south, determined never to see Scotland again. Her aunt and uncle were what they were, and they were too old to change. But Knoydart had disappointed her. She had thought better of him – she might even have come to love him one day. She felt she had made a fool of herself, that *he* had made a fool of her. Well, no more of that. She would never marry. It was a new world now. She would live her life as an independent woman.

CHAPTER SEVEN

Addison's Housing Act was passed, and Addison brought to the building of houses the same zeal he had shown in the Ministry of Munitions. He did not, however, tackle the task directly by creating his own agencies. As the former head of the Local Government Board, he was used to dealing with local authorities, and he simply directed them to build as many houses as they needed and let them at controlled rents. The government would provide an automatic subsidy for any extra cost over one penny on the local rates.

Teddy approved of this approach. 'Addison has the right idea,' he said to Henrietta.

They were taking advantage of a sunny November morning to walk in the rose garden. A sharp frost in the night had killed off the last, too-hopeful buds on the roses. In the shadow of the hedges it was still stiff and white on the grass. It tipped bare twigs and rimmed the rosehips so that they looked diamond-encrusted – like an illustration from a book of fairy tales, Henrietta thought: the elf-king's orb and sceptre. But under the high, pale-veined sky, the gravel in the sunshine was warm underfoot, and the air had an earthy, leafy smell. The dogs swirled around them and ran out ahead, coming back to check their progress, smiling and waving tails: Tiger and Isaac, the pointers Bess and Belair, and Teddy's new spaniel Gossamer. Even the kitchen dog, Roy, had joined them, taking a break from his back-door duties, enthusiastically hunting flies in lieu of anything larger. Everyone likes a sunny morning.

Teddy went on, 'Anything that has to be organised by the central government takes too long to set up. It would be years before anything got done, what with all the arguing about who was to get what, pitting one council against another, holding inquiries and settling disputes. This way, we can start at once and just get on with building.'

'There's no doubt we need the houses,' Henrietta agreed, trying to take an interest for her brother's sake – and, indeed, it was true that there were some terrible slums in York. It was just that she had other things on her mind. Ethel, for instance: her father had died of pneumonia following bronchitis after a long illness; and less than a fortnight later her mother had died quite suddenly of heart failure. Both had been ill with the Spanish flu the year before, and Dr Hasty explained how influenza could weaken both the heart and the lungs. Ethel was distraught; she was staying with her brother Seb for the time being, but Henrietta could not help wondering about her, and hoping she was finding comfort.

And, closer to her heart, Jessie's due date had come, and remembering the hard time she had had with Thomas, Henrietta was anxious about her. She was thinking, not for the first time, that she wished Jessie had come home to have the baby, even as she was saying, 'Diseases run through the slums like wildfire. It was

147

chickenpox in October, but it might just as easily have been measles or even typhus.'

'Well, we can get on with it now, all right,' Teddy said happily. 'They're going to start marking out Tang Hall next week.' The council had bought the Tang Hall estate some years before, but had had no money to develop it. 'And when those houses are finished, we can move the people out of those Walmgate back-to-backs and pull them down. It's a disgrace that we still have houses like that in our city.'

'It won't take much to knock them down,' Henrietta said. 'Some of the walls are only half-brick thick.'

'And it will provide work for the labourers, which is a good thing,' Teddy said. 'There are still more demobbed soldiers looking for jobs than I like to see. We've absorbed the skilled workers, but this will be just the thing for soaking up the rest. And I tell you what, Hen,' he went on, 'we really need more houses in the village, too.'

'I was going to say the same thing to you. I visited Mrs Dalby yesterday, and she still has her son and daughter-in-law living with her, sharing a room with her two youngest while the middle boy sleeps in with her and Dalby, and the eldest sleeps on the sofa in the parlour. And her daughter-in-law has a baby on the way. It isn't right.'

'It's a common enough story. Which is why I was thinking it would be a good idea to take advantage of the Act, and offer the council some land to build on. That part of Chapel Field between West Field and the Wetherby Road. Extend the village along the road.'

'That's good grazing,' Henrietta said. She was surprised – the last thing Teddy ever wanted was to part with any of his precious land.

148

'But we certainly need the houses. And it occurs to me that if I get a fair price for it, I can buy that parcel over beyond White House that Hutton Grange is selling. It will just round off that boundary nicely.'

Henrietta smiled. 'You do whatever you think fit. You don't need my approval.'

He smiled too. 'No, but I like to have it. And another thing—'

She was not to learn what the other thing was, for Gossamer barked a warning, and they were interrupted by the new second footman, a rather scrawny but diligent fifteen-year-old called Albert, hurrying towards them with a buff envelope in his hand. Henrietta's heart turned over from old wartime habit. The telegram was for her; but this time it was not bad news. It was from Bertie.

'"Baby born. A fine girl. All is well. Letter follows,"' she read aloud to Teddy.

'Oh, that's wonderful news!' Teddy exclaimed, and then, 'Why on earth are you crying, old thing? Doesn't he say all is well? That must mean Jessie's all right.'

'I know. It's just relief. But I wish I could have been with her.' Henrietta accepted his handkerchief and dried her eyes.

'It seems to me,' Teddy said thoughtfully, 'that *after* the baby's born is the time a girl needs her mother most. Why don't you telegraph them and suggest you go and stay for a week or so? She won't want to have to run the house while she's in childbed, will she?'

'Oh, Ted,' Henrietta said fondly, 'you do have the nicest ideas.'

'She's awfully crumpled,' Bertie said, trying not to sound too critical. Her little head seemed no bigger than an apple. He held her, a tiny doll in his big hands, sleeping busily, having taken one look at the day and evidently not thinking much of it.

'*You*'d be crumpled,' Jessie said. 'Think of a butterfly's wings. They have to straighten out when it leaves the cocoon. She'll open like a rose.'

'My darling, I have no doubt she'll be beautiful,' he assured her. 'Would that be a good name for her – Rose?'

'Why not Butterfly?' Jessie said derisively.

'I wasn't joking.'

'Oh. I'm sorry. But I don't like Rose. Violet and I were named after flowers. Enough is enough.'

'There are no traditional family names we need to honour, so we have a clean slate,' he said. 'Is there anything you fancy?'

'I rather like the name Alexandra.'

He thought about it. 'But you have to take the surname into account,' he concluded. 'And there is an Alexandra Park in London already.'

She saw the point. 'Oh, yes. Well, I suppose that rules out Victoria as well.'

'And Hyde.'

'And St James's.'

'I'm glad you're feeling well enough to make jokes,' he said.

'I feel like that sock of yours that Bran chewed and left under the bed. But it's all worth it. Let me hold her for a bit.' He passed her over. 'I'm glad we had a girl this time.'

'So am I. But Thomas was disappointed. He was hoping for a kitten.'

'Next time, perhaps. Think of more names. It would have been helpful if you'd had an easier surname, like mine. Everything goes with Compton, but Parke too easily sounds like a joke.'

'Don't you think I know that?' he said, pained. 'I've suffered all my life under the most desperately ridiculous name. She must have something simple and plain that can't be laughed at, our little angel.'

'Angela,' Jessie suggested, but cancelled it instantly. 'No, it begs too many questions. Mary? Elizabeth? Margaret? Anne? They're plain.'

'*Too* plain. Diana?'

'Too fancy. Alice?'

He considered that one. 'I quite like Alice, but I don't think it does with Parke.'

'Perhaps not. What about Catherine?'

'Catherine Parke. Yes, that sounds all right. What made you think of it?'

'I don't know. It just came to me. Does she look like a Catherine?'

He leaned over and drew the edge of the shawl from his daughter's face. 'Catherine?' he called to her. She opened one eye a fraction, and closed it again. 'It means shining clear, did you know that?'

The door opened and the nurse came in. 'Time for Mother to rest,' she said forbiddingly. She looked at Bertie as all month-nurses look at the fathers of their babies, as if he were an invading Goth bent on rape and pillage. 'Too much excitement is bad for the milk.'

'I have to go to work, anyway,' Bertie said, standing up. He leaned over and kissed Jessie, and whispered, 'I'll be glad when your mother gets here. She'll larn her!'

Jessie tried not to laugh – Nurse Cleaver was not one for humour in the bedroom. 'You'd better give Baby to me,' Cleaver said, before Bertie had even got to the door.

He turned, his hand on the door knob, to say, 'It's not Baby any more, nurse. She's Catherine.'

It didn't make any difference to Nurse Cleaver. All babies were Baby, just as the mothers were Mother. But it marked the moment when Miss Parke acquired her name.

Jessie and Bertie had both been delighted when Henrietta's telegram arrived, and Bertie had telegraphed straight back, saying, 'Come!' Though the month-nurse was taking care of the baby and Jessie's physical well-being, and the new nanny seemed to be coping with Thomas pretty well, Bertie hated leaving Jessie every morning to go to work, and he felt she was much too tired to cope with running the house from her bed. Jessie was worried that the servants would abandon their duties if they knew she could not come after them – they were too new for her to trust them – and she didn't want Bertie to have to come home to a cold and dirty house and a badly cooked meal, as well as being banished from her bedroom and the comfort of her arms.

'I wanted to ask you,' she told her mother, when she first arrived, 'but I didn't know if you'd feel able to leave things, and I didn't want to press you.'

'Morland Place will be quite all right without me,' Henrietta said. 'Mrs Tomlinson runs everything anyway. Nobody will even miss me.'

'You know that's not true,' Jessie said. 'But I'm glad you're here.'

'Now, nurse,' Henrietta said comfortably to Nurse Cleaver, 'I shan't interfere with your work, so you mustn't worry. The lying-in room is your domain entirely.'

Nurse Cleaver narrowed her eyes, having had past experience of the mothers of her Mothers, and mentally rolled up her sleeves for battle. But Henrietta had been running a household since she was sixteen, and could sum up her adversary at a glance. She managed Cleaver so tactfully that before the day was out the nurse saw them as companions in arms, pitted against the ignorance of the world. She let Henrietta enter Jessie's room as often as she liked, agreed with her about the management of Baby, and even consented to take an afternoon nap, leaving Henrietta in charge. She told Bertie, when he came home, that her ladyship's mother was a very superior person, and chided him gently for not having brought her to the house earlier.

Bertie had come home to find the hall light on, the fires lit, the furniture dusted and the brass polished, and a savoury smell percolating up from the kitchen, which told him that all was well again; and when he went upstairs he found Jessie looking much more rested. When he sat down to dinner with Henrietta he rediscovered how pleasant it was to have a woman's company across the table, and thanked her for having made the house a home again.

'I don't know what you did to the servants,' he said. 'Yesterday there were fingermarks all over this table, and I found egg between the tines of my fork.'

'Oh, they only wanted a little "telling",' Henrietta said. 'They're good people really. But servants need to know someone is noticing what they do. Why should they clean and polish if no-one sees the difference?'

'It's the same with the men in the army,' Bertie said. 'I think sometimes they let things slip just to test you.'

'Of course they do,' Henrietta said. 'You'd have made a good housekeeper.'

'I take that as a compliment, Aunty,' he said.

Oliver sat his fellowship examination in October, and passed easily. He would have taken it long before, had the war not intervened. Now, as a Fellow of the Royal College of Surgeons, he set aside the once-coveted title of 'doctor', and became a plain 'mister'. It was a custom that had its roots in history – physicians had been educated to become doctors, surgeons only apprenticed to barbers – but now the snobbery had been reversed. In hospitals the consultants, the misters, looked down on the registrars, the mere doctors.

Oliver, however, was not a consultant yet. The army had turned him out, and he had no post at all: he was surviving on the scraps he could glean around London, in competition with all the other doctors tipped out of the army since the Armistice. None of the big hospitals had plastics units. Even Harold Gillies, from whom he had learned his trade, had found himself at a loss when his army service ended in October: he had only been able to get back into St Bartholomew's as an assistant in the throat department. If the father of plastic surgery himself could not get a consultancy, what chance was there for Oliver?

He was fortunate to be able to live in his mother's house, which not only saved him a great deal of money but was just around the corner from Harley Street and the clinics of Wimpole, Devonshire and Queen Anne Streets, and close to the Middlesex and University College Hospitals. And he was sure that he benefited from his mother's wide medical acquaintance, and that he was asked to assist more often than other men in his situation. His mother even paid him an allowance, which at first he had resisted almost angrily, as touching his pride.

But she had said, 'It's just something to keep you going until you come into the earldom. You'll be a wealthy man then. Your father would have done the same.'

'Suppose Thomas comes back? Suppose I don't come into the earldom, as you so delicately put it?'

'Then you can call it a loan and pay me back out of the magnificent salary you'll earn one day as the country's leading plastics consultant. You can pay me interest, too, if you like. Really, Oliver, it's hardly charity – look on it as an investment on my part.'

So he accepted, mainly because the amount his mother had offered was tactfully small; and with the tonsillectomies and the occasional mole removal and skin graft, he kept his hand in and hoped for better days. But he was far from being able to set up his own establishment, and he had fits of depression about the future, common enough in those post-war days in young men who had found their careers stalled. At his club – where his mother insisted he remain a member, even threatening to pay his subscription if he didn't – he often stood at the bar with friends and colleagues, drawn up like horses at a trough, all of them in silent contemplation of the situation, generating a cloud of gloom as noticeable as the cloud of tobacco smoke over their heads.

The Little Season was under way, and he was inveigled one evening into accompanying Violet and Emma to a charity ball. 'You must come,' Violet told him. 'I know you're not engaged because I checked with Mama.'

'I thought Freddie was taking you.'

155

'He is, but there are two of us so we must have two men. It's too horrid arriving at a ball without a man's arm. Emma was going with Jimmy Napier but he's been taken ill, so don't make a fuss, Oliver. And *do* be sociable when we're there. You've been awfully cross recently.'

'I haven't been cross,' Oliver said indignantly. 'I'm never cross.'

'Well, "dour", then, as Emma says.'

'I have a lot to be dour about,' he said with dignity; but he agreed to go, even though it meant the bother of the full soup-and-fish, and his father's former man, Ash, who valeted him when he needed it, was desperately slow.

Almost the first person he saw when they arrived was Lady Verena Felbrigg, looking ravishing – at least to his eyes – in peach georgette with silver-thread embroidery. The new straight style suited her tall slimness, and her dark hair, in a big, soft chignon, made her neck look long and white. He stared at her like a hungry man eyeing a feast through a window.

'Oh, there's Verena,' Violet said. 'Do go and talk to her, Oliver.'

'I'm here with Emma,' he said rather primly.

Emma gave him a shove. 'I only needed you to walk in with me. Go and talk to her.'

'Poor thing, her father's not been well,' Violet added. 'I heard he was in financial trouble, too. If you don't go to her, people will think you're snubbing her.'

Oliver didn't need to follow the logic of this argument, because he was longing to speak to her, and glad of an excuse. As soon as he began to walk towards her she turned her head and looked at him, proving she had known he was there. She didn't smile, however, but greeted him gravely.

'How are you?' she said coolly.

'I'm very well. I don't need to ask how you are,' he said. 'You look ravishing. Is that a new gown?'

'If you had been to any balls recently, you would know that it's not,' she said. 'I've worn it at two already.' An awkward pause followed, when Oliver could not think of anything to say, or anything to do except devour her with his eyes. She said, almost impatiently, 'The music's beginning. Are you going to ask me to dance?'

He bowed and offered his arm. 'Will you do me the honour?' He was a little puzzled. Her manner was not encouraging, but she had asked him to dance. He longed to dance with her, but knew he must keep a rein on his feelings. As they walked off, he looked back at his sister and Emma, and saw they were smiling complacently. What was going on? Had this meeting been engineered? His ears felt hot at the thought.

They circled in silence for a few minutes. Oliver was in a dream of bliss mixed with pain, and would gladly have danced the whole thing in silence, but it was a public ball and some effort must be made to behave normally in case anyone was watching. Dancing in silence was the prerogative of avowed lovers or the irretrievably dull.

He roused himself to say, 'Did you have a pleasant summer? It must have seemed strange to have so much time on your hands, once the Red Cross had done with you.'

He thought it a useful sort of question, opening up an avenue for conversation while emphasising what they had had in common.

But Verena dismissed it with a short breath, almost like a sigh. 'Oliver, why have you been avoiding me?' she asked, with medical directness.

He felt his ears burn again. 'I haven't been avoiding you. How can you think it?'

'Then why haven't I seen you since you left the Queen's Hospital?'

'I'm sure I've seen you since then,' he prevaricated.

'Perhaps, but not intentionally. Only because we happened to be at the same function – like tonight. You haven't so much as written me a postcard. I thought we were friends.'

Her plaintive look as she said the last words was too much for him. Without volition he pressed her hand, and said, 'Oh, Verena—'

'A good start. You remember my name.'

'I'm sorry. I never meant to hurt you. I valued your friendship – I can't tell you how much. But I thought it was better if I just faded out of your life.'

'How could that possibly be better? Did you think I didn't care for you?'

'I never dared wonder. I *hoped* you might, but as things are—'

'Yes, but *how* are things?' she asked in frustration. 'Oh dear, one can't have a sensible conversation on a dance floor. There's a passage through that door at the end. Can we go there and talk properly?'

'If that's what you want,' he said, with apprehension in his heart. They danced to the end of the room, he whirled her neatly to a stop by the door, and they walked out into the corridor in the same movement. There was no-one else there.

'Thank goodness,' Verena said. 'Privacy at last. Now, walk with me, and explain yourself.'

They walked slowly side by side down the passage. 'I don't know what there is to explain,' he said unhappily.

'Don't you? Then you have a very odd way of behaving towards females. You gave me to understand that you cared for me – more than that, that I was an object with you.' She paused for him to speak, and when he didn't, went on, with a hint of anger, 'Please don't put me in the position of having to be more specific. You must know perfectly well what I mean.'

'I did care for you. I *do* care. I can't presume—'

'Oh, please do,' she said, in ironic tone.

He was stung. 'Very well. Since you want plain speaking, I love you, and perhaps I was arrogantly mistaken, but I fancied that you loved me too. I wanted so much to ask you to marry me.'

'Then why didn't you? Why don't you?'

'Because I can't possibly afford a wife. I can't afford an establishment. I'm surviving on a guinea here and a guinea there. I can't get a consultant post and there's precious little assistant work in my specialty.'

'But there will be one day?' she questioned. 'Wasn't there a new hospital being built for you?'

'Not *for* me.' The transformation of the St James and St Ann Free Dispensary in Dean Street into the John Winchmore Hospital was to have given him access to a theatre and beds, but the project had stalled because of the difficulty of obtaining building materials and labour towards the end of the war. He explained this to her. 'It's only just got as far as the architect, and work won't begin until next year. And even when it's finished I'll have to share the twelve beds with the surgeon-in-charge. It's not enough for me to set up a practice.'

'You spoke about it so excitedly,' she said.

'Well, you know how it was when the war ended. We were all excited. The future looked so rosy in comparison.

Somehow the word "peace" makes you think all walls will fall flat and all difficulties will dissolve.'

'Yes, I know,' she said sadly. 'So – what then? You are a struggling doctor and can't afford a wife? Is that the end of it?'

'I can't ask you to marry me,' he said desperately. 'I can't even ask you to wait for me. It wouldn't be fair to you.'

'Fair to me?' she said bitterly. 'Is it fair to make my decisions for me? Oliver, I'm twenty-three. I'm unmarried. Doesn't that tell you something?'

He didn't dare answer that. 'I don't know. I wish I could be sure.'

'Oh, then be sure, for goodness' sake. I love you. You are the person I want to marry.'

'But your father would never agree.'

'Daddy has nothing to do with it,' she said. 'I'm over age. And besides—' She hesitated. 'Things aren't going well at home. Mummy and Daddy would be glad to see me married before they get worse.'

'Oh, my dear, I'm sorry.' He stopped and turned to face her, taking her hand in both his as if to warm it. 'Is there anything I can do?'

She shook her head. 'Some of Daddy's investments have failed. I don't understand that side of it, but the worry is making him ill. Vernon's still at school and they want to protect him, but that will probably mean using my dowry. I've told Daddy it doesn't matter, that what matters is keeping Roughton intact for Vernon. If I were married it would take me off his hands, but with or without a dowry it isn't easy – so many of the young men we used to know fell in the war. I can see that worrying about me is making him ill.'

'I'm so sorry,' Oliver said. Had he made an unbearable situation worse for her? But what else could he have done?

'So you see,' she said, raising her eyes bravely to his face, 'that it's a little late to be saying something would or wouldn't be fair to me. I've pinned my colours to your mast, Oliver. I *will* wait for you, but you have to offer me something to wait for.'

'You mean—'

'Ask me to marry you.' She managed a tremulous smile, and he was breathtaken by her courage.

He gazed at her steadily, his mouth dry. 'Verena,' he said, 'will you marry me? I don't know when I will be able to—'

She put a finger on his lips. 'Hush! The first part was enough. Yes, I will marry you – and, yes, I will wait.'

He caught the finger and kissed it. 'I'll make it up to you. I'll make you happy, I swear it. And as soon—' A thought came to him, and he was so shocked by it he stopped.

She looked alarmed. 'What is it?' He didn't answer, and she urged, 'Don't tell me you've just remembered you have a wife already?'

He shook his head, unwilling to laugh, though he loved her for facing a crisis with humour. 'My brother,' he said. 'The earl.'

'I read that he went missing in Russia. Is that true? I'm so sorry, Oliver.'

'But you see, if he doesn't come back – I don't want to think about it, because I hope with all my heart that he *does*—'

'Of course.'

'It's with the solicitors now. After seven years, if

161

nothing is heard of him, he'll be considered dead, and I will inherit the title and estate.'

'I suppose you will,' she said, eyeing him in an odd way. 'And when will that be?'

'Nineteen twenty-six. March, nineteen twenty-six.'

She gave a short laugh. 'I hope I won't have to wait for you that long.'

'My God, I hope not, too. But why did you look relieved at the date?'

'Because I don't want anyone to think that's why I'm marrying you.'

He looked at her in wonder. 'You are a very remarkable woman.'

'Everyone knows that,' she said lightly. 'One thing, though – it will ease my father's mind to know that, whatever you are now, you may one day be a suitable match for me.'

Oliver emerged from the passage a happier man than he had gone in. He had another dance with Verena, during which they decided that it would be better not to announce an engagement yet, when there was no immediate prospect of marrying.

'Yes, better for you to keep your options open,' Oliver said, 'in case you meet someone you like better than me.'

'Better you don't have to face Daddy,' she countered, 'until you can impress him a little more.'

'But we can still see each other?'

'Of course. That's the whole point, isn't it? We don't need to be engaged to be friends. I'm not a girl with a duenna guarding my every movement. And we both live in London. As long as we don't provoke too much talk and speculation . . .'

'Then would you like to go to the cinema with me next week?'

She wrinkled her nose. 'The cinema?'

'We poor people find it an economical way to pass an evening in a warm, dry place.'

'Goodness, Oliver, you aren't a tramp!'

'Even better, it's dark in there, so no-one can see you and recognise you.'

'I've never been to the cinema.'

'Then you must let me initiate you. Let me see . . . Tragedy with Lillian Gish, or comedy with Gloria Swanson?'

'Oh, comedy for me, every time,' said Verena. 'I like to laugh.'

'*Male and Female* it is, then. It's about rich people marooned on a desert island. Their butler is the only person who knows how to do anything, so he becomes their king.'

'It sounds subversive. I hope you aren't a secret socialist?'

'I beg your pardon, but you are the earl's daughter who wants to marry a poor, struggling doctor.'

'It sounds like a cinema story. Would it be a tragedy or a comedy?'

'Depends on the ending.'

They parted when the dance was over. Another man asked Verena to dance, and Oliver went back to Violet and Emma.

'Well, thank goodness that's settled,' Emma greeted him. 'It *is* settled, isn't it?'

'Did you two plan this?' he demanded.

'Every bit,' said Violet. 'You and Verena were so sweet together last year—'

'—and you've both looked so miserable for weeks now,' Emma concluded.

'What happened?' Violet asked. 'Are you engaged?'

'Only unofficially,' Oliver said, 'so this is a secret, you understand? Don't tell anyone else. I'm not in a position to marry anyone yet, but Verena said she'd wait for me. But we don't want it all over Town. Promise me?'

'We promise,' Violet said. 'I'm so pleased for you. And we won't say anything.'

'We won't say anything,' Emma said shrewdly, 'but I bet *you* do.' And she turned away as a tall, fair young man approached to ask her to dance.

Henrietta had meant to stay only three or four weeks in London. Women were up and about much earlier after childbirth these days, only staying in bed for a week, or two at the most – not like when she'd had her first child, Lizzie, and had been virtually locked in her bedroom for six weeks. But though the birth had been straightforward, it had left Jessie very tired, and even after she got up, she didn't have the energy to take back the reins of the household. Besides, Henrietta enjoyed her daughter's company, and revelled in little Thomas and the new baby. So she stayed on, even after Nurse Cleaver had packed and departed. She instructed the nanny, showing her better ways of doing things, kept the servants up to the mark, gave the cook some tried and trusted Morland Place recipes, and while Jessie was still at the stage of resting in the afternoons, accompanied Nanny Smith to the park with the children.

When Jessie was stronger, they went out together, and even enjoyed some of London's facilities. It was many years since Henrietta had lived there, but she knew her way around. They looked at the shops, went to an exhibition at the Academy, bought some Christmas presents for people at Morland Place in the Burlington Arcade, had tea with Venetia one day and with Violet another.

'It's a real holiday for me,' said Henrietta.

'It's nice being together,' Jessie said. 'It's strange: when you're growing up, you never think your parents could be your friends.'

'It's when a woman has a baby that she and her mother suddenly have things in common,' Henrietta said.

But by the 12th of December the realisation that Christmas was approaching, with all the usual festivities to arrange at Morland Place, impinged upon her state of relaxation, and she told Bertie and Jessie regretfully at dinner that she would have to go home.

'I think you're well enough to manage now, aren't you, darling?'

'Yes, I'm quite strong,' Jessie said. 'I shall miss you, but I know you have things to do.'

'I shall miss you too, Aunty,' said Bertie. In his lonely childhood she had been a second mother to him.

'But you'll be coming to Morland Place for Christmas, won't you?' she said, with the assurance in her voice that the answer was 'yes'.

Jessie and Bertie exchanged a fleeting glance that said many things. Both thought of the strain and effort of moving two small children and all their appurtenances two hundred miles; on the other hand, they thought of having Christmas in this little house, with its various discomforts and inconveniences, and an untested cook, as opposed to the space and comfort and traditional joy of Morland Place, and Mrs Stark weaving magic in the kitchen.

'I shall only be able to stay a couple of days,' Bertie said, 'but Jessie can stay longer if she likes.'

Contrary to her assertion that no-one would miss her, when Henrietta reached Morland Place she was greeted with warm if occasionally reproachful enthusiasm. She had been away too long; nothing had been the same without her; surely she could have come back before now; but they were glad she was home. The dogs said they had despaired of ever seeing her again, and felt the best solution to this was to glue themselves to her knees at all times – at least for the first few hours. Teddy was surprised that she had not brought Jessie and the children back, but was placated by the handsome photograph Bertie had had the insight to have taken, in a studio in Jermyn Street, of Henrietta seated with Jessie standing behind her, baby Catherine on her lap and Thomas leaning against her knee. 'Now this is splendid!' he said. 'I can't believe how much Thomas has grown! And this is little baby Catherine, the newest Morland? I like the name. We haven't had a Catherine in the family for a very long time.'

He was so happy with it Henrietta forbore to point out that Catherine was in fact a Parke, and decided that the hour it had taken to get Thomas into the right position, facing the camera, and with a smile rather than a scowl on his face, had been worth while. And the prospect of the Parkes' visit eased a little the disappointment of learning that Jack and Helen would be celebrating Christmas in Weybridge.

Despite knowing what Uncle Teddy's expectations would be, Helen had not even suggested it. She knew the mere idea would astonish Mrs Ormerod, who expected her children to reassemble at the family home as they had done in happier days before the war.

Besides, much as she loved the people at Morland Place, Helen did not want the trouble of the journey with two small children. Christmas dinner at Fairoaks, with the addition of her brother and his family, would involve a lot of work and organisation on her part, but it was preferable to a day on a train in December with Basil and Barbara.

'You don't mind?' she said to Jack, when they were alone – in bed, where they did most of their serious talking.

'I'm a grown man with my own family,' he said. 'I don't have to spend Christmas with my mother.'

'Oh dear, what does that make of Freddie?' she said.

'I didn't mean any insult,' he said.

'I know, darling. The cases are very different, anyway. They only have to come a few miles, and they go back to their own beds afterwards. And Joan's cook is notorious. I'm sure Freddie would be a much nicer man if he didn't have dyspepsia every night.'

'Will *your* cook be able to manage Christmas dinner for – however many it is?' Jack asked.

'With help,' Helen said. 'The difference is, I know what food ought to taste like. I'm sure Joan had her taste organs removed at some point in her life, poor thing, because whenever I've eaten there she has worked her way through atrocious food with every appearance of complacency.'

He laughed. 'Well, don't exhaust yourself in the process, will you? One meal more or less won't break nations.'

'I shall have to start being careful not to exhaust myself soon, anyway,' she said.

'What do you mean? What are you up to?'

'It's more what you've been up to,' Helen said, into the dark. 'Don't you know? Men can be astonishingly unnoticing sometimes.'

'I've been rather busy,' he defended himself. 'What am I supposed to have done?'

'Darling, use what mother wit God gave you! Not twigged yet? I'm pregnant, you fool.'

'Pregnant?' He sounded bewildered, as if he had never heard the word before. But it was not something he had expected. He supposed he should have 'noticed' but weeks flew by and blended into months and it wasn't something he particularly took heed of at the best of times, though now he *did* come to think of it . . . 'When did that happen?'

'I've been trying to work it out, and I think it must have been that day in September when we went on a picnic on our own – Molly looked after the children, you remember? It was such a lovely day, and that night you were particularly amorous, as I remember, and perhaps *not* particularly careful.'

'You think that was it?' She could almost hear him screw up his forehead in thought.

'The dates fit. But what does it matter? There's a baby on the way, and that's that.'

'You don't sound particularly delighted,' he said cautiously.

'Nor do you.'

'It's a bit of a shock, that's all.'

'It was to me, too. I thought I'd done with all that. I'm thirty-one, Jack, and I don't really want to go through it all again. I was happy with two.'

'For my choice, I wouldn't mind how many more we had – I'd love them all. But you're the one who has to go through it. And then there's the question of finance to consider. We're well placed here, living in your mother's house, but if that were to change for any reason – well, three mouths cost more to feed than two.'

'I know. Don't you think I know that? But here we are.'

'Yes, here we are.' He reached out for her in the dark, and drew her into his arms, thinking that whatever worries the future brought him, she must always come first. As husband and father his job was to provide for them all, but that didn't only mean financially. He had to keep them safe and happy, too, and Helen, his beloved, precious wife, most of all. 'You mustn't worry about it,' he said. 'Everything will be all right.'

'Oh, Jack!'

'I mean it. We'll manage, whatever happens. We're survivors, you and I, and we'll always manage. And even though we didn't intend this baby to come, we'll love it just the same.'

She pressed her cheek into his neck. 'You're a good man, Jack Compton. I don't know what I did to deserve you.' Yes, she thought, they were well placed, living at Fairoaks, but she was as conscious of the fragility of their circumstances as he could possibly be. She was the one who stayed behind every time he took off from Hounslow, and prayed he would come back safely. If he were to die . . . If he were to lose his job . . . Jack said everything would be all right, but he did not know what the future would bring, any more than she did. But here, in his arms, she *felt* safe. And, after all, this was all anyone in the world had: the present, and what they could make of it. She would not waste a moment of being with him, flesh to flesh, heart to heart, in the warm darkness with her head on his shoulder. The new baby would just have to get along somehow.

'You know,' he said, after a pause, 'there is one aspect of your being pregnant we haven't discussed.'

She knew from the warmth of his voice what he meant, but she played innocence. 'And what is that, dear husband?'

'You can't get any *more* pregnant than you are, dear wife, no matter what we do.'

'That's an unproved theory,' she said. 'Don't you think we ought to test it?'

So he turned over to face her, mouth seeking mouth in the darkness, and they did their best.

BOOK TWO

The Cost

O my brave brown companions, when your souls
Flock silently away, and the eyeless dead
Shame the wild beast of battle on the ridge,
Death will stand grieving in that field of war
Since your unvanquished hardihood is spent.
And through some mooned Valhalla there will pass
Battalions and battalions, scarred from hell;
The unreturning army that was youth;
The legions who have suffered and are dust.

Siegfried Sassoon: 'Prelude: The Troops'

CHAPTER EIGHT

By February 1920 the majority of the armed services had been demobilised, though there were still 125,000 men in uniform. Now the full cost of the war had been assessed, and the figures began to circulate: three-quarters of a million men had given their lives. It was an appalling number to a nation that had previously fought wars with small, professional armies, when losses in the ten-thousands would have been regarded as severe.

As a proportion of a population of forty-five million it was not overpowering; that it seemed far worse was a result of two factors. First, the 'Pals' system, by encouraging groups of men to join up and serve together, had concentrated the losses instead of spreading them evenly. In some towns, whole streets had been denuded of young manhood; entire football teams, cricket teams, darts teams had been wiped out; cycling clubs and choirs reduced to female membership. It was natural for those stricken communities to assume their loss had been replicated everywhere. Local newspapers talked of 'the loss of a generation', and the idea spread.

Second, the casualty rate among junior officers had been three times that of ordinary soldiers, and junior officers tended to come from precisely the division of society which was the most articulate; which thought, analysed and wrote; which produced and consumed poetry, commentaries, diaries, novels. The tenor of these writings was first melancholy, and then angry. The war had been won, but there began to be, among the educated, a revulsion not only against the destruction of war but against the system of government, the entire system of civilisation, that allowed such things to happen. Among the educated *bien-pensants*, socialist ideas began to seem attractive for the first time.

The mood of the country had become more sombre as 1919 passed into 1920. The diversion of labour into uniform during the war years had caused domestic shortages: clothes, shoes, furniture, coal, paper, soap were hard to come by, and the prices kept going up. Electricity was in short supply – street lights had to be turned off in some towns. Coal and the railways were still under government management, but they had no answer to the problems. All the easy seams had been exhausted, and getting the coal out was increasingly onerous and expensive. And the railways, after four years of harder wear than they were designed for, were falling to pieces.

With rising prices came rising wage claims, and the workers with unions increasingly turned to strikes. The most strident demands came from the miners and railwaymen, and when they went out, the government saw no alternative to granting them pay increases, which solved the immediate problem but stoked up trouble for the future. Socialist and Communist ideas were rife; and faced with the example of Russia, riven by civil war, and Germany, sinking into red revolution, the government feared Bolshevism more than anything.

Shortage of goods and houses, rising prices, strikes:

these unhappy after-effects of war were added to the grief of loss. And there were visual reminders everywhere, in the war memorials that were being erected all over the country, and in the disabled servicemen seen in every street – one and a half million of them across the nation.

For a year after the Armistice there had been the euphoria of victory, and the joy of families reunited as the men came home, with the post-war boom to soak them up. But now that boom was coming to an end. Unemployment had risen sharply in December, and was still rising; businesses were failing, factories closing as markets shrank. Across the world, the war had caused national bankruptcies. No-one could afford to buy the manufactures the British companies had so enthusiastically pumped out. Warehouses were full of unsaleable goods; and as unemployment rose, domestic demand fell, and a downward spiral was engaged.

Teddy Morland's businesses were not unaffected. He was cushioned to some extent by existing contracts, but he had had to put two of his mills on short-time working; his shops were seeing declining sales; and at home he was having to reduce or forgive rents. But it was not of finance and business that he was thinking as he stood at the drawing-room window one day in February 1920.

It was snowing again: large, soft flakes falling inexhaustibly from a pewter sky. The whole scene was white, the bushes and trees so covered there was barely a dark line to be seen. The surface of the moat was covered with a thin skim of ice, onto which the snow fell, paused a moment and disappeared. The swans were sheltering somewhere – every creature was sheltering, and there was no movement of life out there, just the slow, relentless downward drift of snow. He had been staring out at the scene for half an hour, but he was not really seeing it. He was thinking about Ned.

The War Office had finally closed the files on the Missing. It was a shocking fact that half of all the dead of the war had no known grave. Some might have been buried in places no-one knew about; in some places, burial sites had become battlefields, and the graves had been obliterated by shells, tanks and pounding feet. But a horribly large number had simply disappeared in the destruction of battle, blown into unrecognisable shreds, or sunk into the mud too deeply for any trace to remain. In years to come, he thought unwillingly, a French farmer ploughing his land might turn up bones and recognise them for human. There was a strange harvest waiting in those tortured fields of northern France, and he pitied the poor simple ploughmen who would gather it.

The War Office had written to him to tell him that it had closed the file on Ned, his adopted son, Jessie's first husband. He had disappeared at Loos in September 1915. For a long time Teddy had been haunted by the belief that he was still alive, somewhere, somehow. He had sought him with increasing urgency as the rest of the family gave up hope and accepted that he was dead. Finally, when Jessie had married Bertie, Teddy had had to abandon his search, because to believe that Ned was still alive was to say Jessie was a bigamist. As Henrietta pointed out, one's first duty was to the living.

But the letter from the War Office had taken him by surprise, because he discovered that there was still a tiny seed of doubt buried deep in his brain. So he had been standing here at the window, staring into the blankness of the February snow, wrestling with his own thoughts. Jessie and Bertie were married, they had two children, they were happy: if Ned were to walk in now it would cause terrible complications and heartbreak to everyone. And it was not even that he really thought Ned was alive: it was just that with a strange, atavistic part of himself, *he couldn't believe he was dead*.

He supposed there must be hundreds, even thousands of people all over the country who felt the same. When a person died, you needed a grave and a headstone to make the finality real. That was why, he supposed, there were war memorials going up all over the country. He was having the Monument up at the top of the slope by the mares' field – a folly started by his late brother but abandoned for lack of funds – completed, as a war memorial. All the fallen of the house, the estate and the village would have their names inscribed on it; but there would only be one Morland.

The snow had held up completion, but it was almost ready. He had been planning a dedication ceremony in March, but perhaps April would be better anyway. Easter was an appropriate time, after all, to celebrate heroic sacrifice. There was nothing Teddy liked more than planning a festivity, and thinking about the form of the ceremony, and what they would do afterwards, soothed him a little. But there was still a niggling unhappiness in the back of his mind. Just as having no grave made it harder to accept death, so not accepting the death made it harder to believe that the soul was in Paradise. In his troubled mind there was no deserved Heaven for Ned, because in his mind he *just wasn't dead*.

The same snow was falling in Manchester Square, where Venetia was sitting at the desk in her study looking at a very similar letter from the War Office, telling her it had closed the file on her son Thomas – Colonel Lord Overton – and that no further enquiries would be made. She had given up hoping he was still alive: if he had been, she was sure he would have got a message to her. The last she had heard was in April 1919, and she was not sure even that had been genuine. She had parted with five pounds for it, and it could well have been nothing but a good day's work for a fraudster. Since then there had been nothing. She had let him go in her mind. Mostly she thought about how hard it was for Oliver, caught in this limbo.

She got up and went to the window and looked out. Snow made the grey streets beautiful, muffling the traffic sounds, decorating every pillar box and railing with a frivolous mob-cap. A scrap merchant went past below her, leading his horse and cart, the horse leaning into his collar, their joint footfalls and wheels making no sound, leaving behind a pattern that was quickly filled in with fresh snow. The horse seemed to be wearing a white blanket over its loins. The man huddled down into his collar, under cap and muffler, and every now and then uttered his strange, wild bird-cry – *hanyoh i-e-e-ern!* – which echoed flatly off the tall closed houses like the cry of a sea bird redounding off a cliff face.

She wondered if he was making enough to live on. She remembered the cab horses of her youth: you could tell the jarveys who were thriftless, drunkards, or had been ill, by the thinness of the beast between the shafts. A cabman looked after the horse first. If it was thin, you could bet that his wife and children were thinner. She had seen some thin women lately; and despite the cold season, tuberculosis was increasing.

Hard times were coming. The war had been hard, but

it had had its own momentum, and when you were consumed by working towards a common goal, it was easier to bear the hardships. 'Don't you know there's a war on?' was the response to any complaint. The 'war effort' came first, and its demands overrode any personal goals. It would be harder now to bear shortages and inconvenience. Every little thing would chafe; there would be nothing to distract from sorrow. Already she had heard people saying, *Why did we fight the war in the first place? What did my son, my husband die for?* It was easy to forget, now it was over, and all that was left was to count the cost.

But some good had come out of it. Women had been emancipated: those over thirty could now vote alongside men. Then in November 1919 the Sex Disqualification Removal Act had come into force, meaning that women could now be solicitors, barristers, magistrates, and serve on juries. Women now had access to all spheres, except the Church, the House of Lords, the armed services, the diplomatic corps and higher levels of the civil service.

Perhaps most excitingly, in December the first woman had entered Parliament, when Lady Astor took her seat. She had won in a by-election in Plymouth, caused by her husband's inheriting the viscountcy. A woman Member of Parliament! It seemed almost unbelievable to Venetia, who had fought unthinking prejudice all her life. Nancy Astor was an American by birth, and sat as a Unionist. She had some odd ideas, though, Venetia reflected, watching the snow pile up on the windowsill. She was a Christian Scientist, and had campaigned for Prohibition – a complete banning of alcohol, which those of her persuasion believed to be the ruin of the working classes and an agent of evil. It seemed to be something of an American obsession: they had passed the Volstead Act in October, which meant that from the 16th of January it had been illegal to buy, sell, import or consume alcohol anywhere in the United States, even in your own home. America, she couldn't help thinking, would be a very odd place to live now, and perhaps not very comfortable to visit.

It was a pity. She had toyed with the idea of making a trip, inspired really by nothing more than the possibility, after four years of U-boats and mines, of travelling abroad. Indeed, last July the airship R34 had made the first transatlantic crossing, so in theory one need not even commit oneself to the ocean to get to America. But the thought of a whole nation in the grip of teetotalism was too depressing. She was seventy this year – too old to be changing the habits of a lifetime. Too old, probably, to be travelling so far.

She left the window and went back to opening her post. Some interesting scientific journals, some uninteresting invitations, the usual letters from strangers and madmen asking for her patronage, or merely haranguing her about their hobby-horse. It was so dark, because of the snow, that she had to get up and switch on the lamp; and as she did, her mind lightened, and she thanked God for electricity, and the good, bright fire in her grate, and the useful work that still lay within her competence. She sat down again, put on her hated spectacles, and picked up the first medical journal; and thought that at least Oliver seemed to have thrown off his black cloud, and was more cheerful these days; and that, not living in America, she could look forward to a glass of sherry before dinner.

★   ★   ★

Lennie was finally demobilised at the end of February, and as soon as he was released he hurried straight to Morland Place. The difficulties of a journey on a derelict rail system, further impeded by snow falls, were made light by his joy at going 'home', and seeing Polly.

He was shocked at the sight of her – so pale, so grave, grown taller since he had seen her last. She did not romp and chatter as she once had, and when she smiled it was a sad smile. But the air of mystery and melancholy only made him love her more. He had grown up, too, since the impetuous days at the beginning of the war when he had volunteered as an ordinary soldier, just out of a longing for a good scrap. How innocent they had been back then! He had been in fierce fighting, had seen his companions fall, had accepted, belatedly, a commission, had risen to captain before the Armistice, and had been made up to major since then, as the military presence thinned.

And in this new maturity he did not comment on the change in Polly, or bother her as soon as he arrived with his love and his wishes for their future together. He would take his time to find out what had happened to her and how she felt before plunging in and risking all.

So Polly, who had been rather dreading his arrival, found him gentle, easy and companionable, like the very best sort of brother: undemanding, but interested in everything she did; always ready to attend to her, talk to her, listen to her, play cards with her – but in a sensible, unsentimental way.

The snow, and then the thaw, kept them from riding for a week, but the track was firm enough to drive over. She found herself eager to show off her driving skills to a new audience, so when he said he simply must have some 'civvy' clothes – nothing fitted him from before the war – she drove him into York in the Morris. She waited patiently while he consulted a tailor, then went with him to Makepeace's for socks and ready-made shirts.

'And a hat,' she insisted.

'But there's nothing wrong with this one,' he protested. 'It's the only thing that still fits me – my head hasn't swelled, at any rate. And it was almost new when I joined up, so it's hardly been worn.'

'It may be new, but it's not *new*,' she said. 'It makes you look like an organ-grinder's monkey. Don't you know fashions have changed? You *must* have a new hat. Come through to the hat department, and we'll give you a discount.'

He was charmed by that 'we', and her familiarity with the stock, and noted the respect the shop people showed her. Polly had been studying her business. It touched him, he wasn't sure why – perhaps because she could always have had anything she wanted, so there was no need for her to study for a career like a boy. He bought a hat, under her sharp-eyed supervision, and then as they stepped out of doors again into the misty, dripping rawness of early March, he asked if he might buy her luncheon.

The idea pleased and intrigued her, as he had guessed it would – she still had hardly ever eaten in restaurants. He took her to a very respectable hotel in High Petergate – just opposite the Minster: what could be more disarming? – and absorbed with inner tenderness her delight in the novelty of eating pea soup and cutlets in a public place. Afterwards, they walked around the shops some more, and he stood patiently in the saddler's while Polly chose a new browband for Vesper with the care most girls expended on their own adornment. Then he went into the sweetshop on the corner of Coney Street and bought a paper of chocolate caramels, which he presented to her with a bow, and was rewarded by a smile from her that was close to laughter.

'You are such a fool!' she said.

'I consider that an achievement, and a compliment from you. What now?'

She looked about her. 'We had better be going home. It's getting late, and I'm not used to driving in the dark.'

'Pity,' he said. 'It gets dark so early this time of year.'

'Yes, it is a shame. I've enjoyed myself so much today.'

'Good,' he said, and forbore, with heroic effort, to make any capital out of it.

In a day or two more, the ground was firm enough for riding. A bright, windy day with fast-racing clouds and intermittent sunshine glittered on the wet hedges and beckoned them out of doors. Polly sent to the stables so that Vesper and Hotspur were saddled and ready for them immediately after breakfast. They were fresh from their enforced rest, and the wind excited them even more, getting into their ears and under their tails until they could hardly keep two feet on the ground at the same time.

'It's no good,' Polly said, as Vesper passaged sideways from the menace of a small leaf, 'we'll have to gallop. They'll never settle otherwise.'

'Go ahead,' he answered. 'I'll hold on tight. If I come off, you'll come back for me?'

'If only to bury the body,' she replied, and let Vesper go.

It was a wild ride, and the wind was a cold one, so by the time they stopped he was breathless, and her cheeks were bright as berries. They walked the horses side by side, not pulling now, and Lennie drew out a handkerchief and wiped the flecks of mud from his face, thrown up by Vesper's hoofs. The clouds bowled madly across the sky above the bare trees, and rooks rising from the fields before them were blown about like scraps of paper.

They rode up onto Cromwell's Plump and stopped. Lennie slid rather ungracefully off – he had not been born in the saddle like Polly – and went to Vesper's head.

'I think she'll stand for a bit,' he said. 'Won't you get down? Come and sit with me and talk.'

There was a flat stone at the edge of the rise where generations of people had sat to admire the view. Holding the horses at the end of long reins, they sat side by side in silence for a while. Polly seemed quite relaxed; inwardly Lennie was tense, knowing the moment to speak had arrived.

'I want to talk to you,' he said at last, 'about you and me.'

She glanced sidelong at him, but said nothing, which he took, on the whole, for encouragement.

'You know I've always loved you,' he said. 'Every time I go away I wonder if perhaps it will be different when I come back, but when I see you again, it isn't. You were too young the first time I proposed to you. I know that now. You were just starting to have fun, you didn't want to be serious about anything. *I* was too young, too. I was just a kid in my first long pants, full of myself and my big plans. Well, the war knocks that sort of thing out of you. I see it in you, too. You're much more serious now. And more patient.'

'And you're a major,' she said.

He couldn't tell anything of what she was thinking from the tone of her voice. '*Was.* I'm out of that now. In a way it was quite unreal, especially now I'm out on the other side of it. Something to be forgotten as soon as we possibly can.'

'Some things you can't forget,' said Polly.

'I know. But you can deliberately not remember them. And one thing hasn't changed, Polly. I love you, and I know now I'll always love you. You're the only one for me, now or ever.'

'I know how you feel,' she said.

'You do?' he said, his eyes lighting with eagerness. 'Because I know you're only nineteen—'

'Twenty, soon.'

'I'm twenty-four, and because of the war I've left it late to get started on my life, but I've got plenty of ideas and plenty of "go". I was thinking about going back to America. Things are much easier there – a man with a bit of gumption can really make something of himself. There are fortunes just waiting to be made. I'd work for you, make a wonderful life there for you. You'd have everything you could want.'

'Lennie—'

There was no mistaking that tone. He hurried on, not wanting to hear the fateful words. 'But if you preferred to stay here – I know how much this place means to you – well, I can get ahead here just as well. It may take a little longer, but now the war's over things are going to change in this old country. New ways of looking at things and doing things. The man with ideas will prosper. I'll make it here, I promise you. I'll build you a house, right across from Morland Place if that's what you want. In a year's time, when you're twenty-one—'

185

'Lennie, do stop, please,' Polly interrupted him. She looked at him with a kindness that hurt more than scorn would have done. 'I can't marry you.'

'You're thinking your father wouldn't approve?'

'It's not that. I don't think Daddy would think you good enough for me, but that wouldn't bother me. *I* think you're quite good enough. And in the end Daddy wouldn't stand in the way if it was what I wanted. But it isn't what I want. I can't marry you, because I can't love you. I'm very fond of you, but it isn't enough.'

'Love can grow,' he said desperately. 'If you let it.' She didn't speak. 'When I said I would always love you, you said you knew what I meant.'

'I'm sorry,' she said, with that same deadly kindness.

'You mean – you love someone else?' No answer. 'But then why don't you marry him?' He studied her. 'You seem so sad. Is it someone you *can't* marry? Who is it?'

She sighed. 'Lennie, don't.'

'It's not that oaf Holford, is it? I couldn't bear it if you loved him.'

'No, it's not Holford. Now, please, don't say any more. We ought to move. The horses are getting cold. And so am I.' She stood up.

He stood too, and caught her hand before she could turn away, scanning her face earnestly. 'Who is it, Polly?' he asked gently. 'I see it's making you unhappy. If he's hurt you, I will kill him for you, if that helps.'

'I can't tell you anything about it,' she said steadily, holding his eyes. 'I love him, but we can never marry, and there's nothing to be done, so please don't ask me any more questions. And no-one else knows, so you mustn't tell.'

'I won't tell,' he said. 'You can trust me.'

'Yes, I know.' She managed a smile. 'I really do know that. You're a good person, Lennie.'

He released her hand, unhappy and baffled. He couldn't think his way past the problem. All he knew was that he couldn't give up, even if he must seem to. He walked behind her to Vesper's side and took hold of her cocked knee to throw her up. When she was settled he laid his hand a moment over hers and said, 'I won't say any more about it, I promise. But just remember that I love you, and I'll always love you, and if you change your mind, I'm here.'

'I'll remember,' she said. 'But I won't change my mind.'

Easter was late in 1920, falling on the 20th of April. With the work on the Monument finished at the end of March, Teddy could not wait any longer for its dedication, and the ceremony took place on the second Sunday in April.

The finished memorial was impressive. As originally designed, it had borne a strong resemblance to the Albert Memorial in Kensington Gardens, but Teddy had had a great many of the decorations and curlicues removed to give it a more sober appearance. What was left was the ambitious size of it, enhanced by being sited on the top of a rise, so that the gilded cross on the top could be seen from miles away, especially when it caught the sun.

There wasn't a great deal of sun around on dedication day. During the morning the scattered clouds dragged together like a frown, gradually covering the sky with a grey pall, and by eleven o'clock it was threatening rain. It was windy, too, a sharp breeze bowing the bare trees, bending the wild daffodils along the banks until they touched the ground; flapping the surplices of Father

Palgrave and the thurifer as they walked round the Monument, and fluttering the white cassocks of the waiting choirboys from the village church.

But everyone was there, soberly dressed, the women in black hats and many with veils, the men bareheaded in the damp cold wind, all come to honour the dead of the area, and to remember their own dear sons, brothers, husbands and fiancés. Farmworkers, tenants, villagers, servants, pensioners of Morland Place and former employees, neighbours and friends gathered with the family. Denis Palgrave's words were sometimes whipped away by the breeze, which brought on its intermittent gusts the noise of nesting rooks in the elm trees, and the ever-present clamour of ewes and lambs. Then Teddy read out the names of the dead whose sacrifice was recorded on the panel on the face of the memorial: a long list. Some listened with heads bent, others staring bravely forward, eyes fixed on another place and time; one man lifted his face to the sky when his son's name was read out, as if to let the occasional spots of rain that were coming on the breeze disguise his tears.

The choirboys sang, and at the sound of their young, innocent voices many of the women broke down at last, and some of the men found themselves unable to join in the hymn, 'O God Our Help In Ages Past', for the tightness of their throats. For Jessie it was the line 'Time, like an ever-rolling sea, bears all our sons away' that was too much, and she turned her face to rest it against Bertie's chest so that she should not sob aloud. Helen, noticeably pregnant now, took Jack's hand for strength. Henrietta wept openly for her two sons and her nephew, looking ahead with no attempt to hide her tears, from time to time comforting Ethel who, still in black for her parents, was mourning her husband with simple, honest grief. Maria stood near the nursery-maids, who were shepherding the children, her face grim. She knew people would mutter that she had no feelings, but she would not weep in public.

Finally there was the laying of the wreaths, the first from Teddy, then others from leading families, and finally the simple bunches from the poorer people. The flowers were bright against the stone, brave in the gathering gloom of the sky. Helen thought they were a fitting reminder of the men who had laid down their lives so cheerfully, each a small bright spark of colour in the vastness of eternity, as fragile, and yet somehow enduring.

There were more drops of rain, and occasional spats blown on the breeze, as the ceremony ended and everyone trooped back down the slope. An enormous marquee had been erected in the field opposite Morland Place, where luncheon was to be served. Here the great people were to mingle with the lesser – on such an occasion, Teddy would not countenance a separate luncheon for the gentle-folk. In the war, everyone's sacrifice was the same. So there was a vast buffet from which everyone was to help himself, and everyone was to mingle without regard to rank.

So it happened that Polly found herself standing talking to Mrs Bellerby of White House Farm. She was in her Sunday-best coat and a hat of glazed black straw decorated with cherries, around which, perhaps deeming the cherries to be too frivolous, she had wound a piece of black gauze. 'Eh, Miss Polly,' she said, 'that were a right lovely service. Just what we all needed. I said to Willa Banks as we were walking back, "Trust the maister to know what folks need." He always does right by his own people, does the maister, and there never was a kinder nor better. The War Memorial is really beautiful, Miss Polly, and so everyone thinks, and it's a fitting tribute to all our dear boys as didn't coom back.'

The Bellerbys' son Tom had been killed at the Somme and Joe had fallen at Ypres. Their third son, Christopher, safe at school when the war began, had insisted on joining up as soon as he was able to, in 1918. He had been waiting to go overseas with his battalion when the Armistice was declared, which had saved the Bellerbys, perhaps, from having three names on the Memorial.

So Polly listened to her politely, conscious of her terrible losses. Then, lowering her voice and leaning forward, Mrs Bellerby said, 'I wouldn't say it to just anyone, Miss Polly, but, though you might think me fanciful, I can't help feeling there's another name as ought to be on that Memorial, but never will be. It wouldn't do to say so in front of *soom* people,' she went on, 'but then I make my own mind oop about things, and don't just repeat what other folks say. And to ma mind – as you know, because I spoke about it to you at the time, Miss Polly – a man may be a Christian, whatever country he comes from. I can't help remembering that if ma Joe or Tom had been in his position there'd have been folk ready to believe *they* was bad and evil only for doing their duty as they were bound to. He must have been soom mother's son, and I hope I treated him as she would have wanted, and trust she'd have doon the same by ma boys. He never *wanted* to go to war, you know, as he told me, only he couldn't help it, the way things were. And a better, kinder, more Christian soul you couldn't wish to meet, so I don't care if he was a German, though I dussent say it in *any* company, so I know you won't repeat it, miss.'

Polly frowned in concentration. 'You're talking about – about your prisoner?' she said, hesitating at the end about saying his name aloud, and wondering whether it was safe to admit she knew it.

'Aye, miss, the same,' said Mrs Bellerby, making the cherries under the gauze nod. 'I pride myself on being a judge o' character, and he were an honest worker and a decent man, and did many things for me out o' kindness that he didn't need to. And it breaks my heart to think of him cooming to such an end. He were a victim of the war just like ma boys, and so I say, though it may be fanciful, that he ought to have his name oop there too. O' course, I know it would never do, but I dare say he won't have a memorial in his own land, neether.'

Polly tried to control her breathing. 'What do you mean, about him coming to such an end? What happened to him?'

'Why, miss, didn't you hear? But perhaps no-one would trouble to tell you,' she answered herself, 'seeing what he was. But I heard from Mrs Scaldersby at the post office, who had it from the housekeeper of Captain Standish – who was the superintendent of the prisoners, miss, you remember – that there were a riot down at the docks when they were embarking the prisoners to go back to Germany. Attacked, they were, by a mob, dockers and stevedores and such, armed with great metal poles and spanners and sheave-blocks and the like, and many of them was grievously wounded, and some was killed, our man among them. Which he never deserved such a fate, Miss Polly, and I'll say so to anyone who asks me.'

'He's dead?' Polly said, in a voice that was hardly more than a whisper.

Mrs Bellerby nodded, pleased to have made such an

impression. 'Aye, miss, so I heard. Never even got home, poor Christian soul – murdered by the very people he always said he admired. He always said, Miss Polly, that he loved this country and its people and never *had* wanted to fight us, which is a sad irony, miss, when you think of it. I couldn't have managed without him, and the work he did here on our farm helped to feed our men at the Front, so he was a hero in his own way, and helped us win the war. Poor creature, I wish he had got home safely. Now his name won't be remembered anywhere.'

Polly murmured some comment, and stood looking attentive while Mrs Bellerby continued to speak, on a different subject; but she did not hear a word, and as soon as there was a pause in the flow, she made an excuse and moved away. The sound of people talking all around her was like a roar of waters, the words indistinguishable. She saw faces everywhere and mouths opening and closing and none of it made any sense. It was like being locked up in bedlam. She wandered through the crowd in a daze, until she stumbled into Helen, who caught her arm and said, 'You look pale. It's terribly hot and airless in here, isn't it? Come and sit for a moment. There are seats round the edges for the likes of me.' She guided Polly to a couple of hard chairs and sat with relief. 'I do find it hard to stand for long periods,' she said cheerfully, noting that Polly didn't seem ready to speak. 'It was a lovely service, wasn't it? I'm so glad the rain held off. And the singing of the choirboys was quite ethereal. They sound so touching and innocent, it's hard to believe they are normal human boys, with all a normal human boy's devilment in them. As a mother of a son I can speak to it.'

She chatted gently, thereby keeping anyone else from interrupting their tête-à-tête, while thinking that Polly looked as if she had had a shock, for she was quite white, and her eyes had a blank look. After a few moments, she seemed to recover somewhat, and began to answer Helen's comments, though it seemed almost at random. Finally Helen said, 'I'm beginning to feel a little peckish. I think the crush around the buffet table has eased a little. Could we squeeze in, do you suppose? Would you be so kind as to help me, Polly dear? I feel so clumsy and vulnerable in crowds.'

'Of course,' Polly said absently; and then, meeting Helen's eye – by accident, it appeared – she seemed to register a consciousness about what had been going on. 'Yes, of course I'll help you,' she said more definitely. She took Helen's hand and assisted her to her feet, and said in a low voice, 'Thank you.'

Helen continued to regard her steadily. 'If there's anything you want to talk about, anything I can do, you know I'll be only too glad to help.'

Polly turned her suffering face away. 'There's nothing anyone can do,' she said. And then, with a visible effort, she pulled the mask into place, and they eased their way through the crowd together.

Maria was feeling an equal sensation of detachment from her surroundings, as tenants and villagers who remembered Frank came to talk to her about him, and to praise Frank's son and tell her what a comfort he must be to her and how proud she must be of him. No-one who disapproved of Maria's having married again would have dreamed of telling her so, or even hinting at it on an occasion such as this, though she was sure there must be many such. Palgrave was popular, and to criticise her for marrying him was like criticising him.

And though Frank had been a Compton, he was Henrietta's son and so considered a Morland by the neighbourhood. Today the Morlands could do no ill, and so Maria was protected. Not that she cared in the least what these people thought: she operated by her own judgement, and her own condemnation was the only one she feared; but it gave her a strange, unreal feeling all the same, to receive the polite consolations of these strangers.

Maria was too well aware of her own failings not to know that she was not popular in the district. Partly it was not her fault – she was clever, and clever women were always regarded with suspicion by ordinary folk. But Helen was clever too, and managed to get by. Maria knew that she was too abrasive.

Her background had not prepared her for this sort of life. Helen had grown up in a large house with a lot of servants, had never been poor, and consequently got on with everyone, whatever their station. Maria had learned to value only intellect and intellectual attainment, because they had been the only things in her power to accumulate. She had learned the lesson too well, and simply could not join in the admiration of a pretty face or a new hat as though they mattered, or give deference to someone because of their rank when they had nothing else to recommend them to her.

Denis was her intellectual equal, and he did not defer to rank either, but he had a universal liking for people and a Christian tolerance of their faults. When she criticised anyone to him, he would always find excuses for them. Well, it was his calling: she did not have to be so forgiving. But she wished with all her heart they could have got away from this place. If only he could have left

Morland Place when they got married, and found a living somewhere, preferably in a town.

There was something about Morland Place that oppressed and frightened her. She knew it was unreasonable. She, who prided herself on being rational, was ashamed of her feelings. But what she had said to Denis was true. She felt as if the house was a living thing, and that it had got hold of her and would not let her go. When she woke in the morning she had a sense of dread, as though something were coming to get her. And just lately she had begun to feel ill again, and her troubled mind teased at the idea that the Spanish Lady had introduced some fatal weakness to her system, which was now carrying her off.

She didn't *want* to die. She was still young, she had a new husband whom she loved and a young son she adored. She had everything to live for, if only they could get away from this place. She even thought that being a missionary's wife would be preferable, though she doubted her constitution could stand the climate. Most of all, she wished they could live in some bright, clean, up-to-date place in the heart of a city where the hum of traffic, modern conveniences and unambiguous gaslight would banish the mediaeval shadows from her life. She was a modern young woman and she wanted a modern young woman's life.

She saw the head of Helen appear through a gap in shoulders, talking to someone, and decided to go and stand with her. Helen's was the closest in this tent she would find to a modern mind. She pushed her way through the press of bodies, aware all at once of how hot it was, how airless. The smell of bruised grass, damp canvas and bodies was choking. A sense of abdominal unease made her wonder horribly if she was going to be sick. She hated being sick, with the intensity of a person who loathes any loss of self-control.

She reached Helen and laid a hand on her arm, and as Helen turned to see who it was, the tent began to swing around her like the black mouth of a bell, and the nausea rose up like billows of soft, deadly smoke and closed over her head.

She came to herself to realise, to her horror, that she was lying on the ground, and the first thing she saw were the legs and skirts of people standing round her. Shame scalded her and she tried to get up, but as soon as she lifted her head the nausea and dizziness billowed over her again.

'No, don't try to move, not just yet,' said Helen's voice. Helen's warm, strong hands were on her, one pushing her shoulder back down, the other on her forehead. Her vision cleared and she saw that Helen was kneeling at her side, which couldn't have been comfortable for her. 'Take a moment, or you'll go off again as soon as you sit up.'

Maria was aware now that Jessie was there, too, and Polly, both of them asking the crowds of legs and skirts to move back and give her air. She *hated* being the centre of so much fuss. She wished Denis would come and scoop her up and carry her off to a distant place from which she need never return to meet the people who had witnessed her humiliation.

'I'm sorry,' she said.

'Don't be,' Helen said comfortably. 'It's perfectly natural. It happens to all of us at some time. It happened to me in the middle of a dinner party when I was carrying Barbara.'

Maria frowned, trying to make sense of the words. 'What do you mean? How is it natural?'

Helen's smile grew more tender. 'Haven't you suspected? Perhaps I'm wrong, but, Maria, dear, don't you think you might be pregnant?'

CHAPTER NINE

The tall, fair man who asked Emma to dance at the ball when Oliver proposed to Verena Felbrigg was Peter Gresham: a thin-faced, brilliant-eyed man with quick, nervous hands and a flow of witty conversation that had Emma entranced and amused. He was also a superb dancer, and as the Season of 1920 got into its stride, that was a most valuable skill.

All the young people were mad for dancing. The men who had been through the war had often left university to join up, or had joined up immediately after Oxford; girls had reached coming-out age during the war years when there was no coming out. They had missed an essential part of their youth, and were bent now on making up for it.

The Front had been a place of horror, maiming and death, and everyone who had served had seen things he wished to forget. Some of the women, like Emma, had also served in France; of those who had stayed in England, many had nursed, and all had suffered the shortages, rationing, blackouts, air raids, and the constant fear of the arrival of the Telegram.

They wanted to forget, and dancing seemed to exemplify everything that was not war. Besides, the war for most had been a four-year segregation of the sexes, and the modern dances, like the foxtrot and the one-step, allowed young men and women to get close together and talk intimately. Girls who had missed their come-out were now in their twenties and, while no less eager for pleasure, were old enough not to be closely chaperoned. So the fun was fast and furious, like the rag-time music. Clergymen might rail at modern morality and proclaim the saxophone to be the instrument of the Devil, but balls proliferated that spring, both private and public, and anyone dedicated to enjoyment need never slow down until forced to by exhaustion.

Emma's sheer determination and war-hardened constitution meant that she could stand the pace. Every night had its ball, preceded by a dinner somewhere, and she was a popular guest and never lacked an invitation. Violet enjoyed dancing, but as a married woman and mother of four she was not expected to want to do it so often. She did not go to public balls, except charity events, but accompanied Emma to most of the private balls. When Freddie Copthall took her, she danced almost as much as Emma; but Lord Holkam returned from Paris in April – the peace conference had finally closed in January – and when he took her, she often found herself watching wistfully from the sidelines with the matrons, while he talked politics with the older men.

Emma soon had her court, and was in the happy position of being able to choose escorts. Kit Westhoven was one of them, and they sometimes made a comfortable party of six with Violet and Freddie and Oliver and Verena. Hostesses who invited her to dine for a ball, and who knew Venetia, often paired her with Kit, assuming that was what Venetia would like. But as the Season advanced it was more often Peter Gresham with whom she danced, and went down to supper, or to the breakfast that brought the bigger private balls to a close at around four in the morning.

He was the heir of the Earl of Castleford, who had estates near Leicester and a London house in Upper Grosvenor Street. It was a respectable, two-century earldom built on sheep and coal. Peter Gresham, the third son, had been a brilliant student. At Balliol he won the nickname Quicksilver for his rapidity of thought and speech – though perhaps it also owed something to his prowess in the eights. Balliol was not known as a particularly sporting college, but in his time the boat club had flourished.

He had been studying law, and it was assumed by contemporaries and dons alike that a distinguished career as a barrister lay ahead of him. He was twenty in 1914 when the war broke out. One of his elder brothers, Gerald, was already in the army; the second son, Charles, volunteered at once. Driven by the idealism of youth, Peter wanted to follow Charles's example, but his father forbade him. However, the following spring, when he turned twenty-one, he went against the earl's wishes, left Oxford without his degree, and joined a line regiment.

'The gov'nor was furious,' he told Emma one evening in May, when they had got to the stage of exchanging histories. 'Wanted to cut me off with a shilling, only the mater intervened and told him it was an excess of nobility that drove me, not mere wilful disobedience.'

'And was it?' Emma asked.

'A little of the one and a little of t'other,' he said airily. She had already learned that he tended to make light of serious subjects. 'It's true that I had absorbed all that *dulce et decorum* rot, like the nincompoop I was. Practically brought up on Arthur in the nursery. The chivalric ideal, don't y'know. Brought Nanny to tears every time.' He smiled down at her impishly. 'On the other hand, there was never anything that satisfied me more than taking on authority and beating it. Sheer perversity seems to have been at the bottom of most of my decisions.'

Emma laughed. 'I can't think why you're dancing with me, then. I've never refused you yet. If only I'd known you wanted a fight . . .'

'Oh, I've grown up since then. Mainly, of course, as a result of discovering that war has changed since King Arthur's day. I'm not sure how Lancelot and Bedivere would have coped with mustard gas and shrapnel. Our war was shockingly short on glory. The only Holy Grail at Ypres was a ten-pound tin of bully.'

Despite his taste for perversity, he had served with distinction – 'largely because I relished the sheer imbecility of it all. I took a delight in following idiotic orders to the letter. Later, of course,' his eyes darkened, 'there wasn't so much of that, and it was all we could do to stay alive. Then Charlie went west at Neuve Chapelle, and Gerald caught a packet on Hill 60. And I lost two-thirds of my company in Polygon Wood.'

'I'm sorry,' Emma said.

He looked down at her, with an intensity that made her heart quicken. 'You were out there,' he said. 'You understand. I wouldn't talk about it to any other girl, but you FANYs – we had the greatest respect for you, you know.'

He had been badly wounded in the Polygon Wood action, and it wasn't until some weeks later, while still in hospital, that he had learned of his brother Gerald's death, which had left him next in line for the earldom.

'I can't tell you how furious the gov'nor was that it was me that survived,' he went on, reverting to his normal flippancy. 'Gerry was the man for the earldom – born for it, loved all that chin-stroking and speech-making. And Charlie was the perfect spare, not ambitious, you know, but quite ready to take up the burden if necessary. But everyone was glad when I took to the law, because otherwise, what was to be done with me? The only reason I was born at all was that the mater had a fancy for a daughter. All she got was me, poor creature. And then the jolly old war intervenes, turns the world upside down, and makes me heir.'

'I'm sure your father is glad to have you left to him,' Emma said.

'He knows I'll make a lousy earl. Pretty poor return for all that work and effort,' he said lightly. 'But here we are, and there's no escaping. It's good to know that the gov'nor and I are united in hoping he'll live a long, long life! My greatest regret is that I didn't finish my degree.'

'You'd like a career? Even though you're going to inherit?'

'With, without, or entirely discounting the earldom, I'd like to have proved myself as an advocate. I think I'd have been good at it.'

'Why don't you go back and finish?'

'Oh, streets too lazy!' he exclaimed, executing a neat turn at the end of the room. 'Got used to spending the inheritance now. I couldn't go back and be diligent and dull with a lot of earnest boys fresh from having their curls cut off. Now, really, Miss Weston, can you imagine it?'

'You'd be the boy-king, and they'd adore you.'

'Ugh! Perish the thought! I'm having far too much fun as I am.'

But she had heard the hurt under the laughter, and wondered about that. She could see how he couldn't go back, after what he had done and witnessed. There were a great many men in the same boat, and she met them all the time at the Season's gatherings: young men old before their time, with shadows in their eyes, restless because they had lost the world they once knew and did not fit into the one that was left. A new order would have to be forged for them to feel part of the world again, but how to do it? So for now, they danced and made merry, with the feverishness of children up too late and trying not to be sent to bed.

They were at a ball given by Lord and Lady Farquar at their house in Grosvenor Square – one of the grander balls of the Season, because royalty was expected. Emma had dined first at 143 Piccadilly with Sarah Vibart. Eddie was away with the Prince of Wales on a tour of Australia. The prince had spent a large part of the previous year in Canada and America, where he had been a great success, and he would be in Australia now until August. It was hard on Sarah to be without Eddie for such long periods when they were still practically newlyweds, but the amiable Freddie Copthall acted as host for her when required, so she did not have to miss all the fun of the Season.

Emma had been invited to the Farquars' ball because of her connection with Lord Abradale, and she had come with some trepidation because there was expected to be a large Scottish element. And, indeed, almost the first person she had seen on entering the ballroom was Angus Knoydart, with whom she had exchanged a grave nod.

Fortunately, the second person had been Peter Gresham, who had come over at once and claimed her hand, and now they had had several dances together.

When the music stopped Emma said she was thirsty and they went through to the refreshment room where Gresham secured her a glass of champagne.

'Oh dear! I really was thirsty,' she said. 'I rather hoped for lemonade.'

'Terrible bad for the digestion, lemonade,' he said quickly. 'Better stick to sound wine if you want a long and healthy life. I will say this for the Farquars – they have a good cellar.'

'And no-one's wearing the kilt,' Emma said. 'Such a relief.' She drank the champagne rather too quickly because it gave the illusion of quenching her thirst. Gresham immediately drained his own glass and took two more, and Emma laughed and said, 'I really shouldn't.'

'You really should,' he countered. 'And as a seeker after truth I need to have your comment about kilts expanded, please.'

So Emma told him a potted version of her struggle not to be incarcerated in Scotland. Then, realising that the bubbles had seduced her into being indiscreet, she said, 'Oh dear! I've just realised that if the Farquars invited you, you must have some Scottish connection. You aren't Scotch, or half Scotch, or anything, are you?'

'Would it ruin my chances with you if I were?'

'You're laughing at me.'

'Just a little. But don't worry, I'm all English, as far as I know. The connection is through the Farquars' friend Lord Strathmore, who married a Cavendish-Bentinck, who is first cousin to my mama.'

'Oh. Well, that's a relief.'

'To me, too,' he assured her solemnly. She had inadvertently finished her champagne again, and he found her a third glass. 'Do you know the Strathmores?'

'My uncle is acquainted with them – though his estate is on the west side, and I think theirs is on the east.'

'As remote from each other as Transalpine and Cisalpine Gaul, of course. Yes, Glamis is near Dundee, though they only spend the summers there. They have a place in Hertfordshire, and a house round the corner in Grosvenor Gardens.'

'You seem to know a lot about them.'

'Didn't I tell you my mother's a cousin of Lady S? I used to call her Aunt Cecilia when I was a nipper. Our London house is in Upper Grosvenor Street, and she and Mama are in and out like lambs' tails, so I can tell you all about it. They're busy giving a Season to their youngest daughter, Lady Elizabeth.'

'Is she here? Which one is she?'

'Let me see – yes, over there, just coming off the floor with Prince Albert. I dare say they were hoping for the Prince of Wales to come tonight, but since he's on another of these interminable tours, they had to make do with the spare in the end.'

'Make do? Don't be unkind. The poor prince!' Emma rebuked him.

He looked down at her. 'How tender-hearted you are! But I'm pretty sure he's quite content to come second, and would be horrified if anything happened to his big brother. He no more wants to be king than I want to be earl.'

'He seems to like his partner, anyway,' Emma said. The Strathmores' daughter was a diminutive, dark-haired girl with a fresh complexion, who might have been negligible had it not been for an air of character and determination beyond her years, and her sweet smile.

'Yes,' said Gresham, 'he does seem smitten. I doubt if she'd have him, though. I've met her a few times – when I was convalescing from my wounds. She nursed during the war and I think my mother rather thought we might make a match of it. She's a nice little thing but as stubborn as a donkey when she sets her mind to anything. You wouldn't think it to look at her, would you?'

'Oh, yes, I think I would.'

'She's a superb shot,' Gresham said, 'and quite a scholar for a girl – whereas I gather the prince is something of a duffer, so I can't see that romance going anywhere.'

'What a shame. A nice ball in Mayfair on a fine May evening: it's just right for a romance.'

'Well,' he said laconically, 'I hadn't thought about it until now, but I suppose I could give it a go if that's what you want.'

Emma found herself blushing, though she told herself it could just as easily have been the effects of the champagne. She copied his languid tone. 'Goodness, no – *too* fatiguing. You can shove me round the floor again, though, if you care for it.'

'Don't mind if I do,' he drawled. Back in the ballroom he said, 'By the way, I was thinking of tooling down to Windsor to watch the polo on Saturday. Thought I'd get a party together. Take a picnic luncheon, make a day of it, stop off somewhere on the way back for dinner. Does that appeal to you? Are you fond of polo?'

'I've hardly ever watched it, but I love horses,' she said. 'But there's the Tonbridges' ball on Saturday—'

'I'm invited to that, too. We'll be back in bags of time. Where are you dining for it?'

'The Verneys.'

'Me too. But I know Laura Verney. She won't mind if we chuck. As long as we both chuck, her numbers will still be even.'

Emma was doubtful, never having 'chucked' before in her life. On the other hand, the idea of going on an outing with a party of young people was new to her, and polo sounded smart and exciting. The champagne was coursing through her blood, and as they emerged into the ballroom she saw Lord Knoydart at a little distance, looking at her with a frown she chose to interpret as disapproval. To give herself over entirely to hedonism seemed just then the only rational response to the hand life had dealt her, the only way to keep unwelcome thoughts at bay. Hoping that Knoydart would keep watching, she turned her most fascinating smile up at Gresham and said, 'It sounds like fun. I'd love to come.'

There was no doubt Peter Gresham was the leader of the Season. He had about him that air of sophistication and daring, the aura of the second magnum of champagne, the furiously driven motor-car, the audacious wager and shrewd winnings at Ascot. He gathered around him a smart set, a fluctuating court drawn from a dozen or so of the brightest sparks in London, whom he dubbed 'The Cadets', which, Emma gathered, was an ironic reference to some Greek or Roman organisation, though she did not investigate the meaning further. She was pleased to discover that she was everywhere considered one of the inner circle of the Cadets, which conferred a status on her far more sophisticated than being voted the prettiest debutante of the year, or the girl most likely to marry well, in one's come-out year.

Kit Westhoven was also one of the set, but Oliver and Verena, though they were sometimes at the same functions, were too staid and settled to be Cadets. Others included an American heiress, Flo Vanderbeek, who had driven an ambulance in France bought with her own money; Lady Amalfia Worseley, younger sister of Emma's old friend Ravenna, who had been a VAD; Roberta 'Bobbie' Stainbridge, who was noted for having learned to fly; and Lady Charlotte Ogilvy, whose war work had included collecting Canadian remounts at the docks and taking them, ride-one-lead-one, to the nearby cavalry depot. Among the men, Ronnie Austin, Lord Anthony Leaham and Tommy Beaufort all had fine war records and now were noted for dashingness.

Being among the Cadets did not just mean dancing, though there was plenty of that: they made up a party for anything interesting that was going on. They went down to Ascot and Epsom, to the University Match at Lords, to Oxford for Eights Week (Tony Leaham, who had been at Cambridge, pleaded for the May Bumps instead but was overruled). Gresham knew someone who owned a motor yacht, and borrowed it to cruise up and down the south coast. They motored out into the country to lunch on bread and cheese and beer at a village pub in Hertfordshire, and to watch the local cricket match. They went to air exhibitions at Hendon, to Newmarket and Glorious Goodwood.

In all this Emma found herself constantly at Peter Gresham's side, and saw in the eyes and attitude of those around them that she was considered to be his object. On their motoring parties she was always in his motor, in the passenger seat next to him, watching his long brown hands on the steering-wheel and sometimes struggling with a map that flapped in the wind of their passage. On the yacht she stood by him at the wheel, and he taught her to steer. He always found her seat, helped her with her coat, brought her drink, served her first at picnics. At balls he danced most often with her.

He talked to her constantly, though she often did not understand his references; he read her poetry; when they were apart during the daytime, he would send her foolish notes through the penny post, sometimes with clever but wicked drawings on the back, lampoons of their friends or public figures – he was a talented sketch artist. He sent her flowers in July on her 'half birthday', and a confectioner's box containing a cake cut in half.

She knew herself envied, saw her style begin to be copied. More girls began to bob, though it was still frowned on by the mainstream of society, so she had her own hair cut shorter to stand out from the crowd. She wore what was most fashionable, trying always to be the first with each new idea. Because she so often took Benson with her on their outings, other young women started to be seen with little dogs, and when she bought him a smart tartan collar (it was a private joke with Peter concerning her dislike of the kilt), tartan collars appeared everywhere. She was photographed and mentioned in the society pages and illustrateds, saw herself called 'original' and 'one of the leaders of the smart set', and her name began to be linked with Peter Gresham's in print – something that did not seem to trouble him, only to make him laugh.

Her time was being filled, her mind occupied: she need never think about unhappy things. She was admired, envied, flattered, and had a constant companion in Peter Gresham: together they were at the tip of the pyramid of young society. Yet despite the assumptions of society at large and their set in particular, he had never made love to her or attempted to kiss her – had not even touched her hand in a sentimental way. She felt their attachment growing all the time, but she could not say that she really understood him. He was brilliant, witty, amusing, undoubtedly clever – many of his classical references went over her head – and seemed always ready to laugh; but she sensed behind it a melancholy he rarely allowed anyone to see, which she guessed at and longed to assuage.

Jessie read Emma's name in the papers and noted with amusement that she had become a leader of the *ton*, which, as she said to Bertie, was no more than she deserved, since she was not only pretty and a considerable heiress, but had served unflinchingly in the war in one of the worst places, and had been awarded the Military Medal.

Living a life of retired domesticity – ordering meals, solving small household problems, arranging for the delivery of coal and the mending of a lamp – Jessie was very far from moving in Emma's world. She had only seen her face to face twice that year. She went with Bertie to various functions, but they tended to be military or, if social, involved an older set, which rarely overlapped with that of the Cadets. But more often they dined at home *à deux* – something they never tired of after the long war years of separation – and for amusement slipped out rather shame-facedly to a cinema to watch some melodramatic piece of nonsense that had them laughing as much as the comedy reels of Charlie Chaplin or Buster Keaton.

She didn't see very much of Violet, either, for Violet was very busy with the Season, accompanying Lord Holkam to important functions as he tried to mend the image of their marriage, and mixing socially with the titled set, which held to a completely different orbit that Jessie did not penetrate. Though the wife of a baronet, she made no attempt to be part of the *ton*.

But in May 1920, Violet held a children's tea party for her daughter Charlotte on her eighth birthday, and invited Jessie to bring Thomas and Catherine to it. It was a chance for them to admire each other's children, but Jessie's two were much too young for such an occasion and were soon whisked away, together with little Henry – or Octavian as Violet still referred to him – by efficient nursery-maids. And after ten minutes of smiling fondly at the three older children, and the six friends they had invited to the party, Violet left it to the nannies and took Jessie away to her sitting-room for their own separate tea and said with a happy sigh, 'Dear Jessie, now we can have a lovely quiet chat.'

Jessie and Bertie were invited to dine several times *en famille* with Venetia, and once Jessie accompanied Venetia to a supper party at the Mark Darroways in Soho Square – Bertie was otherwise engaged that evening – which was great fun. It had been Mark who had first encouraged her to nurse during the war. He was proud of her for having gone to France and wanted to know all the details. Oliver was there, too, always affectionate towards her, and it was a pleasant evening of reminiscence and medical chat. She heard with interest how the plans for the John Winchmore Hospital were coming along – slowly, but they were hoping for it to open next year – and Oliver told amusing anecdotes about various surgeons he had assisted, and their foibles.

But oddly – since she didn't even live in London – it was Helen she saw most of. She and Jack often came up to Saturday-evening dinner, and asked Jessie and Bertie down for Sunday luncheons. Sometimes when Helen was bored with domestic life in Weybridge, she and Jessie would meet for luncheon at Selfridges, and go shopping together, or take in an exhibition or a matinée. Then if Jack was away overnight she would stay on to dinner, and Molly would join them from work, and the sisters would take a late train back together. And sometimes if Molly had worked late at the ministry she would call in on Jessie and stay to eat. Jessie enjoyed hearing about her very different life as a secretary, and the snippets of Whitehall inside gossip she picked up.

So it had seemed natural to Jack to ask Jessie to keep an eye on Helen if she should happen to go into labour when he was away. The telegram came at midday on the 22nd of June. Jack was in Paris, Molly at work, and Helen asked her to come 'if it was no trouble'. Jessie had been ready for the call, had a small bag half packed and had already instructed the nursery-maid and the cook on looking after the children and the master. She sent two telegrams back by the boy, one to Helen to say she was coming and one to Bertie to explain she would not be there when he got home, dispatched the housemaid to the corner for a taxi, and ten minutes later was on her way to Waterloo.

As soon as she stepped into the house she was glad she had come, for Mrs Ormerod was in a state of abject panic because the midwife hadn't arrived.

Helen could hardly concentrate on her pains for trying to reassure her. 'Thank God,' she said, when she saw Jessie.

Jessie's coping skills came to the fore as she calmed Mrs Ormerod, directed the maids, saw to the remaking of Helen's bed, and telephoned to find out when the doctor was coming all at the same time. Basil and Barbara were upset by the atmosphere so she sent them off with Nanny Mina to be given tea at the village tea-shop, with ice-cream if they had it, to keep them out of the way for as long as possible. Her calmness and the prospect of the treat took Basil's mind off the idea – gleaned from his grandmama – that his mother was going to die, and where he led, Barbara always followed, so they went off happily.

She instructed one of the housemaids to settle Mrs Ormerod on the sofa with a rug and one of her pills and read aloud to her – she was very fond of Michael Arlen. Then she was free to concentrate on Helen, who was having hard pains, but not yet very close together.

'Dear Jessie,' Helen said, when she was comfortable – or as comfortable as she could be – with the bed suitably stripped, the surfaces of the dressing-table and bedside table cleared and neatly covered with clean towels, and Jessie taking her pulse like a monument of calm. 'I feel so much better now you're here. I hope you didn't mind?'

'I'm glad you asked me,' she said, releasing Helen's wrist and gently wiping the sweat from her brow. 'Would you like the window open a little more? It is warm in here.'

'Yes, please – and a sip of water, if I may.'

It was another hour before the doctor arrived, sweating

213

in the June heat and apologising because he had been at a difficult birth on the other side of town and couldn't get away. He looked sharply at Jessie. 'Who are you? Where's Nurse Gant?'

'She didn't come. I'm Mrs Compton's sister-in-law. I nursed in France.'

He looked harassed. 'A very different matter. But I'm glad you have training. I can't think what happened to Gant. She's usually so reliable. I shall telephone the agency once I've made my examination. Now, Mrs Compton, how are we getting along?'

He examined her, told her she would be a while yet, and went downstairs to telephone. Helen was obviously in discomfort but she wouldn't moan. When the doctor came back upstairs he called Jessie out onto the landing.

'All is clear. Nurse Gant was on her bicycle on her way here when a motor-car brushed her in passing and she fell. The driver took her to the hospital. She seems to have fractured her wrist. The agency is trying to get a replacement. They'll telephone here as soon as they have one. In the mean time,' he eyed Jessie critically, 'do you think you can take care of Mrs Compton?'

'Of course,' Jessie said. 'I came prepared to stay.'

'Good, because I think this is going to be a long job. I shall just take one more look at her, and then I must go and check on my other patient, but I shall be back in two hours. I wish the two houses were not on opposite sides of the town,' he sighed, 'but it can't be helped, can't be helped.'

'Can I telephone you there if anything happens?'

'They are not on the telephone. But I doubt anything will happen before I return. We are not far advanced.'

When he was gone, Jessie took her place at Helen's

214

side and chatted to her to keep her mind off things, holding her hand when the pains came. The children came back from the tea-shop and she gave the nursery-maid instructions, went down to check on Mrs Ormerod, who was asleep, came back to Helen with a cup of tea, which she sipped but could not finish. There was no news of another nurse.

The children wanted to come in and see their mother before bed, but Jessie was against it, and Helen agreed it would only upset them. She sent them a message and promised they would have a new baby brother or sister in the morning.

Helen's pains were severe, but she did not seem to be advancing, and Jessie was worried. She tried not to show it, but perhaps Helen picked up on it, for she said at one point, 'Jessie, if I die—'

'You aren't going to die. You're just having a baby. Women do it all the time.'

'I know. But *if* I do – you'll see my babies are taken care of, won't you? And Jack – he's not as capable as he appears to be. He depends on me so much.'

'I'll see to everything.'

'You promise?'

'I promise. But you're not going to die.'

'Dear Jessie,' Helen smiled, 'you almost sound as if you believe it.' And then another pain took her.

The doctor returned, this time to stay, and Jessie took the opportunity to go down and see about dinner for Mrs Ormerod, who had recovered her equilibrium now that Jessie and the doctor were in attendance, and was driving the servants mad by telling them to be calm when they had no intention of being anything else. She had thought Jessie and the doctor would come down to dinner, and was rather put out by the change to her expectations, but rallied when Jessie asked her to arrange trays upstairs, and became magnificently coping: 'Don't worry about anything. I shall take care of every detail. I'm quite capable of running my own household, you know.' Fortunately Molly arrived home from work just then, and told Jessie in an undertone that she would take care of her mother.

So Jessie was able to go back upstairs with Mrs Ormerod off her conscience. Two trays were sent up, and she and Dr Houseman took turns to slip into the next room and eat while the other stayed with Helen. A telegram came from Jack to say he was on his way home, and a telephone message finally came that another midwife, Nurse Grainger, was on her way, but would not be there until late as she had to come up from her last case. By then Jessie and Houseman had found each other's rhythm and hardly cared.

They had a hard struggle of it. Nurse Grainger arrived at eleven o'clock, a bony Scot with a long face and sparks of ginger eyebrows that made her look like a surprised horse; but she seemed efficient, and did not at once shove Jessie out of the way, as trained nurses were apt to do with VADs – never mind former VADs. She gave her an appraising look, said, 'France?' and when Jessie nodded, admitted her to the medical confidence.

Matters were moving by then, and Helen gave birth just before midnight with a single terrible cry she could not hold back.

When the cord was cut, Grainger shoved the baby at Jessie while she and Dr Houseman attended to the mother – from their muttered conversation Jessie gathered there was some bleeding and Helen was still not out of the woods. The baby was a boy, Jessie saw – small but seemingly well formed, only rather battered and very weary from his struggle. He let out a faint plaintive cry, like a lamb's, and Jessie heard Helen call her name feebly.

She moved to where Helen could see her by turning her head. 'It's a boy,' she said. 'He's beautiful. You shall have him in a minute.' And she took him away to bathe him.

Jack arrived not long afterwards, in time to be the one to place his son, washed, bound and wrapped, in his wife's arms. He had cast one agonised look at Jessie's worn face, and she had replied to his unanswered question, 'She's all right'; but in the time between the baby's arrival and Jack's there had been worrying moments.

The doctor went to wash his hands and Jessie went downstairs to tell Molly the news. She had assumed Mrs Ormerod would have gone to bed, but she was still up, sitting in the drawing-room trying to read, but looking pale and drawn. All her affectations had been cast aside. She struggled to her feet as Jessie arrived. 'I heard her cry out. And the baby. But then it all went quiet,' she said, her anxious eyes devouring Jessie's face. 'Oh, tell me she's all right! Say Helen is all right!'

'Helen is all right,' she said. 'You have another grandson.' She swayed on her feet.

Molly said briskly, 'You need a glass of sherry,' and went to fetch one.

'I was so worried,' said Jack. Helen's hand was folded in both his, and he felt as if he were an unstable balloon only anchored to the ground by it. 'All the way home I kept wondering if I would see you again.'

'Now you know how I feel every day,' she said.

He looked surprised. 'But it's a completely different thing.'

She was sorry to have said it. Flying was his life. 'I know. I was only joking.'

'Joking? Oh, darling! I kept thinking *I* did this to you—' He broke off as she laughed. 'What now?' he asked with a hurt look.

'I think I had something to do with it,' she said. She was light-headed with relief, despite her aches and pains. 'Jack, I'm all right. It's over. Don't make a fuss. We have a lovely boy – or at least, he will be lovely when he's filled out a bit.'

'He's lovely now. Are you glad it's a boy? You didn't want another daughter?'

'I didn't mind either. We'll have to think of a name for him.'

'I was thinking all the way home to Hounslow,' he said. 'I thought of Esther if it was a girl, and Michael if it was a boy.'

'I'm glad it wasn't a girl.'

'You don't like Esther?'

'I like Michael. Michael Compton. It sounds well.'

'Yes. Like an airman.'

'Or an actor.'

'Or a famous barrister – "Compton at the Old Bailey".'

'Or a writer. "The latest novel by Michael Compton".'

'Perhaps he'll be all those things,' Jack said. 'The airman-actor-barrister-novelist Michael Compton.' He leaned down and kissed her forehead. 'You must be exhausted. Don't you want to sleep?'

'Not just yet. I'm so comfortable with you here. Talk to me some more. How was the trip today?'

He began to tell her, but before he had spoken more than a couple of sentences, he felt her hand go limp in his and saw she was asleep. *God, but I love her!* he thought, looking down at her cherished face. And he thanked God humbly for not taking her away.

The next morning, bleary-eyed from too little sleep – he had not got to bed before two, at which point young Michael Compton had decided it was high time to make his presence felt – Jack, having spent the night in Mr Ormerod's old dressing-room, encountered Jessie on the landing on the way downstairs.

'She's still asleep,' she informed him, before he could ask. 'Temperature and blood pressure both normal. Nurse is sitting with her. You can have some breakfast before looking in.'

'I have to go to work,' he said with an air of desperation, 'but I'll see if there's any way they can let me off for a few days, if they can get a substitute.'

Jessie raised her eyebrows. 'Whatever for? She'll be fine now, Jack. She'd be running a temperature if there was anything wrong, and she isn't. All she needs is complete rest. You go to work. You have three children to support, you know. You can't afford to play fast and loose with your employer.'

'But I can't leave her here all alone, with only Mother-in-law and the nurse. She'll fret herself to death worrying about things.'

'Foolish! I'm going to stay. What did you think?'

He clutched her hand. 'Oh, Jess, will you?'

'Of course. I always meant to. I'll stay as long as she

needs me. But she'll be up and about in a week or two, don't worry.'

Jack pulled her close and kissed her cheek. 'Thank God for you! But, I say, poor old Bertie!'

'He'll survive. I'm going to send him a telegram as soon as I've had breakfast. And, yes,' she anticipated. 'I'll send all the other telegrams, too, telling everyone the good news.' She examined him critically. 'I only hope you're not too tired to fly safely.'

He grinned. 'I can do that in my sleep.'

'You look as though you're going to have to.'

Jessie stayed two weeks, not to nurse Helen – that was Nurse Grainger's job – but, remembering how much it had meant to her when her mother had done the same for her, to run the house so that Helen wouldn't be bothered by it. She managed the servants and ordered the meals, supervised the children's regime, sat with Mrs Ormerod, answered the telephone and opened telegrams, acted as a filtering mechanism for visitors so that Helen did not get too tired, and made sure to visit her often with snippets of news and reassurance.

'It's wonderful, having you here,' Helen said one day. 'I feel so comfortable, knowing you're looking after everything.'

'I owe you such a debt for the time you took me in that I can never repay it,' Jessie said. 'So please don't thank me.'

In the evenings, when she had no other engagements, Molly was a great help in keeping Mrs Ormerod amused, and Jack was home most evenings, but all three seemed to feel the benefit of Jessie's presiding over the dinner table and keeping the conversation going – usually Helen's job.

Grandmama took to little Michael in a way she never had to Basil and Barbara – who, in fairness, she had not seen at the same stage, or had a chance to grow attached to. After the first two days he settled down to being a model baby, sleeping when required, crying only when he was hungry and then in a very modest and restrained way. Mrs Ormerod could not have enough of holding him, and called him her 'black baby', because he had such a shock of jet black hair. 'Where's my little black baby?' she would cry. 'Oh, let me hold him, the darling!'

It seemed to suit young Michael to sleep on Grandmama's lap instead of his crib and be cooed over by her when he was awake. It suited Nanny Mina, her hands full with Basil and Barbara, who were feeling a little prickly and unsettled because Mama was absent from her usual places, and because something momentous seemed to have happened without involving them in any way.

And it suited Nurse Grainger to be left free to concentrate on Helen, especially when on the third day she ran a little fever and frightened them all. The doctor came and diagnosed a mild milk fever, which was a relief, but it meant that she could not feed the baby. So the kitchen had to prepare bottles, which Mrs Ormerod was glad to be the one to administer. As long as she did not have to do anything like washing or changing the baby, she was perfectly happy. Never faced with these chores, she was heard to declare that there was nothing to taking care of a baby and she wondered that people made such a fuss about it and paid nannies such ridiculous salaries.

Bertie came down at the weekend, unable to bear being without his wife a moment longer, and brought the children with him, knowing she would want to see them. It stretched the resources of the household somewhat, but Jack was pleased to have them, and Molly said, 'Gosh, the house is nice and full and noisy, isn't it?' Thomas was fascinated by Barbara, and followed her around under the impression that she was some kind of animated toy designed for his own use. Once he could be prevented from poking at her eyes and pulling her hair, he played with her quite nicely, until Basil grew jealous and hit him on the head with a toy spade, and got banished to a corner for ten minutes.

Helen was over her milk fever and feeling much stronger, and it fascinated her to hold Catherine and see how enormous she was compared with Michael – 'In only seven months!' She got up for the first time on Sunday and came down to luncheon, which made it feel like a celebration, though she went back to bed afterwards. Bertie dragged himself reluctantly away on Monday morning by the early train, but Helen urged Jessie to keep the children with her so as to make his life easier at home.

Helen recovered quickly in the week that followed, and was so well by the weekend that Jessie felt no qualms about leaving her. Bertie came down on Saturday night and they went home together with the children on Sunday.

'Jessie was a Godsend,' Jack said to Helen when he went in to say goodnight, wishing Nurse Grainger would let them sleep together. He missed the company, sleeping in the dressing-room. 'She made it all seem so easy.'

'Hmm,' said Helen.

'You are all right, aren't you?' Jack enquired anxiously, of her equivocation.

'Oh, yes. I'm practically back to normal. And, all in all, it wasn't bad, really. But I tell you this, Jack Compton,' she concluded severely. 'Much as I love you, I never want to do it again.'

CHAPTER TEN

Russia was still struggling through a bloody and violent civil war, though the last British armed forces had left the White Russians to fight it out alone. Strikes and bloodshed stalked Germany, and an army marched into the Ruhr to attack the Bolshevik occupation there. Poland was at war with Russia. Ireland was in turmoil, with armed uprisings demanding independence, and British troops brought in to restore order on the streets. Unemployment was climbing towards two million, with engineering, mining and cotton manufacturing particularly badly hit, and there was unrest in several industrial towns. The Communist Party had set up headquarters in the Cannon Street Hotel, and a Labour National Council was threatening the government with a general strike.

But the Season went on, and the young people danced as if it were all that was holding back Chaos. Parliament went down for the summer recess, and the out-of-Town season started: the Cadets kept on meeting but in country houses, for riding, boating, walking, charades and amateur theatricals, billiards and cards, and, of course, dancing every evening, and the flirting that went with it.

Emma and Peter Gresham were invited to the same weekends now, which was comfortable. And in August

224

she was invited to his parents' house party at Kimcote Hall, near Leicester. The sight of the card gave her a fluttering feeling, for she couldn't help wondering if the purpose was to inspect her.

She showed it to Violet, who did not seem unduly interested. 'Kimcote? No, I don't know it. But it's pretty country. Hunting country, too – it will be nice if you're invited in the winter.'

'Should I accept, do you think?' Emma asked, almost shyly. They both had several cards for the same Saturday-to-Monday.

Violet considered. 'Holkam and I are going to accept the Arundels' invitation, because there will be important people whom Holkam wants to meet, but I dare say it will be very dull. I think you're more likely to have young people at the Castlefords'. I think you should go. It will be more fun for you.'

Emma didn't know whether to be pleased or not that Violet seemed to take nothing significant from the invitation.

'But, Emma,' she went on, 'with country-house parties every week from now on, you really will need a maid. I think you should telephone the agency and see if they have anyone available. I'm afraid you've left it rather late. If they can't get you anyone right away, you might try Anna, the under-housemaid, as a temporary solution. She's the most sensible of them.'

As it turned out, she did not need to trouble Anna, for when she telephoned the agency, the proprietor, Mrs Harmsworth, said, 'But what an extraordinary coincidence, Miss Weston! A woman came in yesterday looking for a position, who said she used to maid for you. Name of Spencer.'

'Spencer? Good heavens! Yes, she was my maid for years and years.'

'I hope,' Mrs Harmsworth said, with sudden doubt, 'that you did not dismiss her for any unpleasant reason?'

'No, no! I joined the FANY and then I went to France, so I had no need of a maid. But I thought she was suited. She told me she had a new position.'

'Yes, I placed her with a lady in Kensington, a Mrs Fitzgerald, but she came in yesterday saying she wasn't happy there. Naturally, one is always pleased to have good girls on one's books, but leaving Mrs Fitzgerald so suddenly looked – well, I did wonder if perhaps she was a flibber-de-gibbet.'

Emma laughed. 'Not Spencer! A regular sober-sides! But if she's looking for another place—'

'Yes, indeed, *quite* fortuitous. Shall I send her along for an interview?'

'Yes, do. Dear old Spencer! I shall be glad to see her again.'

Everything was arranged within a day. Spencer, obviously as glad to see her mistress as vice versa, said only that Mrs Fitzgerald was not at *all* the thing, without revealing any details, and that Kensington was *not* what she was used to. So Emma accepted the Castlefords' invitation, and travelled down with the feeling that Spencer's unexpected return was a good omen.

Lady Castleford turned out to be a small female version of Peter – the same fair hair, though mostly grey now, the same features, the same blue eyes, though meshed with lines and sadness. She was charming, but there was a core of steel behind the faded beauty and the pleasant smile. She gave Emma a very keen, though brief, inspection when she arrived, but otherwise did not treat her any differently from the other young guests. Emma did not know whether to be pleased or disappointed.

Lord Castleford was not there to greet arrivals, and when he appeared just before dinner he confined himself to conversation with his own cronies, leaving his wife to bridge the gap between the younger and the older sets. He was a large, shambling bear of a man – Peter had his height, but not his bulk – with grizzled hair and small dark eyes, and a face dragged downwards by disappointment. His presence did nothing to enliven the evening, but fortunately he hardly appeared during the weekend, remaining in his study with the chosen companions of the hour to talk politics, walking with them around the estate, and after dinner returning to his study to smoke cigars with his particular friends, or taking possession of the billiard room. There were in fact two tables in there, but when he was playing on one of them, none of the younger set would have dared offer to use the other.

But the Cadets had each other, so it didn't matter. On Saturday morning they idled about admiring the house – it was a charming Palladian building of harmonious lines, filled with very pretty furniture and chinas, quite feminine in feeling, and Tommy Beaufort, who knew about such things, said the paintings were good. Then as the weather was fine they piled into motor-cars and took off for a drive around the countryside, ending up at the other side of the estate for a picnic by the lake. The picnic arrived in a brake direct from the house, and was laid out waiting for them, with two maids and two men to serve it, beginning, of course, with champagne.

'I say, Gresham,' Tommy Beaufort said, taking a

227

lounging place beside Amalfia Worseley, 'you know how to do a thing properly.' There were large cushions to lean on, and the champagne was well chilled.

'Not worth doing otherwise,' Gresham said, arranging several cushions to his liking and inviting Emma to recline against them. He bowed over her as he handed her her glass. 'That's what they taught us in the army – attention to detail, gentlemen! For want of a horse-shoe nail, and so on.' He imitated a gruff military voice.

'Oh, don't talk about the war!' Amalfia protested.

'Why not?' said Flo Vanderbeek. 'I don't know about you people, but it's the only interesting thing that ever happened in *my* little life. Horrible, yes – but driving that ambulance was a whole lot more fun than sitting around in Mother's drawing-room listening to talk about cousins and babies and who was marrying whom.' She looked around the group for support. She had rather frizzy hair and protuberant eyes, which somehow always made her look like an eager terrier. 'I tell you, I never felt so alive as when I was driving that old ambulance through an air-raid, dodging potholes and thinking my last hour had come. Emma, you'll back me up here?'

Before Emma could speak, Bobbie Stainbridge broke in, nodding her fair, curly head. 'It's like flying,' she said. 'When you first go up and you see all that empty space between you and the ground, you realise you could be killed. But that's what makes it exciting. You feel more alive because you might die. It's a – a—'

'A paradox,' Lord Anthony Leaham supplied kindly.

'A thrill,' Flo corrected. It was a word she used a lot, and which was becoming current slang among young people for anything desirable.

'The brush with death that enhances life,' Peter said.

'That's it!' said Bobbie gratefully.

'Hmph. You females have strange tastes,' Kit Westhoven said. 'I'd sooner not operate with shells exploding around me.'

'I'd sooner not operate at all,' Ronnie Austin interrupted, making a face. 'I don't know how you chaps can do it, dabbling about in other chaps' innards.'

Amalfia squealed. 'Oh, don't talk about things like that! Too gruesome!'

Peter looked at her with amusement. 'You seem to rule out every subject we start. Perhaps you'd like to tell us what we *may* talk about.'

She blushed. 'Oh, I didn't mean – only there've been enough horrid things in the past. Can't we talk about the future?'

'Ah, but I'm afraid that may open up whole new areas of contention.'

'Why should it?' said Ronnie Austin. 'Surely we're all agreed that the future must be very different from the past. The war drew a line under the old way of doing things.'

'Did it?' said Peter. 'I wish it had.'

'But look here, old man,' Ronnie said earnestly, 'what did we fight for, if not to begin a new world order where the old evils will be swept away? We have the best chance mankind has ever had to start afresh.'

'A clean slate,' Flo agreed. 'And *we* won't make the same old mistakes again.'

'Do we know what they are, though?' Kit Westhoven asked her.

'The mistakes? Sure we do! Listen, all men are created equal, right? "We hold these truths to be self-evident", as the good old Declaration says.'

'Ah, yes, when you bloodied our noses back in King George's day,' Tommy Beaufort drawled.

'Right you are, sweetie!' cried Flo. 'To have a better way of doing things in the New World. Just look at the mess the old world got into, with half the people starving and the other half feasting.'

The picnic hampers had been unpacked by the servants, and Emma looked at them and then at Peter, uncomfortable with the implied criticism. But Peter was only smiling with a secret sort of amusement.

Kit Westhoven obviously thought like Emma. 'Well, me for the feasting half, at any rate,' he said lightly. 'Can I help anyone to anything?'

But Ronnie wanted to be serious. He said, 'It's all very well, but the world is so full of riches, it seems to me we ought to be able to share them out a bit more evenly.'

'And what then?' said Peter.

'I don't understand you.'

'All men may be *equal*, but they're not *the same*. If you divided all the wealth equally between everyone on earth, a week later ten per cent of them would have ninety per cent of it, and the rest would be looking bewildered and wondering where it all went.'

'That's human nature,' Tommy Beaufort agreed.

Ronnie flushed. 'That sounds like defeatist talk.'

'And yours sounds like Bolshevik talk.' Tommy returned the ball, still smiling but with an edge to his tone.

Bobbie Stainbridge intervened. 'I can't say I go all the way with these socialists, but I do think they have some good points. I mean, we ought to be able to do more for the poor, especially our returning heroes.'

'Hear, hear,' said Flo. 'Some of the demobbed soldiers are having a pretty raw deal.'

Bobbie gave her a distracted glance and carried on with her own stream of thought. 'And some of them – the socialists, I mean – are really quite respectable. Quite nice people, like the Sitwells. And Siegfried Sassoon – Mummy has a book of his poetry, you know, and she says it's really very good. Only frightfully sad. Daddy says it's subversive, but Mummy tells him he wasn't there – on the Western Front, I mean – so how can he say what it was like?' Having lost her thread she appealed to Kit, who was sitting next to her. 'And it must have been sad, mustn't it?'

'Very sad,' he confirmed solemnly.

'So isn't it just reasonable that we should try to do things differently now, and have a different kind of government?' She looked round at them earnestly, trying to broker a consensus so that there would be no unseemly quarrelling.

'Extremely reasonable,' Peter said kindly. 'There's just one small difficulty in the way of your new world order.'

'And what's that?' Ronnie said suspiciously.

'That the people who have the power are still the people who ran things before, and got us into what you think is a mess.'

'The older generation,' Emma said. She thought of Peter's father and the men of his age, the solid, serious grey-heads, with whom he disappeared into his study to talk politics. The cigar smokers, she called them in her head, with an image culled from an illustration of her youth, of King Edward and other portly, bearded statesmen with thick cigars between their thick fingers, and the fate of the nations in their hands. She looked around the group and thought that, in comparison, they were as light and gaudy as birds, and their words were mere chirpings. How could they affect anything? She caught Peter looking at her and, meeting his eyes, felt he knew exactly what she was thinking.

'The older generation may have the power, but the younger generation have all the ideas,' Flo was saying. 'They'll have to give up the power to us.'

'I don't think they'll want to,' Peter suggested.

'Then they'll have to be made to,' said Ronnie, firmly. 'It's only reasonable.'

'And how will you make them?' Peter asked, in a deadly voice. 'At the point of a gun? "Be reasonable or I'll kill you?" Would you like to start another war?'

There was a short silence. And then Ronnie said in frustration, 'But hang it all! You can't mean you want to sit around and do nothing about anything? Just let everything go to the dogs for want of a bit of effort? Or do you like the way things are? P'raps you don't think anything *needs* doing? That we're living in Paradise already?'

'Ronnie, shut up, there's a good fellow,' Tony Leaham said. 'It's too jolly hot to get excited about the new world order. Can't we have the revolution tomorrow? Have a sandwich.' He held out a plate. '*Foie gras*. Rather good.'

Everyone laughed, mostly with relief, and Ronnie joined in good-naturedly and accepted one. 'I suppose parts of it *are* a bit like Paradise,' he admitted. 'Very pretty lake, Gresham.'

'Man-made. Completely artificial,' Peter said. 'You never get anything quite so symmetrically asymmetrical in nature.'

'Have you seen the lake at Stretton Magna . . .?'

The conversation turned to lighter subjects, but Emma continued to look covertly at Peter. He was joining in, laughing, contributing witty comments, just as he always had since she had known him. But there was something bleak in his eyes, despite the laughter, something hauntingly sad underneath the lightness that made her want to shiver; that made her want to fling her arms around him and protect him, and make him happy.

She realised, with a sense of dismay as well as surprise, that she might be falling in love with him.

They danced that evening after dinner, in what was called the saloon, an octagonal ante-room on the garden front between the drawing-room and the small dining-room, which had french windows onto the terrace. The carpet had been rolled up and removed, along with the larger pieces of furniture, and a gramophone was installed in one corner, presided over by a young footman. The older set chatted in the drawing-room, where Lady Castleford had also organised a couple of tables of bridge, and Lord Castleford and the cigar smokers were in the billiard room as usual.

The Cadets, and the other young people who had been invited for the evening, fox-trotted and one-stepped to the cheery, creaky music with its excitingly uncorseted, American sound. The Cadets led the way, and the other young people watched them admiringly and tried to emulate them. Flo Vanderbeek tried to teach everyone a new dance from America called the Watermelon, which she said was 'kinda like a slow drag, Blind Lemon kinda thing', but was hampered by having never seen it, only having had it described to her in a letter. There was talk of Vernon and Irene Castle, Fred and Adele Astaire;

someone spoke of tap dancing; the tango was mentioned; and someone else said that her mother said black people's dancing was vulgar.

People drifted out between dances onto the terrace to smoke – Flo Vanderbeek, daringly, was the only one of the females who smoked, but she winked at Emma and said, 'There were plenty of us who did in France, am I right, sweetie?'

Bobbie Stainbridge said she'd like to try a cigarette, and choked on it to everyone's amusement. 'It's nasty! I can't think what anyone sees in it.' Servants circulated with glasses of champagne; Ronnie Austin said he'd sooner have whisky and it was sent for, and he added absent-mindedly that champagne gave you gas and everyone shrieked.

Kit Westhoven danced with Emma and said, 'I've been trying to all night. Too bad of Gresham to hog you.'

'He wouldn't have minded if you'd cut in,' Emma said.

'*Wouldn't* he?' Kit said significantly. Then, 'That's a very pretty frock.'

'Do you like it? The neckline is my own idea.'

'Clever.'

'Bobbie Stainbridge is thinking of opening a dress shop. She wants me to go in with her, but I can't think of anything I'd like less.'

'And there is the small matter of your marriage.'

Emma felt herself blush. 'What *can* you mean?'

'My dear child, you'll be frightfully rich, by all accounts, when you come into your fortune. You *must* marry.'

'Why must I?'

He looked down at her solemnly. 'Rich people have a

234

duty to spread the good about. I do dislike it so when I hear of rich girls marrying rich men – such a waste. Heiresses like you must marry impoverished lords faced with losing their ancient seats.'

'Like you?' she said, amused.

'I'm not impoverished,' he said indignantly. 'Not but what one could always do with a bit more, but the old family pile isn't quite on the market yet. However, I can put you in the way of a needy peer or two if you like. Unless things are settled between you and Gresham already?' She didn't answer. 'Thing is,' he added, looking down with interest at the colour in her cheeks, 'from what I gather, Kimcote is pretty solid, so Gresham is exactly the sort of chap you *don't* need to marry.'

'I don't know why you're so concerned,' Emma said, feeling prickly.

'Oh, I'm not, not at all. It's the idlest of idle conversation. And he's a very fascinating chap – one can see that. In fact, I'd be glad to marry him myself if you're not keen.'

She laughed at his joke, and said, 'I didn't say I wasn't keen. But we're just friends.'

He nodded judiciously, as though she had given herself away. 'Snaffle him quickly, dear, that's my advice. That's a market that won't hold up.'

'What do you mean?' she asked, but he only smiled and would not answer.

'Tum-ti-tum-ti-tum. I like this tune, don't you? Good thing, really, because it comes round awfully often. I do think a few more records would have been a good idea.'

The music stopped, and Emma saw that Peter Gresham was alone on the terrace. She was afraid her colour was still too revelatory, but she wanted to be near him.

235

'Goodness, it's hot, isn't it? I think I'll go out for a breath of air.'

Kit smiled down at her kindly. 'Run along,' he said. 'With my blessing.'

Gresham didn't look at her when she arrived next to him, but made room for her without comment, which was even better, for it spoke of an accustomedness between them that said far more. They leaned in silence, while he finished his cigarette, staring out into the darkness. In daylight the view was over the park towards the lake; now it was velvet blackness beyond the short fall of lights from the house, with the shapes of trees – an oak here, a cypress there – cut out against the luminosity of the night sky in the east, where the moon would soon be rising.

Inside the saloon, a slow tune had succeeded the fast one, and Flo Vanderbeek's voice could be heard saying eagerly, 'Now this is perfect for the Watermelon! Let's try it again.'

Emma saw the corner of Peter's mouth curl upwards. 'She's an original,' he said. 'The irrepressible Flo. "Oh could I flow like thee, and make thy stream/My great example."' He looked at her. 'Do you care for Denham? An underrated poet. "Though deep, yet clear; though gentle, yet not dull; strong without rage" – don't you think that fits our Miss Vanderbeek perfectly? I wonder if his subject was at all like her.'

'You said she was an original,' Emma said, trying not to flounder in the intellectual waters. She had never even *heard* of Denham.

'True. And consistency is all. Not like the moon, the inconstant moon. "Packs and sets of great ones ebb and

236

flow by the moon," so the Bard rather mysteriously says.'
Emma nodded, feeling relieved that at least she knew
the Bard meant Shakespeare. 'My father and his friends:
don't you think they're packs and sets of great ones?
What do they talk about in there, in the cigar smoke
over the billiard table?'

'Politics, I suppose,' she said, since he seemed to want
an answer.

'Setting the world to rights?'

She remembered the argument by the lake. 'Or to
wrongs.'

He remembered it too. 'Well, perhaps. But things
happen, you know. Sometimes nobody really means them
to. And then all you can do is respond to them. You do
your best, and it has to be good enough. And if it isn't
good enough . . .' He was staring blankly outwards again.
The leading edge of the moon was just showing above
the trees. 'There's no magical system that has all the
answers,' he said quietly. 'No book of reference for
humanity.'

'You don't believe in a new world order?' she asked,
rather timidly, unsure of his tendency.

'I wish I did. It would make everything so easy.' He
paused, drawing the last of his cigarette, and crushed
out its red winking light on the balustrade. 'I still can't
get used to smoking openly,' he said. 'Especially at night.
"Put that light out!" they used to bellow at us at the
beginning. You only need to see one man shot through
the head by a sniper to learn that lesson. One minute
he's having a gasper, the next you're wiping his brains
from your sleeve. One never gets over the shock of how
easily life is snuffed out. It feels so solid and permanent
inside you – the steady thump of the heart, the gentle

whisper of blood – and then the person two feet away from you is turned on the instant into so much meat. It makes you look at yourself in a different light.'

Emma said nothing. She had memories like that, but she did not want to revisit them.

'Have you read a book called *This Side of Paradise*?' he asked after a moment.

She shook her head.

'It's by an American writer called Scott Fitzgerald. A thoroughly bad book in its way, self-indulgent and uneven, but it has something – a flavour, if you like. What the Germans call *Zeit-Geist* – the spirit of the times. Scott Fitzgerald seems to speak for our age. He says we are the generation who woke up to find all gods dead, all wars fought, all faiths shaken.'

'Do you believe that?' she said.

'I don't believe in a new world order,' he said, as if that were an answer. 'I think we are what we are, we human creatures – flawed, bad, good, hopeful, doomed, merry, wise, sad, destructive geniuses. The war showed us everything we are capable of, from the heroism to the cruelty. I don't believe in Heaven, because I've been to Hell, and it's all man-made.'

He had turned to look at her, and the emptiness in his eyes was like the coldness of the sun going out – the death of everything. But she *couldn't* let it rest there.

'We survived,' she said. 'So many died, but we survived. Perhaps against the odds, but here we are, and we've seen – what we've seen. The horrors.'

'So – what, then? We have to make sure it never happens again?' His tone was ironic, but he was looking at her as if it mattered what she said next.

And she thought, despairingly, How *can* we make

sure of that? We have no power to effect it. We have no voice that can be heard above the old men and the guns. She thought of Fenniman and Wentworth. 'No,' she said. 'We can't do that.'

'What, then?' he asked again.

She felt helpless. 'Just live, that's all. Live our own lives properly. Not waste them.'

And he smiled, the most perfect and yet heartbreaking smile she had ever seen on a human face. 'I like your answer. You deal in truth, like me, not stale shibboleth and simple-minded nostrums.' He laid his hands on her shoulders: they were cold from the stone, but started into heat at the touch of her skin. He looked into her eyes. '"Come, let's away to prison; we two alone will sing like birds i' the cage,"' he said and, leaning down, kissed her on the forehead. The brush of his lips was like the touch of a plum warmed in the sun, sweet, delicious, full of promise. She shivered from the crown of her head to her toes, and it was not from the cold. Then he let her go. 'Let's dance,' he said abruptly.

He walked indoors and she went with him; there was a new record playing, and they moved together, into each other's arms. *Sing like birds in the cage*, she thought, as they stepped about, knowing each other's movements now; letting the music and movement wash all thought away. *We two alone*. She believed he loved her, but he never flirted with her, never touched her, never spoke of love, and that kiss on the forehead was the first he had given her. It had been a lover's kiss, not a brotherly one, but it was on the forehead, and he had almost fled from it to the dancing.

He gave her no reason to believe he would ever ask her to marry him; but she could not move away from him now. She had given some part of herself to him; and she was afraid of what might happen if she did.

For Polly, all the colour seemed to have gone out of life. She went about her daily tasks, ate when food was in front of her, responded when spoken to, sought sleep at night as a thirsty man seeks water, as a relief from the weariness of every waking hour. She realised only now how much she had been sustained before by the idea that one day she might see him again. Now that all hope was gone, life stretched before her as a desert that must be crossed somehow.

Her dogs and her horse were her greatest friends, because from them she had nothing to conceal. She went out for long rides and walks, and had her favourite places to stop, where she might sit, knees drawn up and hands clasped about them, gazing at the land they had both loved, a dog leaning companionably against her or a horse peacefully cropping the grass at the end of the reins. She did not even cry any more. The reservoir seemed to have dried up. What point was there? Weeping seemed to her something that she had done when she was so young and foolish as to think life would come back into balance if only she wanted it enough. She had grown up now. Life was what it was: hoping and wishing and longing made no difference. All that was left was to get across the desert and sleep.

She read a lot more, thinking that not only did it take her away from herself for a spell, but also that it was what he'd have wanted for her. He had valued literature, and music – she asked for more difficult music and her father, surprised but pleased, was happy to provide it. 'Can't do you any harm at all to be a bit more serious about your playing,' he said. 'The piano is a very nice feminine accomplishment.' He noticed her reading in the evening, too, with approval, disarmed of the thought that she might become too 'bookish' by the satisfactory length of time she spent outdoors on horseback. A nice balance, was what he concluded. His little girl was growing up very sensible.

Only Henrietta, noticing how much quieter Polly had grown over the past year or so, sometimes asked her if she was quite well. And then Polly would smile and say, yes, of course she was, and Henrietta was only too glad to have one thing less to worry about. Maria, who might once have wondered about her, was absorbed with her pregnancy and with trying to make a life for herself and her husband within someone else's house, and no longer observed its inmates with much attention.

Lennie had gone back to America in March, before the dedication ceremony for the War Memorial. Oddly, Polly had not missed him at the time, only since the shock of the news about Küppel had worn off. Now she thought of him fondly as someone who had cared about her, and had been a good companion. He was a faithful correspondent, and if her letters were infrequent, short and careless, she did not value his less.

He wrote at first about his family and what they had all been doing and how they had welcomed him back. Henrietta had read these letters with more attention than had Polly, who did not know any of the protagonists. Lizzie and her husband Ashley had recently left Arizona, where they had been living happily since 1912. Ashley had been in the timber business, but he was now sixty-four, and looking for a less strenuous life. His employer, the Culpepper Shipping Line, had allowed him to return to his old job of shipping agent, based in New York. They had moved back with their daughter Rose, now eleven, and had a large apartment in the Paterno, on Riverside and 116th.

Lennie's immediate destination in New York had been the apartment where his father Patrick, an architect, lived with Lennie's grandmother, Ruth, who had more or less brought Lennie up, since his mother had died at his birth. Ruth's second husband had been English, brought up at Morland Place, and she had wanted all her life to visit England. Now, at seventy-four, she considered she was too old, and would never go.

So you can guess that she questioned me pretty sharply about everything I'd seen, and even rapped my knuckles when I didn't give her enough detail. It was due to Granny Ruth that I was allowed back into the United States at all. Volunteering for a foreign army in 1914 meant losing your citizenship, but Granny Ruth got hold of a senator and bent his ear until he got the law changed. She's a spitfire, is Granny! So I didn't mind a bit describing Morland Place over and over to her. Then Pa invited Lizzie and Ashley over for dinner my second night, and I had it all to do again, while poor Lizzie kept sighing, 'Dear old Morland Place,' and getting moist in the eyes because she'd never see it again. So then Granny Ruth wanted to give *her* a rap, and said pretty sharply that instead of blowing like a sick whale she should get Ashley to book a couple of tickets on a Culpepper liner, because that's what *she*'d do if she was a 'miss' of forty-eight like Lizzie. But I guess it would take a couple of dozen teams of wild horses to get Lizzie on a ship again after the *Titanic* business, and then the *Lusitania*, which hit everybody in the States pretty hard. Sighing is all she's got, poor thing, until she 'gets up her pluck', as Granny says – but I can't see that happening.

Ashley and Lizzie's sons, Martial and Rupert, a few years younger than Lennie, had also been in uniform, and he spoke of them in his letters, to Henrietta's intense interest. She had hoped Martial, who had been with the American Army in France, would be able to visit Morland Place before being shipped home, but he had had no opportunity. Rupert, the younger brother, had still been in basic training when the Armistice had ended his chance of fighting. He had been, Lennie revealed, 'sick' about it, though Lizzie had felt all a mother's relief.

But Martial came back without a scratch on him, so she had nothing to complain about. I met them at a family party at Cousin Nat's house, so there was some lively war talk between Mart and me, lots of do-you-remembers about France, and some glowering looks from poor old Rupert, until Granny intervened and told us to talk about something else, because 'war talk was boring'. Then she talked non-stop for twenty minutes (I timed it) about the Civil War! No-one could interrupt her because of being polite to your elders, and she's everyone's elder. But I caught a gleam in her eye when she looked at me so I guess she was doing it deliberately to make the point. She's a tremendous go! I wish you could meet her.

Martial, he wrote, was thinking of following his dad into the shipping business, partly with the desire one day to travel more – 'I guess he's got a bug in his head now he's been to Europe' – while Rupert was going to go back to university to finish his engineering degree.

As to Rose, she's going to a new school here in Manhattan this fall, a pretty serious school from what Lizzie tells me, because you know what an egg-head Lizzie is, and she's determined Rose will be one too. There's no doubt Rosie is pretty bright, and Ashley thinks she can be anything she sets her mind to, but at present what she wants to be is a vamp! She can charm the gold out of your pockets, and if she ever puts that talent to serious use – look out America! But she is a real peach, pretty as a kitten, and can dance and sing worth hearing, too.

His father, he wrote, was working hard and very much in demand.

Everyone wants to build higher and higher sky-scrapers, now the war is over, and Pa's designs are making a name for him. He's presently working on a new headquarters for the Connecticut Insurance Corporation, which was meant to be the tallest building in New York – the Woolworth Building on Broadway presently holds the title – but between the zoning laws and the construction costs, the 'Con I' is having to cut back on Pa's original and it will end up a mere 700 feet, while the Woolworth is 792! I thought Pa would be peeved but he's philosophical about it. He says the race is only just hotting up and he's bound to have another chance to break the record in a few years' time.

He spoke a bit about the general state of the country. The war seemed to have provided a check to natural American instincts, which had only stimulated them now it had been removed.

Everyone's wild to have a good time, and they manage it despite Prohibition. That's a law more honoured in the breach than the observance! Granny Ruth says you can't stop people getting a drink if they really want one, and Pa says the restaurant and club owners simply pay the police a bribe to look the other way. She says it's a bad law because it's impossible to enforce, and he says it's a bad law because it makes criminals of ordinary people, and ordinary people of criminals. Apart from having a good time, everyone is determined to get on, make something of himself, and make a fortune, and knowing Yankee cussedness, many more of them will make it than you might think back there in the old world.

His father had offered to get him into an office somewhere, either as a trainee draughtsman in his own firm, or some other line, but Lennie had thanked him and told him he wanted to make his own way, and that he had an idea he wanted to pursue: 'Radio is going to be the next big thing, and I believe there'll be a fortune to be made out of it. Granny Ruth agreed with me, and said she was willing to lend me money to get started up.'

Teddy was interested in that part of Lennie's letter, when Henrietta mentioned it to him – Polly always gave her the letters when she had finished them. He had read the accounts in the newspapers back in June of an experimental radio broadcast made under licence by the Marconi Wireless Telegraph Company from their works in Chelmsford. Those people who had a receiver could apparently hear, faintly but clearly, two arias sung by Dame Nellie Melba (her fee was paid by Lord Northcliffe as a stunt for his newspapers). The press reported that the broadcast had been picked up as far away as Persia to the east and Newfoundland to the west. As a result of the excitement drummed up by the Northcliffe press over the event, there had been an upsurge in interest in wireless broadcasting, and a number of young men and boys were eagerly building their own receivers, though as yet there was little to receive.

'Lennie could well be right about its being a big thing,' was Teddy's judgement, 'though whether a fortune can be made of it I don't know.'

Things were further along in America, as they always were, and Lennie explained that there were already several radio 'stations' broadcasting regularly, mostly music and some talks and lectures, and more would soon be starting up. There were thousands of amateur listeners who built their own receivers, wrote to each other, formed clubs and issued magazines. It was quite the new hobby.

But not everyone wants to have to make his own set [he wrote in one of his letters in September], and they can be ticklish difficult to 'tune' – that is, to set just right to pick up the signals. I won't go into details, but you can fiddle around with them

246

for hours to get a signal, and just as you're settling to listen, the thing moves and you lose it again! Now I reckon that there's a market of millions out there, especially among women at home with nothing much to do, for ready-made receivers which you can tune just by turning a knob. I have an idea how to construct the insides, and Pa, bless him, has contributed a very nice design for the outer casing, very modern and go-ahead, which is what a new industry needs. So with Granny Ruth's money I am renting a workshop – part of an empty factory that used to make gun parts during the war. In short, I've started to make radio sets! I've had plenty of orders already. At the moment I'm having to have someone else make the covers, but once things pick up I can expand into another part of the factory and make the whole thing.

Privately, Polly thought making radio receivers was pretty small beer. She had never seen one herself, and did not know anyone else who had, and she could not conceive that Lennie would make a fortune that way. But when Ethel made a similar comment, she found herself springing to Lennie's defence. 'You don't understand how things go on in America,' she said. 'Someone has an idea and goes along with it, and the next thing you know they're millionaires. That's how motor-cars got started.' She had no idea if that were true, but it sounded right, and she was sure Ethel wouldn't know any better. 'Imagine if you had got in at the beginning of motor-cars, what a fortune you'd have made.'

Ethel was unimpressed. 'A radio receiver isn't a motor-car. And making things with your own hands isn't what you'd expect of a gentleman. He ought to have gone into architecture like his father. That's a profession, and quite gentlemanly.'

Polly had tired of the conversation. 'I don't suppose Americans care so much about being gentlemen in the way you mean,' she said. 'Anyway, they're all thousands of miles away and I don't suppose we'll ever see any of them again.' And she walked away. Her own words had reminded her of Küppel. What did any of it matter? Lennie might become a millionaire with her blessing, but Erich Küppel would still be dead.

The slump that had begun the previous December continued to deepen through 1920. Unemployment went on rising, enterprises folded, and among the companies to be forced out of business was that of Tom Sopwith. On the 3rd of September the works were closed for a fortnight, but before more than a few days of the closure had passed, employees were sent a notice, which most of them had already anticipated: 'We much regret we find it impossible to reopen the works as the difficulties caused by restricted credit prevent the company from finding sufficient working capital to carry on the business and it will therefore be wound up.'

There was an article about the closure in *Flight* magazine, and Jack had a letter from Sopwith explaining the situation.

I know you will be as sad as we are that we are going into voluntary liquidation. The end is inevitable and I would prefer to wind things up now, while we are still solvent and can pay the creditors twenty shillings in the pound, than wait to be forced into it and have to let people down. You know we have done everything in our power to keep things going when the aircraft market collapsed. We tried motorcycles and we had a fine design in the ABC, but when the sources of credit dried up we could not keep paying out the wages and overheads, which of course always fall due before the income begins to arrive. We were in competition with American firms already up and running. Furthermore the slump has now hit the motor trade as well, and valuable orders from the Dominions and Scandinavia have been cancelled.

You were in at the birth of Sopwith Aviation, my dear fellow, and I shall always think kindly of your great contribution, and the many plaudits and trophies you helped us win. I hope you will always consider you have a friend in me, and that we shall continue to meet socially in the years to come as we have done. And, naturally, if better days should come and *there* is some way of reviving the good old firm, you will be the first person I come to.

'It's the end of an era,' Helen said, handing back the letter. 'It's a great pity that such a great name should disappear.'

'Yes,' said Molly – they were all at breakfast. 'Even I've heard of the Sopwith Camel and the Sopwith Pup.'

'Things are bad all over,' Jack said. 'Martinsyde has gone into liquidation, and Glendower, and Kingsbury.'

'I hope AT&T are better off,' Helen said. She said it quite calmly, but there was alarm within. De Havilland was personally wealthy but then so was Tom Sopwith. No-one could afford to employ people for whom there was no work – and the London to Paris service was not precisely overwhelmed with passengers.

'We'll survive,' Jack said, meeting her eyes. He was referring not to his employer but to them as a family, as she very well knew. He wiped his lips, threw down his napkin and stood up. 'I must be off.'

When he had gone, Molly looked at her sister. 'He's worried,' she said. They were alone – their mother was having breakfast in bed.

'Everyone's worried,' Helen replied. 'Things are bad everywhere.'

Molly shrugged. 'Except in the civil service. It feels good to know one has a secure job in times like these. Perhaps Jack should try for a job at the Ministry of Defence.'

'It would bore him to distraction. But I'm glad you are gainfully employed, at any rate.'

'Shan't be much longer unless I get off to work,' Molly said, rising to her feet.

'You are enjoying it, aren't you?' Helen asked.

'The job? Yes, of course. It's interesting. Why?'

'It's just that sometimes lately you've seemed – distracted.'

'Oh, it's nothing,' Molly said. Then, 'I'm disappointed, if you want to know. With Emma. When the war ended we planned to live and work together, to do important things. Now she's helling all over London with that set of hers as if she never had a serious thought in her life.'

'I did wonder, when you said you were inviting her to stay, back when she was stood down—'

'Oh, I know. I remember. But I thought I knew her better. She wrote to me all through the war, and I thought we were close. Now she doesn't even reply to my letters.'

250

Helen was sorry that Molly should be hurt. But she said, 'She moves in such different circles, living with Violet. And she's going to be very rich. It's natural for her to seek out people in her own sphere.'

'I know,' said Molly. 'But in the war we *were* the same circle. We were working girls. Now I suppose she'll marry that Gresham chap she's always hanging around with and become a countess and that will be that.'

'She can still do good things when she's a countess. Perhaps more so – it's easier for a married woman of position to influence things than an unmarried girl.'

Molly grinned suddenly. 'Then I'll have to get married, won't I? To a man of position. Find myself a nice, unmarried minister. Pity mine's spoken for.' And with a light-hearted wave she was gone.

Helen remained sunk in thought among the eggshells and crumbs until the strident voice of young Michael Compton proclaiming his woes roused her, and she got up to go and see what she could do to restore peace in nurserydom.

CHAPTER ELEVEN

Even before the ceremonies of Peace Day in 1919 were over, there had been calls for a permanent replacement for the Cenotaph. Thousands had laid flowers and wreaths during the week that the temporary one was in place. It seemed that, in some mysterious way, it embodied the nation's bereavement. Four years of pent-up sorrow had been waiting to be released; sorrow too deep to be assuaged by one ceremony. There must be an annual remembrance centred on a permanent memorial, for as long as memory lasted.

The severe beauty of Lutyens's design had been so universally praised that no other was considered; and no other site would now do. The inconvenience to the traffic in Whitehall had to be set aside, because the place was fixed in the public's mind.

But an additional memorial began to be talked about. The vicar of Margate, the Reverend David Railton MC, had been serving in France as a chaplain in 1916. One day he returned from the line at Armentières to his billet in Erkinghen. There was a small garden to the rear of the house, and he stepped out to take a breath of air. It was dusk, and strangely still – the guns for once were not speaking, the birds had fallen silent, and there was no wind. It was silent except for a murmur of voices from inside the house where some fellow officers were playing cards. At the end of the tiny garden was a grave marked by a cross of white-painted wood, on which had been marked in black letters:

An Unknown British Soldier
(of the Black Watch)

The white cross stood out preternaturally in the fading light, and the eerie quiet made it seem suddenly almost unbearably significant to a man who had helped in the burial of hundreds of soldiers, and knew there were thousands more who had no known grave. When the discussion of the new permanent Cenotaph reached the newspapers, he wrote to the Dean of Westminster to suggest that the body of an 'unknown comrade' might be sent home, to represent all the hundreds of thousands of missing men.

The dean passed on the request to the King, changing only the word 'comrade' to the word 'warrior'. The King was not in favour of the idea, as Venetia's old friend Lord Stamfordham explained to her at tea one day. 'Had it been mooted last year . . .' he said. 'But the King thinks it's too long after the event now. It will be two years since the last shot was fired. He thinks people will regard any funeral now as belated, perhaps insultingly so.'

'Not a case of "better late than never"?' Venetia asked.

'One must always tread very delicately in matters such as this,' said Stamfordham. 'One risks offending as many people as one satisfies.'

'You're not in favour yourself, Arthur,' Venetia suggested.

He raised his hands. 'You know I would never seek to influence the King's mind over a decision of this sort.'

'There never has been a decision of this sort.'

'Precisely. Isn't there something rather – don't you think? – *un-British* about it?'

'One can see the French doing it,' Venetia conceded. 'With great panache and high emotion.'

Stamfordham nodded. 'We are supposed to be made of sterner stuff – stiff upper, and all that. The King thinks it risks reopening the wound, just when time is beginning to heal it.'

But the dean had taken the idea to his heart and, undismayed by Stamfordham's letter, wrote to the prime minister, who guessed it would be a popular move and was immediately for it. Under pressure from the Cabinet, the King reluctantly agreed, and a committee was formed under the foreign secretary, Lord Curzon, to arrange the matter. The burial was to take place immediately after the unveiling of the Cenotaph on the 11th of November 1920.

At Horseguards, Bertie was put in charge of the arrangements. They were delicate and complicated and kept him so busy that Jessie hardly saw him: instead of their cosy dinners together he was surviving on sandwiches brought to his desk while he burned the midnight oil, making lists and writing orders.

It was obviously important that the Unknown Warrior should be truly unknown, to avoid any accusation of favouritism, and Bertie toiled long over the method of choosing. One body was to be exhumed from each of the four main arenas of battle – Ypres, Arras, the Aisne and the Somme – each identifiable only as a British soldier, of regiment unknown. The bodies were transported on the night of the 7th of November to the chapel at St Pol. Each was laid on a stretcher and covered with a Union Flag, and the officer in charge, Brigadier General Wyatt, came in and pointed to one at random. The other three were removed and reburied in the military cemetery.

The chosen body was taken under French military escort to Boulogne where it was placed in a coffin of English oak, with the inscription 'A British Warrior who fell in the Great War 1914–1918'. A sword given by the King from his private collection was fixed to the lid. The coffin crossed the Channel on the 10th on the French destroyer *Verdun*, accompanied by six British destroyers, and at Dover was received with a nineteen-gun salute fired from Dover Castle.

Bertie was there to oversee the ceremonies, as six warrant officers, representing the various services, carried the coffin off the ship while the band played 'Land of Hope and Glory'. Bertie fell in behind it, with the GOC for the south-east and the officer commanding the Dover garrison, the mayor and corporation and other dignitaries, and the coffin was carried, along a route lined by troops, to the station for its journey to Victoria. It was put into the same carriage that had transported Edith Cavell's body; behind it, one passenger carriage was coupled up for Bertie and a detachment of fifteen men, and the train pulled out at 5.50 p.m.

There could not have been anyone in the south-east of England who did not know exactly when the Unknown Warrior's train would be passing, and there were crowds at every station, the women in black, the men bareheaded in the rain, as it steamed through on that wet, dark November night. As the train reached the London suburbs and slowed for the multitude of points, Bertie looked out of the window, down into the rear gardens of the houses, and saw the figures of men, women and children silhouetted in the light falling from their open back doors, standing silently, paying their homage as the great black train hissed past in the rain. He felt then that the right decision had been made: this was speaking to something very deep in the people.

After a journey of three hours the train reached Victoria where it was met by an honour guard drawn from the Grenadiers. A huge crowd of civilians had gathered, and as Bertie stepped down from the train he was struck by the eerie silence, broken only by the sound of muffled weeping. The body was to remain in the carriage overnight, watched over by the Grenadiers and a shifting congregation of civilians paying respect. Bertie was able at last to go home, feeling far more exhausted than the physical demands of the duty could explain, and slept in his own bed for a few short hours. He was up again at five. The procession was to start from Victoria Station at ten o'clock, but he had four good hours of work to do before that.

On the morning of the 11th the streets of Westminster were once again crowded and, as in the previous year, many thousands had waited all night to secure a good place. But the mood was more sober than on Peace Day: that had been a celebration of victory; this was a mourning of the nation's loss. The Unknown Warrior was carried to the Cenotaph on a gun carriage drawn by six black horses, the procession led by massed Guards bands with drums muffled and draped, and bearer party and firing party. On either side of the coffin marched the pallbearers, four admirals, four field marshals, including

Haig and French, three generals, and Air Marshal Trenchard. Troops lined the streets, heads bent and arms reversed. Behind them the crowds stood packed, the men bareheaded, many in tears, and all in silence, so that the only sound was of the wheels and hoofs and the slow-marching feet as the procession passed down Constitution Hill, along the Mall and into Whitehall.

The royal party came out of the Home Office and took position on the dais as Big Ben struck the three-quarters and the head of the procession reached the Cenotaph, which was still shrouded in flags. The gun carriage swung round across the road and stopped in front of the King, who stepped forward and laid a wreath on top of the coffin, while the massed bands played 'O God Our Help in Ages Past', with a choir from Westminster Abbey to lead the singing.

Then as the last drumroll died away Big Ben could be heard giving the chimes that precede the hour. As the first stroke of eleven sounded, the King pressed a button that released the flags, unveiling the Cenotaph, and as the last stroke of eleven died away, a profound silence fell. For two minutes, across the land, in every town and village, across the Empire, and on the seas that Britain commanded, all activity ceased and everyone stood still and silent. Traffic stopped, trains halted, ships hove-to; work ceased in shops and factories, plough teams stood still in fields, farmworkers put down their tools and bared their heads; women went to their back doors to stand with their small children, who did not understand but were hushed by the weight of the emotion they sensed. United in a world of grief, a nation mourned.

At the Cenotaph, at the end of the two minutes the clear, haunting notes of the Last Post rang out, and it was then that many who had bitten their lips so far broke down and wept.

After the laying of official wreaths on the Cenotaph steps, the procession moved off towards Westminster Abbey, and Bertie joined the King and the princes and other dignitaries to march behind the gun carriage.

The service in the Abbey was short but very moving, with prayers, two hymns and a reading before the Committal, which was presided over by the Archbishop of Canterbury. The congregation was made up of men decorated for gallantry, and of women whose husbands or sons were among the missing. Jessie was there, as was Venetia; they sat together and drew comfort from each other's presence, for the proceedings were almost unbearably touching. During the singing of 'Lead Kindly Light', the coffin was lowered into the grave, and the King scattered earth from France over it.

When the last prayers and the blessing had been spoken, there was a pause, and then a drumroll began, very softly at first, growing louder and louder until the ancient stones seemed to tremble with the intensity, then gradually dying away into a breathless silence. It held an instant, and then came the heartbreaking sound of the loveliest of bugle calls, the Long Reveille. And when that in turn had died away, it was over.

Bertie met Venetia and Jessie at the Abbey doors. 'I have one or two more things to do, but I shall be off duty in half an hour,' he told them.

'Come and join us, then,' Venetia said. 'I'm taking Jessie home to luncheon.' She held out her hand to him. 'That was the most beautiful and most touching thing I think the Abbey has ever witnessed.'

He took her hand and pressed it. Like many another that day, he had no words. The ceremony had spoken for them all. He looked at Jessie, and saw she felt the same; the glance that passed between them was enough. The wounds of the war, the immeasurable loss, the sacrifice and long struggle were all laid as tribute in that open grave.

The tomb remained unsealed for six days, during which time vigil was kept around the clock, a man at each corner, volunteers drawn from the three services, with senior officers and princes taking their turn. During that time, over a million people filed past the grave, paying their respects: at times the queue stretched almost to Lambeth Bridge. Their wreaths and flowers they left at the Cenotaph, until the steps were completely hidden and the bank of flowers stretched down the centre of the road on either side.

On the night of the 17th of November the tomb was filled with earth brought from France, and sealed with a temporary stone. A permanent one of black Belgian marble had been ordered, to be unveiled the following year on what would be known from here onwards as Armistice Day.

For Jack, thinking about Armistice Day and the burial of the Unknown Warrior had provided a brief distraction from his own cares. He and Helen had gone to the local war memorial for the remembrance ceremony there. Walking home afterwards, sharing an umbrella against the fine, cold drizzle, he said, 'I'm glad Ned has an official memorial now as well. Frank and Robbie have their names on a gravestone, but poor old Ned . . .'

Helen squeezed his arm. 'Your family paid a big price.'

'No more than many others,' he said.

I'm glad it was you who survived, she thought, but she didn't say it aloud. It was one of those things you couldn't say to a serviceman who had lost friends and brothers. They walked in silence and she cast little looks at his face, bent towards the earth. His hair had turned grey at the temples during his time as a prisoner, and lately she had noticed more threads of grey creeping into the rest. In fact, the hair round the back of his neck which she could see below the rim of his bowler was quite grizzled. She knew he was worried, and she knew also he was unwilling to burden her with his concerns. It was ridiculous – if he couldn't tell his wife, who could he tell? – but men were like that; or at least the right sort of men, who took their responsibilities to their families seriously. Male pride could be maddening, but it was also admirable and touching. She couldn't have loved a man who didn't have it.

Still, she was no fluffy little empty-head, like the girls he had courted before he realised he loved her. Their marriage had been predicated as a marriage of equals. So after a suitable pause she said, 'I know you're worried. Is it the job, or is there something else I should know about?'

He glanced at her warily, and then she saw his shoulders go down in surrender. 'It's the job,' he said. 'I didn't want to bother you with it, but I'm afraid things aren't going well.'

'Not enough passengers?'

He frowned. 'It isn't entirely that. Of course, we could always do with more, but, no, it's the financial crisis. The difficulty of obtaining credit. Every business needs a steady flow of money to keep it going, because so many of your costs arise in advance of your income, and some costs have to be maintained at times when there's *no* income—'

'Yes, I understand that,' Helen said.

'But just now either the banks don't have any money or they aren't willing to lend it.'

'Is that what happened to Handley Page?' Helen asked. The month previously, Handley Page had stopped its air passenger service.

'Yes,' said Jack. 'AT&T is in a slightly stronger position because of the link with Airco, but Airco isn't doing well either. And I hear Instone Air is struggling. It's the times, this damned credit difficulty.'

'So what's going to happen?'

'I don't know. We may have to stop the service. And then – then I'll be out of a job.'

'But the service will start up again? When times are better?'

'Perhaps. I don't know. But I can't expect Geoffrey to keep employing me when there's no work.'

She thought of the terrible months when he had had no job. She didn't want him to suffer like that again. But it was, as he said, the times. There were any number of men out of work, all around the country – only last month there had been a mass march on London of the unemployed. And it was not just the working classes but people like Jack, the managers and professionals, the ex-officers.

'You'll find something else,' she said, trying to sound calm and confident.

'It took me long enough to find this job,' he said starkly. 'Oh, Helen, I've failed you so wretchedly!'

'You've done nothing of the sort. I'm happy and healthy and so are the children. We have a roof over our heads and food on the table—'

She wished she hadn't said it as soon as it was out. Of course, he pounced on it. 'The roof is only over our heads because of your mother. It isn't *our* roof. What sort of security is that?'

She sighed. 'Oh, Jack, we've just come through four years of war. Compared with wondering if I was ever going to see you again, this is a heaven of security. I don't much mind what happens as long as we're together.'

He gave a wry sort of smile. 'But I never wanted to be the sort of husband about whom his wife has to say, "All that matters is that we're together."'

'Well, I'm sorry if it hurts your pride, but I didn't marry you on condition you kept me in furs.'

'Fat chance of that.' He looked sidelong at her. 'I hate seeing you being so stoical and level-headed.'

'Then you should have married a woman who has the vapours when she sees a spider, like that idiotic Miss Fairbrother you were so all-of-a-heap about. I'm the stoical sort.'

'But I don't want you to *have* to be stoical, don't you see? I know you must be worried too, but you keep it hidden, and it makes me feel guilty.'

She shook her head at him, exasperated. 'I'm not going to throw a fit just to make you feel less guilty, when you've no reason to feel guilty in the first place. Whatever comes, we'll face it together, and find a way through. But until we know what's coming, there's no sense in worrying about it. It doesn't help.'

'People don't worry because it helps,' he informed her. But she saw his face was a little brighter. He squeezed her arm against his side. 'You might just *occasionally* pretend to be an ordinary, irrational, fluffy-headed female.'

'Still hankering after Miss Fairbrother? Jack Compton, for shame!'

'No,' he said, looking at her with love. 'I know how bored and lonely I'd have been, married to someone like that. You saved me from a horrible fate. You are my soulmate and dear companion and one true love.'

In marriage such things weren't often said aloud, but it was good that they sometimes were, even if it was in a wet lane under an umbrella on a dark, grey November day with the rain coming on more heavily.

A week later, AT&T suspended its air passenger services, and Jack was out of work again.

At Morland Place, Maria went into labour one miserable, wet November day, and Denis Palgrave paced about the house in anguish, unable to concentrate on anything. It was no use for anyone to tell him that childbirth was a natural process which thousands of women went through every day. Like many a man before him he wished he could take the pain himself, instead of her, and irrationally blamed himself for making her pregnant in the first place.

Henrietta said, 'This isn't her first baby. It all went well before.'

'I expect you think I'm a weak-minded fool,' he said humbly.

'I think you're a perfectly normal husband,' said Henrietta.

The words burst forth. 'I wish I could be in there with her!'

'That would never do,' Henrietta said firmly. 'It wouldn't be decent.'

'Shouldn't a father witness the miracle of birth?'

'It *is* a miracle, of course,' Henrietta allowed, 'but it's also raw and undignified. No woman wants her husband to see her like that. When it's over you can wonder all you like.'

He was silent a moment. And then, 'Why is it taking so long?'

'It hasn't been very long. It just seems that way,' said Henrietta. And he was gone, resuming his restless prowling.

Dr Hasty came, and he stayed, which sent Palgrave into another ferment of worry. He was lurking at the end of the passage when, in the middle of the afternoon, the sound of a baby's cry from behind the closed door pierced his heart, and he found himself trembling, with tears on his cheeks. *Thank God, thank God*, he whispered in his mind. But still the door did not open. There were no more sounds from within, and his mind was peopled with horrors. His legs grew unexpectedly weak, and he subsided gently to the floor and sat on the drugget with his back to the wall.

A maid must have seen him, for shortly afterwards Henrietta appeared, prised him to his feet and led him away. 'It isn't seemly, Father,' she said. 'You have a position in the household.'

'But I must know! I heard a baby's cry, and then nothing! Why haven't they come out?'

'They'll come out in their own time. There are things to do, you know, after the baby's first cry.'

'What things?' he demanded, but she turned her face away. It wasn't something ladies discussed with gentlemen.

'We'll have some tea,' she decreed.

It was the longest hour of his life, he thought, and far, far worse than waiting in the trenches for the whistle. But at last Dr Hasty appeared in the doorway. 'It's a girl,' he said. 'Small, but healthy.'

'And Maria?' Palgrave managed to ask, through dry lips.

Hasty's eyes were tired. He accepted a cup of tea from Henrietta, and sipped it. 'There was a small problem,' he said. 'She lost a lot of blood. Such a haemorrhage is not uncommon in childbirth, so don't worry too much. We stopped it, and she's doing finely now, just feeling tired and weak. She'll need good nursing and good food, and in a week or so she'll be her old self again. You can go up and see her now, but don't agitate her, and don't stay too long. She ought to rest.'

Palgrave was gone almost before the sentence was completed, and ran up the stairs, regardless of dignity. He composed himself outside the closed bedroom door, and knocked lightly. The door was opened by the nurse, who had been brought in to help Nanny Emma with her traditional task. His eyes flew past her to the bed, where Maria was sitting up, propped with pillows, the bedclothes tucked in firmly around her in that way beloved of professional nurses, as if in an attempt to control the chaos of illness with tidiness.

Maria glanced up at him from contemplation of the white bundle in her arms. She looked exhausted, and somehow flattened, as if she would not have the strength to lift her head. She was pale, too, and there were dark shadows under her eyes. But her eyes were shining with an almost holy light, and he thought he had never seen anyone look more beautiful.

'We have a daughter,' were her words to him. 'She's beautiful – look.'

He crossed to her, and as she pulled the shawl aside he looked down into the tiny crumpled face in wonder. 'She seems so small to have caused so much trouble,' he said.

'It wasn't trouble, really,' she said. 'It was much easier than with Martin. And much quicker.'

'It seemed like an eternity to me.'

'It's always harder to be the one waiting. It wasn't so very long.'

'Dr Hasty said – said there was a problem.'

'Nothing to worry about.' She freed a hand from the bundle to take hold of his. 'Don't worry, Denis. I'm all right.'

He sat down on the edge of the bed to be closer to her, and lifted her hand to his lips. 'I was afraid,' he admitted.

'It was my fault,' she said. 'I frightened you with my silly talk. I think I was a little mad towards the end of my pregnancy. All that nonsense about the house wanting a sacrifice. I hope you didn't take it seriously. I don't know what got into me. I'm normally such a sensible person.'

'Well, I understand women in that condition do have strange fancies sometimes,' he said awkwardly.

She smiled. 'Strange fancies! Yes, that sums it up. I'm so sorry, Denis, for what I must have put you through.'

'Oh, my darling!'

The nurse coughed, and Nanny Emma drifted up. 'Now, Father, she needs to rest. She's bin working hard. Best you pop off, now, and leave her to me. You can come back this evening, if she's awake.'

He stood up, and leaned down to kiss his wife. 'I'll leave you to your gentle tyrants. God bless you, my love. And our dear little baby. I can't tell you how happy you've made me.'

It was a joyful household that evening. Teddy ordered champagne, and there was a fine dinner: it struck Palgrave as slightly odd that the objects of the celebration – Maria and the baby – were the ones not present. Word had come down from the lying-in chamber that she had taken nourishment and slept, and was doing well. Everyone had seen the baby, still determinedly sleeping, and pronounced her beautiful. Henrietta had said she looked very like Maria but had her father's mouth and chin; Palgrave, for all his puzzled studying of the little creased face, could not see the justification for that. She looked like any newborn baby to him, and it disconcerted him a little to think that he could not reliably have identified her in a room full of infants.

While they dined, a supper of good and strengthening food had gone up on a tray, and the report came back that Maria had eaten everything and would be strong enough for a short visit from her husband before she settled down for the night. He found her a little less pale, but very sleepy, and stayed only a few moments, to kiss her and assure her the baby was everything he could ever have hoped for, before leaving her.

The next morning when he was admitted to the chamber he found her sitting up and looking much stronger, and he was able to sit beside her bed and have a proper conversation with her.

'How are you feeling?' he asked.

'Tired,' she said.

'You've lost blood,' he said. 'You need to eat and rest to make it up.'

'I know. Nanny Emma tells me so every few minutes. I asked for a glass of milk and she managed to beat an egg into it without telling me.'

'What was it like?'

'Slimy. I don't recommend it. But apparently eggs and milk and nourishing broth must be consumed every two hours. And calf's foot jelly. Invalid slops.'

'I shall make them send you up a beefsteak for luncheon,' he said.

She smiled. 'How is my baby? I'm longing to be able to feed her. I wish they would let me have her with me.'

'They will tomorrow. Dr Hasty said you needed to rest today without being disturbed when she cries.'

'I'm just afraid that once she disappears into the nursery they won't give her back.'

He looked contrite. 'I've been thinking,' he said, 'how wrong I was to make you live here, when you wanted a home of your own.'

'You didn't "make me",' she said. 'It was my decision, if you remember.'

He shook his head. 'You knew I wanted to stay here. But I was wrong. We ought to have a home of our own, and you ought to be able to have your children with you the way you wanted.'

'How nice it sounds – "my children".'

'As soon as you're back to normal, I'm going to ask Mr Morland for that house again, and this time we *will* move in, and live like other people.'

'We'll never be quite like other people,' Maria said, but her eyes shone. 'Do you mean it? We'll really have a home of our own?'

'We really will.'

She sighed with pleasure; then said, 'But you must be sure. I don't mind living here – really I don't. All that silliness is past now. It does make sense for you to be here all the time.'

He was firm. 'I'm quite sure. You and I and our two little ones are going to have a home.'

'Thank you,' was all she said, but her heart was in her face. Then she said, 'Can I see Martin today? How did he take to his new sister?'

'He was fascinated by her. He asked was she really *his* sister, as Harriet was John's, and when I said she was, he marched about the room sticking his chest out and chanting, "I've got a sister too. I've got a sister too."'

'I wish I'd seen it,' Maria said. 'I feel I'm missing everything, shut away in here.'

'The nurse wants you to be kept quiet, so you can rest.'

'But I don't want to be quiet. Denis, do come and visit me often, won't you? And send other people in to see me. Never mind what the nurse says.'

'I shall take my life into my hands, defying her. But I'll see what can be done.'

The next morning she seemed a little less well, and Nanny Emma told Palgrave sternly that that was what came of too much excitement in defiance of medical orders. 'She's to have a quiet day today. No visitors but you – and not too much of you, either. Nanny knows best.'

Palgrave, noting that the dark shadows under Maria's eyes were back, agreed rather guiltily. He sat quietly with her, holding her hand. She told him she had tried to feed the baby that morning, but had no milk.

'Nanny Emma said that's to be expected, because you had lost blood. She says the milk will come in in time.' He was feeling much less self-conscious about talking of such things. It had been a short and intensive course for him.

'Yes, she told me that, too. And said it was important that I suckle her even if I don't have anything to give, so as to stimulate production.' She made a face. 'It sounds like an industrial process.'

She seemed rather listless. He said, 'How are you feeling?'

She paused, thinking. 'A strange sort of feeling. Like pressure, here.' She laid her hand against her diaphragm, under her breasts.

'A pain?' he asked, trying not to sound alarmed.

'Not a pain. Just – as I said, like pressure inside. It's uncomfortable.'

'I'll mention it to Dr Hasty when he comes. He's coming this morning, isn't he?'

'Yes, later on.' She smiled faintly. 'I'm not an urgent case now, you know.'

'By the way, as the baby's priest as well as her father, I have to think about a christening. We have to decide on a name. I did have one idea, but it's rather fanciful.

'Tell me,' she said, but she closed her eyes wearily. He thought he should go, but after a moment she opened her eyes again and said, 'Tell me. What is it?'

'Laura.'

'From Laura and Petrarch?'

'Not really. I just like the sound of it. Also laurel is

270

what crowns the victor, and she is the crown of my achievements.'

'Laurel,' she said. 'That's nice.' She seemed suddenly exhausted.

'I'd better let you rest,' he said. 'You mustn't try to do too much all at once.'

'I feel . . .' Her voice trailed off.

He saw she was pale. He pressed her hand with alarm. 'What is it?'

'Dizzy,' she said. Her head sank back in the pillows.

'I'll get Nanny Emma,' he said, starting up. 'And the nurse.'

Her collapse was rapid. Dr Hasty was sent for at once, but by the time he came she was dusky-pale with a rapid, fluttering pulse, her hands damp, unable to speak. After an interminable time the doctor came out to where not only Palgrave but Henrietta and Mary Tomlinson were waiting in the hall for news. 'Has she complained of any pains?' he asked them abruptly.

'Not of pains,' Palgrave said, 'but of a feeling of pressure, *here*. Was that anything important?'

'I don't know. In the diaphragm? If it had been in the abdomen, now . . . Her pulse is low and erratic and her blood pressure is falling. I'm afraid from the symptoms there may be internal bleeding.'

Palgrave felt himself grow very cold, and the world seemed suddenly a long way off, as if he were viewing it through the wrong end of a telescope. 'What can you do?'

Hasty looked unhappy, which was his answer. 'There is very little I can do. I have bound the abdomen and propped up her feet. She is strong and young. If there is bleeding, it may stop of its own accord. The body's powers of healing are immense.'

Palgrave knew it was true. He had seen for himself the things men survived on the battlefield. But this was not a soldier, this was Maria.

He went back in to see her a few minutes later. They had taken away the pillows so that she was lying flat, and she seemed hardly to make a shape under the bedclothes. Her face looked waxy, and the flesh seemed to have shrunk back from it. He took her hand, and it was cold. 'Maria?' he said. She opened her eyes, but it seemed an effort, as though her eyelids were heavy. It was like rolling back a stone from a tomb. No, he mustn't think of tombs!

She looked at him.

'Maria, darling, how are you feeling?'

'Denis,' she whispered. Her lips were dry. She began to yawn, and something inside him broke. He had seen how men bleeding to death will yawn like tired children.

'You must get better,' he heard himself saying. 'You must get well and strong. Please try. For me and for the baby. You must get strong again. Your baby needs you. *I* need you.'

She yawned again, and then her eyes inexorably closed as if it were simply too hard to keep them open. The stone rolling back over the tomb . . .

'Maria!' he said again, pressing her cold hand urgently.

The doctor touched his shoulder and he made way for him. He stood back, watching as Hasty held the wrist in one hand and his watch in the other, then bent forward and placed his stethoscope to Maria's chest, moving it here and there. He placed two fingers against her neck, and felt the wrist again. And then he turned, sought

Palgrave's eyes from among those watching him, and shook his head. 'I'm sorry.'

He heard Nanny Emma behind him begin to weep, and the sound was a distraction. 'She can't be,' he said. 'Not so soon. Not like that. Not so quickly.'

'I'm sorry,' Hasty said again.

'But she looked at me,' he heard himself say. 'She was *there*. She looked at me.'

Henrietta was beside him, and her warm, dry hand slipped into his. 'Come away,' she said.

'No, I need to be here,' he said.

'You need to fetch your things,' she said. 'You need to give her the last rites. While she's still close.'

He thought then that horror could go no further. Maria was his wife, and he was being told he must consign her to death while her last breath was still in the air. While she was still warm, and might wake. The doctor might be wrong. Surely her eyes would open again. She must still be there. If he left the room, the chance would be lost. '*Do something!*' he cried out to Hasty.

Henrietta's small thin hand was insistent. 'Come. It's your duty,' she said.

He cried, 'Oh, God!' and it was appeal and protest and desperation all in one.

His rigid control held long enough to conduct the funeral service, though as the coffin was lowered into the crypt Henrietta could see him shaking so hard she was afraid he might fall down. Maria's mother had been too ill to come, so it was her family by marriage who said goodbye to her. All the women wept, and Teddy looked as though he might break down any moment. He had discovered at once how large a hole she had left in his life. In her quiet way she had implanted herself in his heart all unknowing.

But after the funeral Palgrave's disintegration was rapid. He was silent and withdrawn for the rest of the day, and that night, for the first time in a year, had one of his screaming nightmares. Then began a period of terrible strain for the household. There were the fits of helpless weeping; the long periods of silent inaction, staring at nothing, seeming not to hear when he was spoken to; the nightmares and the sleepwalking. He no longer carried out any of his duties: the children went untaught and the altar unserved. He would not eat, and grew gaunt; spent hours shut up in his room, and emerged unshaven, dazed-looking, hardly seeming to know what day it was. His speech was often stammering and disconnected, and he trembled uncontrollably; sometimes he raved, seeing things that weren't there, imagining himself back in the trenches.

Teddy said hopefully that he would come to himself after a period of mourning, that it had been a terrible shock, that he had been very much in love with poor Maria. Henrietta found a wet-nurse for the baby, and looked on in anguish, helpless to reach the tortured man.

The climax came when, sleepwalking, he found his way out of doors during the night and was found by the post boy the next morning in his pyjamas, soaked to the skin and shivering, wandering on the path in front of the house. Daniel, the footman, brought him in, took him upstairs and attended to him in a calm and efficient way, proving his worth to Henrietta. She met him in the Great Hall when he came back downstairs.

'How is he?'

'Sleeping,' said Daniel. 'I took the liberty of obtaining a few drops of laudanum from Mrs Tomlinson, as he was extremely agitated.'

'We'll be lucky if we don't have pneumonia next,' Henrietta said. 'What was his state of mind?'

'Confused,' Daniel said. 'He didn't know where he was. Thought he was back at the Front. I've seen shell-shock cases before, madam, and this is a bad one.'

They exchanged a long look, and then Henrietta said, 'We can't go on like this.'

'No, madam. There are the children to consider.'

'Yes. Yes, they must be upset – frightened.' Henrietta came to a decision. 'I shall speak to the master.'

Teddy was adamant at first. 'We don't send our servants away when they're sick. We'll look after him here. He'll come out of it by and by.'

'It's not like nursing a fever,' Henrietta said. 'We don't have the knowledge or skill to nurse mental cases like this.'

'Mental case!' Teddy protested. 'He's not a madman.'

'Well, just at present, Ted, he is.'

Teddy looked horrified. 'You can't mean you want to send him away to a lunatic asylum?'

'No, of course not. But there must be hospitals where they treat this sort of thing – isn't it called war neurosis? I'm sure I read about it somewhere.'

'They do terrible things to them in those places – starve them and put electric currents through them.'

'Not all of them, surely. Wasn't there one in a spa somewhere, where they gave them sitz baths and massage and such things?'

'I don't know,' Teddy said. 'I don't like it, Hen. He's our responsibility. We can't just shrug him off.'

'I don't mean that we should. But we don't know what to do for him. And who knows what might happen next?' She met her brother's eyes. 'I'm afraid he might try to kill himself. I've read that they do. You wouldn't want that on your conscience, would you?'

Teddy shook his head in misery. 'He's practically family,' he said.

'He needs proper treatment,' Henrietta said and, feeling she had softened him up enough, added, 'Why don't you consult Colonel Bassett about it?'

Teddy took to the idea. 'Hound' Bassett was his mentor on all matters military, and it was he who had first introduced Palgrave to Morland Place. 'Yes, old Hound ought to know what's best to do,' he said.

The Hound was gravely sympathetic. 'I'm afraid with these cases there's always the chance of a relapse,' he said. 'Poor fellow, what a terrible thing to lose his wife like that. Fairly knocks a feller for six. It was the shock brought on this other business, depend upon it.'

'Yes, but what's to be done? We feel he ought to have proper nursing, by people who know what they're doing, but I won't have him treated harshly – electric shocks and ice baths and suchlike.'

'No, no, I quite understand. There was a lot of that sort of thing during the war, when shell-shock wasn't properly understood, and the main thing was to get the chaps back to the Front as soon as possible. But it's different now. There are all sorts of new treatments. Probably all he needs is a rest cure – peace and quiet and good food and so on.'

'He came to us for a rest cure in the first place,' Teddy said helplessly.

'Hmm. Yes. So he did,' said the Hound, thoughtfully. 'Well, you must let me look into it. I'll ask a few of the chaps and see what's best to be done.'

'But quickly, if you don't mind. I'm afraid for what he might do – you understand?'

Hound protested. 'Oh, my dear fellow, surely not. He's a padre, after all. But I shall certainly make all haste in my enquiries.'

He was as good as his word, and the following day telephoned Teddy and asked him to come over.

'There is a place, a sanatorium for ex-officers suffering from war neurosis, near Northallerton, which I think will fit the bill.' He read the question on Teddy's lips, and said, 'Now don't be anxious, my dear fellow. I put some pretty stern questions and it seems they treat them very kindly there. It's a manor house with a farm attached, and the chaps get lots of nourishing food, and do work on the farm – supposed to help a great deal, healthy labour in the open air, gettin' in touch with nature and so forth.' He coughed to cover his unfamiliarity with such concepts. 'They do other sorts of indoor work, as well – therapy, I think they call it – makin' things, and paintin' and so on. And they have fatherly chats with a medico about what brought the shock on in the first place. They even hypnotise them and talk them out of it while they're "under". Sounds like a lot of mumbo-jumbo, I know, but apparently it works. This place has had very good results – chaps who were quiverin' jellies, or completely deaf and dumb, getting back into the swim and holdin' down jobs.'

'It sounds like the sort of place Henrietta was thinking about,' Teddy said cautiously.

'Only drawback,' said Hound, 'a bit expensive. But knowin' how fond you are of the feller . . .'

'Expense is no object,' Teddy said firmly. 'I just want what's best for him.'

Everything was quickly arranged, and three days later the bewildered man, his thin face set and grim, was driven away in Teddy's big motor, with the excellent Daniel beside him, charged by Teddy to see him safe there and by Henrietta to comfort him. Teddy saw Palgrave settled in the car and closed the door gently himself. 'I'll leave the window down a bit,' he said. 'The fresh air will do you good.' Palgrave looked at him through the gap; his eyes reminded Teddy of an animal caught in a leg trap. His own eyes filled with tears. 'As soon as you're well, you must come back. I'll keep your position here for you. And we'll take care of the baby, don't worry. She'll be safe with us.'

There was no change in Palgrave's expression, but his lips moved. The motor drew away.

'What did he say?' Henrietta asked, as Teddy turned back towards the great door.

'I think he said "laurel". Or perhaps it was "Laura".'

'It must have been Laura,' Henrietta said. 'That must be the name he chose for the baby. It's unusual.'

'It's pretty. I like it. She ought to be baptised,' Teddy said, his face brightening for the first time in days, 'and if we have a name for her, we can have a proper christening. Poor little mite, practically an orphan – she ought to have everything a Morland or a Compton would have. A cake, a party.' He linked arms with his sister and they walked into the house together. 'You'll need to get the christening robe out and have it laundered. And presents – she ought to have presents.'

It was his way of coping. Henrietta felt his arm trembling slightly under hers, and knew how upset he was.

She wondered who was going to teach the children, and who was going to do Maria's secretarial work, and for her own sake, who was going to preside in the chapel. But for the moment she put those questions aside and went along with Teddy's plans to welcome Laura into the family, both of the Church and the Morlands. Time enough to worry about other things later.

CHAPTER TWELVE

The young people kept on dancing. There was a ball somewhere almost every night of the week. And if ever there was a blank, there were tea dances at the Savoy or the Café de Paris in the early evening, and public dances at the Grafton Galleries, which were considered respectable enough for a young woman to attend unchaperoned: though there was a Negro orchestra and the modern jazz music was played, gloves were worn when dancing, and it closed at 2 a.m. And one or two of the young married set, like the Verneys, would sometimes hold an impromptu dance, which needed nothing more than a few telephone calls, a gramophone and a rolled-back carpet.

With the end of summer had come an end to tennis, boating and motoring for pleasure, but winter still had its attractions, and parties were got up for steeplechases, university rugby matches, horse sales and ice skating. The important thing was to keep moving, to be active every waking hour, for that way memory could be kept under control. No-one wanted to think about the past. The past was grim and painful, and everything about it reeked of the failures of previous generations, with their hidebound ideas and ridiculous rules. One had only to look at how one's parents kept talking about the war, when they were the very generation who had caused it. This was a new age, and it belonged to the young. Never again, was the thought at the back of their minds, *never again*, and it applied to almost everything.

Emma had as much to forget as anyone. She danced for her life, and as often as not it was with Peter Gresham, so that hostesses began to invite him for her instead of Kit Westhoven, and the newspapers and magazines began to print photographs of them arriving at places together. The subtle implication was that a marriage would be announced, somewhere down the line, but he had not proposed to her, nor had he kissed her since that one time on the terrace. She *thought* he loved her, but it was implied rather than stated. She wondered sometimes what it would be like to have him make love to her. She had hardly ever been kissed. Fenniman, her fiancé, had had few chances; and Wentworth, whom she had thought she might come to love in the same way, had kissed her only once, at a service dance in an aircraft hangar in France. He had been killed before it could come to anything. But she had felt the stirrings of something that made her believe she could be very passionate if the circumstances ever allowed. In fact, she was almost afraid of the thought of it: she suspected she might burn up like paper if she ever let go.

But she did not dwell on such dangerous thoughts. She was happy in Gresham's company, and just as she would not think about the past, she preferred on the whole not to think about the future. The present was all one could be sure of, and the important thing was to keep busy and occupied.

Winter weekends brought shooting parties. Emma could shoot a bit, having learned at Morland Place when

Uncle Teddy was worried about a German invasion. She was not very accurate, unless the target stood still, and indeed she had no desire to kill birds even if she could have; but at least she knew how to handle a gun, and did not shriek and clap her hands over her ears every time it was fired, like some females. Gresham liked this difference in her and, on one memorable weekend at the very respectable Tonbridges', had scandalised the older company by announcing she would act as his loader. It could not be said that she particularly enjoyed it as a way to pass the day, but it was fun to shock people, and to stand out from the crowd, and it was nice that Gresham was proud of her.

When hunting started, however, she did come into her own, because she could ride well, and looked good on a horse. She was able to take an active part, while the more delicate urban flowers lounged indoors by the fire, yawning, until the hunting party came back. She loved the long gallops, the all-out stretch of nerve and sinew, the mind-emptying concentration. Returning tired out in the pink winter dusk, she sometimes thought that if one could hunt every day, one would never be prey to unwelcome thoughts.

Peter Gresham hunted like a madman, and went to every weekend with three hunters and two grooms to lead the spares, so that he was quite an expensive guest to accommodate. His popularity ensured this was never a bar to invitation. Emma, on a borrowed horse, could not keep up with him when hounds were running, especially when he took his own line. People often commented that he would break his neck one day, but if they said it in his presence he would laugh and say, 'There are worse ways of going west.'

After the hunt and the bath there would come the delicious, languorous feeling of well-being, of every part of the mind and body having been well worked, so that it felt tuned up like a violin, ready to play. On hunting evenings Gresham was always especially brilliant, and Emma felt in sympathy with him, and occasionally surprised herself by her own quickness. After dinner on hunting evenings there would always be dancing, and generally champagne. The young set drank a lot of champagne. Wine in general was only drunk with meals, and sherry and Madeira seemed heavy and old-fashioned and only suited to one's parents. Men might drink whisky but it was not really acceptable for women to drink spirits. But champagne one could drink at any time, and its lightness and fizziness seemed to sum up the mood of the younger set perfectly. Emma was glad to discover that one became hardened, so that several glasses did not result in that swimmy-headed feeling she disliked. Even so, she was always careful not to drink too much. Drunkenness in men bored her, while she thought a tipsy woman a disgusting sight. Fortunately Peter Gresham seemed to have an extremely hard head. Though the other Cadets could get riotous and some of the men had had to be helped to bed on occasion, she never saw him the worse for wear.

In December 1920 she was invited by the Gresham parents to a hunting weekend at Kimcote Hall, Peter promising her his mother could mount her. Lady Castleford was a keen huntswoman and had in her string a useful gelding she could spare.

'The parents are giving the Fernie a lawner on Saturday, so you must come down on Friday in time for dinner,' Peter said. He arranged to pick her up at

St James's Square and drive her down in his sports tourer, with her maid and his man, Spalding, following in his second car with the luggage while the grooms took his horses by train. They didn't talk much on the way down. Peter drove very fast – the second car was soon left behind – but unlike some men she had had the misfortune to be driven by, he concentrated on the task in hand, which made her feel a great deal less nervous. He watched the road ahead, and she was happy to glance from time to time at his stern profile, and his lean, capable hands on the wheel. Though they didn't speak, she felt he was aware of her presence and was happy to have her beside him. In fact, he said at one point, 'Thank God you don't chatter pointlessly like some girls.' It was rather a terse compliment, but in the absence of many others she cherished it.

On arrival at Kimcote she thought Lady Castleford greeted her with a little more warmth – she at least acknowledged that they had met before – but there was still a thoughtfulness in the way she regarded her, almost a calculation. To her surprise, Lord Castleford appeared in the hall – although it seemed that he was on the way from somewhere to somewhere else. He stopped when he saw the arrivals, and then changed his mind about continuing on his path and came over to shake Peter's hand. 'You again,' he said. 'Is it Saturday already?'

'No, Father, Friday. Lawn meet tomorrow.'

'Here? Good God! Why doesn't someone tell me these things? You're not looking well. Too much jazzing and late nights. Do you good to get out on a horse. Fresh air, so on.' He looked at Emma with utter indifference, which transformed into a considering frown. 'I know you. You've been here before.'

'Yes, Father. This is Miss Weston,' Peter said patiently.

'Weston? The MP's daughter? Tommy Weston's girl?' He looked at his wife. 'Is that the one you—'

'Weren't you on your way somewhere?' Lady Castleford intervened firmly. 'Peter and Miss Weston need their baths. We shall all meet at dinner.'

The earl harrumphed and shambled off obediently, and Emma took her red face up to her room. At dinner that evening she and Peter and a couple of cousins were the only ones staying – the rest of the guests were local people invited for the evening – which made it feel rather intimate, as if she were someone special. Talk around the table was dull at first – on the progress, or lack of it, of the League of Nations in Geneva, and the continuing troubles in Ireland – but it got more interesting when one of the cousins mentioned the Prince of Wales, and the dam burst. He had returned from Australia in September and was to be based at home for a whole year, and everything he did was of palpitating interest to the general public and the newspapers. The cousin was inclined to be wistful, as the prince was hunting in Leicestershire that very weekend but going out with the Quorn – a near miss that the cousin seemed inclined almost to resent.

'Well, I hope he dresses properly for it,' was the limit of the earl's interest. 'Dresses like a damned bounder sometimes.'

'Really, dear,' Lady Castleford said, in mild reproof.

'Saw a photograph of him in Biarritz wearing the most frightful checked cap. Looked exactly like a bookie's runner.'

But the cousins and a young couple from the neighbourhood thought the prince was 'romantic' and 'delightful' and his informality and readiness to mix with 'the people' were desirable traits. Then somebody happened to mention that the Dudley Wards were also staying that weekend with the same hostess, and Lady Castleford was obliged to change the subject. It might be well known in their circle that Mrs Dudley Ward was the prince's intimate companion, but that was no reason to discuss such things around the dinner table. It did not stop it being discussed after dinner, in low voices among the young people. What everyone wanted to know was *were they actually lovers?* Though it was not possible to ask the question direct, the topic was hinted at. On the one hand, the prince was – it was to be presumed – a normal young man with a young man's appetites. On the other hand, he was friendly with both Dudley Wards and the husband was present more often than not when they were staying in the same house together.

And someone said, 'I just can't imagine it, somehow – he's so small and delicate, almost like a fairy prince. One can't imagine him doing anything – well, you know – *physical.*'

And someone else said, 'But Freda Dudley Ward is so beautiful and elegant and, besides, why would he be so keen on her if it was a platonic relationship? He can have that with anyone.'

The youngest someone asked, 'What does *platonic* mean?' and was told briskly by her elder sister, 'Never mind.'

Peter said, 'It's a philosophical term, pertaining to Plato. And talking of philosophers, have you heard about that Austrian fellow, Dr Freud, and his theory of the psyche?'

'Is that something to do with bicycles?' one of the cousins asked.

'No, it's a theory about the way the mind works,' Peter said, and Emma, glancing at him, saw from his expression that he was teasing. 'He says you can cure anyone of anything by making them talk about it.'

'I've read about that,' said a neighbour. 'They call it the talking cure. My mother knows someone whose brother did it.'

'What did they cure him of?'

'Can't remember, but I know that's what it was. You lie down and talk about your childhood, and when you get up, you're cured.'

'Why your childhood?'

'Dunno. Apparently that's the way it works. This Freud fellow asks you questions about your childhood and pop! All your troubles go away.'

'Sounds like a good party trick.'

Someone giggled. 'I say, I'd like to try that.'

'Too thrilling!' said someone else. 'Can't we have a go at it? I'm all for something new.'

'Oh yes! Bags me be the one asking the questions. I can think of a few I've always wanted to ask you, Betty.'

'Beast! I'm not doing it if you're doing the asking. But it sounds fun. Oh Peter, can we?'

'Not here, not now,' Peter said, looking amused. 'Can you imagine what my mother will say if you lie down on the sofa for no apparent reason?'

'Next week, at the Orpingtons',' someone suggested. 'They won't mind. Better than charades.'

'Oh, are you going? So am I.'

'So am I. I bet Winnifred Orpington will be game for it.'

'She's a game girl. She's going to have a nigger band for the dancing. Real American ones.'

287

'No!'

'I heard it from a *very* reliable source.'

It was all fascinating to Emma.

The lawn meet the next morning was very elegant, and there were a lot of frighteningly smart women among the hunting party. The hunt breakfast was lavish, served as a buffet in the Great Hall, and Emma soon realised that the presence of so many young and handsome females was a direct tribute to Peter. She was glad her habit was new, and that her maid had a good hand with hair. Lady Castleford was perhaps the most elegant of them all, and Emma felt she ran a critical eye over her as she led her outside to introduce her to her horse. It was a nice bay with a kind look, broad in the chest and with powerful hocks – the sort of horse you felt you could trust to take you over everything.

'He'll take care of you,' Lady Castleford said, as her own horse, a lean grey, was led up. 'Keep behind me, as you don't know the country. Or if you lose me – let me see . . .' She pointed out one or two other stalwarts among the hunting ladies. 'They won't lead you wrong.'

It was a damp, misty day, with mild airs from the south-west – just right for scent. The earl did not hunt any more, but he knew what was required, and was keen to give the Fernie a good day, so he had had earths stopped and wire taken down, and lane crossings packed with tan. After a couple of blank draws, hounds found in a coppice on a slight hill, a wily old dog-fox that led them a dance from one wood to another, and then gave them a grand run almost to Market Harborough before giving them the slip among some pigsties. By then it was after two, and given their

288

distance from home, it was decided to call it a day, say good night and hack home.

Emma's room was in the family part of the house – another telling point, she thought; or at least Spencer thought, and made her opinion known. Emma was not familiar with that wing, and when she left her room to go down to dinner, she somehow turned the wrong way and couldn't find the staircase she was looking for. She turned a corner, saw what seemed to be another flight at the end of a corridor, and went towards it. A door halfway down was partly open, and through it she heard the sounds of voices. Another step, and she recognised them as Peter's and his mother's, and she froze on the spot as she realised, to her chagrin, that they were arguing.

'You most certainly *will* come,' Lady Castleford was saying, her voice cold. 'It is expected.'

'To hell with your "expected",' Peter retorted hotly.

'Moderate your language, please. Everyone knows you are down here this weekend. If you don't go to church they will feel insulted. To say nothing of the insult to the Almighty.'

'To hell with your "Almighty", as well!'

'Do not dare to blaspheme in front of me!'

'Blaspheme? How is it blasphemy if I don't believe in your God – and I don't?'

'I won't have you speak like that, Peter. At the very least you should show respect—'

'Respect to whom?' he interrupted furiously. 'To your church – whose bishops I saw with my own eyes blessing tanks and guns that were going to blow men to pieces?'

'Not men – Germans.'

'Germans who believe in the very same God, with

great sincerity – and no doubt had their tanks blessed in just the same way. Don't you *see* how ridiculous it is? A vile charade of monsters and death's heads. Your pretty parish church built on the rotting bones of lies. Well, I won't be a part of it.'

Emma had already begun to retreat softly backwards, distressed to be a witness to such an exchange. But Peter came out from the open door like something catapulted, slamming it behind him, and had taken two steps towards her before, in his fury, he even registered her presence. He stopped dead.

'I'm so sorry,' Emma stammered, her face burning. 'I got lost going down . . .'

Without speaking he took hold of her upper arm and swung her round, his face grim and his mouth set. He marched her back the way she had come.

'Peter, I'm sorry,' she tried again. His fingers were hurting her arm, and she was afraid of tripping on her long skirt. 'I didn't mean to hear—'

'It doesn't matter,' he said tersely. 'The whole world knows what a disappointment I am to my parents.'

'I'm sure you're not,' she protested.

'It's all right. They are a disappointment to me, too.' He pushed through a door and they emerged onto a wide landing with a massive equestrian painting on the wall, which she recognised. 'Here, this is the main stair-case. You know where you are now.'

He released her arm and seemed to be turning away, and she said, 'Aren't you coming down?' He was fully dressed in evening clothes, as if he had called on his mother on his way. 'The bell has gone.'

He looked blank for a moment, and then said, 'Yes, I – I was on my way, but I need to compose myself. I'll follow in a few moments.' He met her eyes. 'I know I needn't ask you to forget what you heard.'

'I should never mention it to anyone,' she said, rather shocked at the idea.

'I know you wouldn't but – I wish you would forget it, too.' He laughed nervously. 'I find that I care rather a lot how I stand in your estimation.'

'Nothing has changed,' she assured him. 'But, Peter—'

'"But, Peter"?' he mimicked her. 'Are you going to remonstrate with me now?'

'I should not be so impertinent,' she said quietly, and he looked ashamed. 'I only wanted to say that, if it would make your parents happy, why not go to church?'

'That would be hypocrisy,' he said.

'Not hypocrisy,' she countered. 'Just kindness.' She saw him take pause at the word. 'Don't you feel there ought to be more kindness in the world? We've seen enough of the other thing.'

'It's a matter of principle,' he said, rather stiffly.

'Is it? If you don't believe in God, how does it matter? Is it worth so much unhappiness?'

'Thank you for your opinion,' he said with an ironic bow. 'And now, if you will excuse me . . .' He left her, going back through the door into the private passage.

Emma went downstairs, feeling miserable. She had offended him! After saying in effect that it was none of her business – which it was not, there being no engagement between them – she had gone ahead and offered him advice he had not requested. She walked slowly down, thinking that here was an end to their closeness, that he would not seek her out now. His parents would be glad, she supposed, that he was not, after all, going to be marrying a nobody.

★　★　★

Peter was wildly gay that evening, in his most flashing form. Perhaps it was only Emma who felt there was something brittle in his mood. His mother behaved exactly as she always did – nothing marred the perfect veneer she maintained in public. After dinner, when the cigar smokers had withdrawn, they all played charades. Peter chose Emma to be on his team, but he did not speak a personal word to her all night, and she felt he was not looking at her either, his eyes sliding over her shoulder when he was obliged to address her. After the charades, someone suggested dancing, but Peter said it was late and he was exhausted after the hunt and had rather a headache, and asked to be excused. 'But don't let me spoil your fun. I'm going to go up to bed, but please have the gramophone brought in if you like.'

But Lady Castleford said, 'I think we would all benefit from an early night,' and that was that. It was not, in fact, so very early – it was after midnight – but the younger set would have danced for a good few hours yet. Peter bowed and quickly made his exit, leaving Emma feeling heart-sore. She thought that perhaps he had refused dancing because he didn't want to dance with her, or be seen not to be dancing with her.

As they all followed in Peter's wake, Lady Castleford said in her clear, carrying voice, 'A quarter to eleven *sharp* in the hall for everyone who is coming to church tomorrow. Romney will have prayer books for those who have forgotten to pack one.'

Spencer woke her in the morning, drawing her curtains and saying, 'It's a lovely morning, miss. I'll run your bath while you eat your breakfast.' At Kimcote, since the war, it was the custom for breakfast to be served on a tray in the room on the morning after a hunting day. The reason given was that everyone was tired and needed to lie in, but in fact, as Spencer had told Emma the previous day, having gleaned it from the servants' hall, it was really because trays were less trouble to the servants than having to prepare the dining room and lay the table.

Emma didn't mind. She didn't really want to face anyone after the unfortunate eavesdropping incident. She had slept badly, and sat up, rather heavy-eyed, as Spencer put the tray across her lap and then pottered about. Her room, because it was in the family wing, had its own bathroom attached – a great luxury, and one she supposed she would not be enjoying again. The breakfast was excellent, but Emma ate without appetite, chewing list-lessly as Spencer went into the bathroom to start the bath running, and emerged again to get things out of the wardrobe. Only when she realised that Spencer was laying out her dark blue two-piece did she rouse herself.

'Why are you putting the suit out?' she demanded.

Spencer looked surprised. 'Church, miss. You *are* going? You usually do. And her ladyship's maid hinted very strong that it was expected.'

Emma didn't answer. It was part of what had kept her wakeful last night. If she went, after what had passed between her and Peter, wouldn't that be like rubbing his nose in it, parading her own virtue at his expense? But if she didn't go, it was snubbing his parents, and Lady Castleford's opinion of her would diminish. On the other hand, did it matter any longer what the countess thought of her? If things were over between her and Peter . . . But perhaps he would be offended by her staying home, and think she was pitying him.

'Why, miss,' Spencer said, turning to look at her in

293

the middle of these complicated thoughts, 'have you got a headache? You look a bit funny.'

Emma saw a way out and grasped at it. 'I don't feel quite the thing,' she said. 'Perhaps an hour or two in bed . . .'

Spencer came over and laid a quick hand on her forehead. 'You haven't a fever,' she said. 'Best you go, miss. The walk down to the church in the fresh air will do you good. It's a lovely sunny morning, and not too cold. It won't do to get wrong with the Lord without a good reason. And her ladyship expects it.'

Emma yielded. The Lord, in Spencer's comment, was not Lord Castleford, and while Emma was not entirely sure what she believed any more, after what she had gone through in France, she knew it was never wise to get on the wrong side of your maid.

So just before a quarter to eleven she walked down the main staircase, her gloves and prayer book in her hand, to join the obedient guests gathered under Lady Castleford's shepherding eye in the hall. The long-case clock gave a chesty rumble as preparation to striking the three-quarters, and Lady Castleford had actually begun to say, 'Very well, I think we should—' when her eyes went upwards to the staircase behind Emma, and Emma turned her head and saw Peter coming down, correctly attired, silk hat in hand, his man behind him carrying his prayer book. Her ladyship gathered herself seamlessly. 'Ah, Peter, there you are. Well, as we are all assembled, I think we can go.'

Peter came straight to Emma and offered his arm, with a little bow. She looked up into his face and saw contrition and, behind it, a little gleam of amusement. She slipped her hand under his elbow and joined the crocodile behind the earl and countess with a sigh of relief. It was all right.

When they came out of church again, Peter was at once by her side and said, 'Let's walk quickly. I'm stiffening up with all this sitting. Mother will be ages haranguing the vicar, and I can see Father talking to old Oliphant about his cattle. See you back at the house, everyone!' he called to the rest of the guests spilling out from the porch and, grabbing Emma's hand and stuffing it under his arm, he hauled her away, setting a brisk pace.

Once they were out of sight, on the straight estate road that led back to the house, he slowed a little and said, 'Now I can talk to you in private, without all the eyes and ears. I wanted to thank you for what you did yesterday.'

'I don't think I did anything,' she said shyly.

'Yes, you did. You restored my sense of proportion. I was behaving like an ass – not to mention a cad towards my mother. She is what she is, just as I am what I am. But it wasn't worth, as you so succinctly put it, all that unhappiness.'

'It was none of my business,' she said, 'and I'm sorry I overheard.'

'I'm glad you did. Now, painful subject closed? What I thought we'd do was to go through the hothouses and pick everyone a buttonhole to wear at luncheon. Gerald used to do it before the war, and the charming custom has rather lapsed lately. It would please my mother. Will you?'

'I'd love to. But can we please fetch Benson and take him with us? I can be up to my room and back like lightning.'

'Of course. I'll show you the quick way, through the stables and up the back stairs. That way you won't meet anyone and get waylaid.'

Benson was delighted to be out, and frisked about them, his whiskers bristling with emotion. 'He's a fine little fellow,' Peter said. 'Has he been shut up until now?'

'No, Spencer takes him out first thing for practical reasons. But this is his first walk of the day.'

'It must be jolly to have a dog. A lot of you FANYs had dogs in France, didn't you?'

'It was company on the ambulance,' she said. She didn't want to talk about France, and it seemed neither did he, for he did not pursue the thought. The silence that followed between them was companionable. It was a lovely morning, more like November than December, the sky a soft, misty lilac, the sunshine gentle and hazy, the air scented with autumn smells of woodsmoke and leaf mould.

For Benson's sake Peter led her the long way round, through the stables and round the outside of the walled gardens before coming back in through a small wooden door in the wall and emerging beside a potting shed. Here he collected secateurs and a basket and led her to the hothouses. They wandered happily in the warmth, savouring the smells and colours. 'My mother's great passion,' he said. 'Well, one of them. Hunting's another. She loves plants of all sorts, but especially all these fragile things that can't stand the weather outside. Gerald used to talk to her for hours about them. I never knew whether he really cared about floriculture or whether he was just ingratiating himself. For my part, I can't see the point of a flower that can't bear the

English climate. It would be like breeding a pointer that couldn't point, or a hound that couldn't hunt. Things ought to have a use.'

Emma breathed in the scent coming from the gardenias. 'Perhaps their beauty is their use.'

He stopped and looked at her. 'There you are again, seeing the other side. Perhaps if I had you by my side I would get through life without rubbing everyone up the wrong way.'

'But you don't,' she protested. 'Everyone wants to be with you. I've watched when you're in a group, and people jostle to be the one nearest to you. You are loved!'

'Not by my parents.'

'I'm quite sure you are. They lost two children – how could they not cherish the one remaining to them?'

He smiled fondly at her. 'I'm sure that's what you would do. But you are too gentle and good to understand people like them. When they look at me, all they feel is resentment that I am not Gerald. It makes them hate me, not love me.'

She wanted to protest, but it seemed pointless in the face of his certainty. And in any case, other feelings were emerging that were more interesting to her than his parents' state of mind. The warmth, the heady scent, the colours, the privacy of the dense greenery, and above all his closeness, standing almost with his body touching hers, looking down at her, his face so near that she could feel his sweet breath on her cheek – all these things meant she didn't want to talk about the Castlefords.

'What about you, Emma?' he asked her softly. 'Do *you* love me?'

He didn't wait for an answer. He bent his head and kissed her, and as she responded he stepped closer, put his arm round her waist, and now their bodies were touching all the way down. Passion raced through her. She clung to him, their mouths locked, a piercing sweetness streaming from his tongue to hers. She had never felt anything like this before. She was bewildered, almost drunk with it, wanting more, wanting it never to end. All thought was blotted out, and they stood in the green bower kissing and kissing, pressed together, as time seemed to slow and stop.

At last his mouth left hers and she opened her eyes almost drowsily as he drew back his head to look down into her face. 'Emma,' he said. 'I didn't realise. You *do* love me.'

She had no words. She had been taken so far out from herself that it would take time to get back.

'In that case we had better get engaged, don't you think? Will you marry me, Emma? Shall we go in and tell them? My mother's been on tenterhooks for weeks, and Father wants an heir. Shall we put them out of their misery?'

She put her hands up behind his head, threading her fingers through his thick hair – oh, the blissful licence to touch him like that! – and looked searchingly into his eyes for a moment. Then she drew his head down to hers, his mouth to her mouth. She felt his lips, questioning at first, warm into passion, felt as if it were a silken rope coming unknotted as the restraint slipped away from him, and he held her to him so tightly it almost hurt her, and kissed her fiercely, his insistent body hard against her softness. Then she knew it was all right. An unknown time later the control came back to him and he drew back from her again, but this time it was softly and reluctantly, lingering like cobwebs.

298

'I think,' he said, 'that we had better not do that again until we're married.'

In the new year of 1921 Venetia gave up her surgical consultancies. Her hands were no longer strong enough – for from strength comes the essential delicacy of touch – and her eyesight was weakening. She had always known, of course, that the day would come, but she had dreaded it, fearing that without it her life would be a blank. But in the event, what she felt at first was relief, as from a near-intolerable strain. The first morning she awoke facing no 'list', either that day or in the future, she smiled to herself with pure pleasure and turned over and went back to sleep.

Such indulgence did not last long. She had been active all her life, and early rising was bred into her bones. And she still had work to do. Her lifelong research into tuberculosis went on: the Pasteur Institute might be close to creating a vaccine against it, but there was still no cure or even an effective treatment, apart from the sanatorium. And there had been an upsurge in cases during and since the end of the war. Now she would have time to dedicate herself properly to the study.

She would have time to read all the articles and journals that she could normally only skim over; time to read books for pleasure, and to play the piano. Surgery had kept her hands flexible, but she was badly out of practice. She made a point of spending at least an hour a day at the keyboard. She played again the favourite pieces of her late husband, and sometimes seemed to see him, leaning against the piano as he used to do, smiling at her. She missed him so much, every day. Those who said time healed all things were only partly correct. The intensity faded, but not the sorrow itself.

She found time to go for walks, and half wished she was not too old to ride. She liked to stroll out into the little garden behind the house, and enjoy the snowdrops and the winter-flowering jasmine, to see fat buds coming on the cherry-apple, and the thick snub noses of daffodils pushing through. She was never too busy for Oliver, at whatever time he came home, and when the new regime had been in place for a few weeks he commented that he had never seen her so gay, and that she was looking younger every minute. 'If that's what giving up surgery does, I've half a mind to try it for myself. I found some grey hairs the other day – perhaps I can reverse the process.'

She had time to be glad of a visitor in the middle of the morning, where before, if she had been at home, she would have been too busy to feel anything but annoyance at the interruption. She had been comparing sputum slides in her study, but came straight downstairs to the drawing-room with a glad smile and an outstretched hand.

'Helen, my dear! What a delightful surprise.'

'I've been cursing myself for an idiot not to have telephoned first,' Helen said. 'I do hope I'm not interrupting you?'

'You are, but it doesn't follow that the interruption is unwelcome,' Venetia said. 'Let me see, what can I offer you at this time of day? Will you take some coffee, or tea?'

'Thank you, nothing,' Helen said. She looked uneasy, and seeing it, Venetia sent the servant away with a nod, and led her to a small sofa in the bay window. 'I wanted to consult you,' Helen said, settling herself.

Venetia read her face. 'I hope Jack is well?' she said. 'He hasn't had a relapse of any sort?'

'No, he's quite well. It isn't about Jack.' Helen drew off her gloves and smoothed them between her fingers. 'Or – well – not directly. I don't know if you knew that he lost his flying job. All the air companies have stopped passenger flights.'

'I'm sorry,' Venetia said. 'These are difficult times. It must have been hard for him.'

'It was hard,' Helen said, looking up from her hands. 'He hates to be out of work.'

She explained about the job he had found as a motor mechanic in a garage in Weybridge, doing repairs for the passing trade and local motorists, and maintaining the small fleet of vehicles for hire by the day. Sometimes a hirer would want a chauffeur for a particular occasion, which made him extra money. And when an expensive motor broke down outside the town and he had to drive out to it and effect repairs, the grateful traveller would usually give him a tip. Of course, on other occasions they were so annoyed at the delay to their plans they would merely curse him for the time it took him to reach them, almost blaming him for what had gone wrong. He told Helen all these things in the evening over dinner and made jokes of them, but she could see his spirit was bruised, as much by the tips as the cursing; for in both cases they saw him not as an equal, a gentleman – Jack Compton DSO, Air Ace – but as a menial in a cap with oily hands.

And the money was not a great deal. It was enough, given that so many of their living expenses were paid for by Mrs Ormerod, but even so Jack felt the need to supplement it in any way he could.

'On Sundays he goes to Brooklands, and earns what he can in the sheds,' Helen said. He had offered his services as a mechanic, because he could not get any flying. The one school that remained, clinging on by its fingertips with lessons and pleasure flights for the few with money to spare, now had a lady instructor – a pretty, curly-haired girl who had still been in school when Jack was flying at Mons. The novelty of her being a female gave the school just the slight edge that allowed it to survive, if not greatly to prosper.

'It would be enough to make any man feel depressed,' Venetia suggested, still probing delicately for the problem Helen had come to discuss.

She sighed and nodded. 'I think it's the not-flying that disappoints him most. But he does try most honourably *not* to be depressed, the dear man.' She stopped.

Venetia waited a moment, and then said, 'You said it was not directly about Jack that you wanted to consult.'

Helen came to with a start, and looked away uncomfortably. 'Oh dear,' she said. 'I rehearsed it all in my head on the train, but now I come to it, it's very difficult.'

'I am glad to help you in any way I can,' Venetia encouraged. 'Aside from Jack being my godson, I am very fond of you, Helen. So tell me what you want. Is it money?'

Helen looked shocked. 'Goodness, no! I would never—'

'You want my help in getting Jack a position? I'm afraid my influence does not run in aviation circles.'

'No, it isn't that.' Helen clasped her hands and pulled herself together. 'You see, we have three children, and as things are, I really don't want any more. Of course, we could simply not . . . um . . . But it's hard when you love each other so very much, as Jack and I do.'

'You want to know about contraception. Birth control. Ways to make intercourse unproductive,' Venetia said neutrally.

Helen could not read her reaction. 'I hope you are not angry that I asked. I thought perhaps that if you didn't know, you might be able to direct me to someone who did.'

Venetia remembered how, many years ago, she had given advice on contraception to the first wife of Tommy Weston, Emma's father. He had been so angry when he found out, it had caused a breach between them, which had lasted almost to his death. In those days it had been illegal to give such advice and, indeed, several people had gone to prison for publishing pamphlets on the subject. It had also been socially unacceptable: contraception was widely regarded as wicked, shameful, even blasphemous.

Nowadays, the legal situation was unclear. Since the beginning of the century, birth control advice had been disguised as health and hygiene advice, and no-one had been prosecuted for years. But it was still not something any decent woman would discuss, or admit to doing; and in the aftermath of the war, when so many had been killed, there was an extra edge of disapproval of the idea of limiting families. She felt it was brave of Helen to come and ask her about it.

'I'm not angry. Far from it. Tell me, what method do you use at present?'

The words just wouldn't come. 'Oh dear, it is so strangely difficult,' Helen said apologetically.

Venetia helped her along. 'The most commonly used method – I suppose eighty or ninety per cent of married couples practise it – is *coitus interruptus*.' She looked at Helen to see if she knew the term. 'The withdrawal method,' she clarified. 'That is, the man withdraws before—'

'Yes,' Helen interrupted hastily. 'That's what we – um . . .'

'Of course, it is not completely effective. Judging the exact moment is difficult, and even a few stray spermatozoa can be enough. There are two devices that offer better protection: the rubber sheath, and the cervical cap.' She explained these to Helen, whose face gradually resumed its normal colour under the practical tone of the conversation. 'But you know, of course,' Venetia concluded, 'that neither is completely foolproof. And Jack would have to consent. You cannot practise birth control without his knowledge.'

'I understand that. I don't think he will object. I know he worries about any further increase to our family. As long as it doesn't mean total abstinence – I think that would break his heart. Mine too,' she added, with a little burst of frankness.

Now Venetia smiled. 'There is nothing to be ashamed of in enjoying one's husband's embraces. It is one of the great gifts of a beneficent God.'

Helen smiled too. 'I'm glad you see it that way.'

'When I was young, girls were taught that sexual pleasure was for men alone, and that any female who enjoyed it was bound for Hell. I think we are a little more enlightened now – except, of course, that still we never really speak about it.'

'Perhaps that *would* be a step too far. Imagine drawing-room chit-chat about such things! That would be a world gone mad.'

'Quite. Very well, then, do you have the information you need?'

'I understand what you have told me, but I'm not sure how to proceed. The cap you mentioned . . .?'

'You would need to have it professionally fitted, and be shown how to use it. I could refer you to a colleague who specialises in such things – or, as it happens, a clinic has just opened in Holloway to advise on birth control and dispense devices. You might find that more anonymous. Have you heard of Marie Stopes?'

'Didn't she write a book? I seem to remember something – didn't she say that women and men should be equal in marriage? It sounded rather sensible to me.'

'She believes that a woman cannot be free unless she has control over her own body, which must include contraception. No-one would publish the book before the war, but since it came out – what is it? Two years ago – there has been no action against her or the publisher, so I think we can take it that she has opened this clinic with some confidence.'

'I think that *would* be less embarrassing,' Helen said.

'I'll get you the address,' Venetia said. 'I'm glad to be able to promote the clinic. It will be giving free advice to the poor, so it's important that some of the better-off patronise it too, or it will fail for lack of fees.'

Soon afterwards Helen took her leave, carrying the address of the clinic in her pocket and feeling much more cheerful. Venetia went back to her slides, reflecting that times had indeed changed since the 1880s when she had first practised. Contraception, women taking control of their lives, having the vote, travelling about unchaperoned, taking jobs . . . She remembered her own young womanhood, when she had railed against the only role society would allow her, to be decorative and then to become a wife and mother. She had raged about her father's drawing-room like a caged tiger. Helen's little girl would grow up in a very different world; and as in so many things, it was the war that had been the catalyst. Strange to be able to impute any good to that savage evil.

CHAPTER THIRTEEN

Teddy had struggled on for a while without a secretary, though Polly did what she could to help, impressing her father with the business head she was developing. 'Your mother was just the same sensible, managing creature,' he told her warmly.

The death of Maria and the loss of Father Palgrave had shocked the household, and no-one wanted to hurry to replace the chaplain in any of his capacities. The children had a disgracefully long holiday with only the nursery-maids to keep them in check. When things settled down a little, Henrietta taught the younger ones their letters and numbers, and tried to set lessons for the older ones; but for rather a lot of the time, their instruction involved reading a book, writing a story, or even drawing a picture – anything to keep them quietly occupied.

As to the chapel, Teddy read prayers in the evening when he was at home, but on Sunday everyone had to go to the church in the village, or to the Minster. Henrietta was the one who minded most, but she hoped that Palgrave would come back before too long – before it was necessary to find another chaplain, at any rate.

After Christmas it was plain that a secretary at least

would have to be found, even if only on a temporary basis. Teddy had gone to visit Palgrave in the sanatorium and had found him pale and thin, calm-seeming and quiet, but with distant eyes. He had greeted Teddy politely, but had not wanted to talk to him – every conversational opening sank into the sand. Afterwards Teddy had spoken to the sanatorium's director, who had said that he did not think Palgrave would be ready to leave for many months. 'His mind is much disordered. He seems calm, but any small thing can set him off. He certainly could not undertake a salaried position or any responsibility as he is.'

At a family conference early in January 1921, it was decided that James, Roberta and Jeremy ought to go to school. 'They need proper teaching and discipline,' Henrietta said. 'The boys will grow wild if they are left to their own devices.'

'I want my Jeremy to be educated like a gentleman, so that he can get on,' Ethel said.

'I think we had better arrange for them to go to St Edward's,' Henrietta said. 'And Harriet, too – she'll be six in March. That will just leave John and Martin and the baby. Nanny Emma and the maids can manage them.'

'They ought to have a governess,' Ethel said. 'Nanny Emma doesn't teach John anything but nursery rhymes.'

'Let them alone,' Teddy said. 'They'll be old enough for school soon enough. Let them romp while they can. I don't approve of too much schooling too young. Let their minds grow strong first, or you'll stunt them with training.'

'So you agree about St Edward's?' Henrietta asked.

'That's all right for the others,' Teddy said, 'but I always meant James to go to Eton. I talked about it with

Father Palgrave last year. He thought he was too young to go last September, and I agreed, but as things are I think he should go this September. That will mean he will have to go to a crammer, to make sure he knows the same things as the other boys. I'll have a word with a few fellows at the club and see if they can recommend someone in York. Can't have the little chap going up with a disadvantage. Not that he needs to be a scholar, but boys are cruel little beasts and pick on any difference.'

'Eton,' said Ethel, approvingly. 'Yes, that gives a boy an advantage in the world. I'm sure Robbie would have liked our boys to go to Eton too.'

Teddy managed to ignore that. 'What about the chapel?' he said, looking at Henrietta.

'I think we should go on as we are, and see if Father Palgrave improves. You did promise to keep his position for him. We can do without for a while longer.'

'Very well,' Teddy said.

At his club, his enquiries for a crammer were immediately fruitful. Colonel Marchbanks knew of a feller, positive brain-box, who did private tutoring for selected pupils. 'Used to be a don up at the House. Gave it up late in life to marry. Dashed sad business – pretty young thing, died in childbirth. Infant died too. Now he spends his time writing a treatise on somethin' or other, and tutorin' boys. Lives in High Petergate – house with the blue door opposite Precentor's Court.'

Teddy felt for the unknown don, losing his wife in childbed. Still, he could not be too careful with James. 'But what *sort* of man is he?' he asked.

'Oh, he's quite pukka,' the colonel assured him. 'I've dined with him – keeps a dashed fine cellar. Had a

Cockburn 'ninety-six last time I dined there that was quite superb.'

'So he's a gentleman?' Teddy urged.

'Good Lord, yes! Keeps a cook and housekeeper and a very useful sort of manservant. Private income. Does the tutorin' more for the love of it. And still keeps in touch with the college – dines at High Table once a month and so on. He'll bring your boy up to snuff.'

The following day, Teddy went to interview Dr Halliday. He was a tall, lean man with an air of flexible strength, as if he had been an athlete; and he seemed younger than Teddy had expected, though perhaps it was an illusion fostered by his eager eyes. His air was calm and authoritative, but his voice was full of enthusiasm. Teddy liked him, and was sorry all over again about the lost wife. He thought Halliday was the sort of man that women would find attractive.

'I was at Eton myself,' he said when Teddy told him what was wanted, 'so I know what he will need to know. But I hope you will not want me to limit myself to that. Your son is at the age when the mind is like a sponge and will take in vast amounts of knowledge. This capacity soon fades, and in my view it is a shame to waste it.'

Teddy frowned. 'He is to inherit my estate from me in due course. He won't need to be a scholar.'

'It isn't a matter of need, precisely, Mr Morland. It is of what a man might *be*, in the round. I'm sure you wish your son to reach everything that is within his grasp, to furnish his mind richly, to have inner resources that will help him to cope with life's vicissitudes.'

Teddy's brow cleared. 'Oh, you mean *character*! Well, naturally I want him to have character, and I think I can assure you he is a fine, manly boy. But I don't want him overloaded with study so that his spirit is crushed.'

'I hope I have never crushed a boy's spirit. Perhaps I had better meet the lad, to see if we get on with each other.'

Teddy thought that sensible, and brought James to High Petergate the next day. James went with great reluctance. He had been enjoying his holiday since Father Palgrave's departure, and the thought of cramming with some fusty don when he might be out in the field with his pony did not suit him. Seeing the rebellious scowl when Teddy presented his son in the drawing-room, Dr Halliday said, 'If you will permit, Mr Morland, I would like to take James into my study for a few moments and talk to him alone.' He smiled reassuringly at Teddy. 'Won't you have this chair by the fire? I find it's the most comfortable. And let me give you a glass of this sherry. It's a rather fine oloroso. Quite rare. My wine merchant in London sends me odd parcels from time to time.'

The sherry was indeed extremely fine, and the decanter was left hospitably at Teddy's elbow. The chair was comfortable, the fire pleasant, and one of his own cigars completed the moment, so that he did not notice the time passing, and was surprised when the clock struck and he realised James and Dr Halliday had been absent almost three-quarters of an hour. As the chimes died away the study door opened and James almost burst through, his face alight and his eyes shining.

'Oh, Father, Dr Halliday's been telling me about Thermopylae, how the Greeks held the one road through the mountains, only seven thousand of them, and there were *millions* of the Persians, the biggest army ever seen in the world, but the Greeks held them up for *seven days*!

And then a local man betrayed them and showed the Persians a goat-track that led round behind the Greeks, but Leonidas – he was the King of Sparta and the commander-in-chief of the Greeks – he knew what was happening, so he sent away nearly all his force and just kept back fourteen hundred of his best men. Dr Halliday says he'll tell me what happened next when I come again. Oh, Father, can I come again, *please*?'

Teddy's startled eyes met those of Halliday over the excited boy's head. 'It looks as though I shall have to say yes.'

Halliday smiled. 'The boy has been well taught in the basics. It will be no great task to bring him up to scratch. And I think I can say it is a task I shall enjoy.'

'That's settled, then,' Teddy said. He laid a hand on James's head. 'Go and wait in the motor, my son, while I discuss a little business with Dr Halliday.'

It was in the course of this 'business discussion' that Teddy's other problem was solved. He had taken to Halliday so well that it seemed natural to explain the background of Palgrave's illness and Maria's death and express the need for a secretary. Halliday said, 'As it happens, I know of someone who is looking for a position, who might suit you very well. She is trained in Pitman shorthand and typewriting—'

'*She?* It's a female, then?'

'I think, if you will forgive my venturing an opinion, that you will have difficulty in finding a suitably trained man. And if you did find one, you might not find his manner exactly to your liking. Shell-shock is not the only change young men bring back from the war – independence of mind is another.'

Teddy knew exactly what he meant. 'Well, I suppose there's no harm in meeting her,' he said.

Within three days, Miss Husthwaite was installed in the steward's room. Within a week she had made the position her own, and within a month Teddy could not remember how he had ever done without her. She was a woman in – he guessed, because of course he could not politely ask her – her forties, trim of figure. Her fair hair, beginning to grey, was pinned behind in a neat bun, but with a curly front that belied the severity of the dark blue two-piece she always wore, and seemed better to match the gleam of fun in her blue eyes. She had gone to London after her secretarial training and joined the civil service, moving, over twenty years, from a lowly position to one of some responsibility. But when her mother died she had given up her post and gone back to York to take care of her father.

He had been a shopkeeper, but had sold up when his wife began to ail so as to be with her. Now medical expenses and rising prices had put paid to his prosperity, and required his daughter to find another position. They lived, Teddy discovered, in a small flat above a shop in The Stonebow. This Miss Husthwaite kept neat, and here she cooked her father's meals, before she set off on her bicycle in the morning to ride to Morland Place, and after she arrived home on it in the evening. Her father did the marketing during the day, took the clothes to the laundry, returned Miss Husthwaite's books to the library, undertook small repairs around the flat, and heavy jobs like cleaning the windows, making up the fire and fetching in the coal. So they rubbed along contentedly, and the generous salary Mr Morland paid her made up for the long hours she sometimes had to work.

The work itself suited her down to the ground, as she told her father in the evenings as they sat over their dinner together. She had a free hand in the office: Mr Morland had proved very easy to handle, for her career in a man's world had long ago taught her that men would agree to anything if they thought it was their own idea. She could arrange the office and routines to suit herself, and the work, while not difficult, was varied and interesting.

And before long she had been so thoroughly absorbed into the life of the household that she almost felt they were her own family. No-one kept anything from her: indeed, she was often sought out as a sympathetic ear, a dispenser of sensible advice. Her conversation in the evening was as often about the Morlands' concerns as it was about her secretarial duties. For Mr Husthwaite it was a window onto another world, which was as good as reading a novel. His life, it had to be said, was dull, and he could hardly wait for Hilda to come home each evening so that he could have the next episode in the serial.

The transformation of the St James and St Ann Benevolent Dispensary in Dean Street into the John Winchmore Hospital had been delayed by the shortage of manpower in the last months of the war and the shortage of materials since, but the work was finally finished in March 1921, and the opening of the new facilities was planned for the beginning of April.

The upper floors had been completely transformed. Now there was a suite of two theatres on the top floor, fitted with the very latest in steel operating tables and adjustable lights. Between them was a service room

314

containing the trolleys and bowls, sinks, laundry baskets and waste containers, with glass-fronted cupboards to house the instruments and supplies, and drawers full of the clean aprons and caps.

On the floor below was the main ward of twelve beds and, divided from it by a lobby, the nurses' room, sluice and kitchen, and two private rooms for the better-off.

The free clinic was on the ground floor, with a new bright, clean waiting-room and refurbished consulting- and treatment-rooms, and the dispensary was in the basement along with the main kitchen and offices.

'It's all absolutely beautiful,' Venetia said to Mark Darroway, when she went to visit him after her first tour of the new facilities. 'Better than I hoped. I'm surprised at how much space there is inside, compared with the façade. And the private rooms are quite luxurious – though whether we will ever persuade the rich to use them . . .'

'You will. You must,' said Mark. 'Especially with plastic surgery, where asepsis is so vital. Besides, they might be glad of the anonymity, if they're tinkering with their appearance.'

'Oliver is *not* a "beauty doctor",' Venetia said firmly.

'That's what he'll be called,' said Mark. 'The old guard don't take kindly to these new-fangled disciplines. And if you are to have any fee-paying patients to keep the coffers filled, he will have to take on beauty operations.'

'I don't know what the trustees will say about that,' Venetia said.

Mark smiled. 'Don't be disingenuous, my dear. You know the other trustees are mere cyphers, and will do whatever *you* decide. And since you provided the vast majority of the funds, that's only fitting. The Winchmore is your baby, and you shall do with it what you please.'

Venetia looked at him carefully. He had always been a lean man, rather stooped, like a heron, but as the low March sunshine from the window fell on his face she thought he was looking thinner than ever – quite gaunt, in fact. He was not a good colour, and had a look of blueness about the lips that she didn't like. In the silence that had fallen she could hear his breathing.

'You didn't come to show me round,' she said.

'I thought you'd like to be alone and look at everything in your own time,' he said.

'No, you didn't,' she countered. 'Last year you would have wanted to show me yourself – nothing would have kept you from it. What is it, Mark?'

His dark eyes looked into hers ruefully. 'You know perfectly well what it is. Don't you, Venetia?' He saw her pain and knew she had guessed. 'It's been coming on gradually for a long time now. You remember I expressed doubts to you at the beginning that I would be able to be your director.'

'You only said you'd be too old,' she objected. 'And you're hardly any older than me.'

'True. But you have a heart like a steam engine, while mine is worn out. It was slow at first, but now I'm going downhill rapidly. Oh, my dear, don't look like that! I've known about it for months, and I've adjusted to the idea. The old grey horse comes for all of us sooner or later, and I can hear his hoofs on the cobbles outside. It won't be many more weeks.'

'Let me examine you,' Venetia demanded, her mouth

set. Ridiculous, at her age, that she could still find herself near to tears!

'No, Venetia. There's nothing to be done, and you know it. Hearts wear out. It's not a bad way to go, compared with some. I'm glad to have seen the Winchmore finished, and I hope I'll see it open. But I can't be the director, which is a pity. And I shall be sorry not to see how this new world of ours turns out. Not all good, of course – but the tuberculosis vaccine seems close to realisation, and who knows? You may discover a cure in a year or two. There are going to be cures for all sorts of things we've had to live with for centuries, and you'll see them. I trust you to tell me all about them when we meet again up there.' He threw a humorous glance at the ceiling.

'Oh, don't be so damn brave about it!' Venetia cried. 'You must be raging inside.'

'Too tired to rage. That's the thing about my trouble – it makes you feel so tired you don't care about things any more. Now, let's stop talking about my tedious old condition, and talk instead about the Winchmore. You need a director of surgery, and I think you should offer the position to Oliver.'

She looked surprised. 'But he's so young. And he's never held any kind of residency before.'

'I think he's ready,' Mark said. 'In fact, I know he is. It isn't his fault the war intervened, or that none of the major hospitals have plastics departments. He's a pioneer, and pioneers pretty much have to be young – don't you think? Let him make this specialty his own. Let him be the beauty doctor of all beauty doctors, so that his name is the first that comes to mind whenever plastics is mentioned.'

A slow smile came to her troubled lips. 'It will make

the old fogeys at the great hospitals spitting mad to see him get on so young.'

'And that's the best reason yet,' said Mark.

The hospital was formally opened on the 4th of April 1921, and Venetia persuaded Princess Mary to cut the ribbon, which ensured publicity, and photographs in all the newspapers. Christopher Addison was no longer health secretary: he had quit the post at the end of March to become minister without portfolio, his housing reforms having brought him criticism because of the high cost. But the new secretary, Sir Alfred Mond, accepted the invitation: an odd-looking man, bald, but with a huge moustache as if in compensation. He was the son of a Jewish chemist, and had come into politics from industry, was extremely wealthy, a patron of the arts and a great benefactor. Venetia was pleased that he had come, and was even more pleased when he showed an interest in the benevolent side of the venture.

'Burns and scalds are still the most common domestic accident to women and children,' she told him, 'but once their lives are saved no-one seems to care if they go through life disfigured. Here at the Winchmore we will offer them hope. And to those born with hare lips, webbed fingers, missing noses – deformities of all sorts. The innocent victims of inherited syphilis, those needing reconstruction after cancer surgery – the list is endless.'

Sir Alfred listened intelligently, and at the end expressed himself interested in supporting the hospital. To have him as a donor and trustee would be a great coup, Venetia thought: though he would not remain health secretary for ever, he would always, she hoped, be rich and influential. She dedicated as much time to him during the tour and at the reception afterwards as she could politely deny Princess Mary.

It was a further coup that the Prince of Wales called in at the reception afterwards. He had heard of the event from Eddie Vibart and cut short an engagement to come and lend his support – he liked such informal 'droppings in' and enjoyed surprising people, rather than being tied to a schedule and going where he was expected. Venetia hadn't really time for him, as she juggled the princess and Sir Alfred, and was glad to see that he latched on at once to Violet, and seemed extremely happy chatting to her, almost to the exclusion of everyone else.

The more serious papers not only reported the opening, but also detailed the facilities and the work that would be done there, and wrote about Venetia's past public service, and Oliver's career. The latter was what Venetia had most hoped for, for he would need the word to be spread if he was to make a success of his new position. The free side would make up the bulk of his work, but it had to be supported by the paying patients. The rich too had unsightly moles, had children with birthmarks and congenital deformities, and suffered accidents. Oliver had a very good social manner and plenty of contacts in the *beau monde*, where he was universally liked. Venetia could imagine the wealthy coming to him for treatment: perhaps he might even become a craze among the females of the *ton*, who were always looking for something new to be excited about.

Oliver was at her side at the opening ceremony, made a graceful address accepting the directorship, then moved among the guests and reporters in a very accomplished way, looking every inch the consultant. But whenever she caught his eye, he gave her a look of almost stunned delight, like a child seeing its first Christmas tree. The news that he was to be director of surgery, with complete power over the John Winchmore's activities and future, had rendered him speechless when she first told him. Being Oliver, he was not speechless for long, and since then he had been bubbling over with plans and ideas.

But one of the first things he had said, which rather endeared him to his mother, was 'Now I can get married!'

One windy day in late March, Mrs Ormerod had gone upstairs to get Michael up from his afternoon sleep ('Oh, let me. The darling!' she had said). As she lifted the warm, sleep-swollen baby from his crib she suddenly felt most peculiar. She laid him carefully down, crossed the room to the armchair, sat down and quietly died.

Michael's howls of protest brought the nursery-maid, and her shrieks brought Helen running. The doctor was sent for, but it was only a formality – it was plain to Helen that nothing could be done. When Jack got home he found her dry-eyed and stoical. 'I'm glad it was like that for her – so quick and easy. She was always so afraid of being ill. Now she's with Daddy again.'

It was good for Jack to be shaken out of his own troubles in favour of comforting Helen. 'I'll have a little weep later on, after the funeral,' she said to him, when they were alone. 'I don't really feel it yet – there's so much to be done.'

Molly was briskly practical. She had never had a close relationship with her mother: she had been a late baby, and her arrival had perplexed more than gladdened her parents. She had been brought up by nursery staff and had been given, Mr Ormerod had always complained, far too much licence; but the fact was that Mrs Ormerod was too tired and too old by then to take the trouble with Molly that she had with Freddie and Helen. Molly had grown up regarding her mother as she might a caterpillar or ladybird in the garden; had studied her behaviour with a kind of detached amusement. So she put on blacks, agreed with Helen that it was a mercy Mother had gone that way, and expected to cry at the funeral, if at all.

The fact that Basil and Barbara kept asking where Grandmama had gone and when she was coming back was proof of how the attachment between grandmother and grandchildren had grown in the past months. Helen eventually took Basil onto her lap and explained to him slowly and patiently about death. Basil listened solemnly, and when she had finished he asked, 'When's Grandmama coming back?'

Helen sighed and stroked his head, turning the little unruly curls at the nape of his neck round her finger. 'Darling, didn't you understand what I've been telling you? About Grandmama?'

'Yes, Mummy.'

'Where has Grandmama gone?' she tested him.

'Grandmama's gone to Heaven to see Grandpa.'

'That's right.'

'But when's she coming back?'

'Never, darling.'

'Is that tomorrow?' he asked, using his sweet, wheedling look.

'No, Basil, she's never coming back.'

'Can I get down now, Mummy?'

And a few minutes later she heard Basil telling his sister in a joyful bellow, 'Grandmama's coming tomorrow. She's bringing presents for us,' and had to conclude that, with Basil, the wish was always going to be father to the thought.

The great benefit of funerals, Helen discovered, was that they gave the newly bereaved something to do. Mrs Ormerod had had a wide circle of acquaintance, of the generation that expected to be invited to funerals and really enjoyed them. There was also a large cast of cousins and second cousins (privately to Jack, Helen said that whenever they turned up at a family wedding or funeral they always reminded her of a musical comedy). Helen's elder brother Freddie, his wife and their children were the first to be consulted. In deference to Freddie's seniority, Helen asked if he would like to make the arrangements, but he refused with almost unseemly haste.

'No, no, that sort of thing is always better handled by females. And obviously the funeral must go from Fairoaks. But do ask Joan if you need any help. I'm sure she'd be happy to send a ham, or something.'

Helen thought she'd manage very well without Joan, and she was pretty sure that the promise of a ham, if it were forthcoming, would not be followed up: the ham would be present in spirit rather than in the flesh. Anyway, she'd just as soon be busy as not, because there was a niggling worry in the back of her mind that she did not want to have to take out and look at, not yet.

The bombshell fell at the gathering after the service. The musical-comedy cast was falling like a plague of locusts upon the funeral baked meats – Helen had provided lavishly in anticipation – when Freddie cornered her for a private word. He was a tall and bulky man, and looked vaster than ever in frock-coat and black silk cravat, with a cup of tea in one hand – Joan had lately become a total abstainer and was trying to edge her husband in the same direction. If anything could arouse Helen's sympathy for her brother it was the thought of spending evenings with Joan without the softening effect of alcohol.

'Very good "do", this,' he said, as an opening gambit. 'I told you females were better than chaps at this sort of thing.'

'Why, thank you, Freddie,' Helen said, not without irony. 'So you did.'

'Good to see the family all together again,' he said, with a vague glance around. Helen resisted the desire to challenge him to name any one of them. 'Family's important at a time like this. Glad to have mine around me, I can tell you.'

'Yes, Joan must be a great support to you,' Helen said. She told herself she really shouldn't have, but actually it didn't matter. Freddie took the compliment at its face value.

'Excellent woman, Joan,' he said, with perhaps a hint of glumness. 'Absolute rock. Manages everything like a top-notch general, despite all our difficulties. Which brings me,' he continued quickly, preventing Helen from asking what the difficulties were, 'to the delicate matter of when you and Jack were thinking of moving out.'

'What's that?' Helen said, frowning.

'It's not that I'm trying to hurry you, but the sooner the better, don't you think? No sense in hanging things out, and Joan is anxious to get the move over before the summer. I'm sure you'll want the same, to get settled in – wherever you're going.'

'I'm not with you, Freddie. Are you talking about moving in *here*?'

He opened his eyes wider, his face expressionless.

'Well, you do know it's my house, don't you? You do know Mother left it to me?'

Here it was – the thing in the cellar she had heard moving about and had not wanted to open the door and deal with. She made a last-ditch effort at denial. 'How do you know that? You haven't seen the will.'

'Of course I have. Who do you think helped her draw it up? I can't remember all the small details – gifts to friends and so on, and she left you and Molly some personal things – but the house and contents come to me. I don't know why you're pretending to be surprised,' he went on. 'Father left the house and everything to her for her lifetime, but he made it clear he wanted it to come to me when she went, and she would never go against his wishes.'

'But why would Father leave you *everything*?'

'Because I'm the only son,' Freddie said, as if that were obvious. 'And, frankly, he expected you and Molly to get married to men who would support you. Well, I suppose Molly may still marry at some point – she's not *quite* too old yet. At any rate, she's earning her own living.'

'But what are *we* to do? With three little children to take care of?' she protested, though her mind, working furiously, had already gone to the end of the argument.

'You'll have to make alternative arrangements. You've had a good long time living on Mother's charity. Besides, you could never have kept up this house without her: her annuity dies with her, so you'd have to move anyway.'

'Freddie, I can't believe you'd just turn us out like that, make us homeless! You don't *need* the house – you've got a home.'

'The Laurels is much too small for us, now the children are getting bigger. We've been talking for a long time about how difficult it is to manage in such a small house.' Helen could guess who had been doing most of the talking. Freddie was one of those men who came home from the office and, provided his dinner was served and he was let to read the newspaper in peace, noticed nothing of his surroundings.

'So the upshot is that, in order to provide you with a bit more luxury, you're willing to make Jack and me and our children homeless.'

He grew red in the face. 'It isn't a matter of *luxury*. I have to entertain for my business, and Joan has to keep up a certain position in society. The dining-room at The Laurels is quite inadequate. And there's the children's future to think about.'

'Yes, and I'm thinking of my children's future, too,' Helen said.

He grew impatient. 'Well, that's not my concern, is it? I am responsible for providing for my family, and your husband is responsible for providing for his. It's no use taking this personally, Helen. The house lawfully belongs to me and I need it, and there's nothing more to be said. Now, obviously I don't want to throw you out into the street, but it's up to Jack to make whatever arrangements are needed, and I'd be glad if you could manage to vacate the premises by the end of the month. I'm sure that will give you adequate time.'

'Vacate the premises,' Helen murmured. 'You sound like a bailiff.'

He reddened again, but with an obvious effort controlled his annoyance, and was even magnanimous. 'I'm sure if there are any little things – bits of furniture you particularly want that we don't need: some of the nursery things, for instance—'

'You are all kindness,' Helen said, with the sweetest, most poisonous smile she could conjure.

But as she said to Jack later, when they were alone, it was no use railing against it. 'The house is his and he's entitled to do as he likes with it. And we always knew there would be difficulties when Mother died. I just didn't expect it to happen so suddenly.'

'It's not his until the will has been proved,' Jack said.

She looked at him sadly. 'I don't want to play that game. It would reduce us to their level. To Joan's level, I should say, because it's certainly her who's driving him. Freddie wouldn't care what he lived in as long as his comforts were taken care of.'

'But he's *letting* her drive him,' Jack pointed out. 'I think you are excusing your brother too much. I saw him examining things in the drawing-room, inspecting his possessions. He's really longing to move in here and be lord of the manor.'

'It *is* a much nicer house than The Laurels,' Helen said, with a sigh. 'And of course we both grew up here. Perhaps he's been looking forward all his life to owning it. Poor Freddie. He hasn't got much else to be happy about.'

'That's my girl,' Jack said, with a faint smile. 'Naturally a good position and a generous salary and a wife and four healthy children couldn't make a man happy, without his father's house to live in.'

Helen punched him on the upper arm. 'That's for being facetious. Oh, Jack, what *are* we going to do?'

The greyness of worry seeped through his determination to be cheerful. 'Find somewhere to live. But we won't be able to afford much. And, Helen, we won't be able to afford servants. A daily skivvy will be about the limit. Oh, God, if only I could get a proper job! Freddie's right, you know – I am supposed to support you.'

'Don't start that again. We'll manage. And things will get better. These hard times won't last for ever.'

The will was read a few days later, at The Laurels, where Helen, Jack and Molly were entertained in the drawing-room ('so much smaller than Fairoaks') with cups of tea and small, dry biscuits. 'I cannot offer you sherry, I'm afraid,' Joan said, in her affected, fluting voice, 'because we are a total-abstinence household.'

'Good luck with entertaining Freddie's business chums,' Molly muttered to Helen, when Joan had moved away, 'without a spot of alcohol.'

The solicitor, a very elderly man Helen remembered seeing once or twice in her childhood, read the document aloud and offered to answer any questions, but it was all quite clear. Some small trinkets and personal mementoes had been left to friends and favoured relatives. Mrs Ormerod's jewels were divided between Helen and Molly, and Helen had been left her furs. Everything else went to 'my beloved son, Frederick George Arbuthnot Ormerod'. The Arbuthnot, Helen remembered being told, had been added at the christening in the hope of a legacy from an elderly and single great-uncle, who in the event had left everything to a charity for retired cab horses.

At home – or rather, at Fairoaks – afterwards, Helen, Jack and Molly discussed the situation.

'He can't throw us out until after probate,' Molly said, making the same point Jack had raised. 'I'm all for giving them as much trouble as possible.'

Helen said, 'I can't find the energy to fight along those lines. I don't consider myself bound by Freddie's deadline, but I'd as soon have it over with. If we can go by the end of the month, I think we should. Now, it seems to me we have two options.' She looked at Jack. 'We could go back to Morland Place. I'm sure Uncle Teddy would have us.'

He looked unhappy. 'I don't want to do that. It would be admitting I'm a complete failure as a husband and father. But I have to consider you and the children. If you think you'd be more comfortable there—'

'I wouldn't.'

'It would be safe. It would give you security.'

Helen shook her head. 'I only suggested it in case it was what you wanted, but it isn't what I want. The only other option is to find a house to rent. The question is, what do you want to do, Molly? Do you want to come with us, or go your own way?'

The sisters exchanged a frank look. Molly said, 'The question *is*, would I be more help than hindrance? If I come with you, I can help out with my salary. But then you'd need a bigger house, which would cost more.'

'I don't want you to consider that. I want you to do what suits you best,' said Helen. 'You ought to have your chance at life. You're young, with everything before you.'

'I think we should wait and see what sort of a place you can get. I'll live with you if that works out better, or I'll get diggings in London if it goes that way.' She put out a hand and gripped Helen's for a brief moment. 'We won't lose each other, don't worry. I want to be sure those children grow up knowing their aunty Molly.'

★ . ★ . ★

Facing the world without Fairoaks was a large dose of medicine to take all at once. Helen found a tiny furnished house – a red-brick terraced railway cottage in a back-street in Walton, which seemed the best they could afford for the moment on Jack's wages. She did not want to get them into debt at a perilous time like this, and she did not yet know, until she had tried it, how much day-to-day living would cost. If it seemed they could afford something better, she told herself, they could move later on.

The place was small – two rooms and a kitchen on the ground floor, and up the steep, narrow stairs, two bedrooms over the two rooms, and a tiny third over the kitchen, leading off the smaller bedroom. There was a small yard out at the back, with a lavatory, wash-house and coal-shed. There was no bathroom, but a large tin bath hung on the wall of the wash-house, where there was a good copper to provide hot water. The furniture was plain and cheap but the place seemed clean, and the landlord was willing to store his pieces if they had furniture of their own they preferred to use. 'I intend to interpret Freddie's offer of "any little bits of furniture you want" quite generously,' Helen said.

Molly went with Helen to look at the place, and was tellingly silent. 'Three bedrooms, you see,' Helen said. 'The children can all go in together.' Molly was still silent. 'You could have the larger bedroom,' Helen suggested.

Molly hugged her, to hide the tears she did not want her to see. Molly never cried, and it would upset Helen to know how pitiful her sister thought all this. 'I'll find diggings in London,' she said. 'It will save on train fares.'

Jack was also silent when Helen showed him round, after work one evening. 'Basil and Barbara can go in the larger room, and you and I can have the smaller bedroom, with the baby in the little place that leads off it. Ideal, really, having him so close. And there are actually two rooms downstairs. You don't know how rare that is.'

'No, I don't,' he said. He took her in his arms. 'I've failed you,' he muttered into her hair. 'Oh, Helen, I'm sorry!'

'Don't talk rot,' she said briskly. 'This is nice and convenient for your job and the airfield. I'm glad it's small because it will mean less housework. Jack, be sensible. I've thought it all out. Once I see how much the household can be run on, we may be able to move to something better. But it won't hurt us to economise for a bit, and maybe even put some savings aside. Oh, darling, don't look so blue!'

'I can't help it. Look what I've brought you to! Maybe we should go to Morland Place after all.'

'Not on your life! I'm looking forward to taking care of you all in this dear, snug little house. Really I am!' She answered his automatic protest. 'It's what women have done through the ages – it's a primordial instinct.'

He was goaded into a watery laugh. 'Instinct, be damned!'

'You wait and see. We'll be so happy you won't want to move. I'm taking Mother's cook's recipe book and I'm dying to try out her recipes. And I tell you this, Jack Compton – nobody's going to eat humble pie unless it's one *I've* cooked.'

CHAPTER FOURTEEN

Spring came bursting up from under the earth in a torrent of energy: new grass almost clamouring to be grazed, new shoots thick in the cornfield and vegetable plots, new leaves breaking in a pale green wave over the bare black bones of winter. Horses shed their winter coats, revealing themselves as glossy as chestnuts under the rough outer casing. Dogs rushed outdoors and clowned madly, driven wild by the feast of smells. Cows' milk grew richer for the fresh grazing. And everywhere the high, childlike clamour of lambs, and the deep knuckering replies of their dams, made the glad music of a Yorkshire spring.

Polly rode out one morning on Vesper who, though now a matron of eight, nevertheless could not help responding to the vivid scents coming down on the quick little breeze. She danced about, flirting her tail and looking for objects to shy at – blown white blossom petals, the bowing daffodils on the bank, a pair of lambs stotting away from the hedge as if on springs, a blackbird giving his alarm call, hidden in the sweet olive-yellow curdle of new leaves in the oak tree.

'You're such a fool,' Polly told the mare, sitting her bounces with ease. Vesper flung her ears back and forth in acknowledgement, and then decided that a rivulet of water running across the path to the drainage ditch was a dangerous snake, paused to kill it with two fierce stabs of her forefoot, and leaped extravagantly over the corpse, clearing it by several feet in both dimensions.

Polly rode out to Twelvetrees, for the pleasure of seeing the mares with new foals at foot – stilt-legged woolly toys, still surprised by their own ability to run and buck – and then turned aside and rode across the fields to Holgate Beck, to follow its course and make a circuit home across Hob Moor. She never liked to go back the same way she went out.

'And you shall have a gallop,' she assured her dancing mare.

Her mind was a pleasant blank as they went along together, absorbed with the sights and sounds of spring without thinking about anything. She was pulled from this reverie when she reached the place where the beck crossed the track that came up from Tyburn and led to Morland Place, for there was a man standing there, watching her approach. Vesper snorted a warning, and started lifting her legs showily, like a hackney. Polly rode on towards him, unalarmed, though she did not recognise him. There were often tramps and wandering unemployed on the roads these days, but she had nothing about her to steal, and she could outrun anyone on Vesper. Besides, she sensed no danger from this man.

He was tall and thin, wearing nondescript brown clothes like a countryman, with a strange, shapeless hat that shaded his face. As she came near he pulled off the hat, and she drew a breath of surprise. It was Father Palgrave; but he was much changed. He was very thin, his face quite gaunt, and his short-cropped hair had turned completely silver. She reined to a halt beside him, and he put out a hand to the mare. Vesper shied her head away automatically, and then lowered it to snuff his fingers.

'What a surprise to see you here,' Polly said. She smiled nervously, for there was no answering smile in his face. His eyes, which seemed somehow sunk back in their sockets, looked at her with the longest stare she had ever seen, as though he were seeing her from hundreds of miles off. There was a deadness in his face, as if he had been in a place of unimaginable horror.

'I came to say goodbye,' he said. Even his voice was different. There was no music in it, and he had always been a speaker one wanted to listen to. 'But I couldn't get any further. I can't go up to the house. So I'm glad you came along.'

'Goodbye?' she queried.

'I've left the sanatorium,' he said.

She waited, but he didn't seem to be going to say anything more without prompting, so at last she asked, 'Weren't they kind to you?'

He made a little pained movement of his shoulders, shrugging off the question, as if it was not the one he wanted to answer. 'I discovered . . . I should have realised how much it was costing your father to keep me there. I can't justify . . . can't go on taking . . .'

'Father doesn't begrudge. He just wants you to get well,' Polly said quickly.

'I will never be well,' he said.

'Yes, you will. In time.' She heard her own words, and felt stupid. She remembered how she had hated what had seemed to be the arrogance of people who were not suffering when she was. People who told her that everything would be all right, when she knew it wouldn't. 'Aren't you *any* better?' she asked at last, humbly.

'I have bad days and worse days,' he said quietly, staring off into the distance. 'On bad days – like this – I cry a lot. On worse days . . .' He shook his head, having no words for it.

'Is it,' she asked tentatively, 'the shell-shock?'

He paused before answering. 'When I was buried – that time in France – I lay in the dark, waiting to die. I could hear the shells. Feel them sometimes, through the earth. The impact was like a terrible silent noise. I knew what each shell must be doing to men, on both sides. I wondered why God would allow us to do it. I was angry. If we were made in His image, what sort of God was it? But still I prayed.'

'You got out,' she said, trying to follow his sense.

He shook his head again, but it was not a negative. 'I'm in the dark again. But now I think there's no God, only us. There's nothing in the blackness. Nothing but nothing. And I don't know how to get out.'

She didn't know what to say, only half understanding. Vesper flung her head up and down, wanting to be off, and she checked her with a light touch on the rein.

'Where will you go?' she asked.

'To the brothers at Ampleforth,' he said. 'They'll take me in.'

She felt relieved. It seemed a good solution. 'Perhaps you'll find God there,' she said tentatively. The words sounded foolish and inadequate once they were out. She felt oddly ashamed. 'Or – whatever you have lost,' she concluded weakly.

He seemed to see her suddenly – his eyes were no longer a thousand miles off. He took a step closer and

334

laid his hand briefly on her knee. She always rode 'across' on informal rides like this, in breeches and boots, with a divided skirt that covered her legs down to mid-calf. She looked down at his hand – long and thin, but still strong-seeming – pale against the navy serge. At once it was withdrawn.

'You've lost something, too,' he said, as if he had just discovered it. 'You've grown up.'

'I'm twenty-one next month,' she said – foolishly, because she knew that was not what he meant.

'Will you tell them, up at the house, for me? Tell them, thank you. And goodbye.'

'But you'll come back one day?' she urged. He shook his head. 'What about the baby?'

'I have nothing I can give her,' he said hopelessly. 'It's better she believes I'm dead. I can't . . .' He began to cry, but soundlessly, a slow leaking at the eyes, like bleeding to death. Polly's reaction must have been visible in her face, for he lowered his head and put a hand up, wiping at his eyes with the cuff of his sleeve. 'I have to go now,' he said, muffled, turning away. With his back to her, he paused to say, 'I hope you find what you lost.'

She watched until he disappeared through the arch under the railway, feeling raw with his suffering; and disconcerted, as though there were things she should have said or done that she had lost the opportunity for. She thought of the infant Laura – poor little orphan! So far she had just been a baby to Polly, undifferentiated as all babies were, but now suddenly she saw a flash of her growing up, a little girl, motherless and now fatherless too. Poor baby. What had the war done to them? She felt the restless urge to run away from it all, the same urge she had felt before. Vesper, sensing it, began digging with an impatient forefoot.

'Come, then,' Polly said, turned her, and let her spring away into a canter, high-tail in the breeze, leaping over puddles and rivulets of rain and even shadows on the path as if they were three-foot jumps. Polly sat her lightly, and lifted her face to the wind of their passage, and let it dry the tears on her cheeks.

Teddy was away in Manchester and, unwilling to broach the subject that she felt so raw inside her, Polly waited until he came home before she spoke of the encounter with Father Palgrave. By then, a letter had come from the sanatorium's director.

Teddy could not simply leave the matter as it was. He went first to the sanatorium, ready to be angry. Here had been some mismanagement, surely.

But the director – a small, balding man with a worried forehead and mild eyes behind gold-rimmed glasses – faced him without guilt. 'He discharged himself,' he explained. 'We tried to dissuade him, naturally, but we had no power to detain him, so there was nothing we could do. I wrote to you in courtesy because you had been paying for his treatment. I hoped that perhaps he would return to you. He does not seem to have had any other home, or family.'

'You should have stopped him!'

'We did all we could, but he was determined to leave, and we could not use force.'

'But is he *fit* to be wandering around on his own?' Teddy cried.

'He is not insane, sir, just unhappy and disturbed by his memories. We thought he had made some progress.

Lately he wasn't waking up screaming in the middle of the night. Unfortunately we believe now that was because he wasn't sleeping very much any more. But when he told us he was leaving he spoke quite rationally and calmly.'

It was not enough for Teddy, who went back to his motor and told Simmonds to drive straight to Ampleforth, the Benedictine abbey set in the lovely wooded valley off the Helmsley road. He was received courteously and shown into a small parlour, which was so obviously a waiting room it was impossible to imagine anything ever happening there. It was utterly silent – not even the ticking of a clock or buzzing of a fly. At times Teddy felt the urge to check if he was still breathing.

But at last the Father Abbot came in and sat down with him, and confirmed that Denis Palgrave was there. 'He came to us, rather footsore and very tired, and asked for shelter. We follow the order's tradition of hospitality, and always keep some rooms for travellers, but it was soon clear that he needed more from us than a bed for the night. He is very troubled in his mind. He told me that he had been contemplating suicide and, knowing what a grave sin it is, he had come to us to be safe. I think he chose the right place. In the few days he has been here, he has seemed calmer. He follows our routine, attends our services, prays with us. He works a little in the gardens, does his share of chores in the house. It is good for someone with chaos inside to have order around him.'

'Has he spoken to you about what's wrong with him?' Teddy asked anxiously.

'He doesn't speak very much at all, but he has told me a little. Whenever he is ready to tell more, I will be ready to hear him.'

'My daughter met him on the road. He said he didn't believe God existed.'

The abbot's eyes warmed with humour. 'He is angry with God. You can't be angry with someone who doesn't exist.'

Teddy thought about this for a moment. 'Can I see him?' he asked.

'I anticipated that you would want to, and asked him if he would come, but he doesn't want to see anyone from outside. I hope you will not be offended. Inwardly he is very frail. Think of him as an invalid who needs rest and quiet. He did ask me to thank you for all your kindness to him.'

Teddy nodded that away. 'Will he get better?' he demanded.

'He will get better. I cannot tell if he will ever be completely well, or if he will ever be able to leave here. But we will take care of him for as long as he needs us.' He gave a look of sympathy, as if knowing this was not enough for Teddy. 'I think he is in the right place. It was no accident that he came to our door. God sent him to us: He is taking care of him.'

So Teddy returned home, and told the family what he had learned. 'It looks as though poor little Laura may never see her father,' he concluded.

'She has us,' Henrietta said. 'We are her family now.'

'Oh, of course we'll take care of her,' Teddy said. 'There's no question about that.'

'I think she is in the right place,' Henrietta said quietly and firmly, and Teddy noticed, with a vague sense of comfort, that she had unknowingly used the same words as the abbot had about Palgrave.

* * *

338

When Oliver went to see the Roughtons to ask for Verena's hand in marriage, he had not known what reception to expect, but he was surprised at its coldness. The earl, who looked old and ill, scowled at him.

'So you're the pup who's been getting my daughter talked about?'

'Sir?'

'Squiring her all over Town, taking her to damned parties, dancing with her in public.'

'We have attended balls together,' Oliver said cautiously, not understanding the objection.

'I've even seen photographs. In the newspapers. And the gossip columns – my daughter in the gossip columns! They use initials but it's obvious who they mean – "Lady V F, daughter of the E of R." Ridiculous nonsense! Might as well come right out and say it. Everyone knows. You're ruining her reputation, and if I were a well man I'd call you out for it!'

Oliver, taken aback, protested: 'But I assure you, sir, there was never anything improper—'

He got no further. 'Improper?' the earl roared. '*My* daughter? Dare to use that word again and I'll horsewhip you, sick man or not. I've enough strength in my arms for that, I promise you!'

'Please,' Oliver said, 'may I explain? Lady Verena and I have an understanding—'

'No young thruster has any *understanding* with *my* daughter.'

Oliver spoke quickly in the hope of getting to the end of the sentence before another outburst. 'We want to get married. I asked her and she said yes, but I wasn't in a position to support a wife so we agreed to keep the engagement secret.'

'My daughter is *not* engaged, least of all to you! Her mother and I will choose someone suitable for her when the time comes. In the mean time, you can take yourself off, Impudence, and if you come sniffing around here again I'll set the dogs on you!' A violent fit of coughing stopped him. Oliver looked on in alarm as the earl's face turned red and then purple. He wondered if it would tip the old man completely over the edge if he were to touch him or offer him help.

Fortunately the door opened and Lady Roughton came in, followed by Verena. They had been having their own conversation in the parlour next door. Oliver saw that Lady Roughton looked anxious rather than angry and wondered if that was worse – but perhaps she was only anxious about her husband. She hurried to his side, poured some wine from the decanter on a side table and persuaded him to sip it. Oliver wanted to suggest water was a better idea but it didn't seem to be the moment to be putting himself forward. The coughs subsided, a period of heavy breathing followed, and the countess straightened up at last and said, 'Do you understand, Roughton, that this young man wants to marry Verena?'

'Understand? Do you think I'm an idiot?' he bellowed. 'Talk sense, woman! What do you think started me off in the first place?'

'Please don't shout,' she said. 'You know the doctor said you must try to keep calm. And really, Roughton, I don't know what there is to shout about. Mr Winchmore has come very honourably to ask your permission, even though Verena is of age, so he didn't legally have to.'

'*Legally?*' Another explosion seemed to be imminent, but the earl controlled himself with a visible effort. 'We

340

don't know anything about him – except that he's a damned outsider!'

'Daddy!' Verena reproached him. 'You know very well who he is. He's the son of the Earl of Overton and the grandson of the Duke of Southport. I should have thought that was quite good enough for me.'

'Do you think I'm an idiot? I know his name and where he is in the stud book. That's not the point. What do we know about *him*? Apart from the fact that he's been making a figure of you, Verena. And besides,' he went on hastily, seeing his daughter, who was made of the same stuff as him, about to challenge this, 'he's just admitted he can't support you. I ought to fetch my malacca to him for his impudence.'

'I beg your pardon, sir, but I said I couldn't support her *before*. I can now, which is why I've come to ask you for her hand,' Oliver said. And he explained about the Winchmore, and being surgeon-in-charge.

Roughton listened to this without satisfaction. 'A doctor,' he said witheringly. 'It's come to that, has it? My daughter wants to marry a damned quack! And not even a physician, but a surgeon! A jumped-up barber!'

Even Lady Roughton thought this was going too far. 'That's quite enough, Roughton,' she said. 'Consultant surgeons are perfectly respectable people. Look at Sir Andrew Fields. You were glad enough to consult him last year about your – trouble.'

'Didn't say he could marry m' daughter, though,' Roughton growled. 'Fine thing if you have to offer your daughters to every tradesman who comes to the door.'

Verena had had enough. 'Daddy, you may as well get used to the idea. I am going to marry Oliver. You can't stop me, and the only reason we asked you was to be polite – but you can't even be polite in return! You might remember that I have no dowry and I'm twenty-three years old. I'm not exactly a catch any more.'

Oliver suddenly saw the humour in the situation. 'My dear,' he said gently, 'I didn't realise that was why you wanted to marry me.'

She turned to him, stricken. 'Oh, God, I didn't mean that! I love you, Oliver! I'd marry you if I was the richest heiress in Britain. And I'd marry you if we had to live in a hovel.'

'Probably have to,' the earl muttered, but his heart was not in it any more. He was tired, and his stomach hurt. He just wanted to be left alone.

Oliver was smiling at Verena. 'I get the idea. You needn't go on. I don't think it's helping.' He turned to the earl and said politely, 'Sir, I love your daughter, and I believe I can support her in sufficient comfort. My prospects are good and I hope one day to be able to give her the luxury she deserves. Won't you give us your blessing?'

The earl looked at him sullenly. 'There's no dowry. You understand that. Can't give her a penny. Estate's all to pot – got to keep what little I can for the boy.'

'I understand,' Oliver said. 'It's Verena that I want. I love her. She is dowry enough in herself.'

'Sentimental twaddle. That's not how marriages are arranged in the best families. God knows how you've been brought up, if that's the way you think.' Then the earl waved an irritable hand. 'Oh, take her. Take her. Always was a damned headstrong girl. Never would take the bridle. I wish you luck of curbing her. Yes, yes,' he added, as Verena came round the desk to kiss him in thanks, 'go and talk to your mother about it. I wash my hands of the whole business.'

'Thank you, sir,' Oliver said. The three of them moved away, but he heard the earl behind him muttering, 'Doctor's wife. My daughter a damned doctor's wife,' as they went out.

Lady Roughton was more amenable, though still not, to Oliver's chagrin, ecstatic. 'Have you any thoughts about the wedding? I suppose you'll want to get married from here,' she said to her daughter. 'It will be awkward. We can hardly avoid asking people, and who is to pay for it all? The guest list will run into hundreds. I'm sorry to be so blunt, but you know how we are situated, Verena. It isn't that we don't *want* to give you a fine wedding. There simply isn't any money.'

'Actually, Mummy, Oliver and I were thinking of a London wedding. I don't want to upset you and Daddy, and I know a woman ought to be married from her home, but our lives are in London now.'

'But you know the London house is leased out,' said Lady Roughton. 'Even if we could get permission from Lady Stalybridge to use it, I can't see how that would come out any less expensive.'

'No, not that,' said Verena. 'Oliver and I were thinking of getting married from his mother's house. It will only be a small affair – just close family and a few friends, and a quiet wedding breakfast back there. Lady Overton is quite willing to stand the cost.'

Lady Roughton looked despairing. 'It's come to this, my daughter's wedding to be paid for by her mother-in-law.'

'The cost won't be great, you know, not more than an ordinary dinner party. And after all, our children,' she looked shyly at Oliver, who took her hand and drew it through her arm, 'will be *her* grandchildren too.'

343

'I suppose so,' Lady Roughton sighed. 'But I'd always planned how your wedding would be.'

'Don't be sad, Mummy. I'm not. It will be a lovely wedding, and Oliver and I mean to be very happy. And,' she added beguilingly, 'there is one thing you can give me – one very important thing.'

'What's that?' Lady Roughton asked suspiciously.

'Your wedding dress. I've always wanted to be married in your wedding dress. I know that's why you kept it.'

The countess's tired face brightened. 'Do you really mean it, darling? I always hoped . . . It will have to be altered for you. But the material is so good, much better than the silks you can buy today. And the lace cost a fortune at the time. You couldn't find anything like that now.'

So the conversation ended happily. On their way back to London, Oliver asked, 'Did you really always dream of being married in your mother's dress?'

She squeezed his arm. 'Silly. But what does it matter? I'm not sentimental like Mummy's generation. The dress will do very well. And I wanted to keep her from asking where we'll be living. I didn't think it was the time to be breaking it to her that we'll be starting married life in your mother's house.'

Oliver and Verena, having no great occasion to plan, settled on a June wedding. Emma's marriage to Peter was set for July, and was also to be a London wedding, at St Margaret's, with the wedding breakfast at the Holkams' house in St James's Square. (Violet had offered it, as that was where Emma had been living, and Holkam had agreed to it once Violet assured him that Emma would be paying for everything. The guest list featured

344

everyone who was important in society, right up to and including royalty, so the occasion seemed likely to do Holkam credit and reinforce several connections that would be useful to his career.)

The Castlefords had accepted her as Peter's bride-to-be without a struggle, perhaps because of her large fortune, and if her own origins were obscure, her connections were more than good. In any case, they reminded themselves in private, there was a lot more of *that* sort of thing going on since the war. A certain duke's heir had recently married a steel magnate's daughter from Pittsburgh, in order that her fortune should restore the estate. At least Emma Weston had a nice accent and English table manners.

Perhaps it was to reassure herself on the last count that Lady Castleford invited Emma for a Saturday-to-Monday at Kimcote without Peter, partly to grill her on her habits, tastes and intentions, and partly to impress upon her the elevation to which she was being lifted, and school her in the duties and responsibilities she was marrying into.

'You will be countess one day,' Lady Castleford told her grandly, 'and all this will be yours.' She waved a hand to indicate Kimcote Hall and the rolling acres beyond. 'Certain things are expected of the chatelaine of Kimcote. First and foremost, your duty will be to support Peter. An earl is like the king of a small kingdom. He gives the law, settles disputes, takes care of his people. His people look up to him and his wife and expect a great deal of them. They judge *everything* by the standards the lord and lady set. It is a sacred trust, and I understand that it might seem somewhat daunting to someone not born to it.'

Emma tried to look undaunted. She had accepted Peter, but it seemed she was marrying a multitude.

'But I shall be here to help you,' said the countess. 'Place yourself unreservedly in my hands, and I'm sure you will not disappoint. Your responsibilities will be heavy, but always remember Peter's will be even greater one day, and your first duty will always be to him – to be his *rock*.'

She accompanied the last word with a little squeeze and shake of Emma's upper arm. She then went on to talk about the wedding, which she seemed to be having tremendous fun planning. 'I'm so glad, my dear, that you haven't any family. If you had had a mother, she might have got in the way dreadfully. As it is, I can do everything, and make sure it is done right.' Emma had never known her mother, so was able to take this implied insult on the chin.

She was taken on a guided tour of the house. Lady Castleford explained the importance of various objects and gave an exposition of key points in the family's history, while sprinkling words of advice and wisdom, and coaching Emma on the things she must, and must never, *ever* do. But she reverted every few sentences to the wedding, which seemed to mean something more than itself to her.

The truth was revealed when, looking out of an upstairs window at the main drive, flanked either side by lime trees, the countess looked suddenly tired and said, 'I always hoped to have a daughter's wedding to plan, but I only had sons – Peter was supposed to be a girl, you know.'

So this, Emma thought, was her wedding *manqué*. She felt a sympathy for her for the first time, and it made her seem less daunting.

Lady Castleford went on, 'But then Gerald and Charles were killed. It's a good thing, as it has turned out, that Peter was a boy.' She looked at Emma, as if suddenly remembering she was there. 'Peter isn't strong like his brothers. He's sensitive. He thinks too much. But now he has you, and you seem to me very strong – level-headed. I'm glad you will be there to take care of him. And I,' she pulled herself together firmly, 'will be there to help you. Now, I think we should go and look at the strong-room.'

In the strong-room, the countess brought out cases of jewels and laid them on the central table on a cloth of black velvet, which seemed to be there for the purpose. 'These will come to you on your marriage,' she said. 'They are the family jewels, so they will go to your eldest son's wife in her turn. They are part of the estate. My personal jewels I hope to leave to your daughter, if you have one.' She looked hungrily at Emma for a moment, then began taking items out and explaining their history. 'The stones are good, but the settings are heavy. You can have them remodelled, of course, in time, if you wish. I hardly wore any of them, only the diamond set for State Openings and the ruby set when we dined at the palace, or for embassy balls. But this, now . . .' She opened a box and took out a tiara of fine diamonds. 'This I always considered rather light and pretty. I thought you might like to wear it for the wedding.'

Emma touched it with a wondering finger. 'Thank you. It's beautiful.'

The countess looked for a moment at the delicate web throwing sparks of fire from the heart of the stones, and then became brisk. 'I shall meet you in London next week for the fitting of your dress,' she said. Emma's wedding dress – which she was paying for herself – was being made by a leading London couturier, Blanchine, and everything about it – the style, the material, the trimming – had been chosen by Lady Castleford before Emma had even known about it. 'And we shall have luncheon afterwards with one or two friends of mine whom you ought to know. They are important hostesses, and I shall introduce you, so I expect you to make a good impression.'

She was the oddest mixture of kindness and bullying. Emma wondered if she would ever get to grips with her.

She wondered, too, sometimes – a little forlornly – if she would ever get to grips with Peter. She loved him, and believed he loved her, but he hardly treated her any differently since they had become engaged, and sometimes she felt there was something missing, a connection between them on some level she believed must exist but had no experience of: she had been very young when she was engaged to Fenniman, and they had been very little together. She was older now, and wanted something more, without being sure what it was.

Though she was with Peter a great deal, it was always in company. Opportunities for them to be alone together were few, and they had exchanged very few kisses since that moment in the hothouse, and none of the same sort – just snatched embraces in corridors and taxis. She longed for intimacy – physical, yes, but mental also: she longed to tell him everything and have him tell her his thoughts, to be alone with him in the darkness of the bedroom, with no barrier between them. She looked forward passionately not to the wedding but to the wedding's being over, so that they could start their life together.

Peter didn't take the wedding itself seriously at all. He laughed when she told him about his mother's plans, and seemed to regard the whole thing as if it were a curious custom of some Amazonian tribe he was reading about. He said there was no use in trying to thwart his mother when she had her heart set on something: they must just go along with it.

'I'll turn up and be good on the day,' he said on one occasion, 'and I advise you to do the same. It isn't important, anyway, is it? What matters is what comes afterwards.' He looked down at her, and she caught her breath: just for once he seemed really *there*. 'You are my safe haven,' he said softly, 'and I shall come and hide in you.' And then the moment was past, and he grinned and said, 'I hope Mother doesn't get you up like some Druid sacrifice all in white sheets for the wedding. But I suppose Monsieur Blanchine can be trusted. He has his reputation to think about. His creation is bound to be in all the newspapers.'

It was ironic, Emma thought, given her feelings about the place, that they were to go to Scotland for their honeymoon: the Castlefords had a house there on a grouse moor, which in July would be empty, so they could have it all to themselves until the August shooting began. Peter was adamant that he didn't want to go abroad. 'I never want to see France again,' he said bluntly. Emma understood the feeling and had hoped for Italy, but he said Italy would remind him of the war as well. 'We'll have long walks and swim in the burn and be quite alone,' he promised her. 'And I swear I shan't let anyone in a kilt come anywhere near you.'

*　　*　　*

Teddy gave a ball for Polly's twenty-first birthday, hiring the Assembly House for the purpose. Polly designed her own gown for it. She had grown tall in the last year – perhaps too tall for a woman, since she was also very slender. Teddy might privately mourn her lack of womanly roundnesses, and Henrietta might wish – as she did with most people – that she had more flesh on her, but there was no doubt she was healthy enough. She was not thin, but athletic: her figure was supple and strong from all the riding and walking.

And while she was not pretty in the conventional way, as she had been when younger, she had a special beauty that was all her own. Henrietta always thought vaguely that it was like the beauty of an animal, a deer or a wild horse, something clean and clear and indefinable, enhanced by a sort of remoteness or privateness that animals sometimes had. Boisterous young men became quiet in her presence: no-one would ever take liberties with Polly. Her height gave her authority, her opaque blue eyes an air of mystery, her long golden hair drawn back into a chignon, emphasising the length of her neck, a quiet grace.

Polly was taking a closer interest in the drapery business that would one day be hers. She had learned about the financial and managerial side of it, and was now having a say in *what* Makepeace's should be selling, as well as *how*. Already she had influenced window and shop-floor displays, making them artistic and inventive: previously, neat, symmetrical stacking had been the summit of ambition. Now she was proud to know that people stopped to look at Makepeace's windows for the displays themselves, and discussed them almost like works of art. And recently she had begun to draw designs for clothes, which she then took to the seamstresses in the workshop to discuss. When they seemed good enough, she had them made up. Through them she was learning what could be done, and was refining her designs accordingly.

She had a plan, which she was waiting for the right time to discuss with her father, for moving the leather and saddlery department to another building altogether, so that she could expand the women's clothing into the space. Makepeace's had begun as a saddler, expanded into whips, canes and gentlemen's gloves and hats, and from there into drapery, women's hats and underclothing, then ready-made dresses. She now felt that the old saddlery shop struck the wrong note, and that it would do just as well on a different premises. Meanwhile, women's ready-mades and fashions in general seemed to her to be the future.

For herself, for the ball, she wanted something original that would make a virtue of her height and slenderness. The current straight fashions seemed to be made for her, but she wanted her dress to be different from everyone else's, to be noticed. Then her father might agree to her plans, and the leather department might become Polly's Originals, with Polly herself the best advertisement for her wares. So she drew and rubbed out, stared off into the distance chewing her pencil end, consulted the staff and the seamstresses, looked through bales of material and boxes of trimmings. Teddy had told her anxiously that she could have the best mantua-maker in York, or even go to London and have her gown made there, but Polly only smiled and patted his arm and told him not to worry, he'd be proud of her. So he gave in and told her she could have a free hand.

She found the silk she wanted, but had to have it

dyed, since she couldn't find the exact colour. She spent hours with the seamstresses, explaining what she wanted and getting the pattern just right. The result, she felt, was worth it. The dress, of heavy silk the colour of an English bluebell, draped beautifully, like a Greek toga, from the points of the shoulders to the lowered waist, and from there fell to her ankles. The overskirt was drawn up in loose swathes and gathered on one side, held by a silk rosette at the hip, showing the underskirt of a silvery blue. The gown was sleeveless, with broad streamers hanging from the shoulders instead, and as she danced they would move and turn and show the undercolour. Around the neck and the hipline was a band of silver embroidery and crystal beads, giving a frosted look. On the evening she wore a bandeau round her forehead of the same silk, embroidered and bead-encrusted, while her chignon was held at the back by an invisible net sewn with transparent beads, so that they appeared like dew-drops resting on her hair.

Teddy's present for her birthday was a slender strand of diamonds, so beautiful they made her gasp, and perfect to be worn with the dress. She couldn't imagine what they had cost, and hugged him wordlessly before expressing the thought.

'Never mind,' Teddy said, pleased and a little moist at the eyes. 'You're worth this and much more. Besides, you're an important heiress, you know, so you must dress the part. I always meant you to have diamonds when you were twenty-one.'

The ball was a great success. Polly was the cynosure of all eyes, her gown was admired, and she danced every dance and went in to supper with Lord Lambert's son, which was just what Teddy wanted. He didn't really want

Polly ever to leave him, but he knew she must marry some time, and if it had to be, he would have liked a title for her. The Lambert heir was a nice sort of fellow and Lambert Hall was only a few miles away.

It was a few days after the ball that things went wrong for Polly. Catching her father alone at last, while Miss Husthwaite was out of the steward's room for a moment, she asked him if he had liked her ball gown.

'It was beautiful,' he said, leafing through some papers on his desk. 'What is all this? I thought I'd signed everything this morning. And where's that tenancy agreement I asked for? I thought she'd have put it here.'

'Please, Daddy,' Polly said, making him look up. 'The dress?'

'Yes, it was very fine. Are you wanting some more clothes? You know you don't need to ask.'

'I designed it myself,' she reminded him.

'I know,' said Teddy. 'I dare say none of those London people could have done it better.'

'That's rather what I wanted to talk to you about,' Polly said, and outlined her plan for Makepeace's and the ladies' fashions department. But she could see her father was distracted and not really taking it in.

'It's nice that you have plans for the old place,' he said, 'and I expect they're very good. But let's leave it as it is for now. People know what to expect when they go to Makepeace's. They like it the way it is.'

'How do you know that?' she asked, frustrated.

He looked perplexed. 'Because no-one likes change. There's been change enough since the war. What we need now is a bit of time with things settling down and being normal again.'

'I thought you said Makepeace's would be mine.'

'It will be, one day. Don't be in too much of a hurry to grow up, chick.'

'But I am grown up. I'm twenty-one,' she reminded him.

'When you're my age, you realise how young twenty-one is. You just enjoy yourself while you can.'

'But that's the thing, Daddy—'

'I'm sorry, chick – can we talk about this another time? I must find that agreement and get it over to Pobgee.'

Polly gazed at him sadly. 'You won't let me do anything, will you?' she said, with quiet desperation.

He was genuinely puzzled. 'But I let you do whatever you want,' he said. 'Anything you want you can have, you know that. What was it this time? A new dress, didn't you say?'

'No, *you* said that. What *I* want is to change Makepeace's. I want to make it my own business. I want to show you I can manage it and make it successful.'

'It is successful.'

'More successful,' Polly insisted. She changed tack. 'Daddy, I must have something to *do*.'

'You have plenty to do. You're always on the go, as far as I can see. Riding, tennis, dances. And now summer's here you won't have a minute to sit still, with all the fêtes and picnics and what-not. You're the most popular girl in the district – and rightly too.' He reached out and cupped her cheek with his hand. 'You're the most beautiful by far. Now, why don't you go out and get some fresh air – leave frowsting in dusty offices for old men like me?'

'Yes, Daddy,' she said, and went sadly out. She wandered through to the Great Hall where the front door was open, letting in the sweet May airs. Sawry was coming the other way with a silver tray on which a letter lay.

'Oh, Miss Polly – this just came for you in the midday post. Miss Husthwaite has the rest.' Polly reached out a hand for it. 'From the United States of America, miss,' Sawry added conspiratorially.

She knew the writing. 'It's from Lennie,' she said, feeling a little cheered. Lennie's letters were always full of news. 'I'll take it outside to read.'

'Good idea, miss,' Sawry said. 'It's a beautiful day.'

She had hardly set foot out of doors when her dogs, Kai and Silka, found her, frolicking and bowing in the hope of persuading her to a long walk; but when she got no further than the rose garden and sat down on a stone bench, they accepted it philosophically and settled at her feet, blinking happily in the sunshine, and snapping occasionally at flies wandering past. It was a soft May day, golden with warmth and promising all that was lovely about that loveliest of months. The sky was cornflower blue, and the light filtering through the trees illuminated the pale young leaves so that each stood out in individual beauty. One of the stable cats, a large, plushy marmalade tabby, came tiptoeing delicately along the stone edging of the path, placing its white-tipped feet with velvet precision. It paused a cautious moment at the sight of the dogs, then jumped lightly up onto an empty plinth nearby and sat blinking in the sunshine, tail curled tightly around its feet, looking like a statue to self-possession.

Lennie's news was mostly about his business, and Polly read it with more interest than she would have a couple of years ago. His radio factory was 'going great guns': he had so many orders that he had now taken over the whole factory. He was making the cases as well as the insides, and had branched out into different designs and different sizes:

It seems folk snap them up as fast as I can make them. There are twenty radio stations now, and more starting up every day, mostly broadcasting dance music and serious talks, but I've heard they are going to start broadcasting sporting events too this summer. I reckon that will prove popular with the fellows! My sets are being sold in Macy's and Bloomingdales and all the best stores, but I have a new idea which I will tell you about next letter if it works out.

He went on with family news. Martial was engaged to be married 'to a nice girl whose father's in the mining business'. Lizzie, he wrote, was half inclined to be tearful about it – he would never understand why women felt a wedding was the occasion for waterworks – but Rosie was excited about being a bridesmaid.

She's a proper little woman now at twelve years old, and mad keen on dresses, and dressing-up generally. She was in the Christmas play at her school and everyone said she did really well, and now she's scandalising poor Lizzie by saying she wants to be an actress, which Lizzie seems to feel is next door to a fallen woman. But she's a heap of fun, and whatever she sets her mind to do, she'll do well, and enjoy herself mightily in the process.

He wrote about New York and American news in general, and finished two sheets later – his letters were always satisfyingly long – by saying:

I miss you very much, but that's nothing new, so I suppose I don't really need to tell you. I wish so much I could see you again and chat to you instead of writing – we were always good friends, weren't we? I suppose there isn't any chance of your coming over for a visit? Lizzie was saying just the other day that she would love to have you, and that you would enjoy New York. Of course, I think the same. You and New York are just made for each other, and you'd be the queen bee here – everyone loves the English accent! But I suppose your father would never let you come.

Polly folded the letter and stared into space, her mind busy with a revelation. Silka sat up and scratched at her neck with her long hind claws, and Kai yawned so mightily his ears almost met behind. The cat yawned daintily in sympathy, stood up and stretched itself into a croquet hoop, then jumped down into the bushes and disappeared on important business. A fat bee flew past Polly's cheek, so close she felt the fan of its wings on her skin. She looked suddenly around her, and thought there never was a place so beautiful as Morland Place in the young of summer, or a place she loved so much. She got up and went indoors to find her father.

'Daddy, you said I could have anything I wanted,' she began. He looked up, startled. 'Well, I want to travel.'

'Travel?' Teddy said, in blank amazement. 'Travel where?'

She remembered suddenly Palgrave saying, 'I hope you find what you've lost.' She wouldn't, she never could, because Erich Küppel was dead; but perhaps in a new place, in a new world, she might find something else, something at least to fill the emptiness inside.

'I want to go to New York,' she said.

CHAPTER FIFTEEN

Though Helen might make brave noises about it, life without servants was hard, even in a house as small as the one in Walton. Taking care of two small children and a baby – bathing, dressing, feeding them, taking them for walks and keeping them occupied – was a day's work in itself, especially when one of them was Basil. She found herself longing for September when he would go to school, though that would present its own problems – Jack was already fretting about the sort of children he would mix with in the local council school, and what bad habits he might pick up. Helen wanted to tell him he should be more worried about what bad habits Basil would teach the innocents he was let loose on, but she had to be careful what she said to Jack these days: his sense of humour was frayed by worry.

With careful management she could afford a char-woman, who came in each day to do the heavy cleaning. Mrs Kifner – Basil *would* call her Mrs Kipper – also attended to the boiler and would do the fires in winter. Thank God it was a warm summer – no fires yet – and that the little house had gas lighting, so there were no lamps to fill and trim. But that still left the rest of the housework, tidying and bed-making and dusting – and it was astonishing how much dirt and disorder five souls managed to spread in the course of a day. There was mending and darning, too, and the marketing and cooking; and every meal left a pile of washing-up behind it. The laundry she sent out – Mrs Kifner had a sister she recommended – and thank God for that, or she'd have gone mad; but still there were things she had to rinse out herself in the wash-house, because the baby's demands were hard for any laundress to keep up with.

And then having got the children bathed (the large tin bath to drag into the kitchen for Basil and Barbara, but she found it easier to wash the baby in the sink in the wash-house) and to bed at the end of the day, she had to make the house welcoming for poor Jack, and cook a meal and sit down and eat it with him in a cheerful and engaging manner, though she was often so tired she'd as soon have gone to bed without eating. It was a private and unexpressed irony to her that her trip to the Malthusian clinic in Holloway had been largely wasted, for they were both too tired these days to make love.

Everything seemed to take so long. Shopping, for instance: walking from shop to shop, pushing the perambulator with a child walking on either side, the bags getting heavier all the time and the children more fractious, so that when she got home and discovered she had forgotten something she wanted to burst into tears. Sometimes if Basil misbehaved or Barbara spilled her milk, she felt that one more thing would break her heart.

Saturday afternoons and Sundays were the saving of her. On Saturday afternoons, if Jack was home, they would take the children to the park. Jack would play ball with Basil and Barbara and Rug – who was a keen footballer – while she pushed the perambulator or helped

Michael to take his first wambling steps. Or they might take a picnic down to the riverside and watch the boats go by, a perennial pleasure to the children, who had an ambition to make every person on the river wave to them. Having Jack around made it so much easier with the children, and he would help her with their bath-time, and tell them a story in bed while she got their own supper ready. Then in the evening, feeling much less exhausted, she would enjoy talking to him over the meal, and afterwards he would read aloud to her while she got on with the mending – another of those jobs she simply had not thought about before, but which accumulated silently through the week like dust-mice under beds.

And on Sunday there was a little lie-abed, and then church together; then Molly would arrive and help her prepare dinner, which they ate together as a family. She was glad of Molly's visits, bringing a breath of the wider world outside into her cramped domestic sphere. Molly was always such a lively talker that even poor tired Jack was enthused into discussing politics and world affairs with her, and his shoulders seemed to straighten and worries fall off him almost visibly, like dust.

One Sunday when Molly was helping her wash up, Helen said, 'I hate to put so much responsibility on you, but if you didn't come and visit on Sundays I think I would go mad.'

'You're looking tired,' Molly said.

'It's the children, mostly,' Helen confessed. 'It's so hard when you haven't anyone else to take charge of them when you want to do something. I'm sure I could do the marketing in half the time if I didn't have to take them with me. Just getting them ready to go out is like a military campaign.'

'Are you sure you couldn't afford a nanny?' Molly said absently, drying a plate.

Helen looked at her with affectionate exasperation. 'Dear Molly, not possibly! And where on earth would I put one if I could?'

Molly smiled. 'It's just as well I didn't come to live with you, isn't it?'

'I'm managing the finances at the moment,' Helen went on, 'because I had some savings, and I'm eking them out, a few pence here and there to make things smoother. But if anything happened and I had to use them up . . . If I had to get rid of Mrs Kifner . . .' She shuddered. 'And with winter coming there'll be coal to buy, and warmer clothes for the baby. And winter ailments. Coughs and colds I can dose myself, but if we had to call in the doctor . . . We manage all right, but, oh, Molly, what on earth would we do if Jack couldn't work, or lost his job?'

'It makes you realise,' Molly said, 'how narrow the line is for most people, between getting by and disaster.'

Helen washed a few more things in silence, and then said, 'You're right. And people do manage, don't they? Thousands and thousands of them, all the time, every day. My next-door neighbour, Mrs Philips, has five children, and her husband is only a railway worker. And she does her own washing – I've seen her hanging it on the line.'

'No doubt she's used to it,' Molly said, not following.

'That's exactly my point. It's a state of mind.' She straightened up, squaring her shoulders unconsciously. 'I suppose in the back of my mind I've been thinking that this is just a temporary aberration and that everything will get back to normal in a few weeks. I've been doing it all with half an eye over my shoulder looking for rescue. But if I accept that this is my job, and tackle it head on, I'm sure things won't seem so grim. Lots of women cope with far more than I have to.'

'Other women don't have your brain,' Molly objected.

'But that's the point. If I can't work out a routine for all this, I should be ashamed of myself.'

'I didn't mean that. I mean you are an educated woman. You have a mind that needs nourishing as well as a body.'

'There, that's the last plate. All done now until suppertime. That's the worst thing about housework – as soon as it's done, it starts building up again. Why can't someone invent plates that wash themselves?'

Molly looked at her with a frown. 'I hate to see you turning into a drudge. You can't just put your mind into a box, Hel.'

'That's what I'll have to do, for the time being.'

'It's unjust. I hate that old Freddie,' Molly fumed. 'What a beast!'

'He took care of his own first. That's what we all do. The house was rightfully his. You couldn't expect him to give it away to me as if it was a – a vase or a china dog.'

'You're such a hero,' Molly said. 'If it was me . . .'

'Nothing to be done about it,' Helen said. She dried her hands and linked her arm through Molly's. 'Let's go and roust them all out for a walk, while the weather's nice.' And her smile wavered for a moment as she thought of what it would be like in winter, with wet coats and muddy shoes, housebound children, coal to pay for, fires to make up and the layer of soot over everything, colds in the head and handkerchiefs to wash, dark evenings and getting up in the dark. Then she shook the thoughts away.

It's all a matter of attitude, she told herself. *You can get through anything if you approach it in the right way. And didn't you say all through the war that you wouldn't mind anything if only Jack came back in one piece?*

Well, perhaps this was the price. If so, it was worth paying.

The size, expense and glamour of the Weston-Gresham wedding drove the press into a frenzy, and Emma and Peter were besieged by reporters and photographers wherever they went. *She* was pretty, extremely rich and an ex-FANY; *he* was brave and handsome with a fine war record. They seemed to sum up everything that was admirable about the new young people, and their smiling faces as they arrived at parties or emerged from theatres seemed to be in every day's paper and every week's illustrated.

Everything about the wedding plans was discussed in the gossip columns: the guest list – both the Prince of Wales *and* the Duke of York were attending – the wedding gifts, the carriages, the wedding breakfast. She and Peter had managed to keep their honeymoon destination private; and Blanchine was making a great mystery about the dress, which bred a whole litter of speculative designs in the ladies' magazines.

Over the years Emma had grown used to a certain level of press attention, and didn't mind too much. She was happy. As the day grew closer, Peter had become attentive and loving. He sent her letters even if they were meeting later, which they did almost every day, and flowers several times a week. He thought the wedding a gigantic joke. As he said to her one evening when they were dining alone at the Ritz, one of the privileges of an engaged couple, 'The wedding is for other people, my parents, principally. It's what happens afterwards that matters.' He reached across the table and laid his hand over hers. 'I can't wait to get you alone. I love you so much, my darling.'

Their eyes met and a spark of passion seemed to leap between them that made her feel hollow and weak.

'Will we really be alone?' Emma asked, all her longing in her face.

'If we can prevent the press hounds from tracking us. But I can't see them going all the way to Aberdeen, even for a story as gilded as ours. You'll like Barmechin. It always makes me think of Rumpelstiltskin's castle, but all the beds have new mattresses: the mater ordered them when the King and Queen came on a visit from Balmoral. Father had a new boiler put in at the same time so there's plenty of hot water – you see, I understand what civilisation really means.'

Emma laughed, but the mention of Balmoral gave her pause. 'You absolutely promise there aren't tartan carpets, and chairs made of stags' antlers, and a piper playing under the bedroom windows at dawn?'

'Mother loathes tartan carpets – says they're frightfully middle-class – and the only stags' antlers are still on the stags. And no pipers, just a few old servants, who know how to mind their own business, and keep us comfortable.'

'And what will we do all day?'

He pressed her hand. 'Walk, talk, be together. Make love.'

Her cheeks glowed, but she could stand such things from him. She gripped his hand tighter, the longing flowing in her strong like a tide. 'Shall we truly?'

'Most truly. Do you doubt it? I dare say some days we shan't get up at all. We shall make one little room an everywhere. "Love, all alike, no season knows, nor clime, nor hours, days, months" – well, we shan't have months there, but you get the idea. Do you know Donne?'

She shook her head. 'I think he was thought too risqué at my finishing school.'

He smiled. 'Oh, then, what a delight to introduce you to him! We shall lie in bed and I shall read to you the greatest love poetry ever penned. Sometimes I think he took all the words and left none for ordinary mortals like me.'

And there in the middle of the crowded restaurant, holding her hand, he quoted:

O, my America, my Newfoundland,
My Kingdom, safest when with one man mann'd,
My mine of precious stones, my empery;
How am I blest in thus discovering thee!
To enter in these bonds, is to be free.
There, where my hand is set, my soul shall be.

Emma almost felt she couldn't bear it. Her throat was tight. 'Do you really love me so much?' she whispered.

'So very much, my kingdom. I told you, you are my haven, and I shall hide in you from the world's storms. It will be just the two of us, for ever. And that is why, you see,' he said, descending suddenly to the earth again, 'I can't take the wedding seriously.'

She didn't mind the bathos. She was afraid sometimes of feeling too much, hoping too much, and she guessed he felt the same. They had to keep their feet firmly on the earth, or their souls might float off like balloons and be lost.

Emma received a request from Venetia to call on her and, feeling a little guilty at the neglect of her old friends, she went round to Manchester Square at the first opportunity, between a fitting for her going-away outfit and a luncheon with her bridesmaids. She was shown into the drawing-room – pleasantly cool on this hot June day – and very soon Venetia came in, and crossed the room to take her hands and kiss her cheek.

'Emma, my dear, you're looking radiant. What a beautiful outfit.' It was a dusky pink crêpe-de-Chine two-piece. 'You must have great stamina. As I remember, the weeks before the wedding are exhausting for the bride.'

'It has been busy,' Emma admitted. 'But a happy sort of busy-ness.'

'The happiest, when you're in love. As I can see you are. I know young Gresham only slightly, but from all I hear he's a decent man. Had a good war, as they say.'

Emma winced. 'I don't think that's how Peter would put it.'

Venetia led her to a sofa. 'I know, dear. It's a stupid phrase. No-one who was there could ever say it was a good war. But now you young people have the chance to put everything right, correct the mistakes of the past, make sure it never happens again. Had you thought of going into politics?'

'I'm not thinking of anything at the moment except the wedding,' Emma said, with a rueful smile.

'Quite right,' Venetia said. 'Foolish of me. But afterwards – there's a great deal a woman in your position can do. You'll have fortune and rank, which will give you great influence. I hope you'll use it wisely and well.'

Emma was afraid there was a criticism lurking in those words. Did Lady Overton think she had been spending too much time dancing, when she should have been doing good works? 'We're all tired, after the war,' she said, with the faintest hint of resentment.

Venetia heard it and retreated. 'If anyone deserves to have some fun, it's the likes of you and Peter Gresham,' she said. 'I'd like to get to know him – he seems an interesting young man. Will you bring him to see me one day?'

'Yes, of course,' Emma said, pleased.

'And now,' Venetia said, 'knowing how busy you must be, I had better come to the point. I have something to give you.' She rose and fetched from a side table a long narrow box, sat down again beside Emma and opened it. Inside was a sapphire pendant – a large, pale blue stone on a diamond chain. She lifted it out and laid it in Emma's hands.

Emma gazed in astonishment at the lovely thing – she had never seen a stone of that size, and the cut of it created blue fire deep in its heart. 'It's beautiful,' she said.

'It is a pretty thing,' Venetia allowed. 'A Siamese stone, not as valuable as the darker Kashmiri and Burmese gems, but a good colour, and the size and cut are remarkable. It belonged originally to Lucy, Lady Theakston, who was my great-grandmother, and also yours. She is our common ancestor and the reason we call each other cousin.'

'I've heard about her from my father. She was a great lady, I believe?'

'If half the stories are true . . .' Venetia said with a smile. 'She was something of a hero to me when I was young, because she did what she wanted to do, rather than what society expected. Society – and my father – expected me to get married and be a wife and mother, but I wanted to be a doctor. Fortunately, it proved possible to do both,' she concluded, 'but it was a struggle.'

'And this was hers?' Emma said, moving the pendant in her palm so that the sapphire sparked, and the small diamonds glittered. 'It's magnificent.'

'Your father left it to me in his will,' Venetia said. 'But the opportunities to wear it are growing few for me, and it is a piece that ought to be worn. It is time I gave it to you.' Emma began to protest, but she went on, 'It's fitting that it should go back into your branch of the family. Violet has enough jewels of her own. I think it's what your father would have wanted, so you will oblige me, my dear, by accepting it, with my love. Perhaps you'll even wear it at your wedding – the "something blue" of the old rhyme? For your father's sake if not for mine.'

Emma surprised herself, and Venetia, by impulsively putting an arm round her neck and kissing her cheek, but Venetia did not seem to be upset by the liberty. 'Bless you,' she said. 'You'll make a lovely bride.'

'Thank you,' Emma said. 'I shall treasure it always. And I *shall* wear it at the wedding.' *Whatever Blanchine says*, she added in her thoughts.

Oliver and Verena had a fine day for their wedding, which Venetia took to be a good sign, though she admitted to herself afterwards that had it been a foul day she'd have found a way to make that a good sign too. She liked Verena and it was clear that the two loved each other and were well suited. Besides, she had had enough sadness recently: just a few days before the wedding the news had come that Mark Darroway had passed away in his sleep. It was a kind end for a good man, but he had been one of her oldest friends, and she felt the loss.

The wedding took place in St George's, Hanover Square, which was fashionable enough to placate the Roughtons – though the earl probably felt Westminster Abbey a bit of a stretch down for his daughter.

Verena looked very slender and ethereal in her mother's white silk and lace, with a bouquet of white summer roses and Madagascar jasmine. Venetia thought it took a great deal of presence and inner beauty to stand so much white. The church seemed dauntingly large, too, for such a small party. On Verena's side were the Roughtons, her nineteen-year-old brother Vernon, up from Oxford for the day, and her two bridesmaids: her closest friends Amalfia Worseley and Linda Maitland, girls she had come out with, and served in the VAD with during the war. On Oliver's side were his two groomsmen – Kit Westhoven and David Tenby, his friend and gasman – and Venetia, Violet and Lord Holkam.

Compared with what Emma's wedding would be like, it was very small beer indeed; but Venetia thought it lovely. She had made sure there was excellent music, and flowers in the church; and when they came out there was a modest presence of press and photographers, enough to reassure the bride her nuptials would not go unnoticed. Back at the house the servants gathered on the steps to welcome the party in, and there was a most magnificent luncheon. Venetia had spared nothing: the table was beautifully decorated with white roses and greenery, and they began with champagne and went on to the best wines in her cellar.

Venetia thought that twelve was a very pleasant number to have around the table, enough for variety but not overwhelming. The young people were happy and chatty, and there was free-flowing conversation and much laughter. The Roughtons thawed considerably under the onslaught, and the earl eventually mellowed enough to compliment Venetia both on the menu and the wines. When dessert was put on there were speeches from just about everyone. Kit was very droll and had everyone laughing. Oliver called out to him, 'You next!'

When everyone retired to the drawing-room, Oliver and Verena went upstairs to change, and returned in their going-away clothes for the cutting of the cake, before they had to leave to catch their train. Verena kissed absolutely everyone, her eyes bright. 'Thank you for my wedding,' she whispered to Venetia. 'It was quite, quite perfect.'

Oliver took her hand and pressed it. 'Thank you,' he said. 'I couldn't be happier.'

'Oh, you will be,' Venetia assured him.

Everyone crowded into the hall to see them off, and some of the servants threw rice. As they got into the waiting taxi, Kit, standing at Venetia's elbow, said, 'That was the nicest wedding I was ever at. If ever I go in for a spot of matrimony, I shall ask you to do the same for me.'

'I'd be pleased to,' she said.

'Now Oliver's gone, you'll have to look on me as your son-at-home.' He slipped a hand through her arm. 'Let's go and have some more champagne.'

* * *

Helen received a letter by an early post from Jessie.

'I haven't seen you for such ages, not since you moved into the new house. I propose to come and visit you this afternoon, and as you aren't on the telephone, perhaps you'll let me know by return of post if this isn't convenient.'

Helen looked at the house, and at herself, and almost scribbled off a note saying it wasn't; but then thought how nice it would be to have company. Jessie was sensible and would understand the situation. And they couldn't cut themselves off from everyone they knew. So she did some hasty dusting and went out, with her usual entourage of unwilling children, to do the shopping and buy a cake for tea.

Jessie arrived, smiling and affectionate, but expressing herself parched from the train journey. 'And look at my gloves!' she exclaimed. 'Why are railway carriages so dirty? I'm sure I see them being cleaned often enough. Dear Helen, how are you? You look tired.'

'You, on the other hand, look almost indecently well. Married life must be agreeing with you,' Helen said, leading her in.

Jessie gave one quick glance round and said, 'This is snug.'

'It isn't snug, it's poky, so you needn't be polite.'

'I wasn't being,' Jessie said. 'You should see some of the places I lived in as a nurse. Oh, here are the children! Come and say hello, you darlings. Basil, you're growing like a weed!'

'I can do a head-over-heels,' Basil informed her importantly. 'Barbara can't. She's too little. Shall I show you?'

'Not in here,' Helen intervened hastily. 'Perhaps later. Would you like some tea, Jessie?'

Jessie took in the boisterousness of the children's entrance and the size of the house, and reassessed Helen's tiredness. 'It's such a lovely day,' she said, 'why don't we all go out for a walk first? Is there a park nearby?'

'Yes,' said Helen. 'But you said you were thirsty.'

'A drink of water will cure that. I'll enjoy a cup of tea much more when I've stretched my legs. I've been sitting down on a train for what seems like hours. I expect the children would like to go out.' They expressed themselves in no uncertain terms about that. 'Where's the baby?'

'Upstairs, having his afternoon nap. But I was just going to get him up,' said Helen, giving in, with some relief.

With the two of them, it seemed to take no time at all to get the tribe ready to go out, and Jessie held Barbara's hand and chatted to Basil while Helen wheeled the perambulator along the hot pavements. The park was a haven of greenness after the barren streets and noisy traffic. The children raced away, like horses let out of the stables. Michael sat up and looked about him agreeably, and the two women strolled under the shade of the trees, pushing him between them.

'That was gracefully done,' Helen said. 'You should be in the diplomatic corps.'

Jessie did not pretend not to understand her. 'Don't you usually take them out for a walk?'

'Yes, usually. There's only a small yard, so it's the only way to run off their energy. But sometimes it's hard to fit it in. And when the weather's bad . . .'

'Poor Helen,' Jessie said. 'You make me feel guilty, being so prosperous.'

'Well, you mustn't,' Helen said sharply.

'But I didn't know quite how difficult things were for you and Jack. How is he?'

'He has a job, which is more than many people can say,' she answered. 'And we have a roof over our heads and enough to eat.'

'Yes, but—'

'He got so discouraged when he had no job,' Helen went on, overriding the interruption. 'That was the worst thing of all. I couldn't bear to see him sinking under the weight of failure. I know you're wondering why I don't ask for help from Morland Place. But don't you see, it would break Jack's heart? He's supporting us by his own efforts, and that means more than any little inconvenience. So I beg you not to let Jack think you pity us. And that's the last we'll say about this subject, if you don't mind,' she concluded.

'I understand,' Jessie said, after a moment. 'But if things should ever get *too* difficult – you will remember that I owe you a great debt? You wouldn't refuse to let me help if you really needed it?'

Helen's face relaxed, and she managed a smile. 'If ever I really need help, I promise I will come to you first. Is that all right?'

'Yes,' said Jessie. 'That will do.'

'And we are quite all right, you know,' Helen went on. 'It's just – different.'

Jessie nodded, and changed the subject. 'The children look very well.'

'You can tell by the way they behave like hooligans that they're healthy,' Helen said. 'Basil has a streak of pure devil in him. I can't think what he's going to be when he grows up. He has a perfect genius for getting dirty, and where he leads, Barbara follows. Jack calls them Voice and Echo, but it's more like Mud and Muddier.'

Jessie laughed. 'And I can't get over how much the baby's grown. Is he walking yet?'

'He takes a few steps before the force of gravity asserts itself. At the moment he prefers crawling, because he can get up such a speed, but now and then the desire to be on his hind legs overcomes him. Yes,' she addressed Michael, who was burbling and beating his fists on the pram-cover, 'I know you want to get out. We'll stop by that bench and let him show his colours.'

When they were settled, and Michael was standing between them, holding on to their skirts and flexing his knees like a Swedish drill instructor, Helen said, 'Tell me about you. How are your children? How is Bertie?'

'The children are well. Bertie works too hard, but he doesn't seem to mind it. We're staying on in London for another year, you know.'

'Really? Are you disappointed?'

'I was at first. I'd already started packing things up when Bertie said they'd asked him for another year, and my first feeling was that I couldn't bear it. I miss riding, and I want the children to grow up in Yorkshire, and poor Bran only knows parks and streets – where's Rug, by the way?'

'He goes to work with Jack. He prefers the smell of garages. But you've resigned yourself now?'

'There are good things in London too. The theatre and the cinema, and we go out to restaurants sometimes. And as long as I'm with Bertie, nothing else matters so much.'

'I feel that way about Jack.'

'But I am going to Morland Place for a holiday in

August. I'm taking the children for a month, and Bertie will come down for Saturdays-to-Mondays, when he can.' She hesitated. 'Why don't you come too?'

'I couldn't leave Jack alone here,' Helen said at once. 'We don't have servants to take care of him.'

Jessie considered. 'Would you,' she said, even more hesitantly, 'like me to take Basil and Barbara? It wouldn't be any trouble to me, and it would be nice for them to have a holiday.'

Helen's eyes were troubled. 'I'd like it for them, but I have to think how Jack would see it.'

'Surely he'd like them to have a chance to run about in the country. And to see their cousins. Besides, it's hardly charity, Helen. Not when it's family.'

'He might think it was the thin end of the wedge. But I'll talk to him if I can find the right moment.'

'I'll leave it with you, then.' She searched for another subject. 'Did you get a piece of cake from Oliver's wedding?'

'Yes,' Helen said, smiling, 'though I didn't get to taste a crumb. The children wolfed it all. It was nice of Cousin Venetia to send it.'

'She sent us a piece too,' Jessie said, 'with a nice letter explaining that the wedding had been very small, with immediate family only, so that I wouldn't be offended not to be invited.'

'Oh, I had that letter too,' Helen said.

'I'd have liked to see Oliver turned off,' Jessie said. 'I was always fond of him. I think he and Verena will be happy together – she's very sensible. I'm going to have them over to dinner when they get back from honeymoon. Perhaps you'd come, too?'

'Can't leave the children,' Helen said. 'But thank you.'

Jessie was about to suggest a neighbour might keep an eye on them, and then reflected that there were probably other reasons for the refusal.

'Well, then,' she said, after a moment's thought, 'why don't you and Jack *and* the children come over one Sunday, the way you used to? I'll ask Molly, too, and it will be like old times. I know my children would love to see yours. Oh, *do* say you will come. It would be so nice.'

And Helen thought that perhaps it would, and she said, 'I'm sure we could manage that. Thank you.'

'I saw Emma the other day, by the way,' Jessie said, changing the subject before Helen could change her mind. 'She was just coming out of the Ritz with some other people, all looking terribly glamorous and rich. She's in the papers an awful lot at the moment – the press seem to be getting very excited about the wedding.'

'How is she? Is she happy? Did you chat much to her?'

'Oh, I didn't speak to her at all. I was a little way off, and they were just getting into taxis. I didn't want to shout. But she looked happy. I haven't seen her to speak to for ages. She's rather outside my circle now.'

Molly, bumping into Emma in Oxford Street, was less reticent. They met in the doorway of Selfridges and for a moment Emma didn't see her, or didn't recognise her, for she was walking past, followed by an assistant carrying packages, when Molly put out a hand, touched her sleeve, and said, 'Emma!'

Emma stopped, looked, smiled. 'Hello, Molly,' she said, but there was a hint of a guilty blush.

'I never see you any more,' Molly said. 'You seem to have a new circle of friends.'

'Mm,' Emma said awkwardly. 'How are you? What are you doing these days?'

'I have a job,' Molly said. 'In the civil service. I live in London now – in Marylebone Lane.'

'Oh, a flat?' Emma said brightly. 'That must be nice. You always wanted—'

'No, just diggings.' Molly stopped the flight. 'But it's quite comfortable. You should come and visit me.'

It was pure devilment, really, because Emma was swathed in furs and French perfume and wearing a diamond on her finger that Molly thought could actually blind a person if the sun caught it directly, and she couldn't imagine her coming up the narrow stairs in her diggings, or sitting down in her room in the only armchair while she made coffee for her in a tin saucepan on the gas ring in the hearth.

Emma, looking doubtful, said, 'I'd love to, but you know, with the wedding coming up, there doesn't seem to be a minute in the day . . .'

Molly grinned. 'It's all right. I didn't really mean it. You and I are worlds apart now.'

Emma met her eyes. 'I didn't forget that we planned to live together after the war and do great things,' she said humbly, 'but it just didn't work out that way.'

'I know. I'm not angry with you,' Molly said. 'It was different in the war. People were – more equal. But perhaps we should have known it couldn't last. I was disappointed, but I've got over it now. As long as you're happy – and you look happy.'

'I am. Very happy.'

'Good. And I see you still have Benson.' She stopped to caress the little dog, who was wagging away at pavement level. 'But I mustn't keep you; and we're causing

378

a traffic jam,' Molly said, glancing round. She offered her hand. 'All my good wishes, Emma.'

'Thank you.' Emma shook her hand. Her glove was the softest suede Molly had ever felt. 'After the honeymoon, we must meet and talk properly. Come to luncheon.'

'If you invite me, I'll come,' Molly said, thinking it would never happen. 'Just one thing – you won't forget all your good intentions, will you? You won't just wear clothes and give parties? There's so much good you could do.'

And that was two people telling her the same thing, Emma thought, feeling vaguely irritated. Why couldn't she just live her own life, without people telling her what to do with it? But she smiled at Molly and said, 'I won't, I promise,' and as Molly stepped back she continued her way to the waiting taxi.

With just three weeks to go to the wedding, and the whole thing gathering speed like a train that seemed unstoppable, Lord Castleford died in his sleep of what his physician said was a massive heart attack. It emerged that he had been suffering from a heart condition for some years, together with sundry other ailments, which made his sudden death not entirely unexpected, but the effect of it was to derail the wedding in a spectacular and messy way.

Peter came to see Emma two days after a hasty and shocked telephone call cancelled all their immediate engagements. She received him in the drawing-room in St James's Square. He came in looking pale, drawn, suddenly older. He had a skinned look about him, which she had seen on the faces of other people who had suffered a shock

379

or a bereavement, as though they had lost a lot of weight very rapidly, leaving their bones too close to the surface. She had not realised he had cared so much for his father, and said so.

'I didn't care for him,' Peter said. 'He made it clear he didn't care for me, either, so why should I?'

'Whatever your difficulties, you still loved each other,' she suggested anxiously.

'He loved Gerald, if he loved anyone but himself. Charlie barely existed for him, and I didn't exist at all. Don't think I'm sorrowing for a beloved parent, Emma. You know better than that.'

'But you look –' she moved her hands helplessly '– so shocked.'

'It *is* a shock. He was always *there*, you see. He was a monument, my father – a great, indestructible, granite monument. Head of the house, head of the family, lord of the estate, peer of the realm. A public figure, manipulating the government of the day, having conferences – one of those old men in smoke-filled rooms who move the world.'

'The cigar-smokers,' Emma said.

'That's right. Didn't you get an impression of them during the war? Whatever we PBI types at the Front might think, it wasn't us who were making history, nor our generals, nor even the politicians, whatever they believed. It was the cigar-smokers. Every country and every age has them – always there, behind the scenes, pulling the strings. They were there in ancient Rome behind the emperors. I dare say you'd have found them behind Alexander the Great: they probably thought he was just a precocious child, a bit of a mountebank. *They* were the real power. *That* was my father – don't you see?'

Emma thought he was exaggerating, but made allowance for the shock and the filial feelings he would not admit to, but which she felt must exist. 'I see,' she said.

'Do you?' He looked relieved. 'I'm glad. Because then you will also understand,' he took her hand – his were icy cold, unlike him, 'why we have to postpone the wedding.'

She protested. 'But it's still three weeks away. Surely that's long enough. A period of mourning, yes, I understand that, but—'

'My mother won't hear of it. She says it would be unseemly. She says a wedding held under such a shadow would be an unfortunate one.'

'But that's just superstition. Surely you don't believe it.'

'I'm only talking about a postponement,' he said, 'not a cancellation.' The energy suddenly seemed to go out of him, leaving him looking deathly tired. 'There's so much to do. You don't understand what it means when an earl dies. He belongs to more than just us. The servants, the tenants, the villagers. The funeral will be an immense occasion. Then the estate will have to be sorted out. The will alone is hugely complex – the houses, the land, the investments, the pensions, my mother's settlement. God alone knows what death duties will come to. And then there's the title – the College of Heralds wants a meeting. It's a mountain of work – a mountain.' He looked at her helplessly. 'I can't do it in three weeks. And I can't marry you with all that hanging over me. I must – have it – *done with*!' he concluded, with emphasis, through gritted teeth.

She pressed his hand, anxious for him. 'If that's how it has to be, then we'll postpone,' she said, trying to be supportive, though her heart squeezed with disappointment – and something else: fear? 'Oh Peter!'

'I know. I hate the delay too. I want so much to be with you. I wish we could just run away, forget the wedding – just run and run until we find a place where no-one knows us, and to hell with the earldom.' He stared at her. 'I never wanted this!' he cried out suddenly. 'I never wanted the title. God knows—' He stopped, then went on quietly, 'I don't know if I can stand it. If it weren't for you . . .'

'I'll always be here,' she said.

'Yes,' he said, but he looked at her as though she were speeding away from him on a train, leaving him behind. 'Emma . . .'

'Yes, Peter.' She squeezed his hand, trying to put her strength into him.

'I wish something would happen – that someone would take this cup away from me.'

She didn't understand why he had said 'cup'. Only afterwards, when she remembered this scene, remembered it through pain in too-clear detail, did she connect it with the words in the Garden: *if it be Thy will, let this cup pass from me.*

The mechanism of halting the wedding locomotive was as elaborate and exhausting as driving it had been, and inevitably much more of the work devolved onto her because Lady Castleford was in mourning and had estate matters to deal with. Emma had to reassure people over and over again that it was only a postponement, while the newspapers went into an explosion of articles and photographs and headlines that she could not help seeing, even though she tried to avoid them.

But even this came to an end a week later. One day, early in the morning, when she was still in her room, thinking about getting up, Spencer came in looking concerned, to say that she had a visitor. Someone was waiting downstairs to see her.

'At this hour?' Emma said, but her heart had quickened. 'Is it Mr Gresham?' Perhaps he had decided to run away with her after all. She had not seen him since he had broken the news to her. She no longer cared about the wedding. She only wanted him.

But Spencer said, 'No, miss, it's Lord Westhoven.' She was already holding out Emma's wrapper for her. 'He said it's something important. Oh, miss,' it broke from her, 'he looks so queer. I'm afraid it's bad news.'

Emma felt all her blood turn white in her veins. In silence she let Spencer help her into the wrapper and let her begin to brush her hair, but then gently stopped her, took the brush from her hands, and walked out of the bedroom and down the stairs. Two housemaids, interrupted in their cleaning, were hovering in the hall, and their eyes directed her to the small drawing-room.

Kit Westhoven was standing in the middle of the room, turning his hat in his hands. As Emma appeared he put it down and took a step towards her, then stopped.

'What is it?' Emma asked. She heard her voice, but the words seemed to come from far away.

'It's Peter,' Kit said wretchedly. 'Lady Castleford telephoned me last night. She was hysterical – I couldn't make out what she was saying at first. Begged me to come. I went down, but there was nothing anyone could do. One of the groundsmen found him down by the lake.'

'Found him?' Was that small, remote voice really hers?

She turned the hairbrush round in her hands, unable to think what it was, or why she was holding it.

'They brought him in. When I got there they had got him up to bed and the doctor had come. But it was too – there was too much—' He swallowed. 'There was nothing to be done. He died around four this morning. I came as soon as I could. I didn't want you to hear it by telephone, or telegram.'

'He died?' Emma stared, trying to make sense of it. She licked her lips. 'How is that possible? For God's sake tell me. *What happened?*'

'He shot himself,' Kit said miserably. His hands were down by his sides; he looked defeated by the news, the situation. 'He took a gun out from the gun-room, but he didn't take anyone with him, not even a dog. And down by the lake – he shot himself.'

'It was an accident,' Emma said. Kit shook his head, a terrible pity in his eyes. 'It was an accident,' she insisted.

But still he shook his head. 'The way he was found . . . Emma, I'm sorry. There was no doubt. But it will be put out as an accident. The doctor's to be trusted, and the servants. God knows, things are bad enough without—'

'He can't be gone,' Emma said. 'He didn't say goodbye.'

'There was the beginning of a note in his room,' Kit said. 'I wanted to bring it but Lady Castleford took it. He started writing to you, but he didn't finish it. It just said, "Dearest Emma, my kingdom."'

'That's all?'

'I suppose he couldn't go on,' Kit said. 'Oh, Emma, I'm so sorry.' And he began to cry.

The distance between them closed, she did not know

by whose volition. She stood in his arms, hers round his waist, buried her face in his chest, and he rested his cheek on her hair. She felt his tears hot on her head, and it seemed strange that he should be the one crying. She wanted so much to cry – the pain in her throat was terrible – but she didn't seem to be able to. So she held on to him and let him comfort her, while he wept.

BOOK THREE

The New Shoots

I cried for madder music, and for stronger wine,
But when the feast is finish'd and the lamps expire,
Then falls thy shadow, Cynara! The night is thine;
And I am desolate and sick of an old passion.

Ernest Dowson: '*Non sum qualis
eram bonae sub regno Cynarae*'

CHAPTER SIXTEEN

The newspaper headlines said 'Peer in Tragic Shooting Accident' and 'Newly Succeeded Earl Dies in Tragic Accident on Eve of Wedding', but there was inevitably gossip in society circles. The Cadets rallied round, sent Emma letters and flowers of condolence, and spoke publicly about how much the two had been in love; but privately, among themselves, shocked and saddened, they remembered Peter's strange moods and brittle cynicism. Another casualty of the war, they agreed; there was all too much of that sort of thing these days. Every week you could find a small paragraph hidden away in a newspaper about a decorated war hero putting his head in the gas oven in some shabby lodgings. No job, no money, no hope, just a head stuffed full of memories of one's best friends being blown to shreds, and an inability to understand why it had been allowed to happen.

For Peter, they believed, the last straw had been inheriting the earldom, the terrible burden he had never wanted. It was clear enough to them, but it was terrible none the less – beyond terrible for poor Emma. She ought to have been enough to save him, they agreed; and that she had not been must break her heart.

Holkam, who had always quite liked Emma, and had his family's reputation to consider, angrily quashed any rumours he heard about suicide. He secured a police presence – one constable at the door to quiz callers, and one at each end of that side of the square to keep the reporters and photographers at a reasonable distance. Visitors came to the door and left messages and flowers. A few were allowed in – Kit Westhoven, Venetia, Jessie – but Emma would not see anyone. She had shut herself in her room. The flowers Violet sent to the nearest hospitals, the notes she read and replied to where appropriate. One in particular she was glad she had intercepted: Vera Polk wrote of her sympathy for Emma's loss, but added that she might in time regard it as a blessing in disguise because now she was freed from 'the toils of romantic and domestic slavery' and could devote her life to more important things.

Spencer took up trays and brought them down largely untouched. In the servants' hall she whispered that her mistress 'cried most dreadfully, her poor face so swollen', and they all shook their heads in silence, impressed by a tragedy beyond words.

To Jessie, Violet said, 'I wish there were anything one could do. It was hard enough when poor Major Fenniman died . . .'

'But this must be far worse,' Jessie agreed. 'She hadn't known Fenniman for long, and she was younger then. And it was in the war – I think we all became hardened, to an extent, during the war.'

'She really loved him, Jessie,' Violet said. 'She loved him as I loved Laidislaw.' Jessie nodded, remembering. 'There's nothing to be done about feelings like that,' Violet said. 'Time eases the pain, but it never completely goes away.'

'Oh, Vi—'

Violet shook her head. 'It doesn't matter now. It's Emma we must think of. Kit Westhoven comes every day – I wish she would see him. He might be able to comfort her. They were in the same set. At least she could talk to him about Peter.' She brooded a moment.

Jessie thought of the cancelled wedding, the expense of it, the work and misery, poor Lady Castleford. 'Did you hear what will happen to the earldom?' she asked.

Violet looked up. 'I asked Holkam. He said there's a distant cousin – the great-grandfather's the common ancestor. It's a very rich estate but of course death duties will take a large part. Lady Castleford will get her settlement and use of the dower house for life. Poor woman. To lose everything like that – two sons in the war, and then her husband and Peter in such a short time. It makes me realise how lucky I am.'

Jessie looked at her friend curiously. 'You're getting on better with Holkam these days, aren't you?'

'Yes, we're quite friendly,' Violet said. 'The children make a bond between us, and we go to functions.'

'It sounds – lonely,' Jessie said hesitantly. 'I know you and Holkam had a different kind of arrangement. Perhaps one day—'

Violet gave a surprisingly direct answer, for her. 'You know how I felt about Laidislaw. I shall never have another lover.'

It seemed intolerably sad to Jessie for lovely, gentle Violet not to be loved as she should be. *I shall never have another lover.* But time, she thought, can make liars of us all. She turned her mind back to Emma. 'I wonder if it would do her good to go away somewhere. Everything here must remind her so much. Do you think she'd go to Morland Place?'

'I thought of that,' Violet said, 'but I don't think she wants to be near people. She can't bear pity, or even sympathy. I thought of Shawes, but if she was there, the Morland Place people would call and send messages.'

'Yes, you're right,' Jessie said. 'It's just that I'm going there myself in August, and I thought . . . But I can see she'd want to be alone.'

'Holkam would really like her out of the house,' Violet confessed. 'He's sympathetic, but it is unpleasant having the press outside all the time, and the door-knocker going every hour. As long as she's here it disrupts his plans and the household routine.'

'What about your house in Lincolnshire?' Jessie said. 'I know it's uncomfortable in winter, but it's quite nice at this time of year, isn't it?'

'I thought of that too, but Holkam and I are invited to Balmoral and I was going to send the children down there.'

'Well, if the children went to Shawes instead, she could have it to herself. If you think it's right for her to be on her own at such a time?'

Violet looked reflective. 'I remember when Laidislaw died, it was all I wanted – to be quite alone. I think it's what she needs most.'

The arrangements were made, and a few days later Emma left the house for the first time since the tragedy. Heavily veiled, she was smuggled out via the garden and the house next door to avoid the press, and accompanied only by Spencer, holding Benson under her coat, she got into the car waiting at the corner and started on the long journey to Brancaster Hall. There was no-one there but a skeleton staff, and it was too far from Lincoln to attract callers, or even curiosity. Emma could walk with Benson in the gardens that Violet had been planting over the years, and the wider park, without fear of meeting anyone. Despite her abject grief, she was able to feel the relief of being out of doors again. The house at St James's Square had felt like a stifling prison, full of the stench of bereavement.

The Brancaster servants were elderly and incurious, and served her without comment or question; and Benson was the best companion of all, devoted and silent. She walked every day until she was exhausted, and slept through the short summer nights in a black oblivion, waking at dawn to the bitter realisation that this pain would go on for ever. Every step she took alone reminded her of the honeymoon Peter had planned at Barmechin, with 'servants who knew how to mind their own business', where they would walk and talk all day. The agony of his absence from her side did not grow less sharp, no matter how she tried to walk away from it.

And at night in bed, before the blackness of sleep took her, she wept in desolation for her love, torn from her, never coming back.

One day in September, Jessie was walking in Green Park with Thomas and Catherine and the nursemaid, and Bran on a lead. Thomas was growing tall and strong and resented being made to hold the maid's hand – he 'slipped the leash', as Jessie thought of it, whenever he could, and ran about, finding interesting sticks and fallen leaves, trying to catch squirrels, or, that perennial joy of childhood, scattering pigeons. Catherine, almost two, was walking very nicely now, and enjoyed the distinction of holding her mother's hand. Sometimes she caught hold of Bran's tail with the other hand, and he would look back at her patiently and smile. When she had first started walking she had pulled herself up by him, and taken her first steps clinging to his rudder.

They had had a very happy month in Yorkshire, the children renewing acquaintance with the cousins and various dogs, and enjoying the wide spaces of the nurseries, the gardens and the fields. Jessie was happy to be back in the bosom of her family, being petted and overfed, and having glorious long rides on Hotspur, sometimes alone and sometimes accompanied by Polly. Violet brought her children down to Shawes and was there for a few days before Balmoral called. Jessie and Violet sat under the walnut tree at Shawes talking inconsequentially for hours, just as their respective mothers had used to; and when Violet was gone, Jessie oversaw the young Holkams for her, and kept them entertained.

Jessie had missed Bertie, which was the only drawback. He had managed to come down twice, but it was not the same as sleeping in his arms every night. Missing him made her think wretchedly of poor Emma, who would never know that joy. She had written to her twice, saying that the moment Emma felt like ending her isolation, Jessie would come and fetch her in the motor, but there had been no reply. She was a constant topic of conversation at Morland Place. That such a thing could have happened to her after losing poor Major Fenniman seemed the cruellest twist of fate.

Jessie had brought Basil and Barbara with her, and had to answer questions about Jack and Helen and their situation. She painted a vague but satisfactory picture of the little house – very cosy and just the right size for Helen to manage – and said she did not know much about Jack's job except that it was in engineering, which was true if misleading. Uncle Teddy was willing enough to be placated, having many other things on his mind; but Henrietta, with a mother's quickness, smelled a rat, and was persevering with her questions, trying to pin Jessie down without knowing what it was she was suspicious about.

Jessie found she could generally distract her mother either by reverting to poor Emma's plight; or by talking about any of the children, but particularly about baby Laura, who was turning into a very engaging child, nine months old and crawling now. Henrietta felt very much her lack of a mother, and spent more time with her than any of the others. It was Laura's delight to dash away as fast as she could on all fours and be chased by her 'grandmama', and Henrietta's to hear her gurgling chuckles when she was caught and swept into the air. Teddy applied regularly to the brothers at Ampleforth for news of Father Palgrave, but it was always the same: that he was mending slowly, but not ready to leave.

Back in London, Jessie had settled quickly into her domestic routines, though the children had been fractious at first, missing their cousins, and poor Bran had looked at her with a long-suffering expression that said London and the Park were no substitute for the wide-open spaces of Yorkshire.

'Only another year,' Bertie had promised. 'Not even that now – ten months. I shan't sign on again, no matter how they beg me.'

'And then what shall we do?' Jessie asked. Bertie's house in Yorkshire – the Red House in Bishop Winthorpe

– was still in use as a convalescent home, and the lessees had recently asked for a further ten-year lease: there was good money to be made these days from such ventures. Besides, Jessie felt – and Bertie agreed with her – that it was far too big for them.

The land that belonged to the estate was also let out, but that was easy enough to take back in hand. 'We can still farm it,' Bertie said. 'I should like to start again with my cattle-breeding scheme. And I dare say you would like to breed horses. There's always a market for good horses. It would be fun to breed racehorses, and see if we couldn't raise a winner.'

'Saddle and draught horses for profit, racehorses for fun,' Jessie said. 'I like the sound of that. But where should we live?'

'We'll have to find ourselves a new house,' Bertie said. 'Perhaps somewhere between Bishop Winthorpe and Twelvetrees, since our interests will be split between the two.'

'What a good thing we live in the age of the motor-car,' Jessie said.

They had fallen to discussing possible sites for the new house, listing the features it must have to satisfy them both. It was a fascinating topic, which kept them occupied for hours, and she was thinking about it as she walked through the Park, until she was recalled from her reverie with a jerk by the realisation that she knew the woman walking towards her. An instant later, she recognised Beta Wallace.

They both stopped and looked at each other in silence, and Beta's face flushed. They had been 'best friends' as VADs in the general hospital at Étaples – at a time and in a place where friendship was what kept one sane.

Being rejected by Beta when she became pregnant was one of the hardest experiences of the war. Suddenly to be faced with her, here in the Park, made Jessie feel first hot and then cold with shock.

Beta looked older: it was three years since they had last seen each other, but there was more than three years of age in her face, and the sides of her dark hair, drawn back severely under an unbecoming hat, were greying. Her coat, though not exactly shabby, looked old, and her shoes were worn. Jessie wanted to smile in greeting, but there was nothing in the face to invite it: it was closed, almost grim.

'Well, Jessie,' Beta said at last, since they couldn't stand in silence for ever.

'How are you?' Jessie asked, really wanting to know. Painful feelings were struggling within her. She did not blame Beta for rejecting her, but longed for her forgiveness now. She discovered that she still cared very much about her former friend.

'I am quite well, thank you,' Beta said. She examined Jessie with a quick, nurse's eye, taking in the quality of her clothes and the fact of the servant just behind her. 'I can see that you are doing well for yourself.'

'I'm married now. I married – him,' Jessie blurted foolishly. 'His wife died in an accident so there was no—' She couldn't say 'divorce', out loud, like that, in the middle of the Park. 'So it was all right,' she finished, though it sounded wrong – callous, somehow. She hastened to get away from the subject. 'But you: are you – did you—?'

'I'm not married,' Beta said, but did not volunteer more. She stood looking at Jessie, as though there were still something to say.

Moved with a little absurd hope, Jessie groped for another question. 'How is Alpha?' Beta's older brother Alfred: they had been nicknamed Alpha and Beta by their parents when young – Beta's name was Elizabeth. Beta had used to read out his letters to Jessie in the silent, icy depths of night duty. Brother and sister were devoted, and the letters had been erudite and witty – all the Wallaces were educated people.

Beta said, 'He was killed in 1918 at Villers-Bretonneux.'

'Oh, Beta! I'm so sorry!' Her hand went out automatically, but as Beta recoiled slightly she drew it hastily back. 'How terrible for you. And for your parents.'

'My father couldn't bear it,' Beta said, and for the first time her grim control wavered, and something of her pain showed in her face. 'He was never well again. He died a few months later. I had to come home and take care of my mother. I didn't like breaking my contract but there was no help for it. So I didn't see the end of the war either.'

Either: that was one for Jessie. There was so much she could not ask, though she would have asked it of her friend. How were they left financially? What was Beta doing now? Was she working to support them both? How had her mother been affected? Where were they living? Beta's careworn face suggested things were hard. Jessie had seen enough of that sort of outfall from the war – women struggling to get by when the men who had supported the family were all gone – to paint the picture: shabby lodgings, inadequate food, a weary struggle to stay respectable, with nothing left over for the small pleasures that made life worth living.

'I hope . . .' she began, and found it hard to complete

the sentence in any acceptable way. 'I hope your mother finds comfort in you,' she managed at last.

Beta looked quizzical for a moment, as if surprised by thoughts or feelings of her own. Then she looked at Thomas, who had wandered off and now came back, wondering what the delay was. 'Is that—?' she said.

'My son, Thomas,' Jessie concluded for her, aware that Beta would be working out ages and dates. 'And my daughter Catherine.' A piercing awareness of her riches compared with Beta's emptiness brought tears to her eyes. *I have everything*, she thought, *everything I've ever wanted*.

As if it had been forced out of her, Beta said in a low voice, 'I miss my friend.'

It was a shock to hear the words. 'But I'm here,' Jessie said.

Beta met her eyes, and it seemed for a moment there might be a way back. A tumble of memories passed through Jessie's mind – perhaps through Beta's, too. They had been closer than sisters, working together in desperate conditions, sharing the triumphs of saving lives and the bitterness of failing, enduring the cold and dirt and fear and exhaustion, relishing together the small joys – hot water, a mug of cocoa, a square of chocolate, a letter – made more intense by the bleakness of the background.

But even as she thought these things, the light died. 'It's too late,' Beta said flatly.

'Don't say that,' Jessie begged. 'I miss you too.'

'We're not the same people,' Beta said. 'You can never go back.' She drew a breath, squared her shoulders, and said, 'I'm glad you're happy.' And with a nod of farewell, she walked briskly past. Jessie turned to watch her, but she did not turn back. *It's the war*, she thought dully. The war changed everything. No, you could never go back.

For Helen, the break from the children in August was the saving of her. Suddenly she seemed to have enough time in the day, to get on top of the housework and reduce the pile of mending, and also to do things that were not essential but which enriched life. With only Michael to attend to, she actually enjoyed her daily walk in the park, was able to get pleasure out of a fine day and Michael's delight at the new experience of feeding ducks. She taught him things and marked his progress, watched him discovering the world with wonder.

She and Jack had more time together in the evening, and since she was less tired she was able to while away his weariness with bright conversation. Sometimes they took Rug out for a walk together, enjoying the light evenings before autumn set in. Once they even went to the cinema, getting a neighbour's daughter to watch the baby. Mary Pickford and Charlie Chaplin: Helen surprised herself by how involved she became, crying with the one and laughing at the other. Jack held her hand in the darkness of the theatre and, walking home, kissed her when they passed under the shadow of the lime trees.

She found she had time to read the newspaper daily – or, at least, to skim through it in search of things to talk to Jack about. It was rarely a pleasure, however: all the news seemed to be bad. The coal strike had ended at last – miners and railwaymen had been causing trouble all year, and the government had talked of calling in the army – but prices and taxes were still going up and unemployment was as high as ever. The government had been forced to pay out 'uncovenanted' unemployment benefit from tax revenues: the unemployment insurance scheme – which they had extended in 1920 to cover everyone but domestic servants, farmworkers and civil servants – required a contribution from the employed, which did not help those who had been workless since demobilisation. Their plight was so acute that a charitable society called the British Legion had been founded to help ex-servicemen, with Field Marshal Haig as its president.

The USA had at last officially ended the war with Germany and Austria; on the other hand they had passed an Emergency Quota Act limiting immigration – taken to be a sign that they were sinking into isolationism. The troubles were still going on in Ireland, and there were such violent riots in Munich that the German government was forced to declare martial law.

And the airship ZR2 exploded on its trial voyage near Hull, and fell into the Humber estuary with the loss of forty-four of its forty-nine crew, causing the USA to cancel its order for two of them. Jack was, of course, interested in anything to do with flying, though airships did not have his heart as aeroplanes did. Despite the ZR2 tragedy, it looked as though dirigibles were more likely to succeed as passenger transports: the R34 had completed a crossing of the Atlantic in July 1919, and they were already in use across Europe. Though they were slow, they could carry a large number of passengers, while weight was still an insurmountable problem for aeroplanes on long flights: how to carry enough fuel to cross the Atlantic, and still have room for passengers, was something yet to be solved.

The future of passenger aeroplanes – and therefore of Jack's being able to earn a living by flying – seemed in doubt. And it had been a personal blow when in July his old friend Harry Hawker had died, killed in an air crash at Hendon. All his old connections with Sopwith's seemed now at an end. Helen kept to herself the thought that if Tom Sopwith *had* found a job for him, it might have been him who was killed.

She set herself during August to keep her husband from brooding, to keep him cheerful, and make their lives together more comfortable. August was a busy time for him, with holiday motorists on the road, and he made some good tips, which Helen salted away against possible bad times to come. When Basil and Barbara came back from Yorkshire, full of their adventures and chatter about the cousins, the animals and the games they had played, it was September and time for Basil to start school. Helen found a nursery school that would take children from the age of four, and Barbara went there in the mornings, pleased to be doing what Basil was doing, though longing for the time when she would go to the 'big school' with him. The extra time with only Michael to care for made all the difference between a Helen coping and a Helen perpetually running to catch up. It was a better-organised, smoother-running household that autumn.

Once a month they had a Sunday visit to Jessie and Bertie's house, where Molly usually joined them, and there was pleasant family fun and conversation, and for Helen the luxury of a meal she had not had to cook herself. On one occasion when Helen and Jessie were alone together, Jessie remarked how much better Helen was looking – 'You seemed so tired before, I was quite worried about you.'

402

Helen responded that Jessie was looking extremely bonny, and Jessie confided that she suspected she was pregnant again. Helen felt a twinge at the news, and wasn't sure whether it was envy or sympathy. 'You're happy about it?' she ventured to ask.

'Oh, yes,' Jessie said. 'I know Bertie would like more children. Though I do hope in a way that I don't *keep* having more, because if we go back to Yorkshire next summer I shan't want to be losing a year every time, when I can't ride, and can't really do anything around the stables. But I suppose that's in the hands of Fate. Would you like more children?'

Helen said, 'It would present enormous problems. Much as I love my three . . .' She eyed Jessie cautiously. 'Have you thought of doing anything to prevent yourself having any more?'

'You mean – Malthusian League things?' Jessie said. Helen noted with admiration how the question did not make her blush or stammer as it had Helen – but, then, Jessie had been a nurse. 'I've read about such things, of course. There was a conference in New York, wasn't there? They call it birth control.' She smiled. 'Strange idea, science controlling something as natural as childbearing.'

'Better than science making bombs and poison gas and hand grenades.'

'I've read letters in the newspaper saying that, after so much loss of life in the war, it's morally wrong to prevent birth.'

'I suppose it was a man who wrote that?'

'A clergyman,' Jessie agreed. 'He was being outraged by that new Malthusian clinic they opened in London.'

'Oh, you read about that?'

'I'm always interested in anything medical.'

'I've been there,' Helen said – blurted, rather – but managed not to blush.

'Helen! How modern and daring of you! Was it awfully embarrassing?'

'Oddly, it was thinking about it beforehand that was most embarrassing. Once I was actually there and talking to the doctor it seemed quite normal.'

'Does Jack know?'

'Goodness, yes! We agreed we ought not to have any more, and since we do love each other so much – well, you understand.'

'Yes, of course. I'm glad he wasn't upset about it. Men can be difficult about that sort of thing.'

'He was so worried about me the last time, he wasn't hard to persuade. In fact, I manoeuvred the conversation so that he thought it was his idea.'

Jessie laughed; and then, hearing footsteps, said, 'Oh, they're coming back,' and they had to change the subject.

That night, when everyone had gone and she and Bertie were alone together, they talked about the expected baby. Bertie was so happy, she was glad any question along the lines she had discussed with Helen could be deferred for the best part of a year.

Emma returned to London in October, when Brancaster started to be uncomfortable. She had cried herself dry. Now she felt numb. She did not know what she would do with herself; she only knew that she must shut away the feeling part of herself. She had been hurt too often. It must not happen again. So she drifted back to Town, like a leaf being blown at random by the wind, knowing only that winter was coming and Brancaster was not the place to be.

Not feeling she could bear Violet's sympathy, she did not go to St James's Square, but took a small suite in the Ritz. The press had forgotten her, she discovered to her relief. She had been the talk of the moment, but her absence, and the August break, had killed the story, and even the solitary photographer stationed permanently near the hotel door in case of a famous arrival only glanced at her, and decided she did not warrant the expense of flash powder.

The following day she went to see her solicitor, Peter Bracey, to find out the state of her finances. She had come into her fortune in January of that year, but so far had not drawn anything but her usual allowance. Bracey greeted her with a compassionate eye, but when it was obvious that she did not want sympathy he became businesslike. The financial connections that had been in process of being made with the Gresham family had been unpicked, he told her, and everything had been restored to the *status quo ante bellum*. He explained where her money was invested, and added, 'Of course, you now have control over your fortune. You can invest it as you please.'

'And spend it as I please,' Emma said.

'Indeed – though I hope you will be prudent in both respects, Miss Weston.'

'You needn't be afraid for me,' Emma said. 'I shan't fritter it away and make myself destitute.'

'I never thought that you would,' Bracey said. 'I have the greatest respect for your intellect.'

'I'm no intellectual,' Emma said. 'I suppose my fortune has taken a knock this past year or two?'

'Dented rather than fractured. The investments are holding up very well, and should recover what little they've lost when the general recovery begins.'

He gave her the particulars, and she listened quietly, a little shocked inside. She was accustomed to think of herself as rich and hear herself described as a considerable heiress, but she had not realised quite how very rich she was. For a moment it made her sad, because there would not be anyone to spend it on but herself, and no children to pass it to when she died. To be so rich seemed pointless without Peter.

'In fact,' Bracey was saying, 'I would say that, for all intents and purposes, you have enough money to do exactly as you please for the rest of your life.' He paused a second, and went on tentatively, 'Have you thought what you would like to do?'

She had no answers. She suddenly felt very weary. 'Oh, set myself up somewhere, I imagine,' she said indifferently. 'Have a place of my own.' As she said it, the idea lifted her spirits just a little. She need never go back to Violet's house, never be dependent on anyone again. She could be private, keep everyone away. It was all she could think of for the moment. 'I suppose I can afford that?'

'I think you may take it for granted, until warned otherwise, that you can afford everything,' he said.

Though she had not announced her return, and slipped into the Ritz as secretly as possible, it became known that she was back, and she began to receive notes and callers. She ignored the notes and refused the callers at first. But at last, when Kit Westhoven had called several times every day for a week, she realised she would have to see him eventually and told the porter to admit him.

He examined her frankly and said, 'You are as beautiful as ever, only with such a sad look about you. Like Anna Pavlova dancing the Dying Swan. Poor, poor Emma.'

'None of that, please. I can't bear pity.'

'Then I won't offer you any,' Kit said kindly. 'What do you think of my suit? The lapels are my own idea. The Cadets are all mad to copy them. Everyone's been talking about you, wondering when we would see you again. There's a revival on of *The Maid of the Mountains*, with José Collins as the Maid, and we're all going to see it next week. I know I could get another ticket. And we thought afterwards we'd go to the Cecil Club. Have you heard of it? It's a new place in Gerrard Street where you can dance and get champagne after hours. Now do say you'll come.'

Emma recoiled. 'Oh, I couldn't. Don't ask me, Kit. I can't even think about things like that now.'

'You needn't think at all,' Kit said. 'I'll arrange everything for you. It will do you good to go out and see people.'

'I don't want to see people.'

'I know. You think people will say how sorry they are, and stare at you, and prod you with questions like some poor specimen in a laboratory.' She almost smiled, and he felt he had achieved something. 'Well, I won't press you, this time. But be warned – I shall return.'

'Oh, Kit!'

'Oh, Emma! I want my dancing-partner back, that's all.' He became serious. 'What do you mean to do now?'

She was puzzled. 'Now, this minute?'

'No, I mean in general. You can't live here for ever.

Benson wouldn't stand it, to begin with. Are you going back to the Holkams'?'

'No, I want to set up on my own.'

'Here, in Town?'

'I don't know. I want to be quite private.'

Kit threw himself into the problem. 'Well, I've never thought of you as a country girl. Besides, in the country everyone knows everyone else's business. It's hideous. And you can't want to go and fester in the suburbs – Kensington or Hampstead or any such place. If you want privacy, you can't do better than right in the centre of Town, where people know how to leave each other alone. It's a pity you're not a man – a set in Albany would be the very thing.' He frowned a moment, then clicked his fingers. 'Why didn't I think of it before? You've heard about Stretton House in Queen's Walk?'

'The Coventrys' place?'

'Not any more. They had to sell it. They're deep in debt, poor things – death duties, of course, with the last viscount being shot down over Roulers. Death duties are a monstrous invention.'

'But it's a huge mansion,' Emma said. 'What would I want with that?'

'No, you don't understand. It's being turned into flats. I met a very odd woman, a Mrs Perigo, at a party a few weeks ago – she is Brigadier Perigo's widow, Indian Army chap. She is acting as the agent for selling them. She tried to interest me in one, but I'm happy enough at the club, and I can always stay with the Winchmores. They're going to be very modern and luxurious, apparently, with every comfort. Electric lights, lifts, central heating. And you couldn't want anywhere more central, looking over the Park and two minutes' walk from here.'

Emma wondered at his enthusiasm. 'I hope this Mrs Perigo hasn't taken you on on commission,' she said idly.

Kit looked hurt. 'I was interesting myself in your problem, that's all.'

'I'm sorry. It's very kind of you. It's just that – I hadn't got as far as thinking about where, or what. Besides, I suppose these flats will be years in the building.'

'Not at all. They're all going to be ready in the new year. Look here, I won't trouble you about it any more, but if you do think you'd like to look into it, I can get this Mrs Perigo to come and see you. I know where she lurks.' He drew out his watch and said, 'It must be time for lunch. Will you do me the honour?'

Emma shrank. 'I've been eating in here,' she said.

'Oh, but that's so depressing. Do let me coax you out. There's a dear little place in Brewer Street where no-one will know us, and the walk and fresh air will do you good. Or we can take a taxi if you're tired. Check table-cloths, rustic chairs – the proprietor used to run a café in Calais, so it's genuine French food, like we used to have over there. We can take Benson, too – he's very open-minded.'

'You seem to know it very well,' Emma said. 'How come I haven't heard you speak of it before?'

'I haven't told the Cadets. I'm keeping it to myself. It's one of those little gems of a place that will be spoiled if too many people know about it. But I don't mind taking you – you're no chatterbox.'

So she let herself be persuaded. It turned out to be more pleasant than she had feared to be out again, and in company. The restaurant was a small place, and rather dark, so if there had been anyone there who knew her, she wouldn't have seen them. The proprietor greeted them and waited on them himself in the manner she remembered from her time in France, and the food was rustic but delicious. It was the first meal she had enjoyed since Peter died; and it was comfortable being with Kit, letting him do all the talking, feeling no pressure to be entertained or entertaining. He demanded nothing of her, not even to listen all the time, and afterwards she realised that none of it had happened by accident. He had known what she needed. He was a good friend, she thought – the best sort.

Because he had been so kind, she sent a note round the following week to say that she would like to see Mrs Perigo. It couldn't hurt her to talk to the woman, and it would make Kit feel his advice had been welcomed.

She could see why he had described Mrs Perigo as 'odd'. She had evidently been born a lady – she managed to slip it in, during the meeting in Emma's suite, that she had been a Miss Ashby of High Wycombe – and her marriage had been a good one; but being left in straitened circumstances by her husband's death, she had been forced into earning a living in a way that must have gone against the grain. Consequently she was just very slightly *not* a lady now. Her manner was perhaps a little too much of-the-world.

But she was persuasive. She brought with her ground plans and photographs of Stretton House. 'We're keeping the façade, as you see – and the name, as well. No passer-by will be able to tell that it is anything but the mansion it always was. And, of course, as an address it could not be bettered: Stretton House, Queen's Walk. I venture to say, Miss Weston, *that* was a consideration with many of my clients. They are people of the first rank and importance.'

'Then you have sold some of the flats already?'

Mrs Perigo nodded emphatically. 'There is a tremendous demand for accommodation of this sort, and I am confident every single one will be sold long before the finishing date. In fact, I have so many people expressing interest that, had it not been for Lord Westhoven's particular insistence, I should have had to say it was of no use to take up your time showing you the plans. But he is such a particular friend that I agreed to give you first refusal on the few that are left.'

'That's – most kind,' Emma said, thinking that she need not have bothered. But when the plans were spread out on the table for her, and Mrs Perigo explained the features, she began to be interested despite herself. Her life had been one of migration between other people's houses. She had never, since her father died, had anywhere she could call home.

'The flat I was thinking of for you is a two-bedroom, on the first floor – here – a lovely corner unit with windows on the Park.' She marked around it with a pencil. 'Apart from the two bedrooms – here, and here – there is a drawing-room and a dining-room: lovely spacious rooms, interconnecting, with sliding doors between them. Separate small study or library. Luxurious modern bathroom, ample closets, a large kitchen, with pantry, scullery, and the maid's room and lavatory behind, and a separate service door. Fireplaces in the principal rooms. Central heating and electric lighting. A house telephone in every flat. The entrance hall will be very fine indeed, decorated in the first taste, with a porter on duty every hour of the day and night. Elegant staircase, and *two* electric lifts, each with an attendant during the daytime. Laundry collected and delivered to your own

411

service door. And cleaning of the flat can be arranged for a small extra charge, by a reliable concierge.' Mrs Perigo smiled. 'We wish our clients to be comfortable.'

'It certainly seems so,' Emma murmured.

'Now, as to the internal decoration – buying *before* the finishing date means our clients have the option to choose the decorations to suit themselves. I have photographs here of some finished rooms – just by way of example, of course . . .'

Emma found herself looking at a drawing-room with large windows, beyond which was a hint of large trees and green grass (the Park, she thought). The furniture was light and modern, in walnut, the floor was parqueted, large mirrors reflected the light into the room, and everything was done in shades of fawn and cream, very restful and soothing. Suddenly she could see herself there: she could order the furniture and change the colour of the walls to her own taste. No family heirlooms or vast portraits to house, no family history to remember, no family customs to offend against. She would be just herself alone, completely anonymous and free. There was something attractive about the notion. It would be like being reborn as a new person.

And then suddenly she thought of Peter, and her interest in the project drained out of her like grain out of a split sack. What did it matter? What did anything matter?

'Thank you,' she said. 'You needn't say any more.'

Mrs Perigo stopped in mid-sentence and looked at her questioningly. She knew who Emma was, of course – she had done her research beforehand. She saw the greyness and misery come to the pretty face and understood that her potential client had come to the end of her tether. But if she went away now it was doubtful the girl would ever ask for her back, and she still had a great many units to sell. She girded herself for a last effort.

'Then shall I put you down for this unit, Miss Weston? I think it would just suit you, and I should hate you to be disappointed. It's the last of the twos, and I know it will be snapped up by this time next week, because a young married couple was asking about it only yesterday. It will be ready by the fifteenth of January. I have the contract. If you would just care to sign *here*, I can get everything under way for you at once, and need not trouble you any more for the moment.'

And Emma signed, so that Mrs Perigo would go away, and because nothing mattered any more.

But afterwards she was glad she had signed. She had to live somewhere, after all; and the long-suffering Spencer was ecstatic at the idea of a proper home again. That had to be Emma's reward. She stayed on at the Ritz for the time being, which meant that she walked Benson past Stretton House most days. She looked at it as she passed and thought that soon she would be living in the unknown spaces behind its grand façade. All alone. A modern young woman. Sometimes the idea made her want to weep, and sometimes she could only feel a dull resentment at the necessity of finding a home for herself; but sometimes she felt that it would be a sort of haven, a place for her to hide from the world's storms, and then she would look at the house almost with affection.

It had not gone unnoticed by the British government that all commercial air services had ceased by February of 1921; that the nascent industry had failed for lack of access to working capital. After the war, a Civil Aerial

Transport Committee had been set up, which had recommended in 1920 to the minister of war and air, Winston Churchill, that the aircraft industry should receive public financial backing. Despite being known for his 'air-mindedness', Churchill had firmly rejected the suggestion, stating that 'civil aviation must fly by itself'.

However, by the end of 1921 it was clear that no aviation company could manage without help of some kind; and furthermore that the country would do well to invest in it. The British Empire was spread out across the globe, and the advantages of rapid mail and passenger services to its outposts were obvious. And a great mercantile nation like Britain ought surely to pioneer new modes of transport, not follow feebly where other countries led: Britain had invented the railway and had profited vastly from exporting the technology to the rest of the world.

So in January 1922 the government set up a new body, the Civil Air Transport Subsidies Committee, to review the policy. It concluded that the four companies that had been running commercial airlines – Handley Page, Instone, Daimler Airway and the British Marine Navigation Company – should be offered immediate short-term support, to help them start up again, while a longer-term strategy was forged.

Daimler Airway was a new company that had been formed when Daimler Air Hire had bought AT&T in 1921. Because of the AT&T connection, it had a small fleet of de Havilland aircraft; and Jack suspected there had been more than a hint of intervention by his old friend when Frank Searle, the head of Daimler Airway, wrote to him in February offering him a job. The other three lines were to operate inland services, but Daimler was to reopen the Paris route, flying from Croydon Airport.

'The government's keen to have some sort of air service to the continent,' Searle said when Jack met him to discuss the matter, 'starting with Paris, but adding other destinations as soon as possible – Amsterdam, certainly, and perhaps Berlin or Hanover in the next year or so. So they're offering us enough to get the operation going. How would you like to fly the Croydon to Paris route for us?'

'I'd be delighted,' Jack said, hardly daring to believe his luck.

'You are the obvious choice,' Searle said. 'You know the way, you know the airfields. We count ourselves lucky to get you. You're a war hero – frankly, that makes good publicity. And you've flown de Havillands. We'll be operating with DH34s – single-engine cabin biplanes.'

Jack couldn't help asking, 'Did Geoffrey have anything to do with this?'

Searle raised an eyebrow. 'Oh, everyone knows everyone else in this business, don't you find?' And he smiled mischievously. 'I had it on good authority that Fred Handley Page was going to ask you for his outfit, so I thought I'd better get my word in early.'

He had them fighting over him! Jack thought, with a touch of euphoria.

'No more than you deserve,' Helen said, when he told her later that day. 'You've always been too modest about your abilities. Oh, but, Jack, how wonderful! You'll be flying again. I know what that means to you.'

He took her in his arms. 'Can disinterest go any further? Noble woman, you haven't asked what it will mean for you.'

'I presume,' she said cautiously, 'it will mean more money. They must pay you a decent salary, surely?'

415

Jack named the amount. Compared with what they were living on now, it was princely.

'We'll have to move house, to be nearer the airfield,' he said. 'We can afford something a little bigger now – and a servant or two.'

'Oh, Jack! A nursery-maid?'

'And a cook and a housemaid, if you like. We'll have a position to keep up,' he assured her, smiling at her pleasure. 'And on my days off, we can motor down to Biggin Hill and watch the flying.' He released her to arm's length and caught her hands, and she marvelled at how the lines of worry and disappointment seemed to have melted away in an instant. 'The good times are starting again,' he said.

'I'm so happy for you. I'm so happy,' Helen said, ridiculously close to tears.

And in sheer high spirits he began to whirl her around in a dance. They bumped into furniture in the tiny room, and Rug chased round after them, barking madly, until Helen breathlessly called a halt for fear the neighbours would think it was a riot and call the police.

CHAPTER SEVENTEEN

It had taken a long time and much talking to persuade Teddy to let Polly go to New York. Polly had missed Maria, who would have dismantled most of his objections without his even noticing: Polly was sure Maria would have been on her side. It was not so much that he *didn't* want her to go, it was more that he couldn't see why she should want to. Didn't she have everything here at home? New York was so far away. The journey was so long. It was dangerous. She would get homesick. They would all miss her too much.

Teddy was busier than ever during the second half of 1921, dealing with labour problems at the factories, credit difficulties, the necessity for new lines in the stores, and defaulting tenants at home, in addition to the normal work of the estate. Most of all he simply didn't want to think about Polly's request. Was it too much to ask for *some* area of his life to stay the same and require no decisions?

But Polly was not his daughter for nothing, and her determination to engage with him was more than equal to his desire not to. Miss Husthwaite grew tired of having Polly hanging around the steward's room and weighed in on her side, on the reasoning that the sooner it was decided, the sooner Miss Husthwaite could have her office to herself again. Henrietta sympathised with Polly's desire to get away and to travel, though nothing could persuade her that it was safe to cross the Atlantic in a ship.

But Polly had written to Lizzie, and Lizzie had written back with the approbation of the whole American clan, and Henrietta was won over. Though still apprehensive about the journey, she joined forces with Polly to persuade Teddy to give in.

'Hundreds of ships have crossed safely,' Polly pointed out to her aunt, 'both before and since the *Titanic.*'

'It's true,' Henrietta admitted, and later repeated this to Teddy. 'In fact, I believe that was the only passenger ship that ever did founder with loss of life. Perhaps we ought not to condemn the whole idea on the basis of that one tragedy.'

Teddy looked at her. '*You* wouldn't go.'

'Well, no,' Henrietta admitted. 'Though I must admit it would be lovely to see my poor Lizzie again, and the grandchildren.' She looked wistful for a moment. 'But I couldn't possibly leave Morland Place for so long. I've far too much to do.'

Teddy felt the main thrust of the argument had slipped away in an eddy of irrelevances, but he was too busy to want to argue about it with Henrietta. 'I'll think about it,' he said. 'I can't say more than that.' And he hurried out.

But over the weeks, as the correspondence went on between Polly and Lizzie, it came somehow to be that the trip had been decided on as a fact, without any actual pronouncement ever being made on the subject. The argument slipped from *whether* to *when*, and to a consideration of the details. Teddy stalled as long as possible, but overreached himself when he told Polly firmly that she couldn't possibly go before Christmas because it would break her aunt's heart; upon which a seraphic smile came to Polly's lips, and she said, 'So I can go *after* Christmas? Oh *thank* you, Daddy!' and flung her arms round his neck and kissed him adoringly to seal the deal.

So there was nothing left for Teddy but to give in gracefully and iron out the remaining difficulties. Though it went against the grain, he agreed that Polly could travel to America on Cunard's *Berengaria*. Cunard had received her from the Germans as part of the war reparation – she had been the *Imperator*, of the Hamburg-Amerika line (known as Hapag). At the same time, White Star Line had been given the sister ship *Bismarck*, which they had renamed *Majestic*; but *Bismarck* had not been fully finished at the end of the war, and the Germans were so furious at being forced to complete the ship at their own expense before handing it over that they had dragged their feet over the work, and she was still not finished. She would not be ready to sail until April or May, and Polly was adamant (sensing that one delay always gave birth to another) that she did not want to wait that long. Teddy argued that the crossing would be nicer in May than in January; but Henrietta put in a word on Polly's side. The *Berengaria* was a popular ship, and had done the crossing safely many times. It seemed to her too much like tempting Fate for Polly to go on a maiden trip of a new White Star liner.

The question remained of who was to accompany Polly. Polly said indignantly that she was over twenty-one and could travel without a chaperone, but here Henrietta

419

sided with Teddy. It was unthinkable that a gently bred girl should undertake such a journey without the supervision of a sensible older person.

Teddy used his influence to get a look at the passenger list for the mid-January crossing, and found that, luckily, Mrs Innes-Stewart, the sister of Viscount Howick of Heslington, was travelling on the same crossing, with her son Stuart. Teddy knew Howick tolerably well from various committees and public works, and had met Mrs Innes-Stewart once or twice: she was a widow, her husband, Jock, having been killed at Neuve Chapelle. Since then she had been living at Heslington Grange with her brother, who had helped her to bring up her son.

A meeting between Teddy, Lord Howick and Mrs Innes-Stewart went very agreeably, and the lady pronounced herself happy to escort Polly on the ship and see her safely into the hands of her relatives in New York. Teddy was not unmoved by the consideration that Stuart Innes-Stewart, who was just about Polly's age, looked fairly likely to inherit the title, Howick having only two daughters and a wife past child-bearing age. And Mrs Innes-Stewart's complacency was lubricated by the knowledge that Polly was a considerable heiress, and that transatlantic liners were just the place for romance to flourish.

Polly thought that the whole chaperone idea was a bore, but that she ought to be able to evade the widow on a ship as large as the *Berengaria*.

Lizzie wrote that Polly should not bring too many clothes, because she could have everything she needed made up much more cheaply in New York. 'But do bring a warm woollen dress and perhaps a tweed suit,' Lizzie wrote. 'English wool and tweeds are much admired and it is very cold in New York in January.'

'You will definitely need a fur coat,' Teddy said firmly. 'It shall be your Christmas present.' Polly was thrilled: it seemed a very grown-up thing to be having one's first fur coat. Teddy wanted to do the thing properly and wrote to Jessie, asking her to ask Violet's advice, with the result that Jessie and Violet had a very pleasant shopping trip together, and later posted a large, flat box to Morland Place, which Polly opened on Christmas Day. It was a calf-length dark mink with a big collar, and Polly loved it at first sight.

'It's beautiful, Daddy,' she said, caressing it. 'Oh thank you, thank you! You are the kindest father in the world.'

Teddy was pleased. 'I always think a woman can never look ill dressed if she has a good fur,' he said, though he had never considered the matter before. 'A good fur and well-kept shoes are the sign of a lady.'

After Christmas a little melancholy set in for Teddy, with the realisation that his daughter was really going away. She was to stay for five months, or until it started to get too hot in New York. 'You won't want to be there in the summer, from all I've heard,' Teddy said. So she was to come back in May or June. All the same – five months without his darling! 'We shall be very dull without you,' he said pathetically.

Polly kissed him fondly. 'Nonsense, Daddy. The time will fly. You're always so busy, you won't even know I'm gone.'

Teddy did not argue further, but he knew he would.

Polly only came to a realisation of departure when Mrs Tomlinson put away her riding habits in mothballs – 'You won't be doing any riding in New York, miss' – and she was finally brought to tears when she said goodbye to her dogs, and to Vesper. It had been decided to knock her shoes off and turn her out until Polly came back, for there was no-one else with the time to exercise her, and Polly didn't want to leave her to the grooms.

Finally the day came, her trunks were packed and labelled, and Simmonds brought the motor round. Polly stood in the hall, in her new suit (made to her own design, in a lovely tweed that had a thread of her own special shade of blue running through it), with her precious fur coat over her arm, and allowed Henrietta to put her hat on for her.

'Don't cry, Aunty. It's only a holiday. I'm coming back.'

'I'm not crying,' Henrietta asserted, wiping her cheek with the back of a finger. The dogs, sensing something untoward, clustered round, staring up into faces and wagging tails hard, in case it helped. 'You've got my letter to Lizzie?'

'In my handbag,' said Polly. 'I'll give it to her first thing.' She looked around the hall, and said, 'I wonder what will have changed by the time I get back.' She hugged her aunt, said goodbye to Ethel, shook hands with Miss Husthwaite, waved to the servants – several of whom were weeping as copiously as if it were a wedding – and followed her father out to the motor. He had insisted he must take her right on board: 'It would be discourteous to Mrs Innes-Stewart not to hand you over myself,' he had said. But Polly knew it was really because he wanted to see the ship.

Simmonds arranged the rugs over their knees, and they were off, through the barbican and turning out of sight of the waving family, servants and dogs. As her dear home receded behind her, Polly did find it hard to choke back a tear; but as soon as they were on the main road, she thought of the adventure to come, and only wished they were going to Southampton by train, because Simmonds drove very carefully and it was going to take much longer by road.

It was raining in Southampton, but that did not dampen Polly's pleasure. She loved everything about boarding the ship. She loved the dockyard, smelling of salt and tar and oil, the mysterious jears and cranes scratching the sky, and the seagulls cruising and mewing above them. She loved the cavernous Customs shed, redolent of great undertakings, and the sense it gave her of being on the brink of a new world. She liked the fatherly uniformed man who checked her ticket and gave her a smile of complicity with her excitement, as he said, 'First trip to the States, miss?'

She loved the wharfside crowded with see-ers off, and the military band set up there, pumping out stirring music despite the dampness of their uniforms. She loved the vast, stately ship with her three funnels and the row of excited faces along the boat-deck rail. She loved walking up the gangplank with the glimpse of black, oily water surging between hull and dockside, reminding her that this was not just a hotel, despite the hotel smell of warmth and carpets and a hint of soup that came from the brightly lit opening.

She was entranced by the ship. She came from a well-to-do family, and lived a life of comfort and ease, but she had never been exposed to this kind of ostentatious luxury. Everything that could glitter glittered. Everywhere an electric bulb could be fitted, one was glowing.

Everything that could be richly carpeted, upholstered, draped or swagged was so. Mirrors and chandeliers and etched-glass panels flung sparks of light about like a careless rajah scattering diamonds. Stewards in white jackets scurried about like obsequious ants. And passengers in fabulous furs, pearls and diamonds were everywhere, talking in loud voices, calling for service from the ants, greeting friends, gazing about imperiously, generally making it known that the *Berengaria* was here for their benefit, and they meant to take full advantage.

Teddy watched his daughter covertly to see how she would take to it all, and saw with relief that her instinctive reaction seemed to be to want to laugh. She was not overawed, or cowed, or envious, or, it seemed, stirred with ambition to emulate. She gazed around her with a look of merriment in her eyes, as though she saw exactly what was preposterous about this opera-set of a place. He was proud of her.

Polly was glad to discover that her cabin, though on the same deck as that of the Innes-Stewarts, was not next door or even near to it. She had half feared that there might be a communicating door; but Teddy had booked her ticket so much later that there was no danger of that. The cabin seemed to her very large and luxurious, with a sitting-room and a bedroom, and a separate dressing-room containing nothing but wardrobes, drawers and cupboards. Polly was especially impressed that she had her own bathroom, with an extraordinary number of brass taps, handles and porcelain knobs offering hot and cold, salt and fresh, and torrents of different forces and directions, in extravagant combination. With its complexity of pipes and stops it reminded her of a church organ.

She was still exclaiming over the various contrivances when a knock on the door brought in the steward and stewardess to introduce themselves. The former, a middle-aged man named Henderson, reassured Teddy by his calm and capable air and the length of his experience. The latter was a slight but friendly young woman called Hackett, with a faint Lancashire accent. While Teddy was quizzing Henderson, she told Polly she would be looking after her for the voyage, and said, 'Let me take your coat, miss, and hang it up.'

She caressed the fur with an appreciative hand, and Polly could not help saying, 'It was my Christmas present from my father.'

'It's *lovely*, miss,' Hackett said warmly. 'Would you like me to start unpacking your things now? And will you be changing for luncheon?'

'I don't know,' Polly said, suddenly aware of a minefield appearing beneath her feet.

'People generally don't, on the first day,' Hackett said helpfully, 'unless they've got muckied on the journey, or they're not comfortable. That's beautiful tweed, miss – quite suitable, if you didn't want to bother changing.'

Polly saw that Hackett was going to be able to navigate for her, and smiled with relief and said, 'I shan't change, then. And do unpack, please.'

She left her to it and went to join her father, in time to see him slip something to Henderson, which she guessed was an advance tip for keeping an eye on her. The steward gave her a friendly smile and went out, and Teddy said, 'We'd better find the Innes-Stewarts, before I have to go ashore.'

There was a passenger list among the documents laid out on a table in the stateroom (the day's menu, schedule of entertainments, plan of the ship, list of telephone numbers . . .) and Teddy found their cabin number. Their suite, though no less luxurious than Polly's and considerably larger, was in a state of chaos, with luggage and people everywhere. Polly's quick eye soon identified the cast. Mrs Innes-Stewart was the small but very loud lady in a fur coat and smart hat, and her son was the pale, lanky creature with the beaky nose and spectacles. They were each travelling with a personal servant, who seemed to be in dispute with the cabin steward and stewardess about their duties, while the lady herself was haranguing an assistant purser about the importance of keeping her valuables safe, and her son was arguing with a porter about a piece of luggage he claimed was missing.

Teddy's entrance was met with a glance of relief by the ship's staff, glad of the interruption, and a look of annoyance from Mrs Innes-Stewart, quickly replaced with a smile of welcome when she saw who it was. Polly was introduced, suffered herself to be gushed over by the mother, and shook hands with the son – his hand was limp and slightly damp, and she wiped hers surreptitiously down the back of her skirt. Mrs Innes-Stewart told Teddy that it would be a pleasure to take charge of such a delightful, charming girl, and pronounced that Polly and her son would be the greatest of friends, as they had so much in common. In case Teddy should not know what those things might be, she proceeded to tell him in detail what an intelligent, affectionate, sensitive boy Stuart was, so good at his studies, so kind to his mother, the finest rider and shot in the county, a superb dancer, with a fine natural tenor voice, knowledgeable about the countryside, destined for a life in politics or some other exalted field of public life, yet modest and unassuming about his immense abilities, while being the sort of fine, brave, clean-living and manly fellow on which the British Empire had been built.

Polly looked at the voluble widow and the rather drooping son and decided she would have no difficulty in evading them.

After a quick look round the principal spaces of the ship with her father, and a close-to-tearful farewell when the all-ashore hooter sounded, Polly went up on deck to watch the departure. The band played, the crowds below waved; the ship's siren blared, sending rows of pigeons on the Customs shed roof clattering skywards; the tugs hooted in reply, and suddenly the narrow strip of dark, slip-slop water between the ship and the quay was widening and turning grey and the great vessel eased out into the channel. Polly felt a clutch of excitement in her stomach. She was leaving her native land for the first time. Many people around her, leaning over the railings and waving madly, had tears in their eyes, and she thought there was just something about the departure of a great ship that made you want to cry. She found that she was waving madly, too, though she could not see her father or Simmonds and she knew no-one else down there. She thought that perhaps it would be a sad day for mankind if ever people didn't wave madly when a ship set sail.

She stayed for a long time at the rail, after most of the people had gone, watching the various docks slip past, and the seagulls effortlessly keeping pace above, and the grey water widening out on both sides as they got into the roads. Though the air was still damp, the rain had stopped, and ahead, out to sea, there was a strip of yellow along the horizon suggesting the clouds were lightening and there might be better weather ahead. She looked curiously at the green hump of the Isle of Wight sliding into view; then discovered she was extremely hungry, and went back to her cabin to find out what one did about luncheon.

Hackett was there, just finishing the unpacking. 'There was a message for you, miss,' she greeted Polly, 'from Mrs Innes-Stewart, asking if you could go along to her cabin once we'd sailed.' She examined Polly's reaction. 'I think she wanted to fix for you to have luncheon with them, miss.'

'No, thank you,' Polly said firmly. 'I don't mean to be tied to her apron strings the whole voyage.' She looked at Hackett's twinkling eyes. 'Can I trust you?'

'I'm your stewardess, miss, not hers,' said Hackett, obligingly.

'Very good,' said Polly. 'Then, if she ever calls, I'm not here.' The telephone rang again. 'If that's her again, I'm not here now. Wait a moment until I leave the room before answering, and you can say it with a clear conscience.'

'Very well, miss,' Hackett said, amused.

'Thank you,' said Polly, heading for the door. 'I'm going to explore.'

It was not possible entirely to avoid the Innes-Stewarts that day, but the weather seemed to be on Polly's side. The clouds did break up once they were out in the Channel, and the crossing to Cherbourg was made in pleasant if watery sunshine. But once they reached the Western Approaches the weather closed down again, and there was heavy rain and squally winds which got the sea up to a pitch that most passengers found unpleasant. The decks were quickly abandoned, the public spaces near deserted, and both Innes-Stewarts, in common with ninety per cent of the passengers, retired to their beds suffering from seasickness.

Polly felt a little queasy herself from time to time, but would not give in to it, now she could roam the ship free of the fear of being chaperoned. She discovered that going on deck was the best antidote. Hackett borrowed an oilskin jacket and sou'wester for her, and she went out several times a day to enjoy the stinging fresh air and solitude of the deserted decks. A few other hardy souls did the same, and they soon got to recognise each other, and greeted each other like members of a secret society.

At meals there were so few of them it seemed too pointed to sit separately, and with the stewards' encouragement they clustered together like survivors at a single long table. Polly found herself among a very mixed group, of varying ages and stations, united only in having plenty to say for themselves. The others were seasoned travellers, and had many amusing tales to tell of previous crossings, and sojourns in other lands. Polly was the youngest of them by some distance and quickly became their pet. After dinner an orchestra played, but nobody danced; entertainments officers tried to arrange card games or tombola without success. The seas grew rougher, and the band of survivors only wanted to talk, drink and smoke.

On her first night as a survivor, a steward, taking orders for drinks, thought Polly was looking a little pale and suggested a glass of champagne. 'Many passengers find it settling, miss.' Polly tried it, and felt better, and after that, from a kind of superstition, she drank nothing but champagne, which she quickly developed a taste for. One of the other survivors – a large man, bearded like a sea-dog, and old enough to be Polly's grandfather so it wasn't rude – called her Champagne Polly, and sang a few bars of the song 'Champagne Charlie', substituting her name. After that he got the orchestra to play the tune every night at least once. Polly didn't mind. She liked having a nickname, and it made her feel like a seasoned traveller too when the stewards no longer asked her what she wanted to drink, but brought it automatically.

These odd and unscheduled pleasures could not last. On the third evening out, the sea was definitely moderating; on the fourth morning people began to get up, and a summons to Mrs Innes-Stewart's cabin caught Polly off guard so that she felt she had to attend. The widow was sitting up in bed going through a heap of in-board correspondence, looking pale, but enjoying a breakfast, even if it was only dry toast and black tea.

'You poor dear,' she said, when Polly entered. 'This dreadful storm! Have you been terribly, terribly sick?'

'No, ma'am,' Polly said. 'I wasn't sick at all.'

It perhaps wasn't tactful. Mrs Innes-Stewart's eyebrows drew down. 'My dear, you must have been. My stewardess says she has never known a storm like it in twenty years. Half the crew were confined to their bunks. The *captain himself* was unwell.' Polly realised the stewardess must have been telling tactful lies and did not contradict. 'It is wonderful of you to be so brave, but there's no need,' Mrs Innes-Stewart went on. 'There's no shame in succumbing. I myself am known as a particularly fine sailor, as is Stuart, but we have both been devastated.'

Polly only smiled, and said, 'I hope you are feeling better.'

'Yes, a great deal, and I shall get up by and by, but I wanted to say to you, my dear, how very sorry I am you

430

have been deprived of our company – particularly Stuart's. You have been having a very dull time of it, I know, but I mean to make it up to you. We shall be very gay, I promise you!'

Polly resigned herself, reflecting that two days could not kill her, and got what amusement she could out of her chaperone's bewilderment at how many people Polly seemed to know: the survivors stopped to talk to her as they passed, and came across to the Innes-Stewarts' table at luncheon, afternoon tea and dinner, and all seated moments in between. It was like a different ship, Polly thought, now the passengers were out and about, and dinner that night was a pageant of fabulous gowns and jewels, gales of perfume, bedlams of conversation and an endless succession of courses. She might almost have thought the resurrected were trying to make up in one go for all the meals they had missed.

There was dancing after dinner, and Polly was obliged to be shoved round by the damp-handed Stuart who, despite his mother's eulogies, did not seem to have much to say for himself, though he was adequately light on his feet and did not tread on hers. But she was not obliged to dance every dance with him, because members of the Survivors' Club kept coming up and asking her. Mrs Innes-Stewart evidently thought it odd that she should have so many middle-aged and elderly admirers, but she could not object to them if Polly did not. Polly enjoyed dancing with them, since they were all good talkers, and saved her from having to dance with young men who might want to romance her. She had no interest in that sort of thing. Mrs Innes-Stewart had to comfort herself that at least none of Polly's partners showed any propensity for taking her out on deck to look at the moon, which she had braced herself to have to forbid – unless it was Stuart.

It was easy enough to avoid the Innes-Stewarts on the last morning, in the chaos of packing and leave-taking. Polly left Hackett to pack everything for her and stayed on deck, watching the misty mark on the horizon gradually swelling into New York, and exchanging fond farewells with other survivors. The bearded sea-dog came and shook her hand heartily and said she had made the voyage for him. 'You're an unusual young woman, and America will love you. You have just the stuff for them. And if ever I can be of service . . .' He handed her his card with a bow, and took himself off.

On the card was printed *Lord Sommersby*, and a New York address. And on the back he had written, *Thank you, Charlie, for helping us weather the storm. Your devoted servant. S.*

Polly smiled and slipped it into her pocket, and turned to watch the incomparable sight of the Statue of Liberty rising slowly out of the ocean. America would love her, would it? Well, she was perfectly prepared to love America.

Disembarking was as exciting as embarking, because she was setting her first foot on American soil, with everything before her. It was hard to escape the Innes-Stewarts. She was obliged to disembark with them, and out of mere courtesy to introduce them to those who were waiting to receive her, and endure Mrs Innes-Stewart's attempts to further the acquaintance and set up future occasions for meeting. But at last the porters with their luggage grew impatient and the widow and her son were forced to relinquish their stand and follow it, or lose it in the

432

crush. And then at last Polly was free to concentrate on important things.

It was Lizzie and Ashley who had come to meet her: Lizzie grey-haired and motherly and looking so absurdly like Aunt Hen that Polly felt at once at home and safe; and Ashley tall and rather gaunt, his hair between silver and white, his face very brown and lined but still handsome and kind. They hugged her delightedly and Lizzie shed some tears – they seemed to be as traditional to meeting ships as to seeing them off, Polly thought.

And, goodness, was that really Lennie? He looked taller, and somehow handsomer. Perhaps it was his hair, worn longer and thicker than the army haircut she remembered, suiting the planes of his face better. Perhaps it was his expression, relaxed, happy, eager. Perhaps it was just that he fitted in here, which gave him an air of confidence. He was wearing a remarkable large, long coat of very fine-looking wool with a big fur collar, and a homburg hat, and he looked very American.

But his smile, lighting his face in the way she remembered, was just the same. 'It's so wonderful that you're here!' he exclaimed, shaking her hand and kissing the offered cheek. 'I hardly dared believe you'd ever come, and now here you are; and looking just—' He waved a hand over her *tout ensemble* while he searched for the word, and ended with an emphatic 'Just *fine!*'

'We're going to have such fun,' Lizzie said. 'Everyone's so thrilled about your visit, we've had to make up a rota for who gets to entertain you. I kept saying to people, "She's here for months, there's no hurry," but of course no-one wants to wait.' Ashley gave a meaning cough and Lizzie said, 'Of course! Let's get you home, Polly dear. You must be exhausted from all this travelling.'

Polly could only laugh. 'Not a bit! I didn't walk all the way, you know! I've had five days in the lap of luxury and slept every night in the downiest bed I ever saw. How could I be tired?'

'I don't believe Polly is ever tired,' Lennie said.

'Only when I'm made to do things I don't like,' Polly agreed.

The first two weeks in New York passed in dizzying fashion. As Lizzie had said, everyone wanted to entertain Polly, and she was passed around like a delicious treat for family meals and parties, while in the interim being introduced to the sights of New York and learning all she could about her new temporary home. She met the Flint cousins, and dined in their tall red-and-white house and met their four children and their various spouses, and tried her best to remember everyone's names.

Lennie lived in a large apartment off Sixth Avenue with his father Patrick, the architect, and his famous 'Granny Ruth', whom he had spoken of so often. Patrick was tall and kind and had the same sort of unremarkable but very pleasant looks as Lennie. Granny Ruth was so tiny and withered and fragile-looking she reminded Polly of a pressed flower, but her handshake was firm and her eyes were bright, and she quizzed Polly sharply about the journey and things back home with every sign of an alert mind. It amazed Polly to think she had lived through the American Civil War, which to her was something out of history.

She stayed at first with Lizzie and Ashley, in their large apartment in The Paterno, a grand old building on Riverside Drive, where she seemed to make a great impression on their daughter Rose, an enterprising young woman just about to have her thirteenth birthday. She had plenty to say for herself, and seemed almost to think Polly had been invited for her own particular benefit, for she had a whole programme of sight-seeing mapped out in her head, which included all of her favourite places, and did not include anyone but her and Polly. Lizzie was obliged to step in and tell her Cousin Polly would be too busy to play with her much.

'Play?' said Rose, indignantly. 'We weren't going to *play*!'

Polly liked her, and sympathised with the suffering she remembered so clearly of being thought to be too young for things when you knew inside you were not. She encouraged Rose to tell her her secrets and ambitions, allowed her to examine her clothes and possessions, and told her about her war experiences. Rose was bitter that the war had happened too soon for her to play any part; and she was very interested in clothes. Polly had brought her sketching-pad and pencils and amused Rose by drawing outfits for her. Rose asked if she could have the drawings. Polly gave them to her, and a few days later Rose returned them, beautifully coloured in.

'You have a real eye for colour,' Polly told her, and she blushed with pleasure.

Lizzie and Ashley's son Rupert, who had finished his engineering degree, was working away in Chicago when Polly arrived so she did not meet him, but Martial was there, with his new wife, Mimi, a lively and voluble young woman who immediately pronounced Polly 'ravishing' and said they would be the best of friends. 'We're perfect for each other, because I'm so dark and you're so fair!' Polly was not used to such vehemence, but she could see that Mimi was motivated purely by friendliness. She

435

was a svelte, almost thin young woman, with dark curly hair, rather prominent dark eyes, a high-coloured face, and a wide mouth with a large number of very white teeth. She had been Miss Miriam Annaheim, daughter of a very rich man who had made his fortune in minerals and steel. Ashley had met Annaheim senior in Arizona, where Culpepper and Annaheim interests were interconnected. The Annaheims had moved to New York and the acquaintance had been renewed when the Ashley Morlands did likewise. It had flourished into friendship, and the match between Martial, now working in his father's line, and Miriam had been welcomed by both sides, while it was for the Annaheim company that Rupert was working in Chicago.

Lizzie explained that she thought Polly would prefer a younger woman to take her about. 'You won't want to be tied to a grey-haired matron,' she said. 'A young married woman can introduce you and advise you properly. Mimi goes everywhere and knows everyone.'

Another chaperone, Polly thought, but resignedly. She certainly needed someone to show her the ropes, in a strange city in a foreign country.

Lizzie went on, 'Ashley and I mean to keep you for a couple of weeks, but then we thought perhaps you would like to go and stay at Martial and Mimi's. It will be much more fun for you to be with a younger set.'

Polly began to protest out of politeness, but Mimi broke in. 'It's all settled. We talked about it weeks ago, so there's nothing to decide. It doesn't mean you won't see the family. We come over to Ma-in-law's most Sundays, and the Mannings are only a few blocks from us.' She flashed her enormous smile and laughed with what seemed to be sheer high spirits. 'You and I will have such fun! I mean to show you absolutely everything! And Ma-in-law says you'll need lots of new outfits, and there's nothing I like better than shopping for clothes.' She laughed again. She seemed to laugh rather a lot, but she was very good-natured, and Martial, who was plainly very nice and intelligent, had liked her enough to marry her, so Polly thought she would take to her all right when she got used to her.

Meanwhile she was learning about the city: the astonishing 'skyscrapers', which turned the streets into canyons, and the oasis of Central Park (white, now, and sparkling with snow), with the apartment buildings overlooking it like white cliffs; the different districts, which were like separate villages within the city, each with its own flavour, some with a definite national bias – an Italian district here, a Chinese one there. She learned that the avenues went north to south and the streets east to west, neatly arranged on a grid and numbered and lettered so that you could never get lost. Just remember, Lennie told her, that the shadows always lay along the south side of the streets, and you would always know which way you were facing. She marvelled at the shops, like Aladdin's caves, and the wonderful window displays – doing to perfection what she had just started to do at Makepeace's. She marvelled at the restaurants and how New Yorkers seemed to eat out as often as they ate in. She marvelled at the theatres and cinemas and music halls and museums and art galleries, and at the intense pride the New Yorkers took in their culturedness.

She marvelled most of all at how there was no sign anywhere of the war: no damaged buildings, no men with missing limbs or eye-patches, no dole queues, no wretched veterans selling matches on corners – no recession or unemployment. The streets and shops and restaurants and theatres were packed every day and night, and the whole city seethed with activity and cheerfulness. Everyone seemed prosperous, well fed and well clothed, and everyone seemed busy. Polly felt invigorated by sheer contact with so much energy and purposefulness: after the misery of the war and the dead weight of loss and grief, it seemed to fill her with hope, that life could still be worth living. She knew she was going to like it here.

Despite herself, Emma grew interested in her new flat. It was something she could dedicate herself to, with no fear of being hurt. It suited her to be kept busy, to absorb herself in the minute detail of something that ultimately did not matter, and yet which conveyed its own satisfaction: the exact shade of paint, the precise fabric for upholstery or drape, the right electric-light fitting. With Benson at her heels she became a familiar sight going in and out of Stretton House, and those working on her flat, though at first inclined to look at her with suspicion, came to respect her because she knew exactly what she wanted: indecisiveness and mind-changing were what they feared most.

Kit Westhoven was at first puzzled by this new interest: the idea of interior decoration as an end in itself was not something that had ever come his way. You inherited a house from your father and maintained it as required, and the notion that it might make you happier if the walls were a different colour, or the furniture was rearranged, had never occurred to him. But he was glad of anything that made Emma a degree less miserable; and in a short time he began to be interested in it for itself. Emma liked having him to talk to about her ideas, and he liked any excuse to talk to Emma, so he called often at her suite and she showed him what she was doing and how she wanted it all to look when it was finished. He even contributed an idea or two, and discovered himself looking at other people's houses critically.

With all the changes Emma wanted, the flat was not ready until February. By then the Season was approaching, and Kit began delicately to work on Emma to make moving into the flat the occasion of her return to society. Up until then she had ventured out rarely, and only to dine with him in the most secluded of restaurants. She had refused all his beguilements to go to theatres or exhibitions, and had vehemently rejected the idea of visiting other people. He was flattered that he was the one intruder allowed into her life, but he felt it was time for her to face up to the world.

'I don't want to see other people,' she said. 'I don't want their pity. They'll remind me and I don't want to be reminded.'

'But you'll have to meet people sooner or later,' he reasoned.

'No, I won't.'

'Oh, Emma, it would be too sad to hide yourself away like a nun! You can't be like one of those eccentric old ladies, the sort who live in those dark apartments behind the Albert Hall and walk their little dogs in the park and smell of mothballs. You're at least forty years too young for that, and what will you do for forty years?'

She looked at him wearily. 'I don't know. Don't bully me. I don't want to think about anything at all. I just want to be left alone.'

But she didn't any more entirely want that. She liked having him as a friend and didn't want *him* to leave her alone. So he worked on her, by delicate degrees, to persuade her to give a house-warming party.

'A party will be easier than a dinner or anything of that sort,' he said. 'Nobody talks seriously at a party.'

And 'Everyone will be so fascinated by your flat and the fact that you did it all yourself, they won't think of anything else.'

And 'I will speak to everyone beforehand and tell them what subjects are tabu.'

Upon which Emma was roused to say, quite crossly, 'I'm not such a ninny that I have to have my conversations decided for me beforehand. If I'm going to do this, I shall do it on my own two feet.'

Kit noted the crossness gladly. Crossness was better than miserable resignation. And the sentence 'If I'm going to do this' was now lacking the subjunctive mood.

On her first morning in her new home, Emma was just finishing a shockingly late breakfast (her new bed was extremely comfortable, and the flat was much quieter than her room at the Ritz) when Benson barked and the doorbell rang simultaneously. In a moment Spencer appeared and said, 'It's Mr Winchmore, madam. Shall I have him come up?'

There was a little watery sunshine coming in through the window, illuminating the subtle tones of her paint-work, and Spencer had given her sausages for breakfast, to which Emma was partial. In the comfort of the moment she said yes, where another morning she might have said no.

She waited for him in the drawing-room. In a few minutes Spencer announced him, and he came in looking well, and more handsome than she remembered him, wearing an extremely expensive-looking charcoal grey suit with a small gardenia in the buttonhole. He crossed the room in two swift strides and caught both her hands and kissed her cheek before she could decide whether to let him or not. 'Emma, dear, thank you for seeing me. I wanted to be the first to welcome you to your new home.'

'How did you know I was here?' Emma asked feebly.

'Kit told me, of course. We talk every day, even if it's only on the telephone. We both feel a little uneasy if we don't. He's a great one for friendship.'

'I'm glad to have his friendship,' Emma said.

'And I'm glad he has yours,' Oliver said. 'And here's Benson, looking extremely fat and well. How are you, old boy?'

'Can I ring for coffee for you?' Emma asked, remembering the duties of hostess.

'No, thank you. I can't stay more than a minute,' Oliver said, and Emma tried not to feel relieved. 'I'm on my way to the Winchmore and just called in.'

'How are things going?' Emma asked, glad of a neutral topic.

'Very well. Swimmingly, in fact. I'm getting some very interesting cases, and I'm even persuading some of the paying patients to come in for operations, instead of having them done in their own houses. Not the upper classes, of course – they're a lost cause – but the fashionable upper middles can do a lot to change people's minds.'

'You certainly look prosperous,' Emma said. 'The gardenia is a nice touch.'

'Do you think so? Not too dandyish? I find I'm expected to put on a bit of a show for the ladies – helps me to persuade them to go under the knife if I make love to 'em a bit. Verena says I'm too suspiciously good at that sort of thing. But Kit was the real master. I wish I could persuade him to put on the gloves again and come in with me. I'm thinking of taking over a small clinic in Stanmore and there's more work than I can do alone.'

'I've never heard him talk about going back into surgery,' Emma said.

'No, he still insists that he never wants to see another operating theatre, after what we went through during the war. I haven't managed to change his mind yet, though I keep hoping.'

'Can't you find someone else?'

'Oh, yes, there's no difficulty in finding an assistant – too many of us out of a job after the war – but I always envisaged Kit and me setting up together one day. Oh, well . . .'

'How is Verena?'

'In tip-top form. Enjoying playing house – as far as there's any playing to be done. Mother keeps a good staff.'

'It's not awkward, living there?'

'Not at all. We have a floor all to ourselves if we want to be private, and Mother's almost *too* tactful about keeping out of our way. She and Verena get on famously, when she allows herself to be cornered into dining with us. She sends her love, by the way – I told her I was calling here. Verena does too. She hopes you'll come and dine with us some day soon.'

Emma looked away. 'Oh, Oliver, I don't know. Kit keeps trying to persuade me to go out. He wants me to have a house-warming party.'

'I wish you would have one,' Oliver said gently. 'You have to rejoin the world sooner or later.'

442

'I don't *have* to do anything,' Emma retorted.

He looked at her averted face for a moment, and then said, 'You know, during the war it was considered bad form to put on any show of grief or mourning. We've all lost someone, Emma dear. I miss my father every day. I know you had a particularly bad hand, losing two people you were very close to – or perhaps it was three.'

She cast him one scalding glance. 'What do you mean?'

'Oh, just something I heard, out in France,' he said thoughtfully. 'Probably it was all rot.'

'You shouldn't listen to gossip.'

'No, quite right, I shouldn't. But, still, it isn't right that you should shut yourself away like this.'

'Isn't it my business, what I do?'

'There's such a thing as duty,' he said.

Now her eyes returned to him. 'I did my duty in France,' she said.

'I know you did, and I admire you for it. But duty isn't a once-in-a-lifetime thing. You go on having to do it.'

'I still don't see what duty has to—'

'God didn't make you beautiful and intelligent for nothing. And He allowed you to survive, when others didn't. All of us who survived have that same duty – not to waste the life we've been given. I know you don't feel like it now, but if you make the effort, it will get easier with time. Get back into the world, and find out what you've survived for.'

'Oh, Oliver,' she said despairingly. 'It's all so very hard.'

'I know. But have the party to begin with, just that, and see where it leads. We're sociable creatures, we human beings. We weren't meant to live alone in a cave – even an exceedingly smart cave like this.'

★   ★   ★

So she gave a house-warming party. In the end, she invited a very large number, reasoning that the more people were there, the less likely anyone would be able to buttonhole her. Making the arrangements was good occupation, keeping her busy so that she didn't have to think too much about what it meant in terms of meeting people. But at the last minute, on the evening itself, she was overcome with dread, and looking at herself in the mirror as Spencer brushed her hair, she wondered what on earth she was doing. She felt utterly hollow and bereft: what did anything matter, without Peter? How could she greet people, pretend to be glad they had come, pretend to care whether they were alive or dead? How could she do anything but stare into the bottomless black pit of loss?

Spencer must have seen something in her face; she twisted a curl round her finger and said, 'Going to need cutting again soon, miss. Getting quite long at the back – though it suits you a bit longer, if you don't mind my saying so. Which clips will I put in, miss? Or will I put on a bandeau?'

Emma didn't answer, staring blindly at her own reflection. And then Benson put his paws up on her knee and made a little enquiring noise, and she put her hand automatically to caress his head. *Wentworth gave him to me,* she thought. *Fenniman, Wentworth, Peter Gresham. Everyone I love dies. But I just go on.* And then she thought of Kit Westhoven's words. *What will you do for forty years?*

Spencer asked her again about her hair, 'What will I do, miss?' and Emma misheard it as *What will you do?*

They did not die for you to give up, said a voice inside her. Not just Fenniman, Wentworth, Gresham, but all the thousands upon thousands who had died. They were dead but she was alive. What would she do for forty years? Carry on. Not give up. Keep on doing things, that was the secret. Keep moving, never be still.

'Keep on dancing,' she said.

Spencer put in the clips, and sent her mistress out to face the music.

CHAPTER EIGHTEEN

One day in February, Lennie said to Polly, 'There's something I want to show you. Will you come with me?'

'What is it?' Polly asked.

'We have to go out to see it. Put on something warm, because there won't be any heating there.'

'Any heating *where*?'

But he wouldn't be drawn. 'It's a surprise,' he said.

Lennie had his own motor, which was standing on the street at the kerb. Polly had come by degrees to realise, with some surprise, that Lennie was doing very well with his business, and the nice clothes and the motor were bought with his own money. He did not live with his father and grandmother because he couldn't afford a place of his own, as she had assumed at first, but because it suited them all, and they were fond of each other.

'Can I drive?' Polly asked, when they reached the street. 'You can give me directions.'

Lennie liked the fact that Polly knew how to drive, and was proud of the looks she attracted, even in a city where a woman driving was not such an unusual sight. But Polly always stood out in a crowd.

Polly liked the adventure of driving on the wrong side

of the road: it was somehow thrilling, like doing something forbidden. It would be nice to have a motor-car of my own, she thought. She had no idea how much one cost. Perhaps she should investigate . . .

The journey was disappointingly short, only as far as Forty-second Street, where he directed her to stop in front of an empty shop.

'This is it,' he said, jumping out and coming round to open the door for her. She stepped out and looked around. Forty-second was the street for music shops, and one side of the empty shop was a brass-instrument emporium, from the upstairs windows of which there emerged the sound of someone trying out a trumpet, running up and down scales and arpeggios. On the other side was a tiny delicatessen from which the delicate twin aromas of salami and cheese teased the senses.

'This what?' she asked blankly. 'Sandwiches or trombones?'

'Neither,' said Lennie, with a broad grin. '*This!*' He led her to the door of the empty shop and produced from his capacious pocket a small bunch of keys. He opened the door and ushered her inside. It was dark and dusty and very cold; completely empty, only the ghostly marks of shelves long removed interrupting the drab paint on the walls. 'What do you think?'

Polly looked at the scraps of litter and dust-mice on the bare wooden floorboards, and the naked light bulb hanging from an unshaded ceiling fitting. 'It's lovely, Lennie,' she said with feeling irony. 'Perfectly gorgeous.'

He missed the tone. 'Do you think so?' he said eagerly. 'I know it's shabby now, but it's sound – nothing that cleaning and painting won't fix. And it couldn't be better placed.' He turned to smile at her. 'This will be just the

447

first. In a year or two there'll be shops all over New York – all over America. But I wanted you to see the very first.'

'You've bought this shop?' Polly said, catching the thread at last.

'Rented it.' Lennie described a sign with his hand across the air. 'Manning's Radios,' he pronounced. 'It has something, don't you think?'

'Manning's Radios?' She looked around, trying to visualise it.

'I've got my radio sets into all the big stores, and it's time to set up a store of my own. Radio's really taking off now. I heard they've just bought one for the White House, and I'm determined the next president to buy a wireless set will buy one of mine. I want my name to be synonymous with radio – people will look at a set in someone's house and say, "Oh, you've got a new Manning, have you?"'

'Is there really money to be made out of it?'

'You bet there is,' he said. 'And, like with all new things, the time to make the biggest money is at the beginning. Do you know there are nearly five hundred radio stations now, whereas this time last year there were only eight? Wireless sets are selling like hot cakes. I can hardly make 'em fast enough. Now,' he took her arm and turned her to look at the shop, 'imagine this all painted up white and clean.' He used his other hand to make sweeping descriptive gestures. 'Good-quality carpet on the floor, nice polished-wood fixtures, modern lighting – lots of it – and everywhere, as far as the eye can see, Manning radio sets of every shape and size. Small ones, big ones, gigantic ones like ocean liners; mahogany cases, walnut cases, satinwood cases, ebony cases,

448

mother-of-pearl-inlaid cases – heck, even silver cases for rich ladies' boudoirs! Radio sets and radiograms and gramophones – I might even stock gramophone records, maybe sheet music, whatever people want. I want them to come to Manning's Radios first, before they even *think* of going anywhere else. I want them thinking so often about Manning's Radios they even come in here for a sandwich!'

Polly laughed. 'You'll do it. I know you will. A person with so much energy can't fail.'

He looked at her eagerly. 'Do you really think so? You know, the great thing about this country is that a man with enough gumption can really get on, and make something of himself. Doesn't matter who he is or where he starts from, if he's willing to hustle he can make a fortune.' His expression was suddenly serious. 'And when I've made it, Polly, I shall ask you to marry me.'

Polly was dismayed. 'Oh, Lennie, don't say that.'

'Why not? Don't you know everything I do is for you? I know I can never deserve you, but I'll work every minute of every day for you, and no man will ever love you more than I do. If that can be enough one day—'

'Lennie, I can't. Please don't go on. I'm very sorry, because I do love you, but in a sisterly way, not the other sort.'

He looked at her consideringly for a long moment, then said gently, 'You're so young, and you've lived a sheltered life. I know you said you loved someone else, but I wonder if you really know what the other sort is?'

'Yes, I do.' Polly turned away from him abruptly. 'I loved him, and he's dead,' she said harshly. 'It's all over for me now. So please don't go on like this.'

'I didn't know,' Lennie said. 'You told me you couldn't

marry him – but I didn't know . . .' He was contrite, but even so, his heart had lifted a little. A living rival might have presented a problem, but a dead lover's memory would gradually fade, and he didn't mind how long he waited, as long as she came to him in the end.

So he said, 'Forgive me, Polly. I won't talk about it any more. Let's talk about my store instead. What colour do you think the walls should be? You have a good eye for such things. Would you help me decorate it?'

She turned back to him. 'I should like that.'

'And I'll tell you some more about my plans. I'm thinking of moving manufacture to a bigger place across the river – I have to expand and rents are cheaper there. And it's not just manufacture. I have other ideas spinning around in my head.'

'I haven't a doubt of it.' Polly thought how much she liked Lennie when he wasn't trying to be 'spoony', as the Americans said.

Polly was enjoying New York enormously. She now lived in the eighties Westside apartment of Martial and Mimi. Martial – in common with most American businessmen, it seemed – worked very long hours, so she didn't see anything of him during the day. Not always in the evening either: he seemed to have a lot of 'men-only' engagements, which Mimi said were important for his business. She seemed quite resigned to seeing little of her husband, and spoke of it as if it were the norm.

Polly met Mimi's brother, Wendell, who was to inherit the Annaheim family business, and his wife Dottie, a tiny, pretty firecracker of a woman. They often went out in a group together in the evenings, to restaurants or to the theatre. The Annaheims and Mimi were very fond of musical shows, and they took Polly to *Blue Eyes* at the Casino, and *Golden Days* at the Gaiety, and to the Music Box revue. Martial liked plays, too, and they saw *Claire de Lune* at the Empire, and *Mr Pym Passes By* at the Garrick. It was written by an Englishman – A. A. Milne, the *Punch* humorist – which made Polly feel proud and patriotic.

Invariably they ended the evening by dancing, either at a restaurant that had a dance floor, or at a dance hall or nightclub, which in New York was perfectly respectable. Often Lennie joined them, to make the numbers even, so she danced with all three of the men quite a lot: Martial and Lennie were good, and fun to be with, but she didn't like dancing with Wendell. He had a strange, drooping, shuffling style, as if he were exhausted and could hardly move his feet, and he never had much to say for himself. But it was true, as Lizzie had said, that Mimi seemed to know everyone, and Polly never lacked for other partners: wherever they ended up, Mimi would introduce her to 'my great friend so-and-so'; or it was, 'I'm sure you know such-and-such – didn't we bump into him in the Flamingo?'

When Polly first came to live with her, Mimi had been very excited about the idea of shopping for clothes for her, but when she learned that Polly wanted to design them herself she was awed. 'Oh, my! You are *good* at this!' she exclaimed, on seeing Polly's drawings. 'These are just *gorgeous*! I never knew you were so clever.'

She immediately enlisted Dottie's help in finding the right warehouses for cloth and the right dressmakers for making up. 'Dottie knows everything.'

Dottie bought her clothes in a store like everyone else, but in her fidgety, dashing-about sort of way she always managed to find out things, and could track down a 'marvellous little man' who could do or make, or a 'fine little place' which stocked whatever was wanted.

She was just as entranced as Mimi by the idea of Polly's originals, though she examined the drawings with a more critical eye. 'You've made them all too tall,' she said, looking from the sketches to Polly and back. 'I know *you*'re tall, but there never was a woman with arms and legs as long as this. I guess it's a kind of artistic thing, though, isn't it? It does make the women look romantic, sort of. Like Lady Guinevere. I'm glad I'm not tall, though. Men like to kind of *pet* a woman, and they can't do that if she towers over them. But I guess you'll do all right with tall men. What cloth were you thinking of for this coat and skirt? I don't think you'll find any tweed as fine as that darling one you brought from England, but we get some nice wool cloth from Maine and New Hampshire. If I can find out who merchants it, we can see if they have anything the right weight.'

They plunged together into a whirl of activity, hunting down merchants, searching through warehouses, visiting clothing manufactories, workshops and individual dress-makers – strange expert seamstresses in gloomy Greenwich walk-ups. Dottie's chauffeur had to resign himself to driving the ladies to out-of-the-way and unfashionable districts, and waiting for them in grimy streets outside sooty brick buildings where the air seemed to dribble damp industrial fog. But Dottie on the trail of a particular cloth or an expert milliner was like a hound on a coon hunt, and would not be turned aside until she had run her quarry down.

It was natural to move from helping Polly to requesting original designs for themselves. When they went out together and met any of Mimi's and Dottie's numerous friends, the fashions were exclaimed over and Polly brought forward as the originator, so there were soon more people asking Polly to design clothes for them than she would have had time for, even if she was willing. Mimi constituted herself watchdog, and rebuffed the majority firmly, while wheedling the occasional 'favor' for a friend who had a special occasion planned and 'could never be satisfied' now with anything but an original.

In between all this activity, Polly was seeing the sights, getting to know Manhattan, having luncheons and teas with an ever-widening group of acquaintances, and becoming well known in the smart set as 'that handsome Polly Morland – you know, the English girl?' She was developing her own style, for she liked to stand out in a crowd. Though she could not yet quite bring herself to have her long golden hair bobbed, she did have it waved – François Marcel had recently brought out electric curling tongs which heated to a constant temperature, and so took the hazard out of the waving technique. Having her hair cut in a hairdressing shop instead of by a maid at home was a new experience, and Marcel also initiated her into the secret of the chamomile rinse, which was said to keep golden hair bright. The combination of waved front hair and a large chignon behind suited Polly, and was much admired, especially by girls whose fathers wouldn't let them bob.

Many of the women in the smart set smoked, which Polly thought rather shocking at first. But when she got used to the sight of it, she was intrigued enough to try it. She found the taste disgusting but, catching sight of herself in a mirror, liked the way it made her look. So she took to having cigarettes, but never actually smoking them. Having a cigarette lit for you by a man was a nice little ritual, and pretending to smoke showed off your hands and wrists. She had a number of cigarette holders made in different materials to match her outfits, and wore bracelets that caught the light when she moved.

The banning of alcohol, she discovered, had induced a strange split in the population between their public and private lives. Prohibition had been brought in by a certain Representative Volstead, apparently with the intention of stopping the lower classes drinking themselves into ill-health and poverty; so while the law had to be observed overtly, the wealthier classes did not feel themselves to be under any moral imperative to obey it, as long as they were not in danger of being caught. Alcohol at home was provided in the same quantities as ever, but delivered in boxes disguised as other things, from merchants who had to put up their prices to cover the risk of discovery and prosecution. In nightclubs it could be purchased freely, though it was sometimes served in coffee cups. There was much talk of 'raids', where the police broke in unannounced to catch people out, but the better-run clubs and restaurants paid a hefty fee to them to be left alone, and Polly never saw one. It all seemed to be an exercise in futility. People drank all the more, as far as she could see, because it was forbidden – even at luncheon, private flasks would be brought out from pockets and handbags. Nobody need ever go without: doctors were allowed under the law to prescribe alcohol for medicinal reasons, and most were not too particular about it, so if all else failed you could fall back on 'illcohol'.

It seemed shocking at first to Polly that young women

of good class were drinking not just wine and sherry but spirits, often in the form of mixed drinks – the so-called 'cocktails'. She tried one or two but didn't like the taste much, and decided early on to stick to wine, champagne if she could get it. Proper French champagne was expensive, and her preference for it soon added to her reputation for being a very stylish young woman, a leader of fashion. To her surprise, she found other females beginning to ape her.

Lennie said to her one evening, when a woman at a nearby table was waving about a cigarette holder like one of Polly's, and calling for champagne, 'I hope all this nonsense doesn't turn your head. I'd hate you to be spoiled by the wrong sort of attention.'

Polly looked at him, amused. 'Do I seem spoiled to you?'

'No,' he admitted. 'You're as perfect as ever.' Concern for her made him add, 'But it's early days yet.'

'Well, if I ever seem to you to be growing spoiled, I give you full permission to tell me so. In any case, I shall be going home before I've had time to be quite ruined.'

Lennie was unhappy at this reminder. 'I wish you wouldn't go,' he said.

Polly only shrugged, but when she wrote to her father asking for her allowance to be increased – running about with rich women like Mimi and Dottie was expensive – she dropped a mild hint that she might not be coming home at the end of the time slot allowed her. She was enjoying herself too much.

In May 1922, White Star's RMS *Majestic* – the former Hapag Line's *Bismarck* – was completed at last. At over fifty-six thousand tons gross, and nine hundred and fifty feet long, she was the largest ship in the world. She could carry over two thousand passengers and cruise comfortably at twenty-three knots. She was long, sleek and elegant, fitted out inside to a peak of luxury, and Teddy was immensely proud of his connection with her.

In the past he had been invited on the maiden voyage of both *Olympic* and *Titanic*, though he had missed the former because of previous plans, and the latter had turned into the disaster he still could not think about. None the less, when the company invited him to sail on *Majestic*, on her maiden voyage from Southampton to New York on the 12th of May, he was sorely tempted. In the end he decided against it, but the thought of seeing the new ship in action haunted him. He had felt strangely bereft when waving the *Berengaria* out – and not only because it was taking Polly away from him. There was something about that moment of departure . . .

He began to think that he deserved a holiday. He hadn't had one for a very long time – in fact, not since his honeymoon, too long ago to remember the date. He worked hard, no-one could deny that. Gradually his mind suggested a compromise: to sail on *Majestic*, yes, but not all the way to New York. Lots of people got on and off at Cherbourg. That would make a nice little trip, and he would be away only a few days.

He suggested it, tentatively, to Henrietta, who blinked with surprise that he should want it, and then said, 'No-one deserves a holiday more than you. But how will you get back from Cherbourg?'

'I should get the train to Calais or Boulogne and take the ferry crossing.'

'It seems a shame to go all that way for so little. Isn't

there something else you can do on the trip as well? Have a few days in Paris, perhaps?'

'What would I do in Paris, at my age? I shouldn't care to see a show or eat in a restaurant all alone. It would look sad and foolish.' But then an idea came to him. 'There *is* something, though.'

'Something you'd like to do?'

'I'd like to go to Loos,' he said.

Loos was where Ned had fallen, his body never to be found. It seemed to Henrietta unlikely to lift the spirits. And yet she understood. Her son Frank lay in a cemetery in Picardy, her son Robert in Malta, and there was a little part of her that grieved that she would never see their graves.

But Ned didn't even have a grave. 'Is there anything to see?' she asked.

'Just the area the battle was fought over. But I should like to see it. It isn't far from Calais, and I can easily hire a car. And there's a cemetery there, at Dud Corner. A large one. I've read about it. Lots of unknown soldiers' graves. If he *was* brought in and no-one knew him, that's where he'd have been put.'

'But still you'd never know,' Henrietta pointed out.

'No. But I think I'd like to go. Just once. To pay my respects.'

Teddy enjoyed the *Majestic* part of the trip enormously. He managed in the short time available to see over most of the ship – the captain sent a junior officer to conduct him so nothing was barred to him. She was a beautiful vessel, and he half envied the happily milling people who were going to have five days to sample all her pleasures. All too soon Cherbourg loomed into sight on the horizon, and it seemed only minutes after that that he was standing on *terra firma* again, with the great ship, her lights twinkling in the gathering dusk, like a paradise from which he had been unkindly ejected.

He stayed the night in Cherbourg at Le Grand, took dinner there and slept rather badly, his mind unsettled by the new experiences, drifting in and out of over-vivid dreams. The following day, after a *café-complet*, which seemed unsatisfying to a man used to a decent English breakfast, he presented himself at the railway station. Railways in France were still suffering from the effects of the war, and the efficient Miss Husthwaite, after some research, had concluded it would be much easier for him to travel via Paris than to attempt the journey along the coast. So, he reflected wryly, he would get to see Paris after all – or as much of it as was visible from the taxi window on the journey between two termini. It looked grimy and shabby, crowded with people and traffic, pretty much like any other city these days, but he accepted that he had probably not seen the best bits.

From Paris he took the train north via Amiens to Arras, and there, to his great relief, he found the hired car waiting for him as Miss Husthwaite had ordered: he had wondered what he would do if it did not appear. The driver and guide was an Englishman with a careworn face – an ex-officer eking out a living with battlefield tours. Teddy was feeling rather lonely by now, having had no-one to talk to for a whole day, and firmly placed himself in the front passenger seat. Though at home he did a full day's work, travelling alone, in strange places, and without proper food, was much more tiring. He was half wishing he had not set out on a venture that seemed now faintly foolish.

Fortunately the ex-officer, a line captain whose name was Simpson-Daniels, found nothing foolish in it, having conducted many similar pilgrimages, and asked him so kindly and tactfully about Ned that Teddy found himself telling the whole of Ned's troubled history, a long tale that lasted them all the way to Loos. Captain Simpson-Daniels told him that there was a stone in the Dud Corner cemetery dedicated to the missing, and that there was talk of one day putting up a proper monument, when the money could be got together.

The sight of the rows upon rows of headstones almost unmanned Teddy: it was one thing to read the numbers in a newspaper, but to see in pitiful perspective the graves in their symmetrical lines stretching away in all directions brought the reality of the slaughter home. As he stood in the May sunshine, struggling with his tears, he wished he had not come. What good did it do? He fumbled for a handkerchief and blew his nose violently.

Simpson-Daniels, who had fallen back a tactful step, came forward when the handkerchief had been put away again and guided Teddy to the stone commemorating the missing. It was at one end of the graveyard, from which, over the low fence, there was a long view of the bare and unprepossessing countryside. What was it for? Teddy asked himself, as he stared out. This piece of land, so bitterly fought over, fertilised by the lives of so many Englishmen – what crop would it grow? One day, he supposed, men would eat the corn grown out of the sacrificial blood. He tried to think about Ned, but couldn't conjure his face: he was gone, absolutely. He said a prayer in his mind, but it was a mechanical act. Life, in its cruel determination, had moved on and left the dead behind.

'Would you like a tour of the battlefield now?' Simpson-Daniels asked when he turned away from the stone.

But Teddy said, 'No, thank you. I've seen enough. Just take me to Calais, will you?' He was seventy-one, his stomach was grumbling, and he wanted to go home.

He was early for his crossing, so he enquired at the ticket office where he could find some refreshments, and was directed to a hotel across the road where he was promised they spoke English. He was shown to a table in the lounge and requested tea and buttered toast, and it came, at last: the tea in a metal vessel like a coffee pot, and not tasting like English tea – or like tea at all, for that matter – and the toast made from very strange bread, more like cake, which had currants in it. It, however, was not unpleasant, and he was ravenous, so he ate it without a struggle.

During the meal he noticed a woman being shown in to a table near him. She was alone, which struck him because he was sure she was English, and he did not like to see an Englishwoman unchaperoned in a foreign country. She was quite young, too, and reminded him, with a pang, of his first wife, Charlotte – Polly's mother, who had died in childbirth having her. Charlotte had been small and fair like that, with just such a sharp little face – though she had been prettier. This was quite an ordinary little person. He dragged his attention away, before she noticed him staring at her – he did not want to offend. She wasn't really like Charlotte, he told himself sternly: it was just the dead troubling him, after his awakening at Loos. She was wearing a black coat and hat, and he wondered if she had been on a similar errand

460

to his, visiting a grave – brother or father, perhaps. Surely not husband. She seemed too young.

He finished his tea, paid the bill (Miss Husthwaite had even provided him with some French currency in case of need – she thought of everything) and walked back to the docks, where the steamer was now boarding. The evening was fine, though a little breeze had got up as the sun declined, and he decided to stay on deck, leaning on the taffrail and watching the churning wake extend the distance between him and France. He did not suppose he would ever have reason to go back there. He felt a little melancholy.

Someone came up to the rail nearby, and glancing round he saw it was the young woman in black he had noticed before. He felt vaguely glad to know she was going back to England and safety. He would have touched his hat to her, but she was not looking his way: she had taken out a handkerchief and was applying it to her eyes. He was afraid she had been crying.

Suddenly she gave a little cry of vexation, and he looked back in time to see the wind snatch the handkerchief from her fingers and carry it over the side into the sea. He brought out his own large, beautifully laundered handkerchief, smelling faintly of lavender-oil. 'I'm afraid yours is a lost cause,' he said, and presented it to her with a little bow.

There was a hesitation, a doubtful glance at his face, but seemingly reassured by what she saw there, she gave a voiceless 'thank you' and took it. Teddy waited, staring out to sea to give her privacy to dry her eyes and blow her nose. When she finally turned to him, her nose and eyes were pink, which in her pale little face (the impression of sharpness, he realised, came from the fact that

461

she was thin – too thin – as if she did not get enough to eat) gave her a vulnerable appearance, as of a white mouse.

'Thank you, sir,' she said. She looked at the handkerchief, crumpled in her hand. 'If you will give me your card, I will launder it and return it to you.'

He reached for his card case, raising his hat with the other hand, and said, 'I shall be glad to give you my card, but you must not trouble to return the handkerchief. It has served its purpose, if it has been of use to you.' He presented her with a card. 'Edward Morland, at your service.'

'You are very kind,' she said, looking at it. Under his name it had for his addresses Morland Place and his London club. She ran her thumb over the embossing, as if it might tell her something more. She was certainly English, he thought. Her accent was quite pure; her coat, hat and shoes were well brushed, though worn. She was not as young as he had thought – in her late twenties or early thirties, quite old enough to be a widow. Though her face was careworn, her eyes had a quickness of intelligence.

'I'm afraid you are distressed,' he said. 'Can I be of any assistance?'

'Oh – no! Thank you. I've – I've been to visit my husband's grave,' she added in a little rush, as though longing to confide, and being held back only by custom. 'I thought it would help, but it didn't. It is foolish to think looking at a headstone can make things any different.'

'I have been even more foolish,' he said. 'My son doesn't even have a headstone. He was one of the missing. I've been to look at nothing more than a bare field.'

'Oh, I'm so sorry,' she said.

'It didn't help me, either,' Teddy confessed. A longing to talk to her came over him like a wave of passion or the imperative of hunger. 'This wind makes it chilly here,' he said. 'Might I offer you a little refreshment inside?'

She shrank slightly. 'Thank you, but no. I couldn't possibly.'

He liked her for it. 'You have my card,' he said. 'I am well known in York, where I am chairman of the Railway Board. Besides, I'm old enough to be your grandfather.'

She almost smiled. 'I'm sure *that* is an exaggeration,' she said.

He swelled inside with pleasure. 'Visiting that graveyard shook me profoundly, and I'm sure it must have been a shock to you, too. I would be honoured if you would allow me to provide a little restorative. A very small brandy and soda, for medicinal purposes – in the saloon, out of this unpleasant wind.'

After a searching gaze at his face, which Teddy found strangely touching, she gave a little sigh and said, 'I am much obliged to you, sir.'

He offered his arm and she rested the tips of her fingers on it, and he prevented himself from laying his own large hand over her small one.

After the brandy and soda she declined a second one, but allowed him to order a pot of tea, and over the cups the conversation, stilted at first, quickly warmed. For the second time that day he told the story of Ned, and she reciprocated with her own tale. Her name was Mrs Butler – Amy Butler – and her husband had fallen near Plug Street Wood. 'He died without ever having fired a shot,' she told Teddy. 'I don't know why that should make it harder, but it does. He was called up in 1917, and after training he was sent to France and was killed by a shell on his way up to the line. It seemed such a terrible waste.'

By the time the steamer docked, the ease between them was such that it seemed accepted they would travel on to London together. He insisted on buying her dinner on the train – he was desperately hungry now, and it did not take much to discover that she had not eaten all day. As the food restored some colour to her cheeks, he gradually elicited the basic elements of her story. Her parents had died when she was thirteen, and she and her only brother had been split up: he to live with the family of a solicitor, a friend of his father's, with whom he was to take articles when he left school; she to live with her godmother, an elderly woman of precise habits, unsuited to taking on a troubled child at an energetic and turbulent age.

'She wasn't unkind to me,' Mrs Butler said quickly. 'You mustn't think that. She did her duty by me. But she was cold, and I was unhappy.'

She escaped the situation by marrying as soon as possible – at eighteen, to a man ten years her senior, who had a good steady position as an estate agent. They had been happy together, except for the fact that they had had no children. His call-up had left her in a difficult position. By this stage of the conversation she had lost most of her restraint with Teddy, and did not seem to mind telling him of her troubles.

'It was hard enough to manage on his army pay. When he was called up we had to give up our house and I moved into rooms. But when he was killed . . .' She looked at her hands blankly for a moment, and then shrugged. 'It must be a common story. I had to move

464

into lodgings, and find myself a job to make ends meet.' She had hoped to live with her brother after the war, but he had been killed too, at Gallipoli, so she was all alone in the world.

She looked up. 'But I'm very lucky, really. I have a clean room in a respectable house, and my landlady is very kind. And I have a pleasant job in a florist's shop in Conduit Street.' She smiled, and he thought how very pretty she looked when she did that. 'The gentlemen who get their suits in Savile Row come in for their buttonholes.'

'You don't mean Larner's? I've been in there myself, many times, when I've been staying in London.' His expression clouded. 'I don't think I've ever seen you in there. I know I would have remembered.'

'You wouldn't see me in the shop. I work in the back, making up: bouquets for weddings, wreaths for funerals and so on. Buttonholes for the gentlemen. It's quite interesting work, and not at all onerous.'

And yet, he thought, no lady could like having to work for her living; he admired her for her determination to make light of it.

By the time they got to Victoria they were completely at ease with each other and had even laughed together over some of their lighter memories. When they stepped down from the train he felt that he could not bear to part from her so soon, and asked to be allowed to escort her home in a taxi-cab. 'I shall be taking a cab to the club anyway,' he said, 'so it's no trouble.'

She hardly hesitated before accepting. The lodging-house was in Endell Street, and despite the best efforts of the traffic, the journey seemed all too short. Telling the taxi to wait, he walked with her to the house door, lifted his hat and said, 'I wonder if I might be permitted to take you out to dinner one evening?' He expected her to say no: despite how well they had got on together, he was twice her age. Accepting an old man's company on an otherwise boring journey was a different matter from dining with him when you had no need to.

But she said at once, 'Thank you. I should like that.'

It was said so readily that he dared to suggest the following evening, and she said yes, and they parted with a cordial shake of the hand. Teddy went back to his taxi in such a daze of pleasure that the driver had to remind him that he wasn't no mind-reader, guv'nor, and couldn't take him nowhere unless he give an address.

The telegram was brief and to the point –

STAYING ON A FEW DAYS IN LONDON+ SEND BROWN
TO CLUB WITH CLOTHES+ E MORLAND

– but it left Henrietta with a great many questions. 'A few days? How many? And why isn't he staying with Jessie and Bertie? Oh dear, will he want evening clothes, I wonder, or just clean shirts and so on? Brown, what do you think?'

Brown thought he had better take evening clothes as well, and enough for a week. He packed a bag for himself, too. 'I anticipate the master will want me to stay,' he said happily. 'Club servants are very well in their way but he will not want anyone but me to take care of his boots.'

But by the evening Brown was back. 'The master did not require me to stay, madam. He said he would manage without.'

'Oh,' said Henrietta, looking at him in bafflement.

There was a limit to what questions a person could decently ask of a gentleman's personal man.

But Brown had been with the family a long time, and in kindness answered them anyway. 'The master did not say how long he would be staying, madam. Nor did he divulge the nature of the business that was detaining him. But he seemed quite well – indeed, as well as I have ever seen him. Not at all upset by his French trip. On the contrary, madam, I would almost say the master was in high spirits.'

High spirits? What could have happened on the trip to make him jolly? Perhaps, Henrietta thought, it was simply that he had realised the need for a holiday, and was enjoying it. At all events, there was nothing to be done but to wait for him to come back for clarification.

Fortunately Miss Husthwaite had taken charge of everything, co-ordinating her own efforts as confidential secretary with those of the steward, Pickering, Teddy's business secretary, Norris, and the man of business, Mr Pobgee.

'The truth of the matter is that Mr Morland really doesn't need to do all the things he does himself,' Miss Husthwaite explained kindly to Henrietta. 'We all know our duties and are quite able to discharge them. It's only the larger questions of policy that need to be referred to Mr Morland. Day-to-day matters can be taken care of without his supervision.'

'I suppose he has got used to being busy,' Henrietta had said, wondering how Teddy would take to the idea that he wasn't needed.

'Just so,' said Miss Husthwaite briskly. 'But it would be quite in order for him to think of retiring now. One must consider his age.'

'I don't think he does,' Henrietta said, faintly offended, since she was only three years younger than Teddy herself.

At the end of the third week of his stay, Teddy took Amy Butler to dine at Brown's Hotel. Until then, for her sake, he had taken her to little back-street restaurants: she had been adamant that she did not have the clothes to be going anywhere smart. He had gathered that she had expended the last of her savings on the trip to Plug Street: in fact, on the day they met she would have had to go without dinner if he had not fed her, and would have walked home from Victoria, not even having a penny for the bus.

But Brown's it had to be for this evening's purpose: it was respectable, pleasant and discreet, and since he had requested beforehand the quietest table, they were shown to one in a secluded corner. Mrs Butler looked around a little nervously when they entered, but seemed reassured by their distance from other diners. They ate their dinner, and chatted freely as they had done every evening of the past twenty.

At the end of the meal, Teddy told the waiter they would have coffee at the table, and when he had brought it and departed, Teddy said, 'There is something in particular I want to ask you, but before I do, I want to assure you that you need not give me an answer straight away. There is no hurry, if you would like time to think about it.'

Her immediate look of consciousness suggested she knew the nature of this question already. Still, she was able to meet his eyes, which he took as an encouraging sign, and he plunged in.

'To make a long story short, I'm going to ask you to

marry me – but first, I want to explain two things.' He hurried on before she could say anything. 'I want to take care of you. I know what a hard time you have had of it, and I want to make you happy and comfortable. I've told you about my situation, about Morland Place and my businesses, so you know that I am quite a rich man. But I do have responsibilities to my family – in particular to my son and daughter, but also to my sister and the various nephews and nieces I support.'

'Indeed,' she said, as if wondering what this had to do with her.

Teddy explained: 'I wanted you to understand that if you accept me, I cannot make my whole fortune over to you. But I will make a settlement on you that will keep you in comfort for the rest of your life after I die. And everyone will know about it, so there will be no danger of any argument or misunderstanding or anything of that sort. Everything will be fair and open and above-board.'

'Please don't talk about dying,' she said, looking upset. 'You can't think . . .'

He looked distracted by the interruption, having braced himself for his speech, and went on. 'The other thing I must say is that you must not think I am not aware of the great difference in our ages. I have fallen in love with you, and if we marry, I would hope for your companionship and affection, but you must not think that I would ever force myself on you, or indeed bother you at all in that way – you understand me. I shall sleep in my dressing-room and you shall be left in peace, my word on that.'

'No,' she said, and for a moment his heart fell with a painful thump, thinking she was rejecting him outright.

But she reached across the table and laid her slight, work-roughened hand over his, and said, 'We will be properly married. Do you think I would take everything, and then keep myself from you, when I have nothing else to offer you?'

'You don't have to—' he began, and then went back a sentence. *We will be properly married.* 'You mean you would consider it? You might really marry me?'

'I *will* marry you,' she said, smiling.

Teddy looked jolted, like a man who had trodden up a step that wasn't there. 'I didn't think – I hardly hoped – I was afraid you would find me repulsive.'

Tears jumped to her eyes. 'No! How could I? You are kind and good and generous, and I've enjoyed our evenings together so very much.'

'But I'm so much older than you,' he said, almost miserable in his happiness.

'Do you think me a fool? I know that. But you're as vigorous as a man half your age. And our minds are well matched. I've enjoyed our evenings together so much.'

Now he had hold of both her hands across the table. Such a warmth seemed to come through them from her it was like being by a fire. 'You really will marry me?'

'With all my heart,' she said.

He was awash with gratitude. 'I shall love you and cherish you and take care of you all my days, and when I'm gone—'

'You're not to talk of that part,' she said. 'I forbid it.'

The waiters had not been as unaware of Teddy's purposes as he might have thought, and having kept well out of the way until the matter seemed resolved, one now drifted into range at just the right moment for Teddy to spot him and say, 'Bring champagne!' He brought out from his pocket a small box, within which nestled a ring bearing a very fine diamond of medium size: he loved her too much to make a spectacle of her with an enormous stone.

'It's beautiful,' she said. And, mischievously, 'But what if I had said no?'

'I would have taken it back. These things are understood. But I'm so glad you didn't.'

'I am, too.'

He put it on her finger; it was a little too big. 'I'll have it altered for you.'

The waiter arrived with bottle, glasses and ice bucket, and she looked at them with a sort of deprecating humour. 'Is this how my life will be from now on?' she said. 'Diamonds and champagne?'

'Oh, this is only the beginning,' Teddy said airily.

They married on Monday afternoon, the 12th of June, at Caxton Hall, by special licence, the witnesses being the cab driver who had brought them and an ex-officer who was found hanging around outside, eking out a living by being a professional witness in such cases. Teddy would have given Amy any sort of wedding she liked, but she had wanted it to be as quiet as possible, and comforted him by saying it was rather romantic this way, like eloping. She was reluctant to take gifts from him before they were married – though he pointed out this was illogical, since he would give her a great many as soon as they were – but she was obliged to let him buy her some clothes, at least. She would not insult him by going to her wedding in the clothes she wore to work.

So she was married in a coat and skirt of dove-grey *peau de soie*, with a wide-brimmed hat of grey glazed straw decorated with fresh white roses. She carried a small bouquet of white and pale pink rosebuds made for her with many happy tears by her fellow workers at Larner's – who told each other happily that their Mrs Butler had fallen in the cream-pot, all right, but that it couldn't have happened to a nicer person.

On the morning of the wedding, Amy had packed up her few belongings and consigned them to the care of the Paterson's man who called for them by Teddy's arrangement. After the wedding, they went back to Brown's, where he had taken a room, and had dinner, and spent their wedding night there. And early the following morning, Teddy sent off a telegram to Morland Place:

ARRIVING LUNCHEON TODAY 13TH+ HAVE SIMMONDS MEET ONE FIFTEEN TRAIN+ E MORLAND

CHAPTER NINETEEN

The long day was over, and the new Mrs Morland had retired exhausted to her bed, in the rather daunting Great Bedchamber – she definitely saw it with capital letters. She found her clothes had been unpacked and the new nightdress Teddy had bought for her as part of her trousseau had been laid out on the bed. Someone had also put a small vase of roses – crimson and yellow ones this time – on the dressing-table, where Teddy's impedimenta had been cleared away and her own few things were laid out on a clean lace-edged linen runner. It was enough, in her state of emotional exhaustion, to reduce her to tears.

In the drawing-room, Teddy and Henrietta lingered alone together, Henrietta in her chair by the unlit fire, her work in her lap but untouched this long while, Teddy standing by the hearth, one elbow on the mantelpiece, smoking a last cigar, reflecting on the day.

The servants had soon been won round: intense loyalty to the master – combined with a love of romantic stories on the part of the younger maids, and a quick realisation by the older staff that the newcomer was a lady, and did not seem to be putting herself forward – was enough to bring them over onto Teddy's side. He was quick to consolidate the mood by ordering beer and cider for the staff that evening to drink his lady's health.

As soon as the situation was known to her, Mrs Tomlinson had had the bedchamber made suitable for a lady's occupancy, and had jostled Brown, who was slower on the uptake, into moving his master's things into the dressing-room.

Miss Sweetlove, the previous Mrs Morland's personal maid, had been kept on after her mistress's death out of the kindness of Teddy's heart, and given fine sewing and laundering to do, to earn her keep. A new wife for the master, arriving so unexpectedly, had left her tremulous, and with a vague feeling of somehow having been put-upon. She had declared to Tomlinson that she hoped no-one would expect her to maid that person. Tomlinson rather doubted the new Mrs Morland would want to be maided by the ancient Miss Sweetlove, if at all, but warned her that in this house she must do as she was told, like everyone else, and sent her off to the rose garden to cut some flowers for the bedroom, a task Sweetlove felt on reflection she could undertake without wounding her dignity.

Sawry and Mrs Stark the cook kept an inscrutable silence about the whole matter as befitted the dignity of their status. Mrs Stark immediately altered the dinner menu to make it more festive, while Sawry anticipated his master's request for fine wines and champagne and went off with the cellar key and book to make a suitable selection. Afterwards, privately to each other, as they took a last cup of tea in the housekeeper's room before bedtime, they commented that master seemed to have been properly 'caught'. They wondered with gloomy relish what the rest of the family, and the neighbourhood, was going to say.

Henrietta had not been able to conceal her first shock and dismay, and Ethel had been downright hostile, though kept within the bounds of civility by one or two sharp looks from her mother-in-law. Henrietta's immediate suspicion had been allayed by Amy's ladylike behaviour. A fortune-hunter would surely be much brassier about it, and not sit with lowered eyes and cheeks red with consciousness. Henrietta quickly felt ashamed that she had not been more welcoming, and did her best to make amends, reflecting that as awkward as it was for her, it must be far harder for the young woman. She really seemed uncomfortable, and Henrietta set herself to put her at ease, and to keep Ethel from asking the worst questions she could think of.

But now, alone with Teddy, she couldn't help thinking about how strange it all was, what a lot of gossip there was going to be in the neighbourhood, and how unpleasant and difficult things would be. She couldn't understand how it had all come about. There didn't seem to be anything remarkable about the young woman to have captured Teddy, but captured he evidently was. He seemed to have lost a little weight, and his trimmer shape combined with his obvious happiness made him look younger. He was brushing his hair differently, and was wearing a necktie Henrietta had never seen before – really rather bridegroom-like, she thought, touched. But still, the haste and secrecy made it look as though there were something wrong about it – and that was what people were going to say.

Teddy came back from a happy train of thought, looked at his sister's tense face, and, sighing inwardly, said, 'What is it, Hen? We had better have it out now, while we're alone. I know something's troubling you.'

She looked up at him for a moment. It was hard to select one thing from the many, in the face of his refusal to consider there was anything odd about the situation.

'Why did you keep it secret?' she asked.

'Oh, it all happened so fast,' he said lightly.

'But why not bring her here, and let us get to know her, and marry in the chapel? That's what I would have expected you to do. As it is – you didn't even give me warning to get the house ready.'

'I didn't want to wait to get married. As to giving you warning . . .' He frowned, finding it difficult to express himself, and grew a little testy. 'Well, damnit all, Hen, this is my house, isn't it? Why should I have to *warn* people, as if I were breaking bad news? It would sound as if there was something wrong with my wife, if people had to be "prepared" before they met her.' He glared at Henrietta challengingly. 'You like her, don't you?' And then, more uncertainly, 'You *do* like her?'

'She seems a very pleasant person,' Henrietta said, 'as far as I can tell in the short time I've known her.'

'Well, you know *me*, and *I* like her. Can't you just accept my judgement?'

Henrietta hesitated, wondering how to put it delicately. She didn't want to hurt Teddy – but if she didn't say it to him, someone else certainly would. 'I know you like her,' she said. 'Indeed, it's obvious that it's a great deal more than liking. But given that your feelings *are* so engaged . . .'

'You think they've overcome my judgement?'

'Well, isn't it just possible, Teddy dear?' This was so difficult. Henrietta forced herself to go on. 'You've known her such a short time. I'm so afraid that perhaps she has married you for your money.'

She expected an angry outburst but, to her surprise, Teddy began to smile. He answered genially, 'Well, of course she has! Do you think I'm a fool? Do you think I don't *realise* I'm more than twice her age?'

Henrietta was thrown aback. She could only stammer, 'But – surely—'

'Look here, marriage is always a bargain of some kind, isn't it?' he went on. 'Girls with fortunes marry men with titles. Plain girls with rich fathers get handsome men, old men with money get pretty young women. Every woman trades her services as a wife and mother for the security a husband can give her.'

'Yes, I suppose so – in a way,' Henrietta said doubtfully, 'but that's all so – *calculated*. I mean, one would hope these days that there was something more, well—'

He looked at her kindly. 'I think Amy likes me. I know she does. And she'll deal right by me. We enjoy each other's company. And if I can give her comfort and security, that's my pleasure and my privilege, and a very fair price for being her husband. Oh, Hen, I know what people will say – that I'm an old fool and she's a minx! But we'll just have to live with that. It was precisely because we knew people would say such things that we married secretly. And why we'll be going away immediately on a good, long honeymoon.'

'You will?' Henrietta didn't know whether to be relieved or sorry. It occurred to her that such a quick disappearance would only fuel the gossip.

'Amy's never travelled, except for that sad trip to see her husband's grave. And I don't want to stand around patiently while the brickbats are thrown. By the time we come back, the worst will be over and people will have found other things to gossip about.'

'What about the family? Who's going to tell everyone?' Henrietta asked, suspecting it was going to fall to her.

But Teddy said, 'I shall write letters to them all tomorrow. And when we come back, when they've had time to get over it, we'll have a grand family party and everyone shall meet her and see how lovely she is. And,' he continued with a burst of enthusiasm, 'once we're settled I shall do something about this old house. It needs improvement, but with the war, and then Alice dying, and being so busy, I haven't got around to it. Now I have the spur to make it comfortable. Bathrooms and electric light at the very least.' He smiled benignly at his sister. 'While we're away, you can be thinking about what changes *you* want.'

'Hadn't you better leave that to your wife?' Henrietta said. 'She might not relish her sister-in-law ordering things in her house.'

'Oh, Hen, it won't be like that. You thought the same thing when I married Alice, and you see how wrong you were. You're the mistress of this house, and you always will be. Amy won't interfere.'

Henrietta said no more, but she wondered. Alice had been unusual in not caring who ran the house, as long as she was comfortable. Amy was younger and more vigorous, and they all, Teddy included, knew very little about her. A house could not have two mistresses. And suddenly she wondered whether she even wanted to be the mistress any more. Miss Husthwaite thought Teddy should retire – perhaps it was time she did, too.

The next day, while Teddy sat in the steward's room writing letters, Henrietta took Amy on a tour of the house, telling her something of its history, and that of

478

the family. She seemed rather overwhelmed by it all, and listened in a subdued silence, hardly asking a question. When, having gone through the principal rooms, Henrietta asked her if she would like to see the servants' attic or would prefer to go over the offices downstairs, Amy finally spoke, turning to Henrietta with a look of appeal.

'I know what you must think,' she said, speaking quickly. 'I know you all resent me as an intruder, but you must believe I haven't come here to make waves. I don't want to change things. I want Teddy to be comfortable and go on just as he has done, and he couldn't be happy if I were to upset his household and make you all hate me, could he?'

'Nobody hates you,' Henrietta said automatically, though shocked at the idea that Amy could think so. 'And it's your household now.'

'No, really,' Amy said, shaking her head. 'Teddy's told me about how you came here with your husband and family and how you've been mistress of the house ever since. And how the previous Mrs Morland didn't alter that. And I promise you I won't, either.'

Henrietta studied the anxious face before her, and felt she understood better what Teddy had fallen in love with. She was a very *nice* person, and thoughtful of others. Henrietta liked her, and wanted to put her at ease.

'Nobody asks me if I want to go *on* being mistress,' she said lightly. 'Perhaps I would like to take a rest now, and let someone else do the work.'

Amy looked doubtful. '*Do* you want to? Is that how you feel?'

'Would you like to take on the responsibility?' Henrietta countered.

'I've never done anything like it,' Amy said. 'I've never lived in a place like this. I wouldn't know what to do.'

'There's not so much to it, really,' Henrietta said. 'The servants all know their work. Sawry and Mrs Tomlinson and Mrs Stark run everything below stairs. They only need a little guidance now and then.'

'I'm sure there's a great deal more to it than that,' Amy said, shrinking from the idea.

'You'd soon learn. I could help you,' Henrietta said. 'I should like to feel there's someone to hand over to. And I expect Teddy would like to see you take up the reins.'

'But you wouldn't leave?' Amy said. 'You wouldn't go away?'

'No, where would I go to?' Henrietta said, warmed by her obvious anxiety. 'This is my only home now.'

'Mine, too,' Amy said softly, and the two women looked at each other with increased understanding.

'Let's go and look at the kitchen and offices,' said Henrietta.

Ethel had been out in the morning, and returned to luncheon to pass on what people had said when she told them about Teddy's marriage, excusing herself by saying, 'I just thought you ought to know.' Amy kept a dignified silence in the face of the onslaught, wondering what it was that Ethel so resented. Perhaps she didn't know what Teddy had told her, that he was resigned to supporting Ethel for her lifetime, and was happy to support her children until they reached adulthood. She hoped it was only fear that made Ethel spiteful, and wondered whether over time she could get her to trust and like her. Teddy and Henrietta did their best to ignore Ethel and introduce different topics of conversation, but it was an uncomfortable luncheon.

In the afternoon, Teddy took Amy into York to meet the solicitor. Normally, he explained, he would have had Pobgee come to him, but he wanted Amy to have a glimpse of the city. It was only a glimpse, from the motor-car as they eased through the traffic, but she thought it very beautiful and impressively old, and told Teddy she looked forward to knowing it better. She discovered that the solicitor, Sidney Pobgee, knew about her already – Teddy had written to him from London – which was a relief. On the way there, she had caught, or thought she had caught, several strange looks from people who recognised the motor and saluted Teddy as he passed. It was comfortable to have Mr Pobgee greet her with a smile and a handshake and a 'Do sit down, Mrs Morland. May I offer you some refreshment?' as if he had known her for years.

Pobgee had had the settlement drawn up, and explained it clearly and in detail. Amy turned to Teddy and said, 'It's too much. Really, it's all too much. You don't need to have anything written down – I know you will be good to me. And I don't even want to *think* about widows' portions and so on.'

Pobgee answered for him: 'I understand that you may not, madam, but in the case of an estate as large and important as this, the firm of Pobgee, Micklethwaite and Grey *must* think about it. We take our responsibilities seriously, and I assure you the worst thing of all would be for there to be any doubt under the law. And death, madam, is something that must come to all, sooner or later. It is my duty to make things quite clear and indisputable, whether Mr Morland predeceases you, or you

481

him. It must all be set down and witnessed, or there will be chaos. And chaos is not a state over which we at Pobgee, Micklethwaite and Grey can allow ourselves to preside.'

'It's just "in case", dear,' Teddy said. 'Lawyers have to think about "in case".'

She looked at him with a hint of a smile, grateful for the translation. She needed such steadiness as Mr Pobgee went on to outline what different settlements would obtain if she were to bear a child and if that child were to outlive various other family members. At last, with a feeling of having been flattened by the steam-roller of the law, she said meekly that she understood, and watched as Teddy signed and had his signature witnessed.

When they left the solicitor's office and got back into the motor, Teddy told Simmonds to drive around, up the Wetherby Road, across Marston Moor and round by Long Marston and Askham Richard, to show her some of the estate. Teddy didn't talk much, but held her hand comfortably, and now and then pointed out some landmark and told her a bit of estate history.

'When we come back from honeymoon,' he said, 'we'll go over it all properly. I forgot to ask – do you ride?'

'I've never been on a horse,' she said.

He looked faintly shocked that such a condition was possible, but said, 'Oh, you'll soon learn. It's good exercise, and it's the best way to see the estate. When we get back, you shall have your own horse. Jessie will be home by then – she'll pick out a good one for you.'

Yet more people, Amy thought, to meet and be judged by – and no doubt found wanting. She knew about Jessie, who had been married to Teddy's son, and was now married to a tremendous brigadier who was a double

DSO and a VC. Probably she was a martinet like her husband and fiercely impatient of fools. But on the other hand she was Henrietta's daughter, so Amy cherished the faint hope that she might be like her, and not *absolutely* terrifying.

On the whole, though she liked the look of York and its surrounding countryside, and Morland Place itself was a wonderful, historic house, she was very glad they were going away again the following day, and would be staying away for many weeks. She had not quite understood when she married Teddy what she had been letting herself in for.

As if he read her thought, he squeezed her hand. 'Sorry you said yes?' he asked.

'Of course not,' she replied firmly.

And as if she had really answered, 'Just a bit,' he said, 'You'll get used to it. And by the time we get back, we'll be old news.'

Jessie telephoned her mother as soon as she had digested the letter.

'What is she, Mother? Is she a waif, or a schemer? I do hope not the latter.'

'I don't think so,' Henrietta said. 'She is a *little* of the former, and you know your uncle.'

'I guessed it would be one or the other,' Jessie said, 'given the discrepancy in their ages.'

'He told you that in his letter?'

'He was very frank. He said he knew there would be gossip, which was why they were going away, but that he was very happy and he was sure I would like her when I met her. Shall I?'

'I think so,' Henrietta said, trying not to sound too

hesitant. 'She's quite ladylike, not at all brassy, and she says she doesn't want to change anything at Morland Place. I think,' she added, doing her best for Amy, 'that she's quite as embarrassed by the situation as anyone, but she was very needy, poor thing, and she does seem really to like your uncle.'

Jessie sighed. 'Well, all we can do is to hope for the best. I suppose Uncle was lonely after Aunt Alice died. How have the children taken it?'

'He's written to Polly and James, but we won't know how they feel until they come home. Ethel's children, and Martin and Laura, are too young and don't really care about it one way or another. But Ethel is spoiling to make trouble.'

'Oh dear, she is a difficult person,' Jessie said. 'Never mind, I'll be home soon, and I'll try and persuade her into a better frame of mind.'

'I'm so glad you're coming,' Henrietta said, 'and that you'll be staying here at first.'

'It would be silly to stay anywhere else while we look for a house,' Jessie said. 'And in any case, I'd like the baby to be born at Morland Place, with you and Nanny Emma to take care of me. On the subject of which, Bertie thinks I ought to go on ahead of him. He thinks it's cutting it too fine if I wait until he finishes.'

'I think so, too,' Henrietta said gladly. 'So when will you come?'

'The day after tomorrow, if you like,' Jessie said. 'I only have to pack the children's things and mine – Bertie says he'll get someone in to do everything else before he leaves. And as it will be a Saturday he can travel down with me, and stay for Sunday to see me settled. If you can prepare for us at such short notice?'

'Of course I can! There's nothing to it. Can you really come so soon? Oh, it will be so wonderful to have you here! The house seems empty these days. Yes, *do* come on Saturday.'

Which told Jessie that Bertie had been right to think her mother was in immediate need of her.

Helen and Jack were surprised to get Uncle Teddy's news, and Jack naturally worried that he had been trapped, despite the frankness of the letter. 'He's very rich,' he said, 'and I dare say this woman knows it.'

'I think Uncle Teddy has his head screwed on the right way,' Helen said. 'He runs a big estate and several businesses, don't forget.'

'His head may be hard, but you know what a soft heart he has.'

'Yes, and if he's found someone else to lavish his kindness on, who are we to complain?'

'It doesn't matter to us directly, of course,' Jack said. 'We have no expectations. But there are James and Polly to think of. I hope he doesn't do anything foolish.'

'Like signing over his fortune to her?' Helen looked at him with fond exasperation. 'If you think Uncle Teddy would do anything to hurt or disinherit his own children – well, you don't know your uncle, that's all I can say. I hope this young woman will make him very happy. He deserves it. He spends so much of his life caring for other people.'

'Oh, I hope she makes him happy, too,' Jack said. 'It will be interesting to meet her when they get back from this honeymoon of theirs.'

In fact, he met her earlier than that, for Teddy booked himself and his bride a flight on the Daimler service to

485

Paris as the first leg of their wedding tour. He had been longing to try it ever since Jack first got the job with AT&T, and was eager to give Amy every new experience. The meeting was necessarily short – a few minutes snatched from preparing for the flight – but Jack was able to report to Helen when he returned that evening that the new Mrs Morland was about thirty, not a great beauty but seemed like a lady, had a pleasant voice, smiled a great deal, and looked at Uncle Teddy with affection. 'Which, all in all, is the best we could have hoped for,' he concluded.

'Oh, really,' Helen laughed, 'be a little charitable! Can't we accept he hasn't made a mistake, at least until it's proved otherwise?'

The trials of the New York winter – snow and ice and bitter cold, followed by more cold but with sluicing rain or penetrating gritty winds – gave way suddenly to the incomparable charm of the New York spring. Soft sunshine, little warm breezes, the trees breaking out into new leaf, the cherry trees in Central Park breaking out into blossom, and the windows of Macy's and Bloomingdales breaking out into spring and summer fashions.

Granny Ruth told Polly to enjoy it while she could. 'New York has two months of pleasantness between the intolerable winter and the intolerable summer.' She sighed. 'How I miss the South. Even when it was hot – and my, it was hot in the summer! – there was always shade, and fans, and verandahs, and iced lemonade, and watermelon out of the well so cold it hurt your mouth.'

'Couldn't you have gone back?' Polly asked her. She had spent quite a bit of time, one way and another, listening to Ruth's stories about the Civil War. She liked the old lady, and knew she was rather a pet with her – especially since she had made her an embroidered velvet scarf for her birthday: Ruth liked to be fine.

'Oh, my South's gone now,' she said, trying to sound indifferent. 'The people are dead and the houses all burned down. You can't go back, honey. They say the past is a foreign country. Well, when you get to my age, you're an exile for ever.' She changed the subject. 'Did you make that dress yourself? You have a real talent for that sort of thing. That's a pretty length for a skirt, and you have nice ankles. When I was a girl, a man would pretty much have to marry you if he saw your ankles! Now, tell me about your latest beau. Who's taking you out tonight?'

Polly liked telling Granny Ruth about her 'beaux', and hearing in return about how when she was a girl, Ruth could have had the pick of the neighbourhood, except that all she really wanted was to dash about on horseback and climb trees and never grow up. 'And, of course, proposals of marriage were made to your father, never to you, and he was the one who said yes or no.'

Polly had received two proposals of marriage, apart from Lennie's – which was repeated at intervals, but in a light-hearted way, 'just so you know I haven't changed my mind'. The first came in April, from Samuel Mortensen, a very young man who probably didn't have his parents' approval but who was dazzled by her, pressed his suit with passionate urgency and, when rejected, joined Polly's court as a silent and faithful admirer. Lennie laughed about him and called him the Spaniel, and when Polly rated him for being unkind, he said it was only because young Mortensen had such large, soft brown eyes.

'He's got a decent fortune,' Granny Ruth told her. 'His father is Mortensen's Hardware Stores – but I believe there's a girl cousin somewhere intended for him, to keep the money in the family.'

The second proposal, which came in May, was from Cornwallis Huytner, and was definitely made with parental consent, because Corny Huytner's mother had actually been present at the time. It was at a rather grand drawing-room tea in aid of a hospital charity, and Polly had been uncomfortably conscious of being watched from a distance through Mrs Huytner's *lorgnette* as Corny brought her a cup of tea and manoeuvred her into a secluded spot near the window to make his declaration. He was tall and blond with a squarish, pink face and round, chalky blue eyes – like a Dutch doll, she always thought. When she refused him, his face registered dismay, and he descended from the elevated language of the proposal to: 'Oh, gee, don't knock a fellow back right away! I don't know what Ma will say if I can't get you even to think about it!'

He looked so put out that Polly stopped herself from laughing, and said, 'It's not your fault. You can tell your mother I never mean to marry. I have enough money from my father to be comfortable, and I can't see any other reason to marry and have a man telling me what to do when, as it is, I can please myself.'

Corny looked glum and said, 'You're so lucky! I *have* to marry, to get a son to pass the family business on to. It's pretty hard being the only son. It makes Ma nervous to think of all the Huytner money slipping away.'

'Why should it slip away?' Polly said.

'Well, if I don't have a son to leave it to, where will it go?'

'You have two sisters, and I know one of them is married.'

'But her children can't be Huytners, you see.'

Polly didn't. Granny Ruth had told her – she explained everyone Polly met, sooner or later – that the Huytner fortune came from pickles, and that Corny's father had been a self-made man. 'Nothing wrong with that, of course,' Ruth had added sternly. 'Not everyone can come from an old family like ours.'

Just so, Polly thought – but then why worry about the name? Mrs Huytner was very grand, it seemed to her, with nothing much to be grand about. The Morlands had been at Morland Place for five hundred years, but the Huytners lived in an apartment in the Alwyn Court which they had taken only twenty years ago. People in New York were funny, she reflected afterwards. They were all for a man 'getting on' and having 'gumption', and they respected anyone who made a fortune, however humble his background. But they still secretly preferred old money to new, and at the hint of a European title they went weak at the knees. Polly knew that her coming from what was considered to be an 'English stately home' added considerably to her cachet. She was often quizzed about it in drawing-rooms, particularly by the mothers of unmarried sons. It all seemed very silly to her. She loved Morland Place because it was her home, the only one she had ever known, and she was proud of being a Morland, but the idea that she should be valued more because of it was foolish. When in the course of conversation she tried to explain this to Ruth, the old lady nodded and said, 'You'll do. Pride is good when it makes you behave better toward other people. That's how it was in the South – *noblesse oblige*, you know. When it makes you behave badly, it's nothing but vanity, and that's a sin.'

When Polly received her father's letter, she assumed that it would contain the instructions for her return home. She was sorry that her visit was coming to an end, but there was a little piece of her that missed home, and would be glad to see Aunt Hen and the children and her dear dogs, and to go riding on Vesper again, and hear English accents and see green English fields.

But as she read it, she felt her cheeks burn, and tears of shock and outrage came to her eyes. How could he? How *could* he? Her hands trembled as she put the letter down, then picked it up to read it again, as if she hoped she might have misunderstood. Various phrases jumped out from the page as she scanned it, only half taking it in.

'– know this will come as a surprise to you, but I hope it will be a pleasant one.'

'– on the steamer coming back, looking so forlorn –'

'– don't expect her to be a step-mother to you, but I hope you'll come to love her –'

'– travelling for six or eight weeks, so we'll be out of touch until we get back.'

In fury and distress she went straight out and caught a cab to The Paterno to show the letter to Lizzie.

Lizzie already knew about it. 'I got a letter this morning, too, and one from Mother.' She eyed Polly cautiously. 'You seem a little upset.'

'Upset?' Polly was lost for words.

'Well, I know it was rather sudden – I mean, none of us expected him to want to get married again—'

'At his age? I should think not! It's disgusting!'

'Oh, Polly, come now!'

'She's hardly any older than me!' Polly could not articulate the outrage this thought caused her. 'It's revolting!'

'I know it's a bit surprising, but if it makes him happy, shouldn't we be happy for him?'

'She's nothing but a gold-digger, and he's made a fool of himself – of all of us! Just think what people will be saying – the looks, the sniggers! Well, I'm not going back! I'm not going to have people whisper about me and look pitying and laugh behind my back. If he's going to install some adventuress in my step-mother's place, I shall stay here permanently.'

Lizzie looked doubtful. 'Of course, I'd be very glad if you did stay, but you know he could force you to come home.'

'I'm of age. He can't make me do anything.'

'He controls your allowance,' Lizzie pointed out.

It gave Polly pause for an instant, but she went on, 'He wouldn't cut me off. He wouldn't do that. Besides, he says here in this letter he's increasing it – look.' She waved the letter at Lizzie, who caught it in the air and read the bit at the bottom that Polly was stabbing at with her finger. 'You know what that is? It's a bribe, because he knows that what he's doing is wrong.'

Lizzie looked at the angry face before her. Polly had always been her father's pet, and Aunt Alice had been a retiring and negligible sort of person, no threat to Polly's supremacy. But a new young wife, not much older than Polly herself: yes, that must hurt, especially as it had happened when she was away – behind her back, as it were. Was that what it was? Polly was feeling betrayed, abandoned, and far from home. She would come round in time, Lizzie hoped. Meanwhile it was probably best for her to stay on in New York and fill her time with enjoyment and new sights to stop her brooding. Soon enough to go back when the new Mrs Morland was safely installed.

Jessie's third baby was born at Morland Place on the 8th of July 1922, coming easily with the ministrations of Nanny Emma, and Tomlinson, who was delighted to get her old mistress back. Henrietta was reduced to waiting in the background because she had slipped a few days earlier, fallen and sprained her wrist rather badly. 'My right one, too,' she mourned as Dr Hasty examined it.

'It always is, when people try to save themselves,' he said. 'You're lucky you didn't break it. Next time, if you feel yourself going, relax and let go. You'll hurt yourself less.'

She gave him an exasperated look. 'Who on earth ever lets themselves fall? It's against human nature!'

But she was still able to receive the new baby into her curved left arm, and remark that she had her father's eyes and her mother's mouth. 'I think she'll be pretty, too,' she told Jessie, when she had given her back.

'Oh, Mother,' Jessie said affectionately, looking at the little blob of a face, 'you can't possibly tell.'

'When y've seen as many babbies as we huv,' Nanny Emma assured her, 'you get to know all right. That's a masterpiece of a little mawther, Miss Jessie.'

Jessie had no argument with that. Bertie, when he came down at the weekend, agreed. 'I think she's the pick of the bunch. You're getting better at this with practice, my love.'

'*We*'re getting better at this. It was a joint effort,' Jessie pointed out. 'Do you mind another girl?'

'It's what I was hoping for,' he said – and of course she would never know if that were true or not, tactful man that he was.

They decided to call her Ottilie. 'It means "riches", or "prosperity",' Bertie explained to the doubtful Henrietta. 'She's riches to us, and we hope she will always know prosperity, so it's appropriate in both ways.'

Jessie knew her mother better. 'It's a saint's name,' she said. 'There's a Saint Ottilia.'

Henrietta's brow cleared. 'It's certainly a pretty name,' she said.

James came home the same weekend at the end of his first year at school, with a trunk full of crumpled clothes, a holdall and two bags full of other possessions, and a string-and-brown-paper parcel, which was coming undone, containing his pyjamas, a pair of cricket socks and a Latin book. He flew into the house spreading items of clothing and happy chaos, delighted to be home again, wanting to see everything at once, tormenting the dogs and shouting until the chandeliers rang. Nanny Emma 'came down on him middlin' savage' for disturbing Jessie, but Jessie won his approval by saying she wasn't disturbed and liked the noise, so he reciprocated by showing a polite interest in the new baby, and managing not to laugh when told her name. Afterwards, however, she heard him chanting, on his way to the nursery, 'Ottilie what? Utterly awful!'

For the following week, four-year-old Thomas attached himself to James like an adoring shadow, and James allowed him, in a lordly way, to go around with him, since Roberta and Jeremy did not finish school until the Friday. James seemed so completely unconcerned that Henrietta wondered whether he had received his father's news; but when she questioned him tentatively he said, 'The pater's got married again, you mean? Oh, yes, I got a letter all right.'

'And you don't mind about it?'

James only looked surprised, as if 'minding' hadn't occurred to him. After a moment he said, 'A fellow in my class, Belper – we call him the Belcher, but he's all right. He has a white mouse that does tricks – well, his pater got married again, and he got a super bicycle, and a top-hole new cricket bat.' Henrietta could only murmur acknowledgement to this, and James's mind flickered off to more interesting pastures. 'I say, Aunt Hen, a chap in our house has a wireless set he built himself. It's ripping! He gets all sorts of stuff – terrific noises and squeaks and things, but real music too, and once he got a boxing match from Olympia: George Carpenter and Kid Lewis! He let us all listen to a bit of it. It was topping! Do you think Dad would let me have a wireless set?'

Bertie had finally retired from the army, and at the end of July he completed the handing over and packing up, and came down to Yorkshire to make a new home for his wife and family. By then, Jessie was out of bed and pottering, though Tomlinson as well as Henrietta insisted she must take things easily and not rush to return to her normal activities. Jessie was quite willing to be 'invalidish' for a while, as long as she could go for long, gentle walks with Bertie. She had waited so long to ride, a few more weeks didn't make any difference; and she was happy to let Bertie undertake the hard work of trying to find a suitable house for them. 'I'll come and look when you have something that might do,' she told him.

There was a definite change in the atmosphere of the

household when Bertie became part of it. The servants moved more briskly, the food was subtly different, and everything had an air of purpose it had lacked for some weeks. Though he was not the master, various servants, tenants and estate workers brought him questions that they had evidently been saving up for Teddy in the weeks he had been away. Miss Husthwaite bristled at the idea that she could not have answered them herself, but Bertie didn't mind. He was accustomed, as an army officer, to dealing with a wide variety of abstruse and often point-less questions, and could answer most of them almost without thinking. He was so pleasant about it, and brought such a sigh of relief to the household, which had felt itself rudderless since Teddy went away, that Miss Husthwaite forgave him and, finding she liked him and trusted him, even brought him a question or two of her own.

The improved spirits of the house were mostly due to Bertie's presence, but Jessie had contributed one element, for she had made a point of having a serious talk with Ethel before his arrival. She was actually feeling rather sorry for her, for Ottilie's birth must have brought home to Ethel all over again that she was a widow and would have no more babies of her own. She had four children, which was enough in reason, but it was the excitement of a new baby, being the centre of attention, being praised and made a fuss of by everyone, that she missed. So Jessie was gentler with her than she might otherwise have been, and began by petting her a little, asking her opinion about a rash Ottilie had on her chin. She did it so well that Ethel did not point out that Jessie had two other children of her own and ought to know a milk rash when she saw one. She responded to the question and the flattery and gave Jessie the benefit of her wisdom and experience, and so was in quite a smiling mood when Jessie finally brought up the subject of Uncle Teddy and Amy.

'When they come home, I hope you will welcome Amy properly, and be polite to her.'

'I'm always polite,' Ethel said sniffily.

'Mother says you were very unpleasant to her when Uncle Teddy brought her home, so I wanted to be sure you'd had better thoughts since then. I expect it was just the shock, wasn't it?' she suggested generously.

Ethel was not ready for generosity. 'You haven't heard what *I've* heard going around York. Everyone's talking about it. He's making us a laughing-stock!'

'If we all stick together and make it known that we're delighted about it, the gossips will have nothing to gossip about.'

'Delighted?' Ethel said derisively. 'When he marries a girl young enough to be his granddaughter, a girl from God-knows-where that he picks up from the gutter?'

'He's always been so kind to you, taking care of you and the children,' Jessie began.

'And why shouldn't he take care of his own nephew's wife and children?' Ethel interrupted. 'Any man would.'

'I'm not sure that's true. But leaving aside what any other man would do, the fact remains that Uncle Teddy has always been very kind to you—'

'Yes, until this woman decides to clear us all out. What then?' Ethel flashed. 'It's all right for you, with a rich husband, but what will I do?'

'Even if she wanted to be rid of you – which you've no reason to think she would – Uncle Teddy would never let you down, and you know it.'

'Well, I still don't see why I should be nice to her, the hussy,' Ethel said sulkily.

Jessie looked at her reproachfully. 'Oh, Ethel! Why don't you want him to be happy? It's mean-spirited.'

Ethel looked taken aback. She liked to think well of herself, and had never supposed her righteous stand could have any other interpretation. 'I'm not!' she cried. 'Of course I wish him happy, but—'

'No "but". Just be polite and friendly to his wife. That's what he would want, and what will make him happy. It isn't for us to judge whether he should or shouldn't have married her. He did, and that's that. And if she makes him happy, that's all that matters.'

Ethel stared a moment, and then put her nose up. 'I'm sure I have no interest in the matter, one way or the other,' she said. 'He's welcome to marry anyone as far as I'm concerned.'

'But you'll be nice to her?' Jessie pressed. 'And tell anyone who asks that you like her and approve of the whole thing?'

'I hope I know how a lady behaves,' Ethel said loftily.

Jessie hoped so too. She thought she had said enough to keep Ethel in check. And if her objections were based on fear for the future, events would soon settle her mind.

As she started to go out and be seen around York, Jessie heard for herself what people were saying. Uncle Teddy had shocked the neighbourhood before, but this new scandal, having its roots in the exciting subject of sex, was particularly relished by the females of the gossiping persuasion. No-one was so disobliging as to insult her uncle to her face, but several people made a point of telling her what *other* people were saying. 'Of course, I wouldn't repeat such things in a general way, but I thought you ought to know, Lady Parke . . .'

'I didn't want it to come as a shock to you, Lady Parke, and of course it is not *my* opinion, but I have heard it said . . .'

Jessie made her position known and otherwise could only bear with it. Once the couple were home, things would settle down. She did think Uncle Teddy had been unwise in going away and not getting that stage over with at once, but she could understand that he probably wanted a little unblighted pleasure before he faced the music.

'I just hope she really *is* all right,' she said to Bertie.

'I'm sure she is,' he said. 'Uncle Teddy's a downy bird.'

CHAPTER TWENTY

In August 1922 came an escalation of the troubles in Ireland. A treaty had been signed the previous December, giving the southern counties independence within the Empire, while the largely Protestant northern counties remained part of the United Kingdom. A Provisional Government had been formed in January with Arthur Griffith as president and Michael Collins as chairman, and Dublin Castle had been surrendered to them for a headquarters.

But the compromise did not please everyone. While a majority looked on the treaty as a hopeful first step, an extreme minority, under the leadership of de Valera, wanted complete independence of the whole of Ireland at once, and would settle for nothing less. The IRA split into pro-treaty and anti-treaty forces, and violent actions and counter-actions rumbled along until July, when the Provisional Government felt obliged to form a Council of War, and Collins was made commander-in-chief of the national army.

A bloody campaign in July and August drove the extremists out of the towns and cities into the rural areas; but Arthur Griffith died on the 12th of August, and on the 22nd Collins was murdered in an ambush while visiting troops in his home county of Cork. Relations between the Free Staters and the Republicans plumbed a new depth of bitterness, and the fighting descended into repeated cycles of atrocities and reprisals.

In Germany the accredited government was still battling against red rebels who held large areas of the country, notably the Ruhr and Saxony; and Russia was still convulsed by civil war – terrible stories emerged of mass executions, and assassinations by the secret police. Against this background, events in Ireland made the British government understandably nervous. A report from the British Legion said that one million ex-servicemen were unemployed. Creeping Communism and trade-union agitation looked like the precursors of anarchy, and possibly revolution.

But at Morland Place at least, peace and Yorkshire common-sense reigned. The household was running smoothly, the children were thriving, the wheat was ready for cutting, and Jessie had been reunited at last with her darling Hotspur. His age and her recent birthing made for gentle rides rather than energetic galloping, but they were both glad to be together again. Bertie approved of the moderation. He had taken over Teddy's horse Warrior, and he and Jessie took long, leisurely rides about the estate and into the countryside. Hotspur was nineteen, and though he was just as eager for an outing with his mistress as ever, Jessie knew it was only sensible when Bertie said she ought to think about bringing on a couple of youngsters to replace him.

'I can't bear the thought of parting with him,' she said, turning a lock of his mane back to the right side and caressing his neck. Hotspur turned an ear back to her in acknowledgement, and snorted the dust out of his nostrils. 'You see? He agrees with me,' she said.

'I'm sure he'll go on for a long while yet, but you don't want to get left with no horse. And there's hunting to think of. You won't want to tax him too much when the season starts.'

Jessie looked at him in wonder. 'Hunting?' She hadn't hunted since the first year of the war.

'Well, now we're back in Yorkshire for good, we'll want to join in fully with local events.'

'We have to find somewhere to live, first,' she said.

'Wherever we live, there'll be hunting,' he pointed out. 'As to houses – I've been thinking that perhaps the best solution is to build something for ourselves. It may take a little longer, but at least that way we'd have exactly what we wanted. I haven't seen anything suitable to rent.'

'You've only been looking for a week or two.'

'You underestimate me. I've had an agent looking for me all this year. Everything's either much too big or too small.'

'Building a house would be exciting,' Jessie said. 'But where would we put it? Out at Bishop Winthorpe?'

'I was wondering – don't you own some land at Twelvetrees?'

'Just the fields immediately around it. About six acres.'

'Enough to build a house on,' Bertie mused. 'But then we'd have to find more grazing. I suppose we might rent some from Uncle Teddy?'

'It would be nice to live near Morland Place,' Jessie said wistfully. 'I know Bishop Winthorpe isn't far, but it's not the same as being five minutes away. And Mother and Uncle Teddy are getting old.'

'Uncle Teddy ought to be getting younger by the minute, with his new young wife,' Bertie said. 'I don't know what one can infer from the lack of correspondence, but I hope it's merely that he is enjoying every minute.' There had been two postcards from France, but since then only occasional boxes and packing crates of things sent back from exotic places.

'You couldn't expect him to write long letters on his honeymoon,' Jessie said. 'He was never a great one for correspondence anyway.'

'Polly seems to have taken after him,' Bertie mentioned. 'Nothing from her since that wire saying she was staying on in New York.'

'I expect she'll come back when Uncle Teddy does,' Jessie said. 'I was thinking I ought to get Vesper up for her. You needn't worry,' she added. 'I shall lunge her first. I shan't get bucked off.'

Bertie squinted into the sunshine as they thub-dubbed along the dusty track between two cornfields, and smiled at the peaceful scene framed by Warrior's long ears. 'I'm finding it difficult to worry about anything at the moment,' he said. 'No meetings, no uniforms, no politicians, no memoranda – just sunshine, horses, you at my side and Yorkshire at my feet. I'm in danger of sinking into a state of bucolic bliss. Pigs!' he added suddenly, making Warrior jerk his ears in surprise. 'When we build our perfect house, we ought to make room for some pigsties. There's nothing more soothing than leaning over a gate scratching a pig's back with a stick. It induces a sense of proportion in a man's mind. I'm sure Napoleon and the Kaiser and Lenin and all those troublemakers wouldn't have turned the world upside down if they'd kept pigs.'

'Parke's Theory of the Agricultural Origins of Warfare,' Jessie laughed.

Helen had taken the children to Brighton for August, so as to be near enough for Jack to come down at weekends. She wrote that they would visit when Uncle Teddy got back. Violet and Holkam had gone to the South of France where they had taken a house and were hosting a party. The Prince of Wales was to stay with the Vibarts at the neighbouring property for as much of the time as he could get away from Balmoral. But before she left, Violet brought her children down to Shawes to leave them for their holiday. Venetia had gone to stay with her sister at Ravenscroft for the first half of the month, but had promised to come on to Shawes afterwards.

James was delighted to acquire Robert and Richard as more worthy companions – Robert was a year older than him and Richard only a year younger, whereas Jeremy was *two* years younger, and Roberta was only a girl. The boys went off on adventurous expeditions, coming home brown, scratched and hungry at the end of a long day's freedom. Roberta put up her nose at them, and declared herself much happier to play with Charlotte than with silly, dirty boys. Octavian was of an age with Martin, Harriet and John, which left out only four-year-old Thomas, too young for them and too old for the babies. Jessie had him with her a great deal, an arrangement they both found agreeable.

Violet, on her brief visit, made the acquaintance of Ottilie, begged to be allowed to hold her, and told Jessie how lucky she was to have a new baby. 'They're so lovely at this age, and they grow up so quickly. I often think it's the saddest thing when one knows one will never have another.'

Jessie looked at her curiously. 'You really won't?'

'Certainly not,' Violet said. Jessie thought it sad, but Violet seemed content with her life and her detached relationship with her husband.

'I think I shall be quite glad if Ottilie is my last,' Jessie said. 'It does take so much time out of one's life. Tell me about Emma. Is she well? Is she recovering from that dreadful tragedy?'

'She seems to be,' Violet said. 'I don't see so much of her, now she has her own flat, and our circles aren't quite the same, but she goes everywhere, and her picture is in the papers every week. The latest thing is that she's redecorating a house in Cadogan Place for Flo Vanderbeek's parents – Americans, you know, and millionaires. He's very big in copper, or cobalt, or some metal beginning with a *c*, and she's quite a beauty.'

'*Emma*'s redecorating a house?' Jessie was surprised.

'Darling, not with her own hands! She's planning it, choosing the colours and fabrics and so on. She did it with her own flat and everyone was so impressed, and now the Vanderbeeks have asked her to do their whole house.'

'What an odd thing,' Jessie said, puzzled. 'Is she going into business?'

'Goodness, no. It's just something to do. Kit Westhoven says she enjoys it. She and Kit are often together – I can't help thinking they would make a good match, and that it would be the best outcome for her.' She hesitated. 'Oliver says she's burning the candle at both ends. He says it as if it's a joke, but I know he really thinks she's helling too much. I suppose it helps her to forget. But if she and Kit married, it would be the most natural solution. She's had such terribly bad luck, poor thing.'

Jessie and Bertie came back into the stableyard after a long ride together one day, and saw that the footman, Daniel, was standing at the great door apparently looking for them.

'I wonder if Uncle Teddy arrived while we were out,' Jessie said.

But it wasn't that. When they had handed over the horses to the boy, Daniel said, 'A person has come, asking to see you, sir.'

'What sort of a person?' Bertie asked, well aware of the subtle distinction between 'person', and 'gentleman' or 'lady'. Daniel did not approve of the visitor.

'I could not undertake to say, sir,' he said, condemnation in his neutrality. 'Mr Sawry would have sent him packing, but the person was very insistent that you would want to see him. I gathered the impression, sir, that he had been in the military way.' Daniel had been an ex-serviceman looking for work, Jessie reflected, and was perhaps more tender towards such people than Sawry, who had lived all his life in service.

'He asked for me rather than the master?'

'Yes, sir. Brigadier Parke, he said.'

'Then perhaps I'd better see this military sort of person,' Bertie said, with his unfailing good humour.

Along one wall of the hall was a row of small, hard chairs with heraldic motifs painted on their backs. The visitor was sitting on one of them, and stood as soon as Bertie and Jessie appeared. He was very thin – almost cadaverous – with deep-set, glittering eyes, over-sharp cheekbones, a large, uncompromising nose, and failing iron-grey hair. He was wearing a threadbare suit, but in his hand was a hat rather than a cap, signifying a status above that of labourer or domestic servant. While his boots looked worn, they were also highly polished under the light coating of new dust, which, with his carriage, explained why Daniel had thought him an ex-soldier.

Bertie stared at him, and cried, 'Cooper, by God! What brings you here?'

The old man's face wavered between pleasure at the greeting and the desire to maintain military discipline. But when Bertie advanced, offering his hand, he could only take it, and shake it with a passion that told Jessie, watching the reunion, there had been a strong relationship between them. She knew *of* Cooper, of course, her husband's long-serving batman, who had gone through the worst days of the war with him and taken care of him as carefully as a wife, but she had never met him.

'You're looking well, sir,' Cooper said, still pumping the hand up and down. 'I was afraid when I enquired at Horseguards and they said you'd quit that it might be ill 'ealth, but I see now you're looking as fit as a horse, sir.'

'Never better,' Bertie said. 'How did you find me here?'

'Oh, ways and means, sir,' said Cooper, mysteriously.

'Same old Cooper,' Bertie said, with a grin. 'Never any use asking you how you do things.' He turned to Jessie. 'My dear, allow me to present my old batman, Cooper, whom I have told you so much about. Cooper, Lady Parke.'

Jessie offered her hand. 'Glad to meet you, Cooper.'

'Honoured, your ladyship,' Cooper said, bowing slightly. He barely touched her fingertips, but it was out of delicacy rather than disapproval. Close to, she saw how very thin he was – though he was obviously the sort of man who grew more stringy with age, rather than softer. But there had been hardship recently, she thought.

'Well, this calls for a drink,' Bertie said. 'Come on in, and we'll have a wet. Beer, or whisky?'

'Glass o' beer, if it's all the same to you, sir, this time o' day,' Cooper said, flicking a glance at the footman, as if to judge the degree of disapproval this would arouse.

'Good choice. Daniel, we'll be in the drawing-room.'

'I'll leave you alone,' Jessie said. 'I'm sure you have lots to talk about.' Cooper shot her a grateful look, and she knew she'd hear all about it from Bertie later, anyway. 'I want to go up to the nursery to see the babies.'

'Two glasses of beer, then, Daniel,' Bertie said. 'And perhaps some of that pork pie Mrs Stark has in cut.' He did not want to embarrass Cooper by suggesting he was starving, and added, as he led the man away, 'It has to be tasted to be believed. Mrs Stark is a genius. I often think how we would have given a limb for something like that when we were stuck in the front line, contemplating yet another tin of bully with biscuits.'

'Or the times when we was too far in advance for supplies to reach us, sir,' Cooper added. 'Then we'd a' given anything for bully.'

The drawing-room was empty, as Bertie had hoped it would be – Henrietta and Ethel were both out – and he chatted lightly about the war and their memories until the refreshments came. When Daniel had gone again, he raised his glass to his lips and said, 'Well, cheerioh, Cooper. Here's to it.'

'Cheerioh, sir. Down the 'atch,' Cooper said, and sank

half the glass. 'Thirsty business, walking,' he excused himself, wiping his mouth. 'Long way from the station.'

Bertie gave him the plate onto which he had cut a generous wedge of pie. 'Hungry work, too,' he said. 'Eat up, man.' And he settled himself in a chair and waited to see what was coming.

Cooper was trying not to wolf the pie. He was obviously uncomfortably conscious of his surroundings – he kept taking little curious peeks at the ancient drawing-room with its linenfold panelling and massive fireplace, the vast marble clock on the overmantel and the dim family portraits on the walls. Jessie's dog Bran came in, clicking over the polished floorboards and silent on the carpet, and went to Bertie, head low and tail swinging, without a glance at the stranger. Dogs were such snobs, Bertie thought.

When the pie was gone, Bertie refilled plate and glass without asking, and said, 'Well, Cooper, how goes the pub? The Case Is Altered, wasn't that it? Fine old name. Is it thriving?'

Cooper swallowed the mouthful he had just taken, sitting on the very edge of the chair. 'Well, sir, that's rather to the point, sir. It's a grand place, but this here recession they all talk about – well, it's taken its toll, sir. Idle men don't have no money, sir, not for beer nor nothing else. Custom all the time falling off, and when an old soldier on the tramp comes past – well, you can't see a colleague beg, can you, sir? I'm owed money right and left, but the brewery don't take promise notes. Cash on the nail, if I want my beer delivered. In the end I was owing my staff their wages, just to keep open, and I didn't like that, sir. You don't gyp your own men, sir – I don't need to tell you that. Owing a big business like

508

the brewery is one thing – they can take it – but the man behind the bar, what has to go home to his wife at the end of the day, that's different. I had to borrow money from the bank to pay them off, but that only adds interest and puts you worse in debt. And then in the end I couldn't even get a loan. No credit to be had anywhere. I had to sell up just to clear the owing.'

'That's a damn shame,' Bertie said. 'I know how you looked forward to running that pub.'

'Me life's dream. Kept me going, when things was bad in the war,' Cooper admitted. 'It was the times, sir, that done for me. Another time I'd have made a go of it, all right.'

'I'm sure you would have,' Bertie said, and meant it. Cooper was a wangler and a fixer and a shrewd bargainer, and during the war he had kept Bertie supplied with the necessary and made a tidy bit on the side, his 'fortune', which he had sunk into the pub, in his native Hertfordshire, that he had always longed to own. He ought to have been sitting pretty, and building up a business that would support him in his old age. 'So it's gone, then – you've sold it?'

'Lock, stock and barrels, sir,' Cooper said, and Bertie did not know if it was a joke or not. A bitter sort of joke. There was no humour in Cooper's face. It must have been a blow to him. The very fact that he was here telling Bertie about it said that, for Cooper had never been one to show weakness. He had grumbled and complained all the way through the war, but that was just old-soldier grumbling. He had never asked for anything in his life, and had maintained a lordly sort of condescension towards his officer, as if Bertie were a child out of his depth in a man's world. 'I've lost every penny I put in,

509

sir,' he went on, and now, like a soldier, he straightened his shoulders to attention and met Bertie's eyes bravely, as if he were on punishment parade. You take your knocks, and face things like a man. 'Got nothing left but the clothes on me back. So I've come to ask if you can put me in the way of a job, sir.' He searched Bertie's face keenly for distaste, anticipating a refusal. 'If you've already got a vallitt, sir, I'll do anything else. I'm a fair 'and with 'orses, as you know, sir. Or I can do anything around the 'ouse – cleaning silver, making up fires, blacking boots – I've done the lot, sir, in me time. Or outside. Farm labourer. I'll turn me 'and to anything.' It must have been horrible for him to have to ask, Bertie thought, seeing his Adam's apple bob in his naked throat as he swallowed his pride. 'Digging, fetching, carrying – I don't mind what I do, just so long as I can work, sir, and be decent.'

'This isn't my place, Cooper,' Bertie said gently. 'It belongs to my uncle. Lady Parke and I are just staying here as guests until we can find a place of our own. My uncle's away, and I'm not authorised to take on anyone in his absence.'

But he couldn't bear the stark misery of disappointment that dragged lines down Cooper's face, and almost without his volition he heard himself go on, as if this was what he had been leading up to, 'But I don't have a valet at the moment. If you don't mind living a gypsy sort of life, until we find a house to suit us . . .'

Misery was replaced with a fierce, hard sort of joy. 'Thank you, sir. You won't regret it. I'll vallitt you *and* look after your 'orse, sir, if you like. I'll look after you like I done out in France, sir. And anything you want – you or your good lady, sir – you ask me, and I'll get it. You won't regret this, sir, I swear it!'

'I know I won't,' Bertie said, though he wondered, just a little, what he had taken on. A wily old batman who could wangle his way around King's Regs, and barter spare ciggies for unobtainables in war-torn France, was one thing; but a discreet and polished gentleman's gentleman in time of peace was something else entirely. Could Cooper make the transition, or was he, Bertie, throwing a grenade into the servants' hall?

'But what else could I do?' he said afterwards to Jessie, and she said, 'Nothing – just what you did do. Loyalty like that has to be rewarded.'

It turned out that Cooper had his traps with him – just a single bag, which he had left at the gate – so there was no reason not to let him start straight away. Bertie rang and, when Daniel appeared, told him to take him to the servants' hall, and to ask Sawry to find room for him on the men's side. Cooper and Daniel gave each other a look of level consideration before they departed together, and Bertie fled upstairs to find Jessie and be soothed.

Henrietta and Venetia were sitting under the walnut tree in the garden at Shawes, enjoying one of their long, rambling conversations. Venetia had talked about her work on tuberculosis: in the continuing absence of a cure, she was experimenting with vaccination among her most vulnerable families, using her connections to acquire a supply of the BCG vaccine from the Pasteur Institute in Paris. 'They're terribly reluctant to accept vaccination,' she said, with a sigh. 'I have to exert all my force of personality on the tubercular mothers to persuade them to let me vaccinate their children, especially as it can be rather painful, and there can be unpleasant reactions.'

'Do you think it will do any good?' Henrietta asked.

'Hard to tell. We have very little history yet – they only started using it on humans a year ago. But it's such a pernicious disease I believe we are morally bound to try. Look how vaccination has eliminated smallpox. If we could do that with consumption . . . But it would require mass vaccination and we're a long way from there. Still,' she concluded bracingly, 'you don't get anywhere if you don't make a start.'

Henrietta told of her latest letter from Lizzie, detailing Polly's ongoing social triumphs, the possibly interesting condition of Martial's wife – 'My first great-grandchild!' – and Lennie's business success. He had opened three more shops, and was talking of a second factory. 'Wireless is getting to be a tremendous fashion over there. President Harding actually made a speech to the nation on radio recently, and where the President leads . . .'

'I suppose it will take hold over here soon enough,' Venetia said. 'Violet's boys are mad about it, but it seems to be getting to a stage beyond the latest schoolboy craze, like pogo sticks or cigarette cards. I suppose we'll all be expected to "listen in" in due course – you see, I have the jargon already.' She smiled and stretched a little, comfortably, in the sunshine. 'I can't think where we are to find the time for these modern inventions. The time I have left over from work I would sooner spend talking to a friend. There must be a sad lot of people without enough to do, or there'd be no market for these novelties.'

Henrietta smiled. 'You and I are lucky. Our work is our life.'

'I can't help thinking that's the way it ought to be,' Venetia said.

★   ★   ★

'How are you settling in?' Bertie asked Cooper idly one morning as he shaved him.

'Fair to middling, sir,' Cooper said, at his most enigmatic.

Bertie cocked an eye at him round the razor. 'Everything all right below stairs?' he tried.

'Now, sir, you wouldn't expect me to tell if it wasn't. There's such a thing as a code.'

'Code be damned,' Bertie said. 'I pay your wages. You're not part of the servants' hall.'

'In it, but not of it, sir,' Cooper said, moving Bertie's nose out of the way.

'I should have thought you would be hoping to come with us when Lady Parke and I move to a new home,' Bertie said nasally. He let the threat hang in the air for a second, and said, 'I got the impression there was some kind of disturbance going on yesterday. Come on, let's have the griffin. You know I won't tell.'

Cooper sighed and gave in. 'It's that Daniel, sir. He's a handsome devil – and he knows it! He gets all the girls in a tizzy – plays one off against another.'

'You don't mean he's debauching them?'

'No, sir. His interest don't run that way. He likes making 'em run after him – favours one, then drops her for another. They all think he's going to fall for 'em, but he keeps 'em dangling. Yesterday two of 'em has a fight over him – so he makes a fuss over a third and shows 'em both. That's how he operates.'

'When you say his interests don't run that way . . .?'

'He don't care about females, sir. Holds 'em in contempt. There's only one love in his life and that's Daniel Barlow. He's ambitious.'

'Ambitious for what?'

'Well, Mr Sawry's job, for a start. Oh, it's a treat to watch him!' Cooper chuckled, pushing Bertie's chin up to stretch his neck. 'He does a little bit of Sawry's job, and then a bit more. Says, "You look tired, Mr Sawry," ever so respectful. "You should let me do that – it's too heavy for you." Hints away that Sawry needs a rest. And the old boy *is* tired. The war was a strain on him. But Daniel, like, plants the thought in his mind, till it's all he can think about – his aching feet and his stiff knees. He's playing him like a fish. Just waiting for the master to get back and he'll land him all right. He'll be butler this time next year.'

'A small enough ambition,' Bertie commented.

'It don't end there,' Cooper said. 'Butler of a big 'ouse like this gets all sorts of opportunities, meets all sorts of people. He could go far. Could end up in Parliament if he decides that's what he wants. There, sir, you're done.'

Bertie took the towel and wiped his cheeks thoughtfully. 'I should be interested to see him in action.'

'Oh, you won't, sir. He's too subtle for that. But he can't get one over on me. I've watched him courting young Mr James, just in case. And when the master comes 'ome, you watch who's nicest to the new mistress. He'll be persuading 'em both to entertain big, so's he can get to meet important people. But they'll think it was their own idea.'

'Just the way you manipulate me,' Bertie said genially, getting up. Cooper presented his jacket and he backed into it. 'But if there's to be big entertaining, I shall be in a hurry to move out. I like the quiet life.'

'Very wise, sir,' said Cooper. 'But you got where you want to be, sir. Daniel's just starting out.'

*   *   *

514

It wasn't until the end of September that Teddy and Amy came home, announced by a telegram from Dover to say they had just landed, but would be stopping for two days in London on their way. Large amounts of luggage arrived ahead of them, trunks and boxes that had been sent straight on from the steamer, before a second telegram said they would be on the morning train and arriving at York station at noon.

The two days had allowed Henrietta time to make sure the house was spotless and the great bedchamber and dressing-room were prepared, with the finest sheets, towels, flowers, toilet water and such little comforts as fresh writing-paper on the desk and biscuits in the tin on the mantelpiece. It also allowed her to order a delicately delicious luncheon and a fine dinner for the evening, and to have Bertie consult with Sawry over wines, port, sherry and Madeira. Tomlinson had a word with Miss Sweetlove, who had considered her position and realised that if she refused to maid the new mistress she might find herself thrown out altogether. She might be thrown out anyway, if the new mistress wanted a younger maid, but if she had at least shown willing she was likely to have a softer landing.

Jessie thought better of having another word with Ethel, for fear of stirring her up again and making her worse through sheer perversity. She seemed to have been holding her tongue about Amy lately. In fact, she had not been at home very much, spending a lot more time 'out' and 'seeing friends' – she offered no more detailed explanations – which was more comfortable for everyone. But her manner when she was at home was more affable, so Jessie supposed that she must have considered her position too, and come to a better conclusion.

Simmonds went off in the motor he had spent all morning polishing, to drive to the station, followed by one of the gardeners in the Morris in case there should be yet more luggage. James was already back at Eton, and the older children were at school. Martin and John had just started too, which left only Thomas, Catherine, Laura and the baby Ottilie at home. Thomas and Catherine did their best to constitute an excited crowd in the hall, assisted by the dogs who, sensing something was afoot, rushed aback and forth across the yard, standing at the far end of the drawbridge waving their tails hopefully, and then gambolling and tussling in excitement back to the house.

In the end, the big blue and silver Benz turned in under the barbican when the dogs were investigating the possibility of a rat in a corner of the stable and they were taken by surprise. Despite his age and his knees, Sawry beat everyone down the steps to be the one who opened the door as the motor-car slid to a silent halt. And then Teddy stepped out, a trimmer, younger-looking Teddy in a light, biscuit-coloured suit and overcoat, and a Panama hat with a claret and navy ribbon. He looked round him with smiling pleasure at the sight of home, shook the bemused Sawry's hand, beamed up at the family gathered on the steps, pushed various ecstatic dogs down from his chest, then hurried round to the other side of the car to forestall Simmonds from helping Mrs Morland out.

The watchers saw the neat head, wearing a pretty straw hat trimmed with artificial daisies, and the shoulders and upper parts of a tailored outfit of pale blue shantung.

'She's nice,' Jessie whispered to her mother, as the

small, pointed face looked over towards them and smiled hesitantly.

Now they had come round the car and were at the foot of the steps, Teddy cradling his wife's elbow as if she were made of some desperately fragile material. He was quite brown, and even she had a little of a golden colour in her cheeks. 'What a trip!' he said. 'I've so much to tell you.'

'We had your postcards from France,' Henrietta answered for everyone.

'France seems a year away! We've been to so many places. Corsica, Italy, Greece – Egypt! Oh, those pyramids! Impossible to express to you the sheer size of them. We've brought back presents for you all, and all sorts of souvenirs.' He kissed Henrietta, ruffled the hair of Thomas, who had got himself to the front, and said, 'Home looks nice. I'm glad to be back. Bertie – good to see you. Ethel – you're looking well. Jessie dear – I'm looking forward to seeing your new baby.' He looked round smiling, with a nod for the servants, and then said, 'But where's Polly?'

'Still in America,' Henrietta answered. 'She couldn't write to you about it because none of us had a forwarding address, but we were sure you wouldn't mind if she extended her stay.'

'I expect she's enjoying herself,' Teddy said genially. 'Well, it's the right time of her life for that.' He took Amy's hand through his arm and they passed in through the great door together, carried on a bow-wave of dogs. 'Home, my dear,' he said, and she smiled at him. Jessie thought she looked tired, and perhaps a bit apprehensive; but it must be a momentous thing for her to be entering the house ceremoniously under the eyes of such a crowd.

Sawry was there again to take Teddy's hat, gloves and cane, and Sweetlove slipped herself into position to relieve Mrs Morland of anything she wanted to shed.

Henrietta also thought Amy looked apprehensive, and said warmly to her, 'Welcome home, my dear. I expect you'd like to go straight to your room and have a wash before luncheon. I've had hot water sent up already.'

'Thank you,' Amy said, her voice seeming light and insubstantial in the great space of the hall.

Teddy brought her captive hand to his lips and kissed it, and said, 'Yes, you go on up and do whatever you have to do. Don't bother to change. Luncheon will be ready directly – won't it, Hen?'

'In half an hour.'

'And I hope you've had Sawry put plenty of champagne on ice,' he said. 'Because we have a very particular reason to celebrate.' He looked down into Amy's face and she gave a tiny shake of the head, but he carried on anyway. 'Can't keep good news to ourselves, my love,' he said to her, and to the assembled family, 'It's early days yet, but we have reason to believe there may soon be another addition to the family.'

Polly was having a wonderful time. The summer months had opened up new pleasures, for wealthy New Yorkers went out of town, to the countryside or the seaside. The richest owned places on Long Island, sometimes vast estates with private beaches; the second rank rented summer houses there. Lizzie and Ashley always took a place in Oyster Bay, large enough for the family. Granny Ruth went with them; Lennie and Patrick, like Ashley, worked in town during the week and came out at weekends. The Annaheims had a place along the coast in the

Hamptons, and Wendell and Dottie stayed there, and invited Martial and Mimi to join them. They invited Polly, too, and to Rose's disappointment, she preferred to stay with them than with Lizzie.

On Long Island Polly found all the same people she knew in Manhattan, and enjoyed the same society, but with the added pleasure of new activities. There was golf, which was becoming very popular, though Polly couldn't really see the point of it; tennis on the private courts of the various large houses; sailing on the various rich people's yachts; and beach parties and sea-bathing, which was a new delight.

There were smart shops in the settlements along the coast, and Polly was able to buy herself a bathing costume to use until she had time to survey the field and design one for herself. It was like a little dress with a dropped waistband, in sky blue with a sailor collar piped in white, and white bands piped around the arm cuffs and a double band round the wavy hem. Under the skirt was a pair of drawers, sewn into the waistband for modesty. The arms came to halfway down the upper arm and the skirt and drawers to halfway down the thigh, leaving more flesh on display than Polly had ever dreamed of exposing. The first time she wore it she could hardly bring herself to leave the changing-room, and was glad to hurry into the water to conceal her legs. But after a few moments she felt better about it, having discovered at a single glance that her costume was modest compared with many. Some girls wore costumes that clung to their bodies, outlining their figures quite graphically, and with no sleeves, just narrow straps, and no skirt over the drawers. She could imagine what her father would have said about them.

Once she got used to it, however, it was great fun to frolic in the water with so little clothing encumbering her movements. The presence of young men, even more scantily clad, laughing and flirting and throwing large, bright-coloured inflatable balls around, added to the excitement. Mixed bathing was still severely frowned upon in many places, but on Long Island people regarded themselves as sophisticated.

The mixed parties went in for a great deal of splashing and horseplay and ball games, but always ended up with groups and couples sitting under umbrellas on the beach, talking and smoking and – the case of the couples – even spooning. Polly didn't care for the spooning, but she liked beach picnics and playing in the water and learning to swim, and sitting around on rocks being admired.

She soon got the measure of the bathing-suit range, and had several of her own designs run up. With them she wore a brightly coloured silk scarf tied around her head in different ways, and was amused to see the style soon copied. But her outfits were always modest. She knew gracefulness and dignity suited her style, and she did not care for the idea of the young men ogling her figure, as she had seen them doing with some of the wilder girls. The admiration she craved had to be tempered by respect.

The other new pleasure she enjoyed that summer was riding. Several of the wealthier set kept horses at their places on Long Island, and there were lots of interesting tracks and back roads to explore. One of her new beaux, Max Schneider, son of a very wealthy lawyer (and in New York, she had discovered, lawyers were among the wealthiest of all), was staying at his parents' place in East Hampton, where there was a stable of beautiful horses, and he invited her to come and ride as often as she liked. She had thought they might be riding on cowboy saddles with big horns, and wondered how she would get on with that, but she discovered that the rich and fashionable in New York rode what they called 'English style', though few ladies rode side-saddle except on special occasions. Max Schneider was struck by how well Polly rode, and talked about it a great deal among their set, so it soon got about that she was a fine rider. Other girls then discovered they couldn't live without horses, and angled for invitations.

Her visits to Lizzie's house naturally became less frequent, but Lizzie only said, 'I'm glad you're having a good time, dear.'

Lennie, when he came out at weekends and managed to track her down, said, 'You're running with a very rich set these days.'

'Am I?' she said defensively. He was part of home in her mind, and could always make her feel guilty about her racketing around.

'The Schneiders and Annaheims and van Plessets and so on. I hardly know you,' Lennie said. 'I hear you spoken of a great deal.'

Polly put her chin up. 'And what are they saying about me?' she demanded.

He smiled. 'Only that you're beautiful and witty and a demon of a tennis player. And a hard woman to hounds. Nothing I didn't know.'

She laughed with relief. 'There are no hounds. In the middle of summer?'

'And that you're helling around with the best of them,' he added lightly and, seeing her frown, went on, 'But you're looking well. It must be all the healthy exercise and fresh air you're having.'

'You don't think I'm brown?' Polly asked quickly. 'It's really hard to keep one's complexion when one's out of doors so much.'

He was glad of the excuse to examine her face at length. 'No,' he said at last, 'you're as cream-and-roses as any lady could wish. I come with an invitation. The Flints have come out from the city and Lizzie wants to have a family luncheon tomorrow, and especially asks you to be there, as she hasn't seen you in ages. You will come, won't you?'

'Oh dear,' said Polly, 'there's a big party at White Hill – the van Plessets' place – tomorrow. Everyone will be there.'

'You don't have to go, do you?'

'I've almost said I'd go with Max Schneider. Jay van Plesset's uncle who's a senator will be there. And a cousin who acts in moving pictures is staying with them for a rest cure, and they're going to show one of her movies in the library.'

Lennie wrinkled his nose. 'It sounds deadly dull. You'll be glad of an excuse not to go, I imagine.'

Polly smiled, shaking her head. 'Dull? Oh, Lennox Manning! You do make me laugh! All right, I'll come to Lizzie's. It won't hurt Max to be turned down for once – that boy is getting altogether too sure of himself.'

She was still staying in the Hamptons when she received the letter from her father containing the news that he was back home, and that Amy thought she was increasing. In all the sunny gaiety of the summer season, it came as a shock, like having a bucket of cold water thrown over her. She had managed for some weeks not to think about her father and the woman, and now it re-aroused all her feelings of revulsion and alienation.

That her father – her *father* – should not only have married a girl hardly older than her, but that he should have – should have . . . It was disgusting! Old people ought not to do such things. And now there was a child coming! The very notion made her feel sick.

It made it clearer to her than ever that he had abandoned her. He had a new wife and a new family now, and didn't need her. His letter spoke of looking forward to seeing her, but she did not believe it. He must be glad she had stayed away, so he could lavish on *that woman* everything that had previously been Polly's. Well, she would not go back – she would never go back to be humiliated, and to take second place to that – that – *creature*!

She managed to keep these thoughts to herself, so the rest of the family had little idea how strongly she felt. Lizzie received the news separately, from her mother, and tried tentatively to broach it with Polly. She might perhaps have talked her, eventually, into a better state of mind; but Polly put on such a good act of light indifference, Lizzie was left with the impression that she had got over the whole business. So when Polly said she was staying on in New York, Lizzie thought it was simply because she was enjoying herself.

For several days Polly planned a searing reply to her father's letter, but before she put pen to paper a calmer state of mind overcame her, and she felt merely mournful, lost, and very far from home. She wrote instead with the barest minimum of congratulations, and continued that she wanted to stay permanently in New York. She couldn't go on staying with family for ever, and wanted to rent her own apartment, and asked her father to set up her finances in such a way as to make her independent.

'I know you mean me to have Makepeace's one day, but as I shan't be coming back, perhaps you could let me have the value instead.'

Teddy's response was to write first to Lizzie with a torrent of questions. Lizzie replied, no, Polly wasn't ill or upset, yes, she did seem to want to remain in New York, yes, she was happy, no, there was no particular man in her life, and no-one was taking advantage of her. In fact, she fitted in very well and was a leader of society. Yes, it was quite acceptable for a well-to-do young woman to live in her own apartment once she was of age, provided she had a sensible maid, especially when she had so many family members nearby to keep an eye on her. And finally, yes, she did think Polly was quite determined to stay, but young people were always saying 'for ever', and they usually changed their minds later. It was quite probable that if she was allowed to stay, she would have her fill and want to come home in a few more months, a year or two at most.

Henrietta, to whom Teddy showed the letter, said the last part was common sense, and that opposition only made Polly more stubborn. Forcing her to come back would only make her unhappy, and if she was unhappy she would make everyone else unhappy too. Then there was the worry that Polly, forced to return against her will, would find another way of escaping. The thought of his darling eloping with some unsuitable man simply to get away made Teddy shudder. So he gritted his teeth and wrote to Polly that she should have her way, but that the moment she wanted to come home she should say so, and all would be arranged.

Meanwhile, Ashley recommended his own man of business, Samuels, to act as go-between with Teddy's Mr

Pobgee. Samuels was to take care of the money Teddy was settling on Polly, invest it wisely and make sure she always had what she needed, while preventing any fly-by-night suitor from getting his hands on it. Samuels and Ashley were jointly to oversee the matter, making sure Polly did not get into trouble.

Polly received the news that she was to have her fortune filtered through two guardians with equanimity. The amount her father was giving her was ample, and she decided she would start straight away to save a little here and there in case she was refused the money for some particular thing she wanted. Also, she had quite decided to start charging for her original clothing designs, to make it into a proper business. She knew that she would need something to occupy her, besides merely pursuing pleasure. Soon she would start making money from her originals, and that money did not need to go anywhere near Mr Samuels. He need never know it existed.

To begin with, however, Samuels seemed all geniality. He agreed to the apartment she wanted, in the Delft Hotel on Amsterdam Avenue in the fifties, and would pay the monthly bills direct to save her trouble, including the servants' wages. It was a very respectable building, with a porter on duty day and night. It had garages in a mews behind, which inspired Polly to ask if she could buy a motor-car. The readiness with which Samuels agreed made her feel that she would not have much difficulty in handling him.

She hired, through a recommendation of Mrs van Plesset, a lady's maid called Plummer who, she was told, was a 'treasure', because she could sew and do light cooking as well. Plummer had been lady's maid to the bedridden Mrs Oral Connors, and had been accustomed to preparing her invalid luncheons and suppers. At the interview she told Polly it had been a 'very quiet' household, and she seemed to be yearning for a more interesting and social mistress. She was a few years older than Polly, and had a very sensible air, but there was a light in her eyes that Polly liked: she thought she would prove adaptable and friendly. Polly also hired a housemaid, an Irish girl called Kitty; between them they would manage the work of the small household.

She bought a Buick touring convertible and had it painted bright red. The first morning she came out of the Delft's grand entrance, with the uniformed doorman, Henry, touching his cap and saying, 'Mornin', Miss Morland. Fine day,' and saw her red automobile waiting for her at the kerb, she knew she had stepped into a whole new world of freedom and possibilities. And, despite the ache in her heart, she was certain she was going to love it.

CHAPTER TWENTY-ONE

With the return of Teddy and Amy, it became a matter of urgency to Jessie and Bertie to have a home of their own. It was not that Teddy wanted them to be gone – he seemed, indeed, to assume that, now they were here, they would be staying permanently. But though Bertie had enjoyed, in a mild way, the sensation of being master of Morland Place for a few weeks, he could not be comfortable as a lodger. He was looking forward to having his own house, and land to manage and develop again.

Shortly after Teddy's return, Jessie had an official notification that the factory she had inherited from Ned, which had been requisitioned during the war, was to be returned to her. In fact, it had been unused for two years, but the War Office had not removed the last pieces of machinery until a few months ago, and had only just finished decontaminating it.

Teddy was more interested in the factory than Jessie was. 'What will you do with it now?' he asked her.

'I really don't know,' Jessie said. 'It's been out of my hands for so long, I never thought about having it back.'

'The War Office moves slowly, but it gets there in the end,' Bertie said. 'It used to be a paper mill, didn't it?'

'Yes,' Teddy answered for Jessie, 'and it made a decent

return. York has always been known for paper, and it's a thing people always need.'

'But it's just an empty shell now,' Jessie said. 'They took away all the mill's machinery when they requisitioned it. It would have to be completely refitted.'

'In that case,' Bertie said, 'it needn't be a paper mill. It could be anything.'

'Just what I was thinking,' Teddy said. 'In fact, I really need to move my clothing manufacture to new premises. I need to expand and the workshops are too small. And they're dilapidated – no point in putting new machinery into buildings that are falling down.'

'Well, then,' Jessie said, 'why don't you have it? It used to be yours before you gave it to Ned, and I have no use for it.'

Teddy was touched, but said, 'Now, love, you can't go giving away assets like that. You have to get value for them. Bertie will tell you I'm right – eh, Bertie? You have to look after your wife's interests, even if she doesn't know them herself.'

'I agree with you in principle, Uncle,' Bertie said, 'though it seems ungenerous to talk about getting value, considering all you've done for us in the past.'

'Nonsense, nonsense. This is business, nothing to do with family favours. You ought to get the place properly valued, then you can sell it to me.'

Bertie exchanged a glance with Jessie, and said, 'I think something more in the way of a swap would suit us better, if you were agreeable. You see, Jessie and I want to build a house for ourselves, and it would make sense for it to be near Twelvetrees, because we mean to build up the horse business.'

Teddy brightened. 'At Twelvetrees, eh? Well, that

sounds like a good idea. Your mother will like having you near.'

'Jessie has about six acres there, she tells me,' Bertie went on. 'Not enough to build the house on, if we are to keep enough land for the business. So what I propose, if you could see your way to it, is to swap the factory for some of your fields.'

Teddy looked thoughtful. 'I can't see anything against it, but I'd need to see how things could be rearranged.' He pondered a moment, and then went on, 'But I do happen to know there's a parcel of land coming on the market soon, over towards Askham Richard. I could always stretch my boundary that way, if I give up a bit by Twelvetrees. Yes, yes, I think it can be done. We ought to go out and have a look at the ground, see what's the best spot for building. The North Field might be suitable. You don't want to be too near the river, nor yet the railway line. We might go out and have a look this afternoon, if you're not busy.'

Teddy had come home ready to present his new wife to the world, and the autumn and winter were very gay at Morland Place. The plans for refurbishment were put off until the spring, for it was not possible to entertain in a house full of dust and workmen. Henrietta had to do the best she could with old-fashioned cleaning to make the guest and public rooms presentable, and was given Teddy's blessing to hire as many extra staff as she needed. She tried at the beginning to persuade Amy to take over the reins of the household, but she shied away from the idea, and said she had never managed anything like Morland Place, nor entertained on such a scale.

'Nevertheless, my dear, you ought to learn,' Henrietta

said gently. 'I shan't be here for ever, and it's your house now.'

So with Mary Tomlinson's help she began to involve Amy in the decisions and show her the routines of the house, hoping over time gently to slide the reins into her hands so that she didn't notice the change. Teddy felt proudly that anything Amy wanted to undertake, she would manage with credit. Her pregnancy had been confirmed – she expected to be delivered in May – which was such a miracle to him that the mere running of a house paled to insignificance beside it. The astonished delight of being a husband and expecting to be a father again filled his life. He missed Polly every day, and continued to hope for her return; but it was a fact that her absence did not hurt him as it otherwise would have. To that extent Polly was right: she had been replaced.

The neighbourhood had been agog, of course, to meet the woman they had been gossiping about, and the rumours had been so inflamed that the reality was bound to be a disappointment. Instead of a painted trollop, a brassy fortune-hunter, a sly minx or a child bride, they discovered a perfectly ordinary, moderately pretty, quietly spoken, ladylike woman, and had to squeeze what thrill they could out of the fact that she was less than half her husband's age.

But as she continued to fail to outrage the decencies in any notable way, the leaders of the gossiping faction decided a *volte-face* would make them more interesting, and they took her to their hearts. Her story was touching, with the tragedy of losing parents, brother and husband, the manner of her meeting with Mr Morland was romantic, and they were soon competing with each other to invite her to dinner and parties, and claiming loudly that they had always liked her and had never seen anything to wonder at about her marrying Teddy Morland.

Morland Place hosted house parties for cub-hunting, shooting and hunting proper, and it seemed no sooner had one lot of guests departed than another lot was expected. Teddy and Amy went down to Eton one weekend and took James out to luncheon at the Christopher on Saturday and to tea in Windsor, with several of his friends, on Sunday. James and Amy were shy with each other at first, but she remembered what her brother had been interested in at that age and stuck to those subjects, and by the end of the tea all the boys were chattering freely and Amy was obviously accepted as 'Morland's new mater' and a good egg.

Jack and Helen and their children came to stay for Christmas, and once again the house was wonderfully full of children and noise and laughter. The candles on the enormous Christmas tree in the Great Hall were lit on Christmas Eve – the footmen standing by with wet sponges on long poles in case of accidents – and presents were distributed from underneath it to the eleven eager youngsters gathered around. The vicar, Mr Ordsall, brought the church choir to sing carols, and they were rewarded with hot lamb's-wool and parkin and spiced biscuits. On Christmas morning everyone went to church, and in the afternoon the tenants and estate workers came up for their presents.

And on Boxing Day Teddy gave a meet at Morland Place, and he and Jessie and Bertie went out – Jessie on Vesper and Bertie on Teddy's young horse Viking that he was bringing on – while Henrietta and Amy followed to the first covert in a pony trap. James and Roberta also went out, with a groom to bring them back after an hour or two. Basil was deeply impressed by the sight of his cousins in all their glory mounted on their excited ponies, and demanded furiously why he couldn't go too. It was fortunate, Helen thought, that Martin invited him to play with his toy fort in the nursery instead, because the explanation, that he had never learned to ride, would not have cut much ice with him.

Prince Albert, the Duke of York, had proposed to the pretty dark-haired girl Emma had seen him dance with at the Farquars' ball. As protocol demanded, he had proposed through a third party, but the Lady Elizabeth had refused him, telling close friends that she was afraid of never being able to think, speak or act freely again if she married into the royal family.

The prince was so smitten, however, that he would not take 'no' for an answer, and proposed again the following year, having seen her again when she was bridesmaid at the wedding of his sister, Princess Mary. Again he was refused. He told the Queen that he could never think of marrying anyone else, and she was so impressed with such vehemence from her usually biddable son that she went to the trouble of visiting Glamis Castle to inspect the girl for herself, and came away convinced that Bertie was right, and that this was the one girl who could make him happy.

Princes were normally expected to marry princesses, but the fact that she was a commoner did not matter so much for the second son. In fact, as Arthur Bigge, the King's private secretary, said to Venetia, it was rather a good thing, as it showed the establishment ready to modernise itself 'in a way that won't hurt anyone'. The

Prince of Wales, he feared, was all too ready to be modern in the wrong way, and throw aside convention.

So in January 1923 the Duke of York proposed again, but this time, on the advice of a friend, he defied protocol and went to see Lady Elizabeth to propose in person. This time, perhaps moved by his sincerity, or perhaps having had time to think about the advantages of the match, she accepted. The prince sent a telegram to his parents saying simply 'All right', and the engagement was announced formally on the 16th of January.

The Prince of Wales, meanwhile, was not enjoying such a happy period in his life, for his friendship with Mrs Dudley Ward was cooling. She had been regarded by those in the know as his mistress since 1918; now she wanted a more distant relationship, and had said they must see less of each other. While the prince was pleased for his brother's happiness, and thoroughly approved of his choice, it made a stark contrast with his own position. Eddie told Venetia, when he and Sarah were dining at Manchester Square one evening, that the prince was quite in despair, pronouncing that he could never love anyone but Freda, and that his life was ruined. 'He's drinking too much,' he said, 'and generally helling around. Sooner or later he's going to be seen coming drunk out of a nightclub, and if it gets into the papers, the King will have a fit.'

'I suppose I didn't think of it before,' Venetia said, 'but the Dudley Ward was a steadying influence on him.'

'Oh, yes,' Eddie said. 'He always did what she told him, and he behaved himself a great deal better to please her.'

'It was an odd set-up,' Oliver mused. 'Almost like an old married couple.'

'I believe that was exactly the point,' Venetia said. 'The King and Queen have always been very strict with him – the King used to frighten him to fits when he was a little boy, and the Queen has never been in the least soothing. The poor creature is sadly lacking a mother's comfort. Mrs Dudley Ward is married, with children—'

'Whom he adores, by the way,' Sarah mentioned.

'Just so,' said Venetia. 'I think he went to her for a little cosy domesticity. And the fact that he *can't* marry her makes her safe. It must be tiresome to be such a marriage object, and have to watch your tongue with every girl you meet in case she thinks you mean more than you do.'

'Goodness, yes,' Oliver said solemnly. 'I remember how it was – *so* tiresome. Didn't you find it so, Eddie? Though, of course, you were never *quite* the catch I was.'

Verena gave him a stern look and said to Venetia, 'Please rap his knuckles for me, ma'am. I can't reach from here.'

Eddie said, 'Well, I think we should try to cheer the poor fellow up. Sarah, shall we give a dinner for him?'

A date was fixed, and as well as the prince's intimate circle they invited Oliver and Verena for interesting conversation ('Talk to him about plastic surgery – he'll be fascinated!') and Violet for beauty, because hers was just the kind the prince admired. Holkam was free that evening and said he would accompany her, and when Violet looked a little wondering – he usually liked weightier company – he said, 'You should never miss a chance to make your number with the important members of the royal family. You never know where such casual encounters may lead.'

★ ★ ★

Jessie was walking past Kendal's teashop in Stonegate when, glancing in, she met the rather shocked gaze of Ethel, who was sitting at a table in the company of a male stranger. The man said something to Ethel, then looked to see what she was staring at, met Jessie's eyes and half rose from his chair. Jessie had begun to raise a hand in acknowledgement to Ethel, meaning to walk on, not wishing to intrude, but the man said something more to Ethel, and she gestured to Jessie, rather limply, to come in.

Ethel was looking very smart, in her best hat and coat, and she was either very embarrassed, or was wearing rouge. Her companion, a stoutly built man of mature years, had risen to his feet and was hovering attentively, directing towards Jessie a welcoming smile, which featured a set of teeth of improbable evenness and whiteness. He had a large head, on which scanty hair was slicked down firmly, as though to prevent any more of it escaping. His red face was somewhat freckled and sported a reddish moustache. One of his eyes was bluer than the other, and did not move around as freely as its companion. One pudgy, freckled hand held his napkin, while the other seemed to hover hopefully in case it was required for hand-shaking duty.

'Hello, Ethel,' Jessie said. 'I wasn't expecting to see you here. I don't mean to intrude.'

'Not at all, not at all! Delighted!' the man burst in before Ethel could answer.

She gave Jessie a wan smile. 'This is Captain Broadbent,' she said. 'We met at – at a friend's.' She cast what seemed to be a pleading look at the man, who was leaning forward now in his eagerness to welcome Jessie. 'My sister-in-law, Lady Parke.'

'*Lady* Parke. Delighted to make your acquaintance.'
Jessie could not now avoid shaking hands, but did it as
briefly as possible. She couldn't think where Ethel could
have picked up such a vulgar-looking man, or why she
was having tea with him alone. 'Any friend of Eth – of
Mrs Compton's is a friend of mine,' he exclaimed. 'Sit
down, do, and I'll get the girl to bring a cup.'

'Please don't trouble,' Jessie said, though she sat down
in order to make him sit. 'I can't stay.'

'No, no, I insist. A cup of tea and a muffin. Kendal's
muffins, I venture to say, are second to none.' He had a
curious accent, mostly rather flat Yorkshire, but with the
occasional strained vowel as if he were trying to torture
it further up the social scale. 'I used to dream of Kendal's
muffins when I was in the trenches. A dream of home,
d'ye see?'

'Captain Broadbent is one of our heroes,' Ethel said
quickly. 'He was wounded at Passchendaele.'

'Lost a leg,' he said modestly. 'And an eye.' He gestured
to the bluer organ. 'Glass, I'm afraid.'

'I really hadn't noticed,' Jessie said kindly.

'He won a medal,' Ethel put in, 'for conspicuous
gallantry.'

'My congratulations,' Jessie said. 'There was some
hard fighting there. What regiment were you in?'

'Oh, just a humble foot regiment,' he said, with another
baring of the china. 'I'm not one of your glamorous
Guards or Hussars. But let's not talk about that. It's the
folk back home who showed the real heroism – people
like Mrs Compton.' He looked at her fondly. 'Little ladies
like her I can't admire enough. Widowed in that cruel
way, having to bring up her children without a father,
not to say running that big house all alone, but she carries

536

on without complaint. I don't know how she does it, really I don't.'

Ethel's smile was ghastly, but if she had exaggerated a little, Jessie wasn't going to betray her. 'We're all grateful for her courage,' she said drily. 'Have you known each other long?'

'Yes,' Ethel said, at the same moment as Captain Broadbent said, 'No.' She coloured, and he went on, 'Not long enough for me, but sometimes when you meet someone it feels as if you've known them all your life, don't you find that, Lady Parke?'

'Oh, indeed,' Jessie said. 'And you met through a friend?'

'That's right. At a—'

'Bridge party, at Mrs Ellwood's,' Ethel jumped in.

Broadbent coughed. 'Do you play bridge at all, Lady Parke?' he said.

'I'm afraid I don't have much time for cards,' Jessie said.

'Oh, quite, quite,' Broadbent said. 'I dare say you and Lord Parke have a big estate to look after. In fact, I fancy I've read about it somewhere. Wasn't there something in the *Sunday Pictorial*? How many acres was it?'

This was sufficient to rouse Ethel, who said sharply, 'Perhaps you could catch the waitress's eye, Donald. A fresh pot – this is quite cold.'

Jessie had no desire to indulge in bear-baiting. She rose, saying, 'Not on my account, please. I really must be going. I only stopped in to be civil, but I have a great many errands this afternoon.'

Broadbent had also climbed to his feet, and she said, 'It was nice to meet you, Captain. My husband was at Passchendaele – Sir Bertie Parke.'

'I don't think I ever had the pleasure,' Broadbent said vaguely. 'Doesn't ring a bell.'

'What regiment did you say you were with?'

His eyes slid away – or one of them did, at any rate. 'Oh, er, I moved around, you know. Seconded here and there. This regiment and that.' He laughed. 'Never quite knew where I'd wake up in the morning. Can't recollect exactly who I was with at that time.'

Jessie made her escape. She was pretty sure Captain Broadbent hadn't been at Passchendaele. Bertie's escapade there, which had won him the Victoria Cross, had been the talk of the division, but he had obviously not heard of him. She wondered if he had really been decorated. But then Ethel had seemingly told him she ran Morland Place single-handed.

She had called him 'Donald', and he had almost called her 'Ethel'. It was plain there was something more than friendship between them. Jessie couldn't think what Ethel saw in him, but it was easy, from the security of marriage to the man she loved, to forget how lonely widowhood could be. Some women could not function without a man, and men were thin on the ground these days. Perhaps he had other qualities that made up for the tortured accent and dubious provenance. Perhaps just to have someone admire her and compliment her and take her out to tea was balm to Ethel's soul. It certainly explained why she had been so elusive lately, and why she had been so much better-tempered.

As she turned into Petergate, Jessie wondered if, in fact, Broadbent had ever been in the army at all. What man could not remember which regiment he was in? If she were to check up . . . But it was not her business to protect Ethel from unsuitable friendships. She dismissed

538

'Captain' Broadbent from her mind, with the final thought that Kendal's had only opened in 1919, so he could not have dreamed of their muffins in the trenches; though it was a nice poetic touch, the sort of detail that added verisimilitude to an otherwise unconvincing narrative.

The building of Jessie and Bertie's new house was due to begin in late January or early February 1923, as soon as the ground was workable, and Teddy's plans were to be put into operation at the same time. Henrietta sighed a little at the thought of the dirt and disruption to come, and actually felt rather hard done by when Teddy said that he and Amy were going to Town in March for a month or six weeks to avoid the worst of it.

'But why don't you go too?' he said. 'Go and stay with Venetia. I'm sure she'd love to have you. See some shows, visit Helen and Jack, find out how Emma is.'

Henrietta didn't see how she could leave Morland Place at such a time, but Jessie urged her to go. 'Bertie and I have to stay to oversee our own building work, and we can take care of everything. Do go, Mother, if Cousin Venetia will have you. I'm sure nobody deserves a holiday more.'

'Don't you deserve a holiday too?' she asked Jessie, with a last burst of conscience.

'Bertie and I are going to the February sales at Tatt's, to look for a stallion,' she said. 'That will be holiday enough for us.'

Venetia expressed herself delighted with the idea, and so it was decided.

★   ★   ★

By the time Henrietta went to stay with Venetia, the date for the royal wedding, the 26th of April, had been announced, and it was causing much excitement in the capital.

'I've seen her once or twice,' Venetia said. 'She seems a nice, steady girl. I think she'll be good for him. He has a good heart, but he's very nervous. He's afflicted by a dreadful stammer, which makes public events a trial for him.'

Henrietta found it fascinating to hear the distant and glamorous royals talked about in such human terms by someone who had actually met them. All she knew was what she read in the papers. 'It's a good thing, then, perhaps, that he won't be king,' she ventured.

'Well, perhaps. Although his marriage – particularly if he produces an heir – takes some of the pressure off the Prince of Wales. *He* doesn't look any closer to doing the right thing. The King and Queen are fuming that, instead of applying himself to some suitable foreign princess, he does nothing but mope over the Dudley Ward female.'

'I know that name – I think I've heard something about her,' Henrietta said tentatively, hoping for fuller enlightenment.

'I'm sorry, I forget how out of the world you are down in Yorkshire,' Venetia said. 'Freda Dudley Ward is an MP's wife, daughter of a lace manufacturer – American mother – and she's supposed to have been the prince's mistress. She's a perfectly nice, good-hearted, quite smart little woman: nothing exceptional, but the prince idolises her. He's been in a ferment of romantic passion these four years, like a sixteen-year-old falling madly in love with the headmaster's wife. *Quite* unrealistic. In fact, I firmly believe she was never his mistress in the technical sense:

if they had been physical lovers, I'm sure the spell would have worn off by now. *I* think he just likes to worship at her feet. Now she's got tired of stumbling over him at every turn and told him to leave her alone—'

'Dear me!'

'Oh, not in so many words. She did it kindly – said they should just be friends in the ordinary way – but he still declares she's the only woman he could ever love. Exasperates the King to madness. But, of course, that's probably a good deal of the point,' Venetia concluded. 'Being in love with a woman he can never marry takes him out of the running, so to speak. Eddie believes he's so terrified of the whole business – marriage – that he deliberately puts himself *hors de combat*.'

'Goodness, what strange lives you all lead,' Henrietta said. 'It seems miles away from our dull circle.'

Venetia smiled. 'Don't include me in that. I loved Beauty and married him and that was that.'

'Allowing for a few minor excitements, like being the first woman doctor and scandalising everyone,' Henrietta reminded her.

'You and I,' Venetia said, 'have always been too busy to get up to much. Now, the prince is a prime example of a young man without enough to do. They try to keep him occupied with all those foreign tours – Canada and America and Australia, India in 'twenty-one and Japan last year, and there's talk of South Africa next. It's a good thing we have a large empire, or where *would* people send troublesome sons to get them out of the way until they come into their inheritance?'

'Should you talk about him like that? He *is* the heir to the throne.'

'Yes, and it's a pity, now I think of it, that it *isn't* York.

Wales is too popular with the newspapermen – and now he's got a new equerry who is simply leading him astray. Eddie says Major Metcalfe is quite wild – a mad Irishman. Though he did have a good war.'

Venetia's prediction about the rise of the wireless seemed vindicated when in October 1922 a new company had been formed called the British Broadcasting Company, licensed by the GPO, and with share capital of £100,000. The shareholders were large American and British electrical companies such as Metropolitan-Vickers, Marconi, Thomson-Houston and General Electric, and the headquarters were two small rooms in the GEC building in London.

Members of the Radio Society of Great Britain had been mounting pressure on the postmaster general to allow the resumption of test broadcasts, ever since they had been stopped because of alleged interference to military communications. Those early broadcasts had been put out with the call sign 'Two Emma Toc', by two ex-officers, from an old army hut in Essex. They played gramophone records, interspersing the music with the sort of facetious humour familiar to anyone who had watched services shows during the war. One evening after a particularly good dinner, Captain Peter Eckersley, ex-Royal Flying Corps, did not play any records at all, but broadcast a 'Night of Grand Opera', playing the piano and singing all the parts himself, including the female ones. The suspicion had always been that the GPO stopped the broadcasts because everyone concerned was simply having too much fun.

A director general was appointed to the new broadcasting company, a dour Scotsman called John Reith, who looked likely to prevent anything like that happening again. His stern belief was that the purpose of wireless was to educate and uplift. Broadcasts began in November from station 2LO on Savoy Hill – the first proper radio station in England – and a broadcasting licence fee of ten shillings was introduced. News reports and weather forecasts, music, short stories and talk were included in the output, and there was coverage of the general election in November, when the Conservatives won a working majority.

Audiences were limited at first, because few people yet had receiving sets; but as 1923 advanced, sales of sets increased rapidly. 'It was a case of chicken and egg,' Oliver said to his mother. 'No point in having a set until there was something to listen to; no point in broadcasting until there were people out there to listen to it.'

He bought a set in March, and drove his mother mad with the strange noises he seemed to be able to make it produce, until she put her foot down and banished it to his private rooms. 'I thought you'd be interested,' he said in wounded tones. 'You were always so progressive-minded.'

'I see nothing progressive about the sound of chickens being strangled.'

'Ah, but that's just the beginning. Remember Dame Nellie Melba? You'll want me to bring it back downstairs when they start broadcasting symphonies and operas.'

'If I want to listen to an orchestra I can go to a concert,' Venetia pointed out. 'And the Royal Opera House is only a taxi-ride away. It's one of the joys of living in London.'

He smiled at her fondly. 'Luddite,' he said.

It soon emerged that the BBC had requested permission to broadcast the wedding of the Duke of York from

Westminster Abbey in May, but had been refused. There were heated debates in the newspapers about whether it would be improper thus to defile the sacred spaces of the Abbey, or disrespectful to the royal family, or whether, indeed, in the new post-war age of informality and democracy, the people had the right to be allowed to participate in this way.

'If it was the wedding of the Prince of Wales,' Venetia said, 'I suppose there might be an argument for it. But York's wedding is really a private family affair.'

'You can say that because you have a ticket anyway,' Oliver teased her. 'If you weren't going, don't you think you'd want to hear it all on the wireless?'

'Not at all. I'd use my imagination,' Venetia said firmly. 'If you've been to one wedding in the Abbey, you know exactly how it goes.'

And Oliver laughed and told her she was a lost cause.

The newspapers made a great fuss of the wedding, which was just what everyone wanted to cheer them up – world news was still bad, and though the national finances were gradually improving there were still strikes, and taxes were high. Besides, the Duke of York was very popular, having undertaken the less glamorous tours around the industrial north and Wales while his brother was abroad. He was president of the Industrial Welfare Society; and had instigated an annual summer camp for boys from mixed backgrounds. The new duchess was universally adored as being pretty, charming and full of fun.

Henrietta had come back refreshed from her sojourn in London, prepared to face the mess and inconvenience of building with equanimity. Teddy and Amy would be two weeks behind her, and she hoped to get their part of the house clean and ready for them, at least. They had called formally on Venetia while she was there, and Venetia had said afterwards that she liked Amy and thought the arrangement an excellent one. 'A perfectly nice young woman has acquired a home and protection, and a good and generous man has acquired companionship and affection.'

Jessie and Bertie's house was coming along apace, despite indifferent weather. By the time Henrietta got home the foundations were in and the walls were going up, and by the end of April the roof was on, and Jessie was talking about being in residence by the end of June. She and Bertie had bought a stallion at Tattersall's, a four-year-old black thoroughbred, and two mares, which were to be the core of their new breeding plan. Bertie also meant to raise beef cattle on his land at Bishop Winthorpe, and was planning a buying trip in the summer.

The work Teddy had ordered in Morland Place was more complicated than a new build, and it looked as though it would not be finished before the end of summer; but Teddy, when he came home, pronounced himself satisfied with progress, and said that as long as they could entertain in the autumn he would be satisfied. He was paying to have a cable laid so that electricity could be piped to the house. Very few houses, especially country houses, yet had electricity, and it would mark out the Morlands as people of distinction. He meant it to be used for lighting and for certain exciting innovations on the kitchen side, such as an electric iron for the laundry.

'And a wireless, Dad,' James said eagerly, when he

came home for the Easter vacation. 'You must get a wireless. All the fellows' people have them back home.'

There were now eight regional companies broadcasting music and talk, including comedy programmes, for several hours on six days of the week – broadcasting on Sunday was forbidden.

Teddy thought it a good idea. 'We must move with the times.'

Jessie and Bertie were having electricity in their new house, benefiting by a spur from Teddy's cable, which brought down the cost considerably.

Other innovations in Morland Place included the installation of bathrooms, which involved a lot of pipe-work having to be laid in, and improvements to the servants' attics, including two bathrooms for their use, one on the men's side and one on the women's. Teddy insisted on those, though Henrietta worried that some of the servants might not bathe at all if they weren't supervised. Tomlinson reassured her that a proper check would be maintained.

And Teddy was having the gentlemen's wing, which had burned down in his brother's day, rebuilt, to house a smoking-room, billiard-room and gun-room. 'It was such a convenience,' he said. 'The one change my brother made that I thoroughly approved of. If we are to entertain properly, we must have them.'

Jessie had told Bertie about Ethel's gentleman friend – 'Though he seemed more than a friend and less than a gentleman.'

Bertie agreed that he sounded like a scoundrel of some kind. 'Bogus,' he said. 'Definitely bogus. I wouldn't be surprised if he had never been in the army at all.'

'I did wonder,' Jessie said, 'when he wouldn't say what regiment he'd been in.'

'Well, his military record will be easy enough to check, at any rate.'

'Oh, but please be discreet,' Jessie said. 'I should hate Ethel to find out you were asking questions and be hurt.'

'Of course I'll be discreet,' Bertie said, but he looked worried. 'I can't think what he's after – Ethel hasn't any money.'

'Well, that's a good thing, isn't it? As long as she isn't being deceived.'

'Or not more deceived than women usually are by the men courting them.' Bertie smiled. 'You must give us fellows leeway for a little exaggeration.'

'You never needed it,' she said, kissing him. 'You're a natural-born hero.'

With so much else to think of, Jessie had almost forgotten about the matter, when one evening in April, as they were waiting in the drawing-room for dinner to be ready, Ethel announced suddenly that she was intending to get married.

After a moment of surprised silence, the questions came tumbling from Henrietta and Teddy – who was he, how did she know him, why had they not met him? – while Bertie and Jessie exchanged a thoughtful glance. Ethel answered, in as vague a way as possible, that she had met him at a bridge party and they had been partnering each other since then; but Teddy, ever hospitable, had already moved on. 'We must have a dinner for him, so we can meet him. Ethel, my dear, I am pleased for you.'

'You – you don't mind, then?' Ethel asked uncertainly, looking mostly at Henrietta. 'You don't think it wrong of me?'

'Of course not,' Henrietta said, as if she did not remember the fuss Ethel had made when Maria wanted to marry again. 'It's the most natural thing in the world for a woman to want to be married. I'm sure it's what Rob would have wanted for you.'

Jessie, remembering Captain Broadbent's more dubious features, thought a dinner would be too much of a strain on everyone as a first contact, and privately suggested to her mother that she invite him for tea first of all.

Henrietta looked at her sharply. 'Do you know him? Is there something wrong with him?'

'I wouldn't say that,' Jessie said. 'I only met him once, and I don't know anything about him, really, but he seemed – well, rather unpolished.'

'Oh dear,' said Henrietta. 'Has Ethel got herself into bad company? Your uncle will be upset – you know he feels responsible for her.'

'I don't know that there's anything wrong with him. It's just that he's – a diamond in the rough.'

Henrietta put her hand to her cheek. 'Perhaps you're right, then – tea might be better. But if he is *really* impossible—'

'There's nothing we can do about it, Mother,' Jessie said. 'If Ethel wants to marry him, we can't stop her.'

'No, but she might be swayed by our opinion.'

Fortunately, Ethel seemed equally relieved that there was not to be a dinner – or not immediately. Jessie felt sorry for her – it must be wretched to have to worry about whether your family would accept your lover. But she did more urgently want to know if there was anything really bad about Captain Broadbent, for if he was a wrong 'un, fear of exposure at Morland Place might provoke him to jilt Ethel, and she wanted to be in a position to warn her and cushion the blow.

'Have you found anything out?' she asked Bertie that night in their bedroom.

'A little. I haven't been pursuing it because I didn't know there was any urgency, but I shall step up my enquiries now. I'm fairly sure, however, that he wasn't in the army – or, at least, he wasn't an officer. The only Donald Broadbent on record is an artillery major who was killed at Second Ypres.'

'Oh dear, poor Ethel. Not a captain.'

'And not decorated either – no military awards to anyone of that name. That's as far as I got with the military authorities.'

'But someone in York must know something about him. He can't exist in a vacuum.'

'I shall do a little ferreting – or, wait, better still, I'll put Cooper on to it. He can go into places and ask questions that I can't.'

'Good idea. But I still can't think what he could be after, if he *is* a bad lot.'

'Perhaps hoping for something from Ethel's wealthier relatives?'

'I suppose that's possible. He did seem interested in your estate. He asked me how many acres Lord Parke had.'

Bertie snorted with amusement. 'Oh dear. Poor Ethel – is he really clownish?'

'I expect he was just nervous,' Jessie said defensively.

The serpentine Cooper was pleased to be sent on a sleuthing mission. Life below stairs was rather boring, and he didn't have enough to do. 'I'll find out what you want, sir,' he assured Bertie. 'I'm not known around York yet. I'll visit a few pubs, get people talking.'

'Then you'll need some funds to buy drinks. Here, make a start with this. Let me know if you need more.'

'Thank you, sir. I'll soon get a line on him, don't worry. York's a small place.'

Bertie's worry was that Cooper might not report back before the day of the tea party, which would be awkward, but it only took him two evenings of buying drinks and bon-homming to 'come up with the goods', as he put it.

'Well, Broadbent *is* his name,' Bertie told Jessie, 'as far as anyone knows. He's not from York – he's originally from Huddersfield.'

'I thought his accent was strange,' Jessie said.

'Cooper got hold of a window-cleaner whose wife's sister-in-law lives in Huddersfield and recognised him when she was visiting them one time. It seems he was well known in his home town.'

'Oh dear – what had he done?'

'Nothing disgraceful,' Bertie said. 'That's the good news. But he was never in the army, as we suspected. He was a tram inspector, and he lost his leg and an eye in an accident. It was an icy day, and a tram was stuck on the rails. He was on the spot at the time, and when an old woman started to cross in front of it, he dashed forward to help her, just as the tram came unstuck and lurched forward and caught him.'

'How dreadful!'

'He saved the old woman, so he was in the local papers as a hero. The Humane Society gave him a medal – so he was decorated, you see, in a way. A subscription was got up to give him a cash award, and the tram company gave him a pension, so he was comfortably off. But evidently he didn't find that glorious enough, what with all the war heroes coming home. So he moved to another town – Leeds – and claimed to have been wounded at Passchendaele. I suppose a war hero gets better treatment.'

'Yes, and free meals and cups of tea and so on,' Jessie said. 'Free entry to the cinema. Free rides on buses and trams.'

Bertie shrugged. 'Let's be generous and suppose it was the warmth of adulation he craved rather than the financial benefits.'

'So why did he come to York?'

'Cooper says the suggestion is he got rumbled in Leeds and had to move on. But here's a thing – Cooper found another chap who knew Broadbent, and he said he met Ethel at a spiritualist meeting.'

Jessie's eyes opened wide. 'You mean – a séance? Table turning, ectoplasm and all that sort of thing?'

Bertie nodded. 'It seems she's been going for years, trying to get in touch with Robert.'

'Oh, *poor* Ethel!' Jessie said, not for the first time. 'But Mother and Uncle Teddy will be so disapproving – they think that sort of thing is sacrilegious.'

'Presumably that's why she's kept it secret. At all events, this other chap's wife goes to the meetings – their son was killed at Arras – and knows Ethel by sight. The Broadbent fellow joined last year.'

'Has he lost someone?'

'Cooper said his fellow didn't know. It's possible he just went there to meet women. They mostly *are* women at these things, and a lot of them are widows.'

'Yes, lonely, unhappy women,' Jessie said. 'The sort

551

to be preyed on.' She looked at Bertie. 'We'll have to tell Ethel.'

'I suppose it is necessary,' he agreed. 'We can't let her be imposed upon. But I'm afraid it will make her very unhappy.'

And Jessie sighed and said, 'When you say "we", of course you mean me.'

'It would be better coming from you – the woman's touch.'

Ethel listened to Jessie in silence, her face rather pale, her mouth set, and a spark of something in her eyes – though whether it was anger or pain Jessie couldn't tell. Jessie had invited her out for a walk in the gardens for privacy, and they were sitting on one of the benches under a rose arbour, with the heady scent and the sound of bees all around them. She hoped Ethel would not ever afterwards associate the smell and sound with disappointment.

At last she spoke. 'How dare you go spying on us, and asking questions, as though we were – were *criminals*? What business is it of yours? How dare you interfere like that?'

'It wasn't interfering, I was afraid for you,' Jessie defended herself unhappily. 'I guessed when I met him he had not been in the army, and when Bertie confirmed it, we felt we ought to find out something about him – only to protect you.'

'I don't need protecting, thank you,' Ethel said angrily. 'Donald told me himself that he wasn't a captain.'

Jessie blinked. 'He did?'

'He told me everything when he proposed. He only said those things because he'd longed to do his bit in the war and was so disappointed that he couldn't. You don't know how badly people who weren't in uniform were treated, even when they had good reason. He couldn't join up because of his injuries, though he would have gone if they'd let him. And he *does* have a medal for bravery.'

'I know,' Jessie said gently. 'There was a tram accident.'

'He told me all about it. He asked me to forgive him and I said there was nothing to forgive, because we all exaggerate sometimes.'

'You'd told him you ran Morland Place yourself, single-handed?'

She blushed. 'Well, what of it? It didn't hurt anyone. It's nobody's business but mine and Donald's. He knows the truth now. We've got everything out in the open between us, and that's all that matters, so I'll thank you to mind your own business – you and Bertie.'

'I'm sorry,' Jessie said. 'I didn't mean to hurt you. I was only anxious for you.'

'Well, you needn't be.'

'But, Ethel, why did you keep it so secret? If I hadn't happened to see you that day . . .'

Ethel's eyes sparked angrily. 'Because I met him at Madame Rowena's. I suppose you know all about that, too, if you've been snooping on us.'

'Madame Rowena is the spiritualist, is she?'

'And now you're going to tell Mother-in-law and Uncle Teddy about it.'

'No, of course not. It's not my business.'

'I'm glad something isn't,' Ethel said bitterly.

'I won't say a word about anything to anyone. Please believe me, I was only worried for you. But if everything's all right between you and Captain – Mr Broadbent—'

'It's Captain. He can't change now, or people will know. But when we're married we're going to go away and live somewhere else, and start again with the true story.'

'You really are going to marry him, then?' Jessie said unguardedly.

Ethel reddened with anger. 'And why not? You don't like him – I can tell that. You think he's common. It's all very well for you, married to your grand brigadier-baronet, with all the money in the world.'

'Oh, Ethel, I didn't—'

'You don't know him. He's kind, and he loves me – worships me, really. You don't know what it's like for me. I want a man in my life. I'm so *lonely*. You don't really *like* me, any of you. I live here, but it isn't my house. I have nothing to do in it. I don't even bring up my own children. I'm *nothing* here. Well, Donald likes me. I'm important to him. And he'll give me my own home. So go ahead and snigger all you like that I'm marrying a man with one eye and one leg. Make fun of us. I don't care.'

Ethel stood up to leave and Jessie stood too, and tried to lay a hand on her arm, but Ethel shook it off.

'I'm sorry,' Jessie said. 'I never meant to hurt you. I do understand how you feel, and I'm really glad you've found someone to care for. And I promise you no-one will laugh at Captain Broadbent. There's nothing in the least funny about a kind and brave man offering honourable marriage to the woman he loves.'

Ethel gave her one searing look, tossed her head and walked away, leaving Jessie thoughtful.

What was the difference, she pondered, between Amy's marrying Uncle Teddy and Ethel's marrying Donald

Broadbent, except that one was a wealthy landowner and the other a former tram inspector? All over the country lonely widows were marrying where they could, in a land depleted of men. She must find a way to explain it all to her mother and Uncle Teddy so that they would understand. And Mother must make the servants understand – without saying too much, of course – so that Ethel's beau would be received with kindness by everybody.

CHAPTER TWENTY-TWO

The tea-party went better than Jessie had feared. Captain Broadbent was evidently nervous: he sweated a great deal, had to mop his forehead, and had a nervous gesture of sweeping his moustache with his hand; and Ethel was nervous too, which made her alternately rigidly silent and conspicuously chatty. But Henrietta had been giving tea-parties to shy Tommies all through the war and knew how to put people at ease. She was the consummate hostess; and Amy's intense sympathy for Ethel made her talk more than she usually did, in an effort to keep things going.

Uncle Teddy was detained on business and only arrived halfway through, which was probably a good thing, as having to face Bertie, a genuine brigadier, was hard enough for the bogus captain. But Bertie kept the conversation determinedly away from the army and the war. They talked about the weather and the crops, local matters, cinema films, the news that the dancing couple Adele and Fred Astaire were coming across the Atlantic, at Noël Coward's urging, to perform in a show called *Stop Flirting*, opening in Liverpool. Nobody asked any awkward questions; in fact, nobody asked any questions at all until it was nearly time to go, and the visitor had relaxed, seeming to Jessie almost touchingly grateful for not having been ambushed.

The question Teddy finally asked was, 'Have you decided on a date for the wedding?'

Broadbent threw a glance at Ethel. 'Um, no, not exactly – not yet. We – er—'

'You will marry here, of course,' Teddy said – it was barely a question. 'I view myself rather *in loco parentis* to Ethel, and this is her home. I think we could have rather a pleasant affair here, in the chapel, and then, if you choose a summer date, perhaps a reception outside, with a marquee and a band—'

'We want a very quiet wedding,' Ethel broke in firmly. 'Just a few of our friends, and immediate family. And we'll marry in the register office. It will be more convenient for our friends in York.'

Broadbent looked at her. 'If you're sure, my dear. You don't think it would be nicer – I mean, this wonderful old house – so grand . . .'

'We should start as we mean to go on,' Ethel said.

'Oh! Quite. Quite.' He looked put out, brushing his moustache again with the back of his hand.

She turned a defiant gaze on Teddy. 'We shall be comfortable, but not rich, and there's no sense in pretending to be what we're not.'

Teddy was disappointed, but rallied to say, 'Well, Mrs Morland and I shall come down with a handsome wedding present, you may be sure. And we shall dance at your wedding with light hearts – whenever it is – and wish you the very best of everything.'

With an heroic effort he suppressed all the other questions he wanted to ask. Broadbent took his leave, and Ethel said she would walk part of the way back with him.

When they had gone, Teddy said anxiously, 'I hope he's able to support her properly. Where will they live? And what about the children? Has he even met them? How will they like such an odd little man for a step-father? I can't help thinking this is an awkward business, look at it whichever way you can.'

'He *is* an odd little man,' Henrietta said, 'and I'm afraid not a gentleman, but I don't think there's any harm in him. I suppose if Ethel likes him . . .'

'She's a grown woman,' Jessie said. 'She can make up her own mind.'

'But those children are in my nursery,' Teddy said. 'I'm responsible for them.'

'I'm sure everything can be worked out in time,' Amy said. 'With good will on all sides—' She stopped abruptly, with a little frown.

Teddy looked at her sharply. 'Is everything all right, my love? You look tired.'

'I am, a little,' she said. 'I think I'll go up and have a rest before dinner.'

The following day Ethel's beau was driven from every-one's mind because Amy, after a restless night, went into labour early. Teddy was frantic with worry, despite anything Henrietta or Nanny Emma or Dr Hasty could tell him. His feelings were in a turmoil, with an old man's guilt over having a young wife compounded by the whole issue of Polly and Polly's mother. If Amy were to die it would be his fault. He had taken her into his house, as he had taken Charlotte all those years ago, rescuing her from poverty, and had brought her to this pass. Could Fate be so cruel as to strike in the same way twice?

In vain Jessie tried to persuade him to come out for

a ride; in vain did Miss Husthwaite bring him business problems to solve and letters to answer. He sat like a stone in the drawing-room, his hands clasped in his lap, waiting for the blow to fall. Sawry came to the door from time to time to look in at him in mute sympathy, or ask him if he could bring him anything, but he did not respond. He was hollow, wordless, thoughtless, an empty shell abiding on Fate.

The house was old, the walls and floorboards thick, and he heard nothing of the struggle upstairs; until, two hours after noon, light footsteps heralded Henrietta. He looked up in dread to see her at the door, but knew at once from her expression that all was well.

'A boy,' she said. He crossed the room to her – he did not remember how – and took her hands, and they looked at each other in silence, lost for words.

Soon afterwards came Nanny Emma, slow-footed and careful, with a white bundle in her arms.

Now he found his tongue. 'Is she all right?'

'That's a booy, sir,' said Nanny Emma, indignantly. 'Masterous little feller, that is!'

'I meant, is the mistress all right?'

'Lord bless you, she's adoon finely. You can go on up and see her in a bit. Will you houd the babby now?'

Teddy held out hungry arms, and looked in wonder at the tiny wrinkled apple in the folds of wool. 'A boy,' he breathed. He was afraid he was going to cry again. He looked up at the smiling women – that very particular smile that belonged to days when babies came. 'He should be an Edward – don't you think?'

Emma had a visit from Mrs Perigo in April, when the Season was at its peak and she was waiting for Kit

Westhoven to arrive to drive her down to Windsor for a polo match. The Prince of Wales had come back from his Indian tour mad about polo, and now ran several ponies of his own, which had given the sport a fillip.

So she received Mrs Perigo with the information that she could only spare her a few minutes.

'Yes, I know that you are busy, Miss Weston. As I am, myself, so I shan't keep you long. Business had always better be conducted briskly, don't you think?'

'Business?' Emma queried.

'I come to you with a proposition,' said Mrs Perigo. 'I don't expect an immediate answer, of course – you will want to mull it over and then, I expect, you will have further questions. I shall hold myself at your convenience. For now, I will be brief.'

'I wish you would,' Emma said, bewildered.

'I don't know if you have heard that Greyshott House in Hanover Square is up for sale.'

'What of it?'

'It is ideal for turning into flats, in the same way that Stretton House has been, and I would like to be the one to do it. But this time I want to control the process from first to last – hire the architects, the builders, the decorators, everything. See the entire process through. I saw it all with Stretton House, and I have a great many ideas I would like to put into practice.'

'But what has this to do with me?' Emma asked impatiently.

'I need someone to put up the capital,' Mrs Perigo said, her bright eyes on Emma's face, to read her reactions.

Emma felt a stirring of interest, but said, 'And why should I want to do that?'

'Because it will be a first-rate investment. The McNeills have to sell because of death duties and there aren't many buyers around for houses of that size, so it will go for less than its value. Labour is plentiful and cheap at the moment. And rich Americans are arriving every month, wanting apartments just like these, and ready to pay high prices for them. They like our old buildings, Miss Weston, but they don't like our old plumbing and no electricity or lifts! Now I happen to know that Stretton House turned a ten per cent profit, but I am convinced I can do better. I could make it twelve, and that, Miss Weston, is a very good return on your capital.'

'I have a man to manage my investments for me,' Emma said. 'And I don't need more money. I say again, why should I want to do this?'

'I've seen what you did here,' said Mrs Perigo. 'I've seen photographs in the magazines of the Vanderbeeks' house, and I know you designed that. I think you have a talent for this sort of thing. And, what's more important, I think you enjoy it. With Greyshott House you would have a much larger canvas for your ideas – a whole house to play with. You and I, I'm sure, can work well together – there's room for my ideas as well as yours and we shan't quarrel over a detail. And besides all that,' she continued quickly, as Emma made to speak, 'when the flats sell at an enormous profit, I think you will thoroughly enjoy showing all the dull men of business that you have a sounder head than theirs.'

Emma couldn't help smiling. There was something in that. And she had enjoyed refurbishing the house for Flo Vanderbeek's parents more than anything she had done since the war ended. It had been just enough of a challenge to keep her busy, a mixture of artistic expression, the solving of problems, and plain hard work. And the end result was satisfying, giving her a sense of achievement. It was a bit like planting a garden and watching it grow, she thought; or raising a child.

She had rather missed it since she had finished it, though social events had occupied her: hunting and shooting parties all through the winter, race meetings, Christmas parties, charity balls, and then the Season proper beginning again. She could be occupied every waking moment with social engagements if she wanted to; but the fact was that she had discovered, in spite of all her efforts, that dancing was not quite enough. Sometimes in the middle of a dance floor with the music blaring and her friends whirling like leaves around her, she felt empty; and in the emptiness there were dark thoughts she didn't want to have to face. She needed something more. She wanted some work to do.

'Your proposition is not without interest,' she said, 'but I shall have to have time to think about it.' She glanced at the clock.

'Naturally,' Mrs Perigo said, taking her cue. Standing up, she placed her card on the table. 'A simple message will bring me to you to discuss it further. Good day to you, Miss Weston – and I hope we shall have the means of doing each other a great deal of good.'

She talked about it to Kit as they drove down to Windsor. 'You? Go into business?' he said in surprise. 'My dear Emma, why ever would you?'

'Why not?' she said. 'It would be fun, and I'm not so delicate. Goodness, when there are former air aces selling motor-cars on commission, I can't see that I have anything to be fussy about.' She gave him a sidelong look. 'You and I saw things in the war our parents' generation would not have dreamed of.'

'Fair enough,' he said. 'And one must do something. It's true one can get bored with the same old round all the time.'

'You could go back to surgery,' she pointed out. 'I know Oliver would like you to.'

'No,' he said, 'never again. I have closed that book. But this idea – it's certainly attractive. I suppose you wouldn't let me help?'

'What can you do?' she asked, amused.

'Oh, I have ideas, as much as the next man,' he said, mildly offended. 'I could tell you how to fit out a gentleman's dressing-room, for instance – you wouldn't know about that, would you?'

'True,' she said. 'Well, I shall think about it. I shall have to talk to someone about the financial side of it.'

'Bracey's the man for that,' Kit said, changing down and overtaking a wobbling bicyclist with a roar. He had the same solicitor as Emma. 'If he doesn't know an answer, he will always put you on to the person who does. I must say,' he said, changing up again, 'it does sound great fun. I wish you *would* do it, Emma.'

'We'll see,' Emma said, but in the back of her mind she knew she had already decided. If Bracey thought the financial and legal sides were all right . . . It would be a challenge and a change, and she wanted both.

Violet and Holkam were staying with the Bracebridges at their house in Datchet for a Saturday-to-Monday based around the polo match in which the prince was actually playing. The Bracebridges gave a dinner in the evening to which both the Prince of Wales and his lively younger

563

brother Prince George were invited. There was a posse of pressmen lingering at the end of the drive to note down the names of the guests and to acquire, if possible, a photograph of the Prince of Wales and Lady Holkam arriving or leaving together.

That she was the Prince of Wales's new object had been known by the inner circle for some time, and was now being hinted at by the press. The part of the third estate that concerned itself with society gossip approved of the development. It had always vaguely felt that Lady Holkam, who had so amply rewarded them a few seasons ago, was due to pay out again. And their own adored Prince Charming certainly deserved someone as superb as Violet Holkam who, though a wife and mother, had never lost the exquisite, almost ethereal beauty that had won her the accolade of loveliest debutante of her year. As she was married, and the newspapers could not openly approve of adultery, even for princes, the columnists could only hint about friendship and admiration, and allow their readers to interpret that as they wished.

Much of the relationship happened well below the level of public consciousness, though Violet and the prince were seen together at 'shows', dining in restaurants and attending sporting events in small intimate parties. The gossip columnists' sources reported them dancing together – a great deal – and attending the same dinners and parties, invited on purpose by hostesses who knew. But only the inner circle knew that he called in at Holkam's house in St James's Square at odd hours, and only the household knew that he wrote her little notes several times a day, and telephoned her late at night.

Violet was bemused by it all. She had known the prince for years, of course, and had met him tolerably often. Eddie's being his equerry meant that they moved in the same circles, and she had long realised that he admired her. But his rejection by Mrs Dudley Ward had made him see her with new eyes. It was Eddie's dinner party after York's engagement was announced that had done the trick. He needed someone to fill the vacuum, someone to depend on when his beloved Freda made herself unavailable – someone who was on his side.

He courted Violet assiduously, and it was impossible not to be flattered by his attention: he was the future King of England, after all. She had resigned herself, when Laidislaw died, to living without love; but she was still young, and that part of her was lonely. In the face of his extravagant adoration, her natural feeling of awe and respect for the institution warmed into affection for the individual. Though he was three years younger than her, there was something oddly appealing about the slight, fair young man with the eyes of a tired child. He was handsome and charming, a good dancer, and in company was vivacious and amusing – and he was very generous both with gifts and compliments.

When they were alone together, he talked a great deal about the horrors of his situation, his loneliness and misery, his intermittent black clouds of depression. It was not, perhaps, the language of courtship; but as he also said he had no-one but Violet to confide in now, that only she understood him, and that he could not have faced the world without her sweet sympathy, she found herself caught up in his strangely slanted view of the world, and was proud to be, so to speak, on the inside of it looking out. He spoke passionately to her of love, and in the face of his fevered declarations she would have had to be heartless not to be moved into reciprocating.

In the whirlwind of her sudden elevation, the thing that most puzzled Violet was Holkam's attitude. She had been apprehensive, but not only did he not object, he seemed positively to encourage the relationship. He was present with her on many of the occasions when she and the prince met, but when he could not accompany her, he would say, 'You go, my dear, and enjoy yourself.' When necessary Freddie would escort her to maintain the decencies. Freddie was rather gloomy about the whole thing, but took it philosophically as he took everything.

One day the prince arrived at St James's House late in the evening, after dinner. Holkam and Violet were for once alone. Holkam saw to drinks, chatted to the prince for a few moments, then made an excuse and left Violet with him in the green parlour.

Hours later, when the prince had left, Violet went to find her husband. Holkam was in the library, and looked up from the newspaper to say, 'Has he gone?'

Violet regarded him, head slightly tilted. 'Did you deliberately leave us alone?'

Holkam raised his eyebrows. 'I'm sure you didn't want me there.'

'Holkam, I don't know what you think is happening,' Violet said.

He folded the newspaper and put it down. 'It really isn't my concern. You know we agreed that there would be no recriminations, as long as matters were kept discreet.'

'It's not what you think,' Violet said, frustrated.

'Really, Violet, there's no need for this,' Holkam said. 'I know the matter is not entirely secret, but I don't blame you. Whatever the prince does is news, and there's no way to keep it out of the papers. But don't let it trouble you. I entirely approve.'

'You approve?' Violet looked bewildered.

'Of course. It does us both great credit. King's mistress is an ancient and noble calling. No husband would object. I know he's not king yet—'

'And I am not his mistress.'

'Please, dear, there's no need to protest. You may go ahead with my blessing. It can only be good for me.'

Violet shook her head. 'I don't understand. How is it good for you?'

'It gives me influence in the right circles. Don't forget, we have children to place in the world.' He stood up and took her small, cold hand, smiling down at her. 'We agreed to be friends and work together for the family, didn't we? I think we've been doing very well. Our troubles are behind us, our position in society is secure, we are welcome wherever we go. And now this! It couldn't be better. That young man needs a strong woman to guide and advise him, and the Dudley Ward is a mere bourgeoise. You are much more suitable.'

'Holkam, nothing has happened between us,' Violet said desperately. Somehow it was terribly important that he should know she had not broken her marriage vows. And yet – was that entirely true? The thought gave her pause. Was not talk of love – was not accepting David's declarations, his presents, his kisses – in breach of the spirit of the vow? Just now he had been kneeling beside her, resting his head in her lap while she stroked his fair hair, and he had caught her other hand and kissed it and held it against his cheek. It was not something either of them would have done in front of Holkam.

'He's lonely,' she said. She hadn't meant to say it out loud, but having just come from him it was uppermost in her mind. How often their conversations, and his letters, dwelled on that theme – the unique misery of being Prince of Wales, trapped in a routine he found boring and pointless, performing meaningless rituals, bullied by his parents, surrounded by hostile relatives, spying servants and false friends who cultivated him only for his patronage. Having said it aloud, she felt she had to expand. 'It may sound absurd to say that of someone surrounded by people all the time . . .' He cried a great deal, especially when he had been having 'a row' with his father. His tears moved her dreadfully.

'Not to me,' Holkam said abruptly. 'I understand entirely. It is the loneliness of rank.'

She looked at him wonderingly. It was hard to imagine Holkam ever feeling lonely; and yet it would explain so much about him. 'Everyone wants something from him,' she said. 'No-one cares for him as a person.'

Holkam studied her face with a twinge of concern. He found suddenly that he did not want her to be hurt. Besides, a woman could manipulate a man better if her emotions were not involved. 'Are you in love with him?' he asked abruptly.

Violet did not answer for a moment. Then she said, as though it were an alternative, 'He troubles me. And I feel . . .' She searched for the right word. 'Responsible.' She looked up at Holkam. 'He seems to need so much from me. It's a long time since a man needed me in that way.'

Holkam nodded. 'Well, I'm delighted. If you can keep him for a year or so, I should be able to consolidate my career. But he *will* move on to someone else eventually, you understand that? It's in the nature of kingship.'

'I understand,' Violet said.

'Meanwhile, give him whatever he wants,' Holkam concluded.

Polly received the news of her half-brother's birth in a letter from her father in which the almost bewildered joy was followed by a wistful enquiry as to whether she would be coming home soon, as she was much missed. Polly's lip trembled as she read it, but then her expression hardened. So he had another son? Well, he would not care any more about a mere daughter; and James had better look out, too, or he'd find himself disinherited by the newcomer. Deep down she knew her father would never do anything to hurt James, but the only way she could cope with the feelings of loss and rejection was by cultivating such hard thoughts. She would not go back to watch her father fawning over a wife young enough to be his own granddaughter. And the baby – she didn't even want to think about that. It was disgusting! No, she would never do it. She would never go back.

In this new determination, she went to see Lennie. Lennie's business was thriving to an extent that still surprised Polly, though she had been in America so many months now. Wireless as entertainment had taken off like a rocket and was soaring ever upwards. Popular music, variety shows, plays and comedy routines had joined regular news bulletins and the coverage of political events to fill air time. Even church services were now being broadcast. Baseball was a staple, too – the voice of the leading commentator, Graham McNamee, was now as well known to a generation of American men as those of their own fathers and brothers – and commentary on football games was due to follow soon.

There were so many radio stations there was a shortage of wavelengths. In the previous year sixty million dollars' worth of radio sets had been sold – a figure that Lennie confidently predicted would be doubled in the present year; and he would be taking a significant share of it. He had opened a third factory in April, and had a string of shops all through New York. Now he was talking with his Boston cousins about finding suitable retail sites in that city, and he had an agent looking out similarly in Philadelphia.

'And there's something else I'm thinking about,' Lennie said to Polly that day. He had taken her out for coffee and cake at Lindy's on Broadway, and so far she had not mentioned her own business: the news that precipitated it was too painful and she didn't want to talk about it yet. 'I'm thinking of expanding into broadcasting.'

Polly looked up from the piece of cheesecake she was toying with. Lindy's had only been open two years and already its cheesecake was famous in Manhattan; but she had no appetite today. 'Isn't that a very long step?'

'It's a logical one,' Lennie said. 'From making the sets to selling them to putting out the material.'

'Like owning the sheep and selling the cloth,' Polly said obligingly.

'Exactly,' he said, pleased she understood.

'But is there any money to be made out of it?' She had been in America long enough to feel comfortable about asking such a question.

'Gee whiz, yes!' Lennie said. 'Don't you know that the radio stations let air time to advertisers? Commercial companies set great store by advertising. They're willing to pay big bucks to get on the air. They even sponsor whole programmes. Anyone who gets in now, before it gets too crowded, stands to make a fortune.'

'I thought you already had made a fortune,' Polly said idly.

'I have,' he replied seriously. 'But there's never any harm in making another. I shall be a millionaire by next year, Polly. Now, if you were to marry me—'

'Oh, don't, Lennie, please,' Polly said. 'Not today. I'm feeling too delicate to have to hurt you again.'

'What is it?' he said with quick sympathy, pushing down his own disappointment – after all, he had hardly expected her to say yes. 'Have you had bad news?'

She found herself still unready to talk about the baby. He would hear about it soon enough from the family. She said, instead, 'I'm thinking of setting up in business myself. In fact, that's why I came to see you. I wanted your advice.'

'You did?' he said, pleased.

'There's nobody I'd trust more. Look how well you've done in a couple of years, from a standing start. I know you'll set me straight.'

'I'll do my best. What business is it?'

'My clothes, of course. My original designs. I'm tired of dressing the smartest people in New York simply out of the goodness of my heart. Baby van Plesset wore one of my gowns to the Met last month and a dozen people asked me to design for them. If I said yes to everyone I'd never go out anywhere myself. So I thought it was time I started charging people. But, like you, I don't want just to control one part of the process. If my ideas are to be made into reality, I want to control every step.'

Lennie was enthusiastic. 'You'd do the drawings, send them to your own pattern-makers, then to your own

571

seamstresses . . . You already have connections with people of that sort, don't you?'

'Yes, and I could get much better deals from the cloth warehouses if I were doing it as a business.'

'You'd need a workshop with your own cutters and sewers. You'd have to buy fabric, thread, trimmings, and the tools and so on. And you'd need a showroom or shop or what-have-you. A smart place the rich ladies will come to. That would mean fitting out, sales assistants, and you'd want to have some seamstresses on hand to do alterations. Electricity, heating, wages . . . It's a big investment.'

It sounded rather daunting now he laid it out for her. It had seemed a simple thing when she thought of it. 'Yes, it would be,' she said, disappointed. 'I don't suppose I have enough money for all that.'

His heart quickened. 'Now, don't be downcast. All businesses need a capital investment to start with. That's understood. Granny Ruth put money into my first little workshop, and I paid her back handsomely. There are always rich people looking for somewhere to put their spare money. The first thing to do is to write down your plan, and work out what's needed.'

'But who would invest in me?' Polly said. 'I've never done anything like this before. I can see that making gowns for a few friends is not the same as running a real business.'

'Only because you've never charged for it,' Lennie said. 'As to who would invest in you – I would, for one.'

Immediate pleasure was followed swiftly by doubt in Polly's eyes. 'Oh, Lennie – would that be wise?'

He gave her a dignified look. 'I hope I can tell the difference between matters of business and matters of the heart. I wouldn't be doing it to put you under obligation. And if you don't like my money, Granny Ruth has capital to spare, and you know she likes you heaps.'

Polly brightened again. 'You think she'd invest in me?'

'I know she would. Between us we can find the capital you need.' He smiled. 'I think it would be good for you to have something interesting like that to do. I don't like to see you fritter away your life with dancing and cocktails and all the rest of it.'

She smiled mischievously. 'I should have to do all the more frittering in order to get the customers,' she said. 'The very reason people will come to me is that I run with the fast set. I shall be selling an idea of glamour of which I shall be the main advertisement.'

'Yes, but—'

'Don't worry, I shan't have my head turned. Don't you know I refused an offer of marriage from Jay van Plesset last week?'

'I had heard,' Lennie said.

Jay van Plesset was one of the richest young men in Polly's set, a definite catch, and his proposal to Polly had set her at the pinnacle of fashion. Lennie didn't know whether to be happy or sad that she had refused. He was glad that she was still free for him to hope for; but he didn't want her to be unhappy, and he feared that her continuing singleness, since it obviously had nothing to do with him, was a sign that she was still nursing a broken heart. He loved her so much he'd have given up all hope of her in an instant if it would guarantee her happiness. She had recently had her twenty-third birthday, and most girls were married by that age.

He had to say something, so he asked, 'Have you thought of a name for your business yet?'

'The House of Polly,' she said, half joking. 'Like the House of Worth in Paris.'

But he nodded seriously. 'I think that sounds just spiffy.'

In May, the Prince of Wales undertook a tour of Yorkshire, which had the local people in a ferment of excitement. Despite the popularity of the Duke of York, a visit by the heir to the throne fell into a different category altogether. He was handsome, charming, lively, and their future king: in short, he was adored. Any dissatisfaction with him was confined to the Court and nobility, the small circle who knew him personally; and even of those, many dismissed his weaknesses as mere youth, and looked forward to a good reign whenever he should succeed his father. For the rest of the country, he was what he seemed. Most of them had never even heard of Freda Dudley Ward.

When Violet opened Shawes at the same time as the prince was staying with the lord lieutenant, Jessie thought it was just a coincidence. Her surprise was that Holkam accompanied his wife – the first time she could remember him staying at Shawes. A small house-party was invited to stay, and of those at Morland Place, only Jessie and Bertie were invited to a dinner.

Jessie could not help remembering that there had been an awkward history between her and Holkam, but she had long put it behind her, and she had an idea it had meant so little to Holkam at the time that he would not remember it at all. So she was a little surprised when Violet drove over one morning – early, for her – to beg her to accept the invitation.

At Jessie's suggestion – mostly to save Violet's

Pekingeses from being overwhelmed by the Morland dogs – they went outside to walk around the moat. The little silky dragon dogs trotted ahead eagerly. They were old gentlemen of eleven now, and Lapsang's eyesight was poor, while Souchong suffered from rheumatism when the weather was damp, but this change of scene was as good as a tonic to them.

'I do so want you there,' Violet said anxiously. 'I know you and Bertie like a quiet life, and I was afraid you might refuse.'

'No, not at all,' Jessie said. 'We don't go out a great deal, but of course I wouldn't refuse an invitation from you. I don't see enough of you as it is.'

'The prince will be there,' Violet said abruptly.

'The Prince of Wales? But how exciting for you! How did you manage that? I know the Greys wanted to give a dinner for him and they were told his diary was quite full.'

Violet looked at her carefully. 'So you haven't heard anything, then? I thought Bertie might have – from his army friends. Some of them are in Court circles.'

'Heard anything about what?' Jessie said.

'About me and David.'

Jessie looked into Violet's beautiful, violet-blue eyes, and saw a nakedness of emotion she had not seen since Laidislaw died. Along with the use of the family name for the prince, it told her what Violet must be referring to.

'No,' she said slowly, 'I hadn't heard anything about that. I thought – that is, when I was in London, I did hear some talk about a married lady . . .'

'No, that was Freda Dudley Ward,' Violet said simply. 'She was the great love of his life. But she tired of him and insisted they could only be common friends in future. And, Jessie, he does so need someone to love him.'

Jessie was silent a moment, astonished and worried. 'But do you – have you – I mean, is it—?'

Violet did not pretend not to understand. She blushed and looked at her hands, but said quietly and firmly, 'We're not lovers in that sense. He doesn't really like that sort of thing. His love is on a higher plane. I wanted you to know that, Jessie,' she added, looking up at her. 'It's not something either of us would ever discuss. But you are my oldest friend. I didn't want you to think . . .'

Jessie took her hand impulsively. Even on this warm day it was as cold as a river-washed stone. 'Dearest Vi, I would never judge you. I know you and Holkam have a different sort of arrangement, and that's nobody's business but yours. Does he know?'

'Holkam thinks we are fully lovers, and he doesn't mind. He says king's mistress is an honourable position.'

Yes, Jessie thought, that's just the sort of thing Holkam might well say. 'But are you happy? Does the prince really love you?'

'He adores me. He tells me so all the time. He says I am the only thing that keeps him from despair. Sometimes he has thoughts of doing away with himself—'

'Violet, no!'

She shrugged. 'I don't know if he really would. But he says it. I suspect,' she said painfully, in a small voice, 'that he said all those things to Freda in her time. And will say them to others in the future. But I know he means it now when he says he loves me.'

'And do you love him?'

'I must do, don't you think?'

576

Jessie thought a moment. 'You might be bewitched by him, or flattered, or mesmerised.'

'All of those, I suppose. But he needs me, and it's good to be needed like that. Holkam and I get on very well now, we're friendly with each other, and we have the children in common. He's even accepted Octavian, though he still calls him Henry. I think he actually loves him. He tries not to admit it to me, but with Robert and Richard away at school so much of the time, Octavian comes in for more of his attention, and they seem quite attached to each other.'

Jessie found that uncomfortably touching.

'But it's not the same as being loved,' Violet went on. 'David buys me presents and sends me love-letters and tells me how beautiful I am and how he thinks about me all the time. It's – nice,' she concluded inadequately. The dogs spotted some ducks ahead on the moat and ran at them, barking, and the ducks paddled away disdainfully, not bothering to hurry. 'The dogs adore him,' she said inconsequentially. 'He plays with them on the floor for ages when we're alone.'

Jessie contemplated this scene in her imagination with amazement. 'Well, thank you for telling me all this,' she said at last. 'I'm glad you're happy.'

'You're my dearest friend, so I wanted you to know. And I want you to meet David. I've told him about you. But you know it must be kept secret as far as possible. David doesn't care, but I don't want to find myself a public figure. Fortunately, it's only our immediate circle that seems to know, and the newspapers only hint at things.'

'But I can tell Bertie?'

'Yes, but no-one else. I trust Bertie. And I'd like him to know that – that I'm not as bad as he may think.'

577

It turned out Bertie already knew. 'That Violet is Wales's mistress? Yes, I had heard something about it. I didn't say anything to you because it was just gossip, and I was afraid you'd be upset.'

'I would have been, but now I've spoken to her I feel better about it.' She explained the true state of affairs.

'Poor Violet,' Bertie said at the end. 'I'm afraid she'll be hurt when he grows bored with her and finds someone else. As he's bound to.'

'I thinks she knows that. And at least she'll have nothing to reproach herself with, beyond a few kisses.'

The dinner was more enjoyable than Jessie had expected, and unusually informal, given Lord Holkam's presence. Jessie did not know the other people there, who were all London friends from the prince's intimate circle, but she was seated beside Major 'Fruity' Metcalfe, who looked after the prince's horses, so there was plenty to talk about. He was interested that she used to breed polo ponies and urged her to take it up again, and the prince overheard them and joined in, and said he would love to visit Twelvetrees, but it would have to be on another occasion as his diary for this trip was completely full. 'Ridiculous handshakings and factory tours! I'd much sooner look at your horses, Lady Parke.' Jessie told him about their new house, which was nearly ready, and said he'd be welcome to come and stay any time, and he gave a most charming smile and said he would not forget that invitation.

There was no withdrawing, which Jessie liked because women so often missed the best conversation when they had to leave the table, and after dinner there was dancing to gramophone records. The prince danced only with Violet, and seemed to be murmuring into her ear the whole time. Bertie and Jessie continued to chat to the Metcalfes – 'Baba' Metcalfe was a daughter of Lord Curzon, very charming and much younger than her husband. The major had been in the Indian Army, so he and Bertie had reminiscences to swap, as well as much polo talk. They managed to establish eventually that they had once been at the same polo match, though Bertie had been playing and Metcalfe merely observing, and it was enough, in the way of men, to cement their mutual approval. Later Metcalfe asked Jessie to dance, but she didn't enjoy it as much as talking – he held her too close, and his breath smelled of whisky.

They went home at last to a Morland Place agog to hear about how they had met the Heir to the Throne, and what was he like? Jessie was glad that there were positive things to say, and that she need not think of any surreptitious bedroom-creeping going on after they had left.

The spring and summer of 1923 were dominated by all things Egyptian. The opening of the tomb of King Tut-Ankh-Amen in Thebes had been the sensation of the previous November. It had somehow escaped the grave-robbers who had emptied the other royal tombs, and promised untold wonders of antiquity. When the archaeologist Howard Carter had looked in through the first hole broken in the wall, he had cried out, 'I can see wonderful things!'

Now those wonderful things were coming out, and drawings and photographs were coming back every day to an excited public: artefacts in gold and marble, lapis and precious stones; jewellery, furniture, wine jars, vases, goblets and statues, a treasure laid in for a king over three thousand years before and never seen by human eyes since. The *Daily Express* had secured an exclusive relationship for its correspondent H. V. Morton – while other reporters had to wait back at the hotel, he alone was allowed on site, and the paper was selling thousands of extra copies on the strength of his reports. The *Illustrated London News* was full of photographs, and the British Museum was receiving an unprecedented number of visitors searching for more information on the ancient world.

Already the Egypt-mania was feeding through into fashions. Egyptian-style hats, dresses, costume jewellery and furniture were appearing in shops. Wealthy hostesses were giving Egyptian parties, the bolder young women were wearing black lines around their eyes, and Egyptian patterns were all the rage in fabrics, scarves and wallpaper. 'King Tut's Tomb' quite eclipsed the major eruption of Mount Etna in June, which flooded vineyards, fields and forests with molten lava, overran towns and villages and made sixty thousand people homeless – a story that would have dominated the papers at any other time.

'I almost feel,' Jessie said to Bertie, 'that we ought to have some sort of Egyptian-style object in our new house: a chair made like a pharaoh's throne, perhaps, or a set of gold and lapis goblets for serving wine at dinner.'

'Do you think King Tut will be snubbed by our lack of interest?' Bertie queried. 'You aren't afraid of his ghost haunting us? Surely the curse works the other way.'

There had been much talk about a curse on anyone opening, entering or defiling the tomb. It had been fuelled to begin with by a story that Howard Carter's pet canary had been eaten by a cobra on the day the tomb was opened – an event almost unbearably loaded with significance. A newspaper had reported, without any evidence at all, that there was an inscription in hieroglyphics inside the tomb saying *They who enter this sacred tomb shall swift be visited by wings of death*, which caught the public imagination. And when Lord Carnarvon, who had jointly headed the expedition with Carter, had died in April, barely five months after he had entered the tomb, the whole thing was set going again. It was said the lights of Cairo went out at the moment of Carnarvon's death – though that was not an unusual occurrence in Cairo. Still, Sir Arthur Conan Doyle publicly pronounced that the death could well have been the result of the curse, and put his seal on the story.

'Oh, do you think it would be unlucky to have anything Egyptian in the house?' Jessie asked, humouring Bertie.

'Perhaps to be on the safe side we should just have a pair of those wonderful pointed-eared dogs, one either side of the entrance,' Bertie said. 'That wouldn't count as inside the house.'

'Foolish,' she said, pinching his arm. 'I can't believe it's almost finished. It will be wonderful to have a house of our own at last.'

'And one we've chosen for ourselves, with everything just as we want it,' he added.

'The only thing we haven't done is choose a name for it. I suppose it ought to be Parke House – or Parke Manor, perhaps.'

'Parke is such an awkward name,' Bertie said. 'Parke House immediately makes you wonder why not House Park? And we are not going to call it anything *manor*.'

'You're not a bit grand,' Jessie complained. 'Sometimes I think it's hardly worth being *Lady* Parke.'

'You'll see the point one day, when Thomas grows up with the prospect of a title.'

'Since it's a title he can only acquire by your death, I shall reserve the right not to be thrilled by the prospect,' Jessie said.

The last stages of the building and fitting went quickly, and suddenly it was June, and they were having the topping-out ceremony. A small branch of oak was fixed with wire to the chimney for good luck, and a new penny, with the date 1923 on it, was placed on the top corner brick of the chimney and the flaunching mortared over it. The vicar, Mr Ordsall, led prayers of thanks, and there were toasts to the house and its owners, while the name plate was fixed to the wall beside the door: Twelvetrees House was what they had decided on in the end. James said they ought to break a bottle of champagne against the door and say 'God bless her and all who live in her', but Roberta said it was an awful waste of champagne – now she was nearly twelve she was hoping to be allowed a taste.

Finally there was a feast for the builders, on trestles set out on the front sweep, with which the family joined in.

'And if we don't have good luck after that . . .' Bertie said to Jessie.

'We already have our good luck,' she said, bouncing Ottilie gently on her knee.

It was a nice, square, plain and handsome house, with a sweep at the front and pleasure grounds at the back – new-planted and rather bare as yet, except for a splendid oak tree that had been on the site already. There was a large entrance hall and fine staircase, with a morning-room, dining-room, drawing-room and library leading off it, and a separate service wing. On the first floor there was a grand bedroom for Jessie and Bertie, with a bathroom and a dressing-room, and three other fine bedrooms. On the second floor was the nursery suite and 'bachelor rooms', and the servants' bedrooms and bathrooms were in the attic. The house had electricity laid in everywhere, and a modern telephone system.

Apart from a faint smell of new paint and plaster, which Jessie did not find offensive, the house was perfect, and the first night she slept in her own bed in her own bedroom in her own house, she felt she could not be happier. 'Oh, don't say that,' Bertie murmured, nibbling her ear. 'It leaves no room for development.'

Jessie had badly wanted to have Mary Tomlinson for her housekeeper, but she would not ask for her, knowing what a help she was to her mother, and Tomlinson had likewise repressed the desire to ask Jessie if she could go with her to Twelvetrees House. It fell on Henrietta, who perfectly well knew what they must be feeling, to break the impasse and suggest to Tomlinson that she ought to go.

'Oh, but, ma'am, I'm needed here,' Tomlinson said, but with her heart in her eyes.

Henrietta patted her hand. 'She needs you more. I have Sawry and Mrs Stark to keep things going until I replace you, but all her servants will be new, and will need knocking into shape. Do go, Mrs Tomlinson, dear, if you want to. I shall feel happier knowing Miss Jessie has you by her side.'

So Jessie started with an experienced housekeeper who was also a friend, which was a great help; and she had Nanny Emma interview the applicants for the place of nanny, and ended up with a local girl called Annie Maiby, who was young but bright and energetic, and whom Emma approved of. Housemaids were easy enough to find – there were still plenty of young farm girls ready to go into service for their first job away from home – but a suitable cook and butler would take longer. However, Cooper and Tomlinson, who got along miraculously well, could always fill the gaps.

'And we needn't think much about entertaining until October or November,' Jessie said, 'so we have time to try people out.'

Meanwhile, there was the Twelvetrees stud business to organise and develop. Jessie was busy all day long and, despite what Bertie had said, did not see how she could possibly be happier.

CHAPTER TWENTY-THREE

The thing Teddy dreaded most about Ethel's marriage was that he would lose the children. He never liked anyone to go away, but children were the life of a house, and if Roberta, Jeremy, Harriet and John were taken away from him there would only be his own two and Martin and Laura left, and James was away at school for much of the time. The old place would be desolate, he thought.

There had been a meeting between Captain Broadbent and his potential step-children, but it had not gone well. To the magnifying eyes of children, his oddities of appearance were grotesque, and the moustache and the glass eye held their horrified gaze, while the awkwardness of his gait, because of his false leg, made them want to back away. Broadbent himself, though a kindly man, was not over-fond of children, having had no experience of them beyond a certain amount of name-calling and teasing by the urchins in Huddersfield. He felt awkward, faced by Ethel's brood, did not know what to say to them, sensed their uncertainty as hostility, and was as glad as they were when the interview was over.

Afterwards they exclaimed passionately to the nursery staff that they did not want to go and live with that man, until Nanny Emma felt obliged to say sternly they would go where they were told, and be grateful for having a nice home, when there were children living on the streets and eating dirt.

'I'd sooner live on the streets,' Roberta cried passionately. 'I don't *like* him, he's got a funny *eye*,' which made Harriet burst into tears.

'For shame!' Emma scolded. 'Making fun of a person for a misfortune! I'd 'a' thought better of you.'

'But why can't we stay here?' Jeremy asked. 'We've always lived here. Why can't we stay with Grandma and Uncle Teddy?'

'Don't you want to goo and live with your mother?' Emma asked, feigning astonishment. 'Unnatural children that you are!'

Jeremy looked stricken, Roberta stuck out her lip, and Harriet cried harder, which set John off; but the fact of the matter was that though they loved their mother, there were other ties that were stronger. It was Nanny Emma and the maids who had taken care of them, and Morland Place that held their hearts. They had made friends at school, too. In the deeply conservative way of children, they didn't want anything to change.

As the wedding day in August drew nearer, Ethel grew ever more apprehensive. She knew the children had reacted awkwardly to her intended, but she did not know how strongly they felt, for the nursery staff had naturally not mentioned it. Her discomfort stemmed from her own feeling that she would rather not have the children to live with them, the guilt the feeling engendered, and the dread of what everyone would say if they found out. They would call her an unnatural mother; but, really, she had never been allowed to bring up her own children, so why should she start now? Broadbent had his pension

586

and the interest from his capital sum, and they could live comfortably on that, but in a small way. The children would make a huge dent in it, if they had to keep them at home.

Besides, she had seen a delightful house in Knaresborough that she had set her heart on – they had decided on Knaresborough because no-one knew them there, and it was an attractive place, handy for Harrogate and not far from York. But the delightful house, while being perfect for her and Broadbent to start a new life in, would be horribly cramped with the addition of four children. And how could they afford any nursery staff? She would have to do everything for them herself, and never have any time for going out and visiting and having tea-parties and playing bridge. She would turn into a drudge, and that was not at all what she had wanted to marry for.

Fortunately for all concerned, Teddy broke the unknown impasse by confronting Ethel, looking anxious and apologetic, and begging her not to take the children away.

'I know you are their mother and you must want to have them with you, but they are settled here, and the house would be empty without them. And it would be a shame to take them away from school and their friends and so on. I'd planned to give Roberta a pony for her birthday – you know how she's been longing for one of her own. I thought of giving Jeremy one, too. They wouldn't have anywhere to ride if they left here. They're country children, really. They wouldn't be happy in a town.'

Ethel, her heart beating with hope, felt constrained to say, 'But I'm their mother. Their place is with me.'

Teddy spread his hands placatingly. 'But think of them, Ethel dear. This is the only home they know. And you would be able to see them any time you wanted to. You wouldn't be far away. You could have them to stay at weekends and in the holidays. I know it's a lot to ask any mother . . .'

A vision of child-free happiness unfurled in her mind. Shopping, luncheons, bridge drives with dainty refreshments, tea-parties, elegant little dinners . . . Their budget unstrained, their nerves untested, their nice new house unscuffed by clumsy boots. And meanwhile, she told her conscience sternly, the children would have every attention, and far more luxury than she could ever provide. Roberta so wanted a pony. They had fields to roam over, dogs to play with – how could she take all that away from them? It would be cruelty to make them come and live with her.

'Well,' she said at last, with suitable reluctance, 'I only want to do what's best for the children. I shall ask them what they feel about it. If they would be happier here . . .'

And so the matter was comfortably settled. Roberta, with natural perversity, burst into tears as soon as everything was arranged at the thought of losing her mother, but Nanny Emma's sharp retort that she was *not* losing her mother, that she would see her practically every day, combined with the joyful news of the impending pony, soon eased her mind.

Teddy assuaged his feelings of guilt by giving the happy couple a very large cheque as a wedding present, and Ethel assuaged hers by letting him. The wedding, though small, was sufficiently cheery, with a reception afterwards in the Station Hotel, from which Captain and Mrs

Broadbent took a train for a fortnight's honeymoon in Scarborough, before starting their new life together as Mr and Mrs Broadbent in River House, Knaresborough.

Things were still very bad in Germany. France and Belgium had sent in troops to occupy the Ruhr in an attempt to force Germany to pay the reparation that had been promised; but the country had no money to pay with. Strikes, unemployment and civil unrest were rife, and inflation had reached such extreme levels that the small-denomination banknotes had become worthless. It was almost impossible to buy anything: prices could rise out of reach between setting off from home and reaching the shop. The Weimar Republic was issuing banknotes and even postage stamps with a face value of fifty billion marks, and one of the companies employed to print the new notes sent an invoice to the Reichsbank for thirty-three quintillion marks. The people were starving, even those who had jobs; racketeering and crime rates soared; and the miserable, depressed population looked for someone to blame – Marxists, capitalists, Jews, politicians, America, the French, it hardly mattered. It was a fertile breeding-ground for new ideologies and new political parties – anyone who could offer a solution that was even faintly credible.

One of these, the extreme leftist group called the National Socialist German Workers' Party, attempted a coup against the government in November 1923. Under its chairman, Adolf Hitler, and the distinguished former general Erich Ludendorff, it mounted a putsch in Munich, declaring itself the new government. The rebellion was crushed and Hitler sentenced to five years' imprisonment for treason, though Ludendorff was acquitted. The chancellor, Stresemann, then made an effort to get a grip on inflation by issuing a new currency, the *rentenmark*, with an exchange value of one trillion old *papiermarks* to one *rentenmark*. As the *rentenmark* was based on land, and Stresemann firmly refused to print any more money, confidence began to trickle back.

'Things are still very bad out there, though,' Bertie said to Jessie, reading her extracts from the newspaper. 'And there are a lot of hot-headed German nationalists who still believe they actually won the war, but were betrayed by the civilian leaders into making peace on the worst terms. They call it the "stab-in-the-back" legend. I'm afraid the business of the Great War is far from over. Even moderate Germans resent the loss of Poland, and it makes me wonder how long it will be before they try to take it back. Once they get out of these economic difficulties . . .'

Jessie trusted Bertie's instincts about these things, but the idea of going to war with Germany all over again was too horrible to bear thinking about. Surely the national leaders must feel the same way. She thought of the hospital at Étaples. They had nursed German soldiers there, too, wounded and dying boys who only wanted to go home, who were grateful for kindness, and did not understand why they had been sent to kill people who had never done them any harm. Surely the combined wishes of all the populace of Europe could not be ignored by a few leaders in such a way. It could not be allowed to happen again.

Having waited fifty years for the vote, Venetia now found herself being asked to exercise the right almost too often. The general election of November 1922 had returned a

Conservative government with a good majority, but its leader, the Canadian-born Scot Andrew Bonar Law, had resigned through ill-health in May 1923, and the King had sent for Mr Baldwin. Bonar Law died in October 1923, and since Baldwin had changed his mind about tariffs and wished now to bring in protectionist measures, the only honourable thing to do was to hold another general election, to give himself a mandate.

The election was held in December 1923, and as proof of the adage that no good deed ever goes unpunished, the Conservatives lost ninety seats. The main beneficiary was the Labour Party, which won fifty more, taking it to 191, with the hopelessly divided Liberals on 159.

Baldwin held on to power into the new year, but on the 21st of January 1924 he lost a vote of confidence in the House, and the King sent for the leader of the next largest party, James Ramsay MacDonald, and asked him to form a government. The old political classes reeled in horror as the first Labour government in history was formed, and predicted a socialist nightmare that would bring the country to its knees and deliver it into the hands of red revolutionaries.

As if to echo these thoughts, on the same day Lenin, who had been bedridden and paralysed since the previous March from a stroke, died. Now he was dead, it was safe for his enemies to honour him, and his successor, Stalin, gave him a state funeral and pronounced that St Petersburg should be renamed Leningrad in his honour. His death paved the way for Britain to recognise the Soviet republic, which it did formally on the 1st of February. Venetia was gloomy that evening, and Oliver tried to cheer her up in vain. He knew she was thinking about his brother, and about the Romanov family,

591

especially those four innocent, pretty girls. No-one wanted to talk about them any more. They had been rubbed out like pencil marks on the page of history, and the murderous red republic had become respectable. So the world turned, Oliver thought, but he couldn't expect his mother to see it that way.

The Hambling Committee's report on the best way to encourage commercial aviation concluded that the difficulty with the present subsidy arrangement was that the companies concerned had not been given sufficient security of tenure to encourage investment. Also that they were individually too small to create the successor to the British Maritime Empire: an empire linked by air. To the government, the principal reason the nation needed civil airlines was to facilitate settlement, trade, and administration in the colonies. At the head of a mighty empire, Britain would be able to withstand any future attacks from old enemies (was Germany really knocked out for good?) or new (the Soviet Union covered a huge area and had a vast population – who knew what a threat they might one day become?).

The answer, the Hambling Committee decided, was to merge the present four companies into one. So on the 31st of March 1924 the Imperial Air Transport Company was formed, with Fred Handley-Page as chairman and a one-million-pound subsidy guaranteed for ten years – the 'Million Pound Monopoly', *Flight* magazine called it. Not everyone was convinced that a monopoly was the best thing, but the Hambling Committee did its best to foresee and iron out any difficulties that might arise. Besides, the present four could not continue without government help, so there was really no choice but to do as they were told.

So on the 1st of April 1924 the new company took over Handley Page Transport, Instone Airline, Daimler Airways, and the British Marine Air Navigation Company. It also took over their fleets: three Handley Page W8Bs, seven de Havilland DH34s, one Vickers Vimy Commercial – the *City of London* – and two Supermarine flying boats. It was a motley collection, and all the aircraft were old and decrepit. Investment in new craft was much needed.

Jack was happy to learn that the base of operations was to be Croydon, and even happier to learn that his services were to be retained. He would have hated to uproot his family again. The new airline was to re-establish routes between Britain and Europe and also to develop air communication between Britain and the Empire.

'That will be a challenge,' Jack remarked to Helen. 'None of us has experienced what the flying conditions are like out there, but they're bound to be very different – extremes of climate and so on. I'm not sure any of our buses could stand up to it. The variation alone between here and, say, India would rack an old DH34 to bits.'

'Hmm,' said Helen. 'You give me great confidence. I can't wait to wave you off on a trip, darling.'

It didn't happen all at once. There was so much to be sorted out that there were no services for most of April, and Jack was able to spend a glorious amount of time with his family. Basil and Barbara were both at school, but he had fun with them when they came home, and enjoyed taking Michael off Helen's hands when she had things to do. At weekends they went on family trips together, and Helen said it was wonderful to have all his attention for such a long stretch. He even managed to get up a little interest in gardening, and started building a rockery which, however, was doomed never to be finished. And he and Helen had some trips on their own, without the children, driving down to Biggin Hill and borrowing a two-seater to take up – 'Love in the clouds!' Helen commented.

Imperial Airways began operations on the 26th of April, the first of what was to be a daily service from Croydon to Paris, with Jack in the pilot's seat. 'Back to the old grind,' he said cheerfully, as he set off for the airport that morning.

'Our second honeymoon is over,' Helen said, in tragic tones, as she waved him goodbye with Rug in her arms. But she was glad at least that he was on a familiar route. When she thought about the dangerous and hostile terrains that would have to be flown over to get to the remoter outposts of the Empire, she quaked at the idea. Suppose he came down in a desert, or among wild African tribesmen?

Other European routes were the immediate objective of the new airline – London to Southampton and Guernsey, London to Ostende, Brussels and Cologne, and in the summer the Paris route was to be extended to Basel and Zürich – Jack was excited at the thought of that. The distant empire services would take years to set up. New aircraft would have to be commissioned, the route surveyed, landing strips built or improved, ground staff and ticketing arrangements made. It would be a long time, Jack said, before they were up and running. He said it almost wistfully, and Helen knew he was hoping as fiercely as ever that he would be chosen to fly some of them. It seemed there was a certain sort of man who always had to be risking his life to be happy, though he would have told her, and probably convinced himself that he believed it, that flying was no more dangerous than driving a motor-car – less dangerous, in fact, given the idiots who regularly got behind the wheel.

Well, it was a couple of years off, and she was willing to put the thought out of her head, and be glad Jack was employed, with a well-paid position that was guaranteed for the foreseeable future. They had a nice house and three lovely children, and a circle of agreeable friends which included the other Imperial pilots and their families. After the agonies of the war they had reached a stable place in their lives, and she knew she had a great deal to be thankful for.

The sensation of the year was the British Empire Exhibition, which opened in April 1924 in Wembley Park in Middlesex, seven miles north-west of London. It was somewhat reminiscent of the Great Exhibition of 1851, except that it was on a much grander scale, and all the exhibitors were from the one great family of the Empire. The Empire consisted of fifty-eight countries, and only two of them did not manage to send an entry, so it was the biggest exhibition that had ever taken place anywhere in the world, a thing of intense pride to the British people. Everyone in the country wanted to see it. Clubs and associations of all sorts – darts teams and church choirs and works socials, parish councils and individual streets in industrial towns, women's and walkers' and tennis and bicyclists' clubs – got together and took subscriptions and made plans for a group outing to London to see the wonders.

And wonders they were. Three vast buildings were put up – the Palaces of Industry, Engineering and Art. In the Palace of Industry there was a model coal mine with real pit ponies. The Palace of Engineering was the largest reinforced concrete structure in the world, six and a half times the size of Trafalgar Square, and among its exhibits was the beautiful new Gresley A1 locomotive called the *Flying Scotsman*, which was to do the London to Edinburgh run for the newly formed London and North Eastern Railway.

There were fifteen miles of streets, so a detailed map had to be given to each visitor, and the advertisements proclaimed, 'You cannot see it all in one day!' Light railways connected the various parts of the site, and externally a whole new railway station called Wembley Park had been built, with a line connecting it to Marylebone station in London, while an eight-platform bus station could handle twenty thousand passengers an hour.

There were conference halls for films and lectures, a swimming-pool, a stadium where a grand Pageant of Empire was to be staged, with music specially written by Sir Edward Elgar. There was a reconstruction of Old London Bridge, a scale model of the Niagara Falls, and an Indian Pavilion based on the Taj Mahal. There were life-size models of Jack Hobbs and the Prince of Wales made entirely out of butter. There was a whole street of Chinese shops, including a working restaurant, representing Hong Kong. There were gardens containing a hundred thousand tulips and five thousand delphiniums and an ornamental lake. There was a Canadian rodeo, with bucking broncos and steer-roping, which everyone naturally associated with the Wild West of America, causing some confusion. There was a man-made beach complete with donkey rides. There was a whole set of cigarette cards, with views of the Exhibition, to collect, and for the first time ever, special postage stamps were issued to commemorate the occasion.

Naturally, there was a Tut-Ankh-Amen exhibition, held in an enormous concrete building, a replica of the original tomb, which was so impressive many people thought it was the original shipped at enormous expense all the way from Egypt.

At night the entire ground was lit up ('floodlit', the advertisements said – a new word), which was an exciting enough novelty on its own, with the blackout fresh in people's memories, and most houses still being lit by oil lamps or gas; and there was a palace of dancing with modern bands. But best of all, as far as the younger and the more frivolous sections of the population were concerned, there was the Amusement Park, with roundabouts and swing boats, a miniature railway and 'dodge 'em' cars, the Caves of Mystery and the unforgettable, huge and terrifying switchback ride called the Grand National.

The Exhibition was opened on the 23rd of April, St George's Day, by the King, and his speech was permitted to be broadcast by the BBC, so that an estimated seven million people (there were by now one million receiving licences in existence) for the first time heard a monarch's actual voice. Sir Edward Elgar himself conducted massed bands and choir in a rendering of 'Land of Hope and Glory', and it was a hardened person who could hear those words to that soaring music without a lump in the throat.

The Exhibition ran until October, and despite a disappointingly wet summer, twenty-seven million people went to see it; while *Punch* invented a new verb, 'to Wembley', with a definition along the same sort of lines as the old verb 'to Maffick' – to have a riotously good time.

* * *

In the autumn of 1923, when Polly had launched her dress business, she had finally got up the courage to have her hair bobbed; in the spring of 1924, when things really started to take off, she had it cut even shorter. With her tall, svelte figure, long neck and cropped head, she was the epitome of the fashionable woman of 1924. She was what everyone wanted to look like. She chose the slenderest girls to be her mannequins, and such was her growing reputation that some girls deliberately went without food to become thin enough to be taken on by her.

Cloche hats, which had been around for a couple of years, were perfectly suited to short hair – in fact, it was impossible to wear them successfully otherwise – and she adopted them, and made them her own. The close-fitting, clean outline they gave to the head accorded perfectly with her 'style'. As the year advanced everyone was wearing them, almost to the exclusion of other styles. Hems gave evidence of creeping up a little, so Polly slashed an extra inch off hers and brought them to mid-calf, or just above, mostly so that she could show off her newest idea: coloured silk stockings. Until now stockings had been either black or white, but now she had them dyed to go with her dresses, either to match the main colour or to contrast with it. The innovation was received with gasps of delight by her clients: deliberately drawing attention to females' legs was something new and daring.

Egyptomania showed no sign of dying down – indeed, a lecture tour of the States by Howard Carter in 1924 looked set to whip it up even more, so Polly introduced some Egyptian themes into her costumes that spring. She enjoyed using rich colours – peacock, gold, ochre red, sea blue – and had her mannequins paint their eyes like the figures in Egyptian friezes.

Her fashions were being talked about now, and she had been interviewed several times for magazines and newspapers: she had appeared in *Life*, and had even had a paragraph about her in *Forbes*, to Lennie's intense pride. She was beginning to make money, which made her feel better about the – as it seemed to her – immense amount Ruth had invested in her to set up. Ruth said she wasn't at all worried about her money: she was in no hurry, and she knew Polly would make a fortune in due time. Besides, she said, she hadn't had so much fun in years. To Polly's surprise, Ruth wanted to be involved in the day-to-day business – not that she interfered, but she liked to be around and see what was going on. She enjoyed going with Polly sometimes when she visited warehouses or suppliers. And she had ideas, too – she contributed her own designs, some of which Polly found she could incorporate into her style.

'You needn't sound so surprised when you say they're good, miss,' Ruth scolded her one day. 'I've lived a long and rich life, and I've seen more fashions come and go in my time than you can dream of. I've got a big library up here,' she tapped her head, 'and if you've any sense you'll make use of it.'

Rose was the other frequent visitor – whenever she could get away from school. She longed to be a mannequin, though Polly, with a thought to Lizzie's horror at the idea, did her best to discourage her. 'It isn't much of a job, Rosy,' she would say. 'You have far too much intelligence to settle for being a human clothes-hanger.'

'You're intelligent,' Rose would point out indignantly.

'Yes, but I don't walk up and down in the clothes – I design and make them.'

'Well, then, can I come in with you when I leave school? I've got lots of good ideas about costumes.'

Rose's interest had always been more in theatrical costume, but she presented Polly with sheaves of drawings, and occasionally there was something Polly could use. It did help, as she solemnly assured the delighted Rose. It required a great many ideas to keep supplying a fashion house. Fortunately her head was always teeming with them, and she had a magpie ability to take features from everywhere – other people's dresses, paintings, illustrations, museums – and adapt them to her purposes.

She did not know that Lennie had postponed his plan to start up his own radio station in order to help finance her business. He had given the money to his grandmother and asked her to invest it in her name: it took more capital to start up than Polly had envisaged, and Lennie did not want Ruth to be over-exposed – though Ruth said, 'All my money will come to you when I die, anyway – who else is there? If you want me to put it into your pet lamb's pocket I will.'

'She's not my pet lamb. I wish she were.'

'Ah, don't despair, honey,' Ruth said, patting his arm. 'I don't know how that hard-hearted girl can keep rejecting a fine, handsome specimen like you, but she can't keep it up for ever. You have to keep on pitching.'

Lennie smiled. 'I will, Granny. I'll never love anyone else, so I just have to.'

Premises on Broadway, Fifth and Madison, where Polly really wanted to be, were very expensive, but Lennie found her an empty building on 34th Street just round the corner from Fifth, which was practically as good and much cheaper. It was a nice building, too, with handsome windows and attractive stone details outside, and just about enough room inside. It had to be fitted out to a luxurious standard, for Polly meant to charge a very great deal for her dresses – 'A high price serves to keep off ill company' was her maxim. She had a shrewd idea that more people would want to buy her clothes if they were startlingly expensive: the rich liked to be exclusive. Thick carpets, pale walls and a great deal of gilding, velvet curtains and massive mirrors, crystal chandeliers and spindly little Louis XVI chairs – that was the look she wanted.

Though her business now took up a great deal of her time, Polly still 'ran with the fast set', as Lennie put it – for, as she had told him, she was the advertisement for her own clothes. She attended social events, and since now she was invited everywhere she could afford to pick and choose and only go to the most prestigious. She was seen at the opera and the theatre but, like other fashionable people, only arrived when the performance was halfway through. She went to the best parties and, with a select group of the fashionable and wealthy, visited the best restaurants and clubs, always exquisitely dressed.

Something, of course, had to be left out. Lennie said, 'If I didn't come and seek you out at work, I'd never see you any more.'

And Rose said, 'Mummy asked me to ask you if you would like to come to dinner on Sunday.'

She rarely saw the family any more, though she sent them fond messages; but she excused herself that she was rarely in her own home either, except to change her clothes, and to snatch a few hours' sleep between coming back from the latest club or dance or party, and getting up to go out to her business.

But she was happy – or, at least, she was too busy ever to be miserable. The uncomfortable gaps there had used to be, when the whirl of her social life had dropped her into stillness, no longer occurred, so she never had to think about old, unhappy, far-off things. She felt full of energy and purpose. She was twenty-four, in fine health, she was beautiful and admired, she never wanted for an escort or dancing partner, and she was beginning to be famous and rich on her own account and by her own efforts.

One evening in May, just after her birthday, she arrived at a party in an apartment in the Dakota, the home of one of her new friends, Julie Gilbert Margesson, the mayonnaise heiress – Gilbert's Ready-Made Mayonnaise was sold in jars, and found in every kitchen, behind the counter in every deli, and under the counter on every hot-dog stand in the land. She had married the eldest Margesson, Franklin, who shortly after their marriage had inherited his fortune, which came from his grandfather, who had been a Chicago beef baron.

So between them the Margessons had vast amounts at their disposal, enough for Julie to afford Polly's gowns, however much she charged for them, and to elevate themselves above the origins of their money and become generous patrons of the arts. Julie was particularly interested in the ballet, which was not well served in New York. Her mother-in-law knew Adolph Bolm, and she was trying to set up something along the lines of Chicago Allied Arts, which was going to put on ballet performances in Chicago, and even talked of having Tamara Karsavina perform there.

Julie assumed, in that generous way of New Yorkers, that Polly, being English, would automatically be cultured and know a great deal about the arts, and have a passion for them as well. Polly was happy to go along with it, especially as Julie liked to talk so rarely asked awkward questions. Besides, she was a very good customer, and she had often said that if only she could set up her own ballet company, she would have Polly design the costumes.

Julie's parties were always very elegant, well supplied with the very best of food and drink, and with more interesting and, frankly, less drunk people to meet than at some of the fast set's social events. Polly was wearing one of her Egyptian-style dresses, in sea-green and gold chiffon, with emerald stockings, and round her freshly cropped head she wore a gold circlet with a small rearing cobra at the front, which she knew was going to cause a sensation. The dress was low-necked to give room for the broad lapis and gold Egyptian necklace. She wore a gold snake bracelet wound several times round her forearm, and had her longest gold-plated cigarette holder with which she meant to draw attention to her hands and arms.

Julie greeted her warmly, kissed her on both cheeks and said, 'My darling, you look ravishing! The colour of that dress is heavenly! I must have something in that shade – it's almost balletic. Will you make it for me? And what a cunning headdress! Too delicious! You are such an advertisement for your own designs, you clever thing.'

A servant came up with a tray of glasses and Julie pressed a glass of champagne on her. 'Now, come and meet some people. You know most of them, but there are one or two new faces for you. Oh!' as she spotted someone across the room. 'Of course! You must meet Ren Alexander. He's been asking about you.'

She drew Polly across the room – Polly nodding and smiling and exchanging hellos as she passed – and brought her to a halt in front of the biggest man Polly had ever seen. He was not only tall, he was massively made, with broad, strong shoulders – as though he were a template for some kind of new, superior type of man.

'Renfrew Alexander,' Julie said. 'Polly Morland.'

Polly looked up – though she was tall, she still had quite a way to tilt her head – and caught her breath. It was a dark face, almost swarthy, but finely chiselled, with cheekbones that gave it an almost foreign look, a straight nose, strong chin and a mouth so beautifully sculpted a woman would have been proud of it – though there was nothing in the least effeminate about it. Above the broad forehead was a thick mass of Indian-black hair, smoothed and controlled for the evening with oil, but looking as though it longed to escape and be wild. The eyes looking levelly into hers were extraordinary: bright, intense, and of a colour unfathomable, seeming sometimes gold-brown and sometimes green.

'Allow me,' he said, and produced a cigarette lighter, which he struck and held out to Polly. She had forgotten about the unlit cigarette in her holder, 'came to' almost with a jerk and allowed him to light it. Power and masculinity were coming off this man like the blaze of a fire.

'Ren's part Apache,' Julie was saying. 'Isn't that too thrilling?'

'A very small part,' he said.

'I always think he looks only half tamed,' Julie said, patting his arm. 'Oh, I must go and rescue Senator Black – he's been buttonholed by Mary Davies and I don't want him annoyed before I've got him to promise to support my ballet.'

She left them, and Polly for once couldn't think of anything to say – mesmerised by this man like a mongoose in front of a dancing snake. There was so much of him, not just physically but in the aura he projected.

'I've been wanting to meet you,' he said, looking down at her. 'I've heard so much about you.'

'Have you?' Polly said, and then, thinking it feeble not to have something to say for herself, managed, 'I can't imagine you are interested in women's fashions.'

'I'm interested in business of all sorts,' he said. 'But it was the idea of you that captured my imagination. The lone Englishwoman taking Manhattan by storm. And now I see you, it seems even more remarkable.'

'How so?' Polly asked.

'I imagined a tough, mannish female in tweeds. But you are so young and beautiful.' She felt herself blushing. Why could she not drag her eyes away from his? He laughed, and his teeth looked very white against his dark skin. 'I've embarrassed you. I beg your pardon.' There was music from the adjoining room – Julie always had dancing as well as conversation at her parties. 'May I ask you to dance?' he said, holding out his hand.

Without her volition, her own had gone out – it looked very small and white against his – and his fingers closed over it. She felt a jolt, as if she had touched an electric wire. This man seemed so full of vigour, she felt he must devour life in great savage bites. He was a lion of a man.

Delicately the fingers of his other hand removed her glass and cigarette, putting them down on the nearest table, and he led her towards the music. She glided along beside him, and for the first time in her adult life she felt small: almost fairy-like, in comparison with his great size. Delicate and white and fragile, the unicorn to his lion.

The Labour government, perhaps because it was a minority government, seemed moved mostly by a desire not to frighten people about socialism, and did not actually do very much, apart from introducing a measure to address the still-acute housing shortage. John Wheatley's Housing Act – which, importantly, was passed with cross-party support – provided for subsidies for the building of 190,000 new council houses in 1925, with more to come over a ten-year period until the total reached 450,000. It was in the nature of things that it was mostly the prosperous working classes who benefited from the new houses, but as the slum dwellers tended to move up into the houses they had vacated, there was an overall improving effect.

But the period of the Labour administration was blighted with strikes, by engine drivers, dockers and then London tramwaymen. Eventually the government threatened to take out Emergency Powers and the strikers backed down rather than fight their 'own' party, but it left an ugly feeling between them. The Labour government was defeated in the Commons in September, and on the 29th of October another general election returned the Conservatives under Baldwin with a large majority, the Liberals having lost a hundred seats to them. Winston Churchill was made Chancellor of the Exchequer (a surprise to many, since he was famous for knowing nothing about finance). He called for a return to the gold standard – a move welcomed by many, and seen as marking 'the real end to the war'.

*   *   *

In the summer Emma went, with a party, to Wembley, mostly to see the Tut-Ankh-Amen exhibition, because the Egyptian influence was rife in furniture and decorations and she needed to keep up to date with the fashion, and to garner ideas. The films of the moment were *The Tents of Allah* and *The Thief of Bagdad*, both riding the coat-tails of popularity of Rudolph Valentino's *The Sheik*, which had been the sensation of a couple of years back. Most people did not particularly understand that there might be a difference between Araby and Ancient Egypt, nor would they have cared if they knew. It was all generally eastern, exotic, had to do with sand and camels, and meant rich colours and gold.

Greyshott House had been finished and the flats sold. The first redecoration scheme she had done had been a restrained business of light colours and lots of mirrors; but when, in early 1924, one of the flats was sold to an American couple, Ted and Mipsy Oglander from Baltimore, they asked her to redecorate it along the lines of 'The East'.

'I don't mind what you do, my dear,' Mipsy Oglander said breathlessly, 'as long as it's very Egyptian and gorgeous. I can't tell you how I melt whenever I think of Rudolph Valentino! I saw that movie three times, and all I can say is that Agnes Ayres is the luckiest girl alive, though why she should even *think* of resisting him I can't tell! I wouldn't say so in front of Mr Oglander, of course. He went with me to see it once and simply *laughed*. He said no sensible man would behave like that. Well, my dear, what's *sensible* got to do with it?'

'And have you any particular ideas as to what you would like?' Emma asked, pencil poised.

'Oh, no, my dear, I'm simply hopeless about that sort

of thing. That's why I'm asking you to do it. I give you a free hand – I know I can trust your taste because Edith Vanderbeek simply sang your praises to me, and she's the most elegant woman I know. As long as it's very eastern and gorgeous . . . And I'd like some of those divans with Turkish carpets over them – you know the sort of thing – and a boudoir for me, with billowing muslins at the windows. Oh, and I once saw some Chinese lanterns with gold tassels that were terribly sweet.'

'So I have to design something Turkish, Chinese, Arabic and Egyptian all at the same time,' Emma said afterwards, at dinner with Oliver and Verena and Kit Westhoven. 'I'm not sure she wouldn't like a few Greek statues thrown in as well, for good luck.'

'You have your work cut out,' Verena said. 'I can't imagine how you'll do it.'

'Boil the lot down to soup and strain off a cup,' Oliver said. 'Eastern bouillon.'

'Meanwhile,' Kit put in, 'she has her second house for turning into flats coming up.'

'Oh, really? Tell us about that,' Oliver said, and paused a moment to look at the dish being handed to him. 'Darling, what *is* this?'

'Lobster Newberg,' Verena said. 'It's done with cream and eggs and Madeira and—'

'Seems to me like cruelty to lobsters,' Oliver said.

'My fault,' Emma said. 'Bobby Emden pressed the recipe on me – it's very popular in America – and I shuffled it off on Verena.'

'It *is* rather rich,' Verena said, putting down her fork. 'Go on about the house, Emma.'

'Oh! Well, it's Turnberry House in Piccadilly – Frank Turnberry has to sell because of death duties.'

'Damned shame,' Kit said. 'It's an old title, goes back to the Wars of the Roses.'

'Mrs Perigo found it, of course. It's not huge, but it will make twelve nice flats: one six, one four, two threes, four twos, and four ones. And she has customers for most of them already, before we've done a thing. Even with the highest level of fitting-out it ought to turn in a fifteen per cent profit.'

Oliver laughed. 'It's so strange hearing you talking business so briskly, just as if you weren't pretty little Emma, my mother's ward and almost my little sister.'

Emma ignored that. 'It's just a shame that Turnberry can't do it for himself and keep the profit,' she said.

'But then you wouldn't have a business,' Kit pointed out. 'And, besides, Frank Turnberry couldn't do it. Have you seen his suits? He's the worst dressed man in London – in a very wide field.'

Oliver shook his head at him. 'I hate it when you talk like an idiot. When I remember your surgical technique in France . . . It's such a waste.'

'Don't start that again, please,' Kit said primly. 'No more blood and guts for me – I beg your pardon, Verena. How you can go slicing about at people's faces when there's no need, I can't imagine.'

'I did two hare lips yesterday,' Oliver said. 'Two children with a decent life ahead of them, where before they were freaks of nature.'

'I'm very pleased for you,' Kit said. 'And when they put you up for a sainthood I shall certainly give you my vote. In the mean time – how about a little dancing after dinner? Shall we go to the Forty-three? I can get Emma to teach you to tango – she does it rather nicely.'

Oliver laughed, but said, 'Rudolph Valentino has

nothing to fear from me. But I'm afraid we shall have to decline. Verena has been told by the doctor that she must go gently and rest a lot for a few weeks.'

Emma's eyes jumped to Verena, who smiled, blushing a little. 'Yes, it's true. I'm having a baby.'

'Oh, I'm so pleased for you!' Emma cried. She knew that Verena had been wanting a child, and worrying that one had not appeared before now. 'When is it to arrive?'

'December, the doctor says. Perhaps even a Christmas baby.'

'I've always felt rather sorry for chaps born at or near Christmas,' Oliver said. 'There was one in my class at school – presents were such a thorny issue for him. And then nothing to break up the year in between. I'm afraid our timing was off.'

'I don't mind,' Verena said, giving him a look that would have melted a sphinx. 'I'm just happy he's coming.'

'She's very generously promised me a boy,' Oliver explained.

So Emma and Kit went alone, leaving a little early so that Verena could rest. 'I really am pleased for them,' Emma said, as they sat in the taxi, speeding through the dark.

Kit thought she sounded wistful. 'Envious?' he asked.

The answer was a long time coming. 'Oh, I don't know. Sometimes it seems . . .' He thought she wasn't going to complete the thought, but at last she went on, 'Do you ever feel that we all lost our way, somehow, when the war ended?'

For a moment a shadow almost like fear passed through his eyes. But then he said firmly, 'Never. But if you feel like going in for a spot of matrimony and motherhood, old thing, I couldn't do less than offer myself up for the sacrifice. Just say the word and I'll step into the breach.'

'Don't be silly,' she said, and changed the subject. 'It's too early for the Forty-three. Shall we go to Sylvia's? She's having a mah-jong party.'

'Mah-jong?' Kit said, in tones of horror. It was all the rage that year.

'You don't have to play, actually,' Emma pointed out.

'Very well. And Sylvia's drinks are always good – actually.' He leaned forward and tapped the glass, and redirected the cab driver. It was fortunate that, if you moved in the right set, there was always a party to go to.

Oh, the parties! Fancy-dress parties, masked parties, Egyptian parties, Olympian parties where you dressed as Greek gods and goddesses, Venetian parties, historical parties. River parties at Maidenhead hotels. Baby parties where you came dressed as a nursery-rhyme character and the drinks were served in mugs. Sing-for-your-supper parties where everyone had to 'do a turn'.

But most of all, just parties where you got together with your friends and drank and smoked and danced to gramophone records. The gramophones were played loudly so that there was no need – and not much chance – of conversation. For who wanted to talk? Talking came from thinking, and thinking was to be avoided, because that's where your memories lurked. You had to keep the memories at bay, and so you filled your life with noise and movement: jazz music, blues, ragtime, anything you could move to; and the dances, fox-trot, one-step, two-step, tango – jig-jig-jig until your feet were sore and your hair grew limp and your mind grew numb.

Keep moving, because that way you could recapture the innocence of youth, which you had lost in the mud of Flanders or Picardy; that way you could outrun your memories, and life could not catch up with you.

As long as the music lasted, keep on dancing.

Read the next instalment in the Morland Dynasty *series*:

Dynasty 34: The Winding Road
Cynthia Harrod-Eagles

1925. England is prosperous; the nation has put the war behind it, and hope is in the air. The Jazz Age is in full swing in New York, where Polly Morland is the most feted beauty of the day. But a proposal of marriage from the powerful, enigmatic Ren Alexander takes her by surprise. Her cousin Lennie, expanding his interests from radio to television and talkies, worries that no one knows much about Ren; but his attempts to find out more threaten disaster.

In London, the General Strike gives the country another chance to show its stiff upper lip, as everyone turns to and helps out. Emma drives an ambulance again, while Molly runs a canteen, and each unexpectedly finds love, and a new career.

But the whirligig is slowing, shadows are gathering over Europe, and the good times are almost over. Morland Place is threatened by the worst disaster of its history, and the Old World reaches out a hand to pluck Polly from the New. The Wall Street Crash brings the fabulous decade to a shattering close, and nothing will ever be quite the same again; but new shoots emerge from the ruins, hope is reborn, and the Morlands prove again that family is everything, and will endure.

978-1-84744-143-0

The Complete Dynasty Series by Cynthia Harrod-Eagles

The prices shown above are correct at time of going to press. However, the publishers reserve the right to increase prices on covers from those previously advertised, without further notice.

--- sphere ---

Please allow for postage and packing: **Free UK delivery.**
Europe; add 25% of retail price; Rest of World; 45% of retail price.

To order any of the above or any other Sphere titles, please call our credit card orderline or fill in this coupon and send/fax it to:

Sphere, P.O. Box 121, Kettering, Northants NN14 4ZQ
Fax: 01832 733076   Tel: 01832 737526
Email: aspenhouse@FSBDial.co.uk

☐ I enclose a UK bank cheque made payable to Sphere for £ . . . .
☐ Please charge £ . . . . . . to my Visa, Delta, Maestro.

Expiry Date ☐☐☐☐   Maestro Issue No. ☐☐

NAME (BLOCK LETTERS please) . . . .

ADDRESS . . . .

. . . .

. . . .

Postcode . . . . Telephone . . . .

Signature . . . .

Please allow 28 days for delivery within the UK. Offer subject to price and availability.